D1130195

The Flame of Life

By the same author

FICTION

Saturday Night and Sunday Morning
Loneliness of the Long Distance Runner
The General
Key to the Door
The Ragman's Daughter
The Death of William Posters
A Tree on Fire
Guzman, Go Home
A Start in Life
Travels in Nihilon
Raw Material
Men, Women and Children

POETRY

The Rats and Other Poems
A Falling out of Love and other Poems
Love in the Environs of Vorenezh
Storm and other Poems

TRAVEL

Road to Volgograd

PLAY

All Citizens are Soldiers
(with Ruth Fainlight)

The Flame of Life

ALAN SILLITOE

W. H. Allen · London

A division of Howard & Wyndham Ltd

1974

PRINTED AND BOUND IN GREAT BRITAIN BY
RICHARD CLAY (THE CHAUCER PRESS) LTD, BUNGAY, SUFFOLK
FOR THE PUBLISHERS, W. H. ALLEN & CO. LTD, 44 HILL STREET, LONDON W1X 8LB
ISBN 0 491 01921 1

Author's Note

The present novel was begun in August 1967, and finished in January 1974. This is a long time for one book, though during that period other items were written that were more urgently pressing. They elbowed the present work aside, which may have been compliant in this because the plot and form of the book weren't so absolutely clear in my mind as they subsequently became over the years.

During its progress three other novels were written, as well as two books of short stories, two filmscripts, and a volume of poems.

Earlier versions of chapters three and four were printed as part of a novel in progress entitled CUTHBERT in *The Southern Review* (Louisiana State University) in the summer of 1969.

Chapter One

Albert Handley left his car in a meter-bay behind Oxford Street, and went into a shop to buy a transistor radio.

'How much is that?' he asked.

'Costs twenty-seven guineas,' said the young salesman.

Ash dropped from his thin cigar. He'd smoked all the way down that morning. His daughter Mandy had asked him not to, otherwise he might die of cancer. 'Who'll make the money to keep us in the sort of idleness we've got used to if *you* get carried off? The trouble is, you think of nobody but yourself.'

'Looks good.'

He twiddled a knob though it was not switched on. There were no batteries in any, and they were chained by their handles to the wall. He was eating himself so hard that cancer wouldn't get a look in.

'It's very fine,' the salesman told him, as if he weren't a serious customer, but was passing the time before going to a pornographic picturedrome down the street.

Handley unbuttoned his short fawn overcoat. He was tall and spruce-looking, with brown eyes, and a face more reddish than the ruddy glow it had when he'd been poor and walked everywhere. Yet he was still thin. No matter what food he shovelled down, and in truth it was never much, he did not put on weight. There was something intelligent and ruthless about his face, until he smiled and spoke, when whoever he was addressing might make the mistake of thinking him an easy person to get on with.

'I want something powerful,' he said. 'A good radio with lots of short-wave. I live in the country, and like to feel cut off from the one I'm in!'

His brother John had been a wireless enthusiast, and so Handley wasn't as unfamiliar with radios as the salesman thought. But John's dead, you fool, he snapped at himself in his momentary abstraction. What do you mean dead? Of course he's not. Why do you say that? He never was dead nor will be dead. He can't be. If he died I wouldn't paint another picture. I'd die myself, in fact. But he *was* dead, all the same. Killed his bloody self.

He saw a black, complex, heavy model with a multiplicity of wave-bands, switches and aerials. 'What do you rush for that one?'

'A hundred and ten guineas. It's a Philips, from Holland.'

'You look as if you could really communicate with it. Turn it on, will you?'

He unlocked the chain, and fixed in batteries.

'It's a good smart model.'

'Can you get police bands?'

'Everything. Fire-brigade, aircraft, radio-taxis, ship-to-shore in morse and telephone. Anywhere in the world, providing you adjust the aerials.'

The tone was good, trilled with spikey clearness when he spun the wheel over short-wave. 'Pack it up, then. I'll take it with me.'

He got back to his car and found a ticket fixed on the windscreen. He supposed it must be a two-pound fine because—as he now realised, looking at the meter—he'd forgotten to put money in. He drove off without touching it and, going smoothly along Oxford Street, flicked on the wipers till the little cellophane envelope flew out of his sight forever.

He cursed his carelessness—as well as the vindictive warden so assiduous in his packdrill duty—and picked his way through the traffic. His sleek black Rambler Estate made easy progress, but it still took some time getting to the Arlington Gallery after finding a vacant bay in Hanover Square.

String-wire-and-tinfoil sculpture that formed the basis of the current exhibition looked flimsy but interesting, something between Futurist muck, Surrealist crap, and a heap of socialist-realist junk thrown out of a builder's yard. In other words, it didn't lack imagination but had no talent whatsoever, only a demonic persistence on the part of the artist to create something or die. The man's name was famous in the art world, and though Handley couldn't begrudge him that, he was annoyed at the fact that he didn't know what it was about, feeling insulted because the sculptor hadn't done something that his by no means simple intelligence could understand.

Still, maybe it was only a bit of obstinacy on Handley's part, because many people were paying high prices for it, and countless critics were vomiting words in order to explain it to each other. It kept them out of mischief, though he felt that the more words a picture needed the worse it was.

Sir Edward Greensleaves, large and affable, stood up from his desk. Handley was a few minutes early and this disturbed him but, due to reasonably good breeding, it got no further than his own thoughts. Known as Teddy to Handley and his friends, he was at the pinnacle of several hundred years of family history—a genealogical cutting tool. The Greensleaves had one of the oldest pedigrees in England, which meant they came over as vicious narrow-eyed plunderers with Norman from France. Handley could have reminded him, however, that his clan were in England even before the Norman Conquest and even, maybe, prior to the Roman Invasion, but such length of service can be a positive disadvantage especially if, instead of mixing and breeding only with the best names as Teddy's lot had done, you mucked in with all the jailbirds and riff-raff feeding on fur, feather and fin that happened to come your way. Teddy was the last of the Greensleaves, and being of a certain nature, was not likely to extend the name for another generation. Handley, with a family of seven kids, seemed set for a few more centuries at least, unless the world blew itself up in the meantime.

Greensleaves often boasted how he had pulled Handley from the gutter of direst hardship and turned him into a man of the world. He had given him his first show two years ago, and made him rich and famous. Handley didn't see it like that. He had always been a man of the world, and was no different now in either talent or spirit to when he was without money or recognition. His wife and seven kids had got along on national assistance, poaching, begging-letters, and raffling paintings now and again in the Lincolnshire village they'd lived in. He shook Teddy's warm, pudgy hand. 'I need money, that's why I've come to see you.'

'You had a thousand last month. Are you sure?'

'There are a score of us living in our self-styled community, and that means twenty idle mouths to feed. I'm *not* idle, because I happen to be the breadwinner, but I don't mind that because it stimulates me for my work.'

'I wonder if you're making a mistake, living in a community?' Greensleaves ventured.

'Of course I am,' Handley said. 'I'm just one big twenty-two carat mistake like any other human being. It's not many months since my brother John died, and it seems like we buried him only yesterday. Living in a big group helps me to get over it a little bit.'

Edward didn't like Handley to be so much at the mercy of ordinary emotions. If the artist's brother died he should swiftly absorb the fact, however tragic it might be, into the mainstream of his creative powers—he suggested.

'We'll never see eye to eye,' Handley said. 'I enjoy coming to see you because it makes me feel so civilised. I mean, it amazes me how cultured people like you can live so far down in the mud.'

Teddy laughed. 'Let's not go into that.'

'Or we'll never get off it,' Handley said, pushing his face close, 'will we?'

'I mean,' Teddy said, 'wouldn't it be better for you to live in Majorca, or some place where the sun is warm, and living cheap?'

He grinned. 'You want to get rid of me?'

'I want you to be happy.'

'I thought so. You want me to stop painting.'

Greensleaves flushed, as if caught in a secret criminal thought, which deepened when he realised there was no basis for it.

'Don't take me seriously,' Handley said, 'or I'll cry. I'm the only one who knows how I can live.'

'You're painting well?' Teddy said, pouring two brandies. He had the look of a man who had his vices under control, but who also knew exactly what they were—which was something.

Handley sat in a leather chair, his feet on the long mahogany desk. 'Never better, in my humble opinion. You can put another show on as soon as you like.'

'It's only three months since the last. We don't want them to think you're too prolific.'

'Afraid they'll stop buying?' Handley jibed.

'They may want them cheaper. We can't afford that.'

'Why not? It'll hurt you but it won't hurt me. I'm working as if I'm on piece work. Bull week, every week. Grab, grab, grab. Call it inspiration if you like.'

Teddy pushed the brandy over. 'Leave the tactics to me.'

'Cheers! I suppose you might get thin if you didn't make so much money.'

He sipped and laughed. 'I don't think you realise it, Albert, but I like being fat.'

'There'd be nothing left of you if you weren't.'

'It's good to be fat in this business. A thin art dealer isn't trusted. A thin painter, yes, but not someone like me.'

He's trying to reassure me, Handley thought, that he'll never run away with my money. He's devious and corpulent. His eyes are shifty and incompetent. I'm sure he's robbing me. But he's good-natured, and I like him. 'Have you always been fat?'

'Generally, yes. People make way for a fat man. They respect him.'

Handley lit a cigar. 'Unless there's a war on.'

'No danger of that.'

'Civil war, I mean.'

Teddy laughed. 'When I go into a restaurant the waiters smile. I'm always served first, whether they know me or not. I get bigger helpings, what's more.'

Greensleaves' office made him uneasy because three of his paintings hung on the well-lit walls. They seemed out of place, set there for dealers and customers who saw them only as so many square yards of investment. Handley knew, however, that his attitude was a bad one, indicating a lack of detachment and even backbone. He was, after all, happy enough when Teddy took out his cheque book and passed a chit for three thousand pounds.

He put it in his wallet. 'That'll get me through the weekend! I don't need the other for the moment.'

They were disturbed by the buzzer, and when the door opened Handley recognised Lady Daphne Maria Fitzgerald Ritmeester (names he'd seen in an up-to-date *Who's Who* which he'd bought to get basic facts on people he bumped into now that his paintings sold at the proper prices).

'You've already met, I believe,' Greensleaves said.

'Twice,' Handley stood up, 'and both times I asked her to kiss me, but she didn't.'

'On the first occasion you were drunk,' she said, with half a smile. Her charming and grating voice was the sort that would make you feel unsure of yourself if you thought there was a chance of going to bed with her. She was a thin middle-aged woman with dark hair piled over a splendidly intelligent face. Her grey eyes seemed over-exposed due to skilful make-up and care, and her faintly spread nostrils created a subtlety for her lips that they might not otherwise have had. Handley sensed that men would have to be a hundred times more gentle before such women would come to like them.

She turned to Greensleaves. 'I just popped in to give you this,' taking an envelope from her Florentine leather bag.

Teddy blushed at money instead of sex. There has to be something that embarrasses him to the marrow, Handley thought. Lady Ritmeester had bought some of his work, including the Lincolnshire Poacher, that star piece of his one-man show at which they'd first met.

'How long are you in town?'

'Depends,' he said. 'Till tomorrow, perhaps.'

She lit a cigarette and sat down. 'How's the country?'

'Restful, as long as I can get away.'

'I hear you run some sort of community?'

'An extended family, really. A five-star doss-house.'

'I thought the revolutionary thing nowadays was to eliminate the family.'

He laughed. 'That sort of theory's for young people who haven't got families. I have seven kids, so who could get rid of that lot? There would have been another but my wife lost it after our house caught fire in Lincolnshire. I'm afraid to make up a manifesto against the family in case she gets pregnant again. If you can't beat 'em, join 'em. The only thing is to make it bigger. It drives me up the zigzags.'

'You could simply walk away,' she teased, much to Teddy's enjoyment as he opened her envelope, and put the cheque in his drawer.

'If a man's up to his neck in a bog how can he get up and crawl off? He needs a tractor to pull him free, and then it might yank both his arms out and he'd bleed to death. Still, there is some good in the family. The State's helpless against it—or one like mine. Any system that screams against the family only wants to abolish it for its own ends—good or bad. It wants such power for itself. Who wouldn't? Will you have lunch with me?'

Launched in the same tone as his speculations on the family, the request took her by surprise: 'What a strange idea!'

'It would be if we went to a fish 'n' chip shop for a piece of grotty cod washed down with a bottle of high-powered sauce,' he said. 'But I mean real lunch at the Royal Bean up the street.'

She was an expensive production with the palest of porcelain skin as if, should you start to take her clothes off, she'd come to pieces in your hands. 'You fascinate me.'

'You're like a woman,' she answered. 'Full of tease. A real man, I believe it's called.'

No response was good enough, at least not while he expected it. 'I'd be delighted if you'd have lunch with me.'

If he thought about it he couldn't imagine anything more grisly, but it was too late to back out now. 'As an experiment, then,' she said, still with that damaged but maddening smile.

Teddy wondered if they'd need to use his desk to make love on—they were getting along so well—and had an impulse to begin clearing it, so as to inch himself back into their talk. They had forgotten him, and only such rude and crude behaviour could make them pay for it.

Chapter Two

Handley suggested a taxi, but she preferred to walk the two hundred yards. They had the luck of a table near the curtained window. He offered a cigarette from his packet. 'Do you eat out much?'

'Reasonably often.'

'I usually get stomach poisoning, though this place looks all right.' He snapped his finger, but no one heard it.

'That's the disadvantage of a restaurant,' she said. 'Not good for one's self-confidence.'

She was enjoying herself, and what man could want more than that? He knew he was not very strong on courtship, and Daphne Ritmeester sensed it, too, and was trying to make him pay for it. But time was on his side, and they were no longer close to the prying ears of Teddy Greensleaves, which made them somewhat easier on each other.

'If a man is eating alone,' he said, 'and he complains about something or other he gets good treatment. But if he dines with a woman he doesn't because the waiter's back goes up, since he thinks he's only trying to impress the woman. Even if the man is justified in his complaints the waiter thinks he should show solidarity with the male sex and not mention them, especially in front of a woman. You can't win. They've got the class war in one eye and the sex war in the other. If I had my way there'd be nothing but counters where you had to go up and get your own.'

'How perfectly horrible,' she said. 'I'd never eat out.'

'You could bring a maid,' he suggested, 'and she'd queue for you.'

Had he really done the paintings she so much admired? It was like having lunch with your chauffeur simply because he was a good driver. And yet, not quite. This might turn out more interesting. 'Tell me about your life,' she said when half a melon, big enough to float away on across the blue lagoon, had been set before them. 'How did you become a painter?'

'My life's simple,' he replied. 'Always will be, I hope. After prep school, Eton and Oxford, I got a commission in the Brigade of Guards. Fought in France, back through Dunkirk, went to Egypt and got wounded—though not in the groin. I rejoined my battalion and went to Italy, wounded again, invalided out, nothing to do except draw my pension and paint pictures.'

She laughed. 'That's not what you told the newspapers.'

'You've got to make up a good story,' he said, pushing his melon aside because it tasted like marrow. 'Uncle Toby would disown me if I didn't. I love you. But you must forgive me—not for saying that, because I can't imagine anyone not coming out with it—but for being so blunt and common. I can't make pretty speeches. I paint, not talk. I've never been good at weaving snares of words around women. If I'm so tongue-tied that I can only say "I love you", you'll have to forgive me.'

It seemed impossible to get through to him. There must be a gap in his armour somewhere. He knew she was thinking this, and saw that if he kept up his rigmarole long enough she might come to bed with him. 'Do you paint all the time?'

'Every minute God sends.'

'Don't you get bored?'

'I love you, Daphne.'

'Don't you get bored with that?' He was too impertinent to be her chauffeur.

'Let's go to Paris for a couple of days.'

'Certainly not.'

'Venice, then.'

It was ludicrous. She laughed. He rubbed his hands under the table. Wiping them on the cloth, she thought, pointing to the napkin. He drew it across his moustache.

'You haven't got your passport,' she said.

He took it out of his pocket. 'I never leave the house unless it's on me—even if only to the pub for a packet of fags—in case I decide not to go back. I always do, though. You only vanish when all the ends will be left hanging.'

'You're a very destructive person.'

'Not really. To myself maybe.'

'You make my blood run cold,' she mocked.

'Here's the horsemeat,' he said, glad to end such a note.

For a thin woman she showed great appetite, and if he kept up with her it was only to get his money's worth, and because he'd left home with no more than half a grapefruit and a thimble of black coffee under his belt.

He filled her empty glass close to the brim, hoping she'd bend her lips to the table to sip it, so that he could look down her dress. But he'd underestimated her dexterity, for she lifted it easily without spilling a drop.

He apologised: 'I'm no good at serving people.'

'You'd never make a waiter,' she smiled. 'When did you last go to the mainland?'

'Fortnight ago. Got so bored with my community I lit off in the car. Drove five hundred kilometres to this posh hotel south of Paris. Cost fifty francs for a room and bath. Same again for something to eat. I got sloshed over dinner, so daren't use the bath I'd paid for in case I drowned. I climbed into bed with my boots on to make up for it. After all, fifty francs is four quid. I really do love you.'

She jumped, though not, he noted, with annoyance. He imagined it might be due to his quick change of voice and because he touched her warm, silken kneecap under the table. 'Why do you keep on?'

He sensed she'd be disappointed if he suddenly lost heart. She hadn't been entertained at lunch for a long time, and so unexpected.

'Listen,' he said confidentially, eyes lit as he leaned closer, 'I can get all the women I want, just by telling them I love them. If I say it earnestly enough—but not like a beaten dog—no woman can resist it. It always works, even if you do it only ten minutes after meeting them.

Often that's more effective because they think that if you can fall in love so quickly you'll never be able to see their faults. A thing like that almost persuades them they're in love with you. But only the best women believe you when you say you love them, and they're the ones you want.'

She noticed how impeccably dressed he was, how lean-faced and handsome, with his well-chiselled head, short hair and clipped moustache. 'You may not know it,' she said, attempting to divert him, 'but I'm married.'

'Your husband's on the board of fifty-four companies.'

She tapped her empty plate. 'Fifty-six.'

'My stud-book's out of date.'

She picked up the menu to choose dessert.

'He's afraid the country's heading for a Labour Government.'

'It'll shoot rapidly out as soon as it gets in,' he reassured her. 'There's nothing predictable about the English, bless 'em. I was in the butcher's the other day buying the daily cow, and he was bewailing the power of the trade unions and said what England needs is a dictator to put a stop to 'em. He was in raptures at the thought of it, so I said: "Yes, I'd love that as well. That would really ruin the country. Blokes like you would go down first. I'd bloody love that, because as soon as it happened I'd be on my way to Switzerland." You should have seen his face drop. Because I'd got money he thought I was on his side.'

'Poor fellow!' she said.

'You know,' he went on fervently so that she couldn't interrupt, 'I can normally look people in the eyes, but when I'm in love I can burn anyone off the face of the earth. Your eyes are generous and clever. Don't think I don't fall in love even though I am forty-three. My brain may get soft, but the charge is still there. It's not lust or wick-fever either because when I'm in love, as I am now, my slonker isn't so ready to stiffen though it burns like a poker in the fire when it gets there at last. My sight is clearer and I wear glasses less when I'm painting. I'm not shy and devious anymore when I'm in love, even though I have more to hide because *I'm* married as well!'

Her hand shook at the menu. The smile left her. She was glad the waiter came, and they ordered a dessert which, he reminded her, was as high and ornate as the hat she'd been wearing when he first saw her two years ago: 'I'll do a picture when I get home. The idea's forming in my third and visual eye. Lady Ritmeester's hat! It won't be a big one, but its colour will dazzle the world!'

She'd heard more loving speeches in the last half hour than from her husband in fifteen years. The skin under her make-up was burning. 'I'll order more wine—no, champagne,' he said, 'to toast the way I feel about you.'

He felt a hand on his wrist. 'Pay the bill,' she said. 'We'll get a taxi to my flat on Mount Street.'

It was a last ploy to call his bluff, but she knew it wouldn't work, and hoped it wouldn't, and it didn't, though under her confidence she wondered where it would lead—if anywhere.

So did Handley as he helped her into her coat and caught another whiff of her subtle expensive perfume, and a glimpse of the pearls laying along the pale flesh of her neck.

From the long corridor he could see it was the sort of flat that cost a hundred pounds a week to rent furnished. Everything was Harrod's best, tables of expensive rosewood, dark green panelling, heavy half-drawn curtains, an elaborate dressing-table with a pink marble top, built-in wardrobes (a bad touch that, he felt) and a high, enormous bed which redeemed everything. She'd led him straight into the bedroom so that the maid wouldn't twig.

He stood alone, smoking a cigar and blessing such unexpected luck, his back to the empty fireplace. Or was it luck? There was no saying, though he couldn't think she'd shown him to her bedroom for a drink of beer. There were no pictures or ornaments on the walls, and only a faint sound of traffic through the double windows.

She clicked the door to. 'I hate cigars. Do put it out.'

Sitting at the dressing-table, she lifted off her wig. Its sudden absence diminished her face, made it slightly less thin, and dark hair underneath was so short she resembled Joan of Arc.

'Don't kiss me,' she said, when he went to her. 'And don't undress me. Just take your clothes off.'

He didn't trust her, though he had nothing to lose so could see no reason for it. But he got out of his jacket, shirt and trousers, watching her observing him through the dozen mirrors, and noting the slightly exaggerated curve of her lips, as if she too didn't know why he was there. If you couldn't kiss her, how else could you lead up to it?

Her short wispy hair made her look younger and more vulnerable, as if she ought to be glad of having him in her bedroom rather than trying to make him feel so privileged. Her face was also a little hard in its thinness, and the mix-up gave to her eyes a mocking air that he wanted to get rid of.

'It's a fine bedroom. It suits you.'

She took off her pearls and bracelets. 'I camp here. You should see the bedroom at Flaxton, my country place. It would make your mouth water, I'm sure.'

'I like this one.'

'It's mine,' she smiled, standing to let her skirt fall. 'My husband is allowed to visit me in it now and again.'

The transformation from the elegant Lady Ritmeester with the elaborate and high-piled coiffure to the short-haired naked thin woman with a smile like a Hampstead housewife off for an afternoon with her boyfriend was so disconcerting that he found it erotic, and went towards her. The remains of her personality had retreated into her voice. She backed away and said in the normal Ritmeester timbre: 'Don't. I'll come to you.'

Since they weren't more than a few feet apart he could afford to wait, though to pass the time he took off his pants and stood naked. She reached out and touched him in the only spot that seemed to matter, for under her delicate fingers it lifted, a very obedient horn. Her small breasts lured him because he had never seen any so perfectly white. Even the nipples were pale and merged into the flesh. The rest of her body was firm, and only slightly less pale, and he bent forward and kissed her slender neck, his hand on her stomach.

They stroked each other, and Handley was locked in the circle of her as if gripped by fatigue. His dream made him feel she was the most powerful woman he'd ever met, and he was disturbed at his liking for her, though his ready mechanism of self-preservation pushed it immediately away. 'Don't let's burst,' he said, noticing her eyes were closed, and pressing her gently.

'Don't touch me *there*,' she said, when his hand went between them. He wondered if they were to do it by extra-sensual perception, or some such mystical stuff, but he wasn't prepared to enter a brother and sister act either, so pushed her firmly towards the bed. She let herself on to the counterpane, eyes staying closed.

'Not yet,' she said, opening her legs. He knelt beside her on the bed, able to stare because she still refused to look at him. Her fingers rippled at herself, and suddenly her whole body played with some sensation he wasn't allowed to share.

Unable to resist, and he assumed he was not meant to (you had to be careful with such a woman), and being at full height, he slid lusciously into her. Whenever he tried a kiss she moved her face, so he had to be satisfied with neck and shoulders, shifting gently as if afraid of breaking her, none of the usual forceful thrusting, but slowly and tenderly, one hand spread under her buttocks until another trembling broke deeply inside her, so that this time he got the force of it. Her dry breath jerked strongly out of her nostrils and against his cheek. A few moments later he also came, a weird flood that filled her narrow tunnel. It was an issue too soon for his taste, but he was never at his best on a fed stomach and a bottle of wine.

'Get off me.'

He lifted himself. 'Thank you.' There seemed nothing else to say, though he would rather have lain a bit longer.

'Get dressed.'

'Why do you keep your eyes closed?'

'It's much better,' she said. 'I get my enjoyment more quickly. I go into other worlds.'

'What worlds?'

'Wouldn't you like to know?'

'Of course I bloody well would.' He put on his underwear and shirt, grateful for some explanation at least. While his back was turned for his trousers she leapt silently off the bed towards a grey silk dressing gown.

'Does your husband know you carry on like this?'

She sat by the dressing-table and lit a cigarette. 'He thinks I have lesbian relationships, and that's all right.'

'Do you?'

'Sometimes. Just to allay his suspicions—or to head them off.'

The encounter had left him feeling deprived, as if it had been too civilised. 'I expect he likes to watch.'

She frowned. 'He's not perverted. As long as I tell him about them.'

He was half-way to lighting a cigar, but remembered she didn't like her bedroom stunk up—which made him want to get on the street where he could be free and in peace.

'One has to live,' she said. 'And there are many ways of doing it.' Her wig was back. 'Perhaps you'd better go.'

He put his coat on. 'How do I get to kiss you?'

'You'll have to marry me.'

'You already are,' he grinned.

'Exactly.'

'Well, so am I, come to that.'

He had lost his patter, which was another gauge of her success. 'What does your wife do while you're out with other women?'

'She doesn't know.'

Lady Ritmeester laughed. 'Have you asked her?'

'No.'

'Then how do *you* know?' She had found his weak spot. He trusted too much in his own strength. And what a big weak spot it was—such non-existent strength! 'Still,' she said, not wanting to warn him of the disaster she saw in store, 'you can hardly complain if she does the same as you.'

'I won't. But how do we keep in touch?'

She smiled. 'We don't.'

'You serious?'

'Don't ever telephone me.'

'I'll walk up and down outside with a sandwich board over me, saying DAPHNE, I LOVE YOU on one side, and KISS ME, DAPHNE on the other.'

He was almost back on form, so she could be more indulgent. She hated men who became serious afterwards.

'Perhaps we'll meet at the gallery.'

That was enough. Why push too far? He blew a kiss, and she sent one back. Sweethearts at least. 'Do let yourself out,' she said. 'I feel a headache coming on.'

He crossed the street and nearly got knocked over by a taxi. The driver cursed. Handley thought of shouting back, but why bother? He made his way to the car in Hanover Square. With Teddy's cheque in his pocket he could go back to the bosom of his community without a soul being any the wiser.

Two more parking fines had been attached to the windscreen by a rotten little Hitlerite traffic warden, and it was more in sorrow than in anger that he set the car moving up the street, and once again flipped on the wipers so that they went off like a pair of birds in freedom, narrowly missing a Rolls-Royce behind.

It was the last real carefree day he could remember.

Chapter Three

Cuthbert came downstairs in his green-and-white striped pyjamas, switching on lights at every turn. If there was one thing the Handleys loved it was light, and in this at any rate he was no exception to his father.

Formerly, in the Lincolnshire house—called The Burrow when they were destitute, and The Gallery after the old man had struck it rich—bulbs had burned all the time, as if they lived close to an immense inexhaustible powerhouse of a dam. But the family hadn't made much of an impression on Myra's place in the south Midlands, where they had come to live after the Gallery had been burned to the ground by mad Uncle John. They seemed subdued by a subtle combination of middle-class economy and bourgeois abundance.

The décor, the pictures, the smell, even the creak of stairs underfoot made Cuthbert see how much of a trap the freedom-loving Handley family had fallen into by accepting the bonds of this puerile community of twenty souls. Roundabout the house Myra had kept the lawns smooth, the trees pruned and bushes trimmed, and therefore safe against free-booting Handleys who had been so free they had finally imprisoned themselves in the middle of it. The shining motor-mower ready for instant action, primed and fuelled in its centrally-heated garage, was a threat to everyone, and from his stance by the kitchen door Cuthbert pictured rose bushes and fruit trees surrounding and enlacing the house, with their aroma of damp tea leaves and delicately rotting bark, clad with ivy and wistaria gently crushing bricks and mortar to death.

He felt hunger, but no appetite. If voracity is the spice of life, eat on. He tried to smile, but failed, so cut bread and cheese, and came back into the living room. Drummed out of theological college, he'd been glad of this refuge which he now despised. The spine and purpose had gone from his life, and he'd been near to doing away with himself, not because the dismissal had made him particularly unhappy (that was all over and put behind) but because it was a situation he'd been unable to control.

Thoughts of suicide had been tempered by curiosity at the mechanism of this community to which the others imagined he loyally belonged. He was amused at the intensity with which they worried about the world. Such concern seemed merely the premature onset of middle age. People only form this kind of togetherness out of fear, as if they never had father or mother to kick all that crap out of them.

He would appear as a devoted member of the community, though to cultivate the necessary subterfuge—which shouldn't be hard after three years of trying to become a priest—would mean speaking as little as possible, because while you talk you cannot think, and he preferred to indulge in the fruitlessness of his secret thoughts. There was wisdom in silence, acquiescence to one's innermost desires. If you smiled, everyone trusted you. Open your mouth, and you betray yourself. Speech is thought that kills itself as soon as it races aloud from between the lips.

He looked in the mirror, swilling down Nescafé between bread and cheese. The framed prints of early nineteenth-century huntsmen floundering in ditches seemed to have enticed Handley the Lincolnshire poacher to an early spiritual death. An artist did not need a settled base in which to work, so his father should have loaded tools and easels into the Rambler and taken to the road (after installing his family, as was only right, in some opulent bungalow), rather than accept this frigid nullity of communal life.

Looking round the white-walled room, it was hard to imagine a naked man with a penis in full bloom chasing a bare woman between plush chairs, and then going upstairs to rampage in one of the cool, impeccable bedrooms. You fucked quietly in this house, or not at all, didn't even grunt between the sheets, which was why he supposed Dawley had installed himself like General Montgomery in one of the caravans to write his memoirs.

Two months ago he had no notion of staying long in his father's establishment. The prodigal son had never been part of his make-up, and certainly no fatted bullock had been roasted on his tentative return. His life had cost little in the way of straight cash, for like all Handley's children, he was a child of charity, the eternally promising youth of scholarship and patronage.

The nearest he came to a rebellion at school was one winter afternoon when he decided that if he heard another word about King Arthur and his screwy knights he'd go off his head. This state had been lately repeated at theological college when he had found himself beginning to accept the principles of Christianity that had been panned at him during the last three years. He dreaded losing his sacred assets of cunning and hypocrisy.

Over the affair of King Arthur he had throttled his indignation because it only increased his interior scepticism, but the more recent threat to his lack of faith he took so seriously that he entered into months of lying, cheating, perjury and screwing. He hadn't gone into precise details of his expulsion with Handley, yet saw them chuffing into their beers over it one jovial night, in which case the simile of the return of the prodigal might have some relevance after all, and he knew Handley in his heart wanted nothing more deeply than this.

Under the livid strip-lighting he sliced more black rye and Camembert. During the day he could eat nothing, so throughout the night he was unable to overcome his insomnia while the wolf-rat of hunger pranced around in his stomach. At college he slung a loose cloth bag over the toprail of his bed so that when the famishings began he could dip in for biscuits and corned beef, slab cake and fruit—all the goodies he remembered wanting in childhood but hardly ever getting. In his hasty departure this precious piece of equipment had been left behind, so by night he turned into a shoeless marauder and made a sardonic trek for the icebox.

Any change made him bitter, especially one over which he'd had no control. Yet the more he thought of it the less could he remember any over which he had been in charge. This made him realise that his bitterness was misplaced, a spectacle which awed him slightly.

Even the acts which led to these alterations, carried out with much forethought, had somehow happened against his will—a will that was the most threatening part of him because he had never been united with it. Whenever he did something, he wondered why he had done it, and knew that this was not the best way to order your existence. His will was irresolute, disobedient and pernicious, and whatever happened in his life had never been connected to it.

Being without will, almost without desire, momentous events happened to you, but he was too busy eating at the overlit kitchen table to consider them now. It was as if matters of volition and decision were a thing of the past. Having no will created self-regard, led him to suppose that if it had perished in him then it must also be on its way out for the rest of the world. Whether it were or not didn't concern him, for he felt in no way influenced by it.

The fact that he was without will did not mean that he could be manipulated by those who possessed it. Quite the opposite. He felt safe from the world, more his own master than if he were clutched by a rabid will-to-power. And under cover of your own pale lack of will what could not be perpetrated against friends and enemies alike?

He didn't know why he suffered so much from lack of will, yet thought it might be because he'd come into the world unable to remember his dreams. It may not go together with everyone, but it did with him. And having no will he was sometimes resented by people who said he was harbouring a secret and wicked will against them, a will-lessness that went so far into his core that they saw a deep disguise, a trick, a threat of such forceful intent that they would be powerless against it when its aims became known.

Thus his father, whom Cuthbert suspected of having taken his share of both dreams and will—for what they were worth—and woven them into the fabric of his artistic life, distrusted his lazy contempt of all that went on in the house and its environs. He accused Cuthbert of brewing up black-souled mischief that boded ill for everyone.

At dinner when he was seen to eat nothing, Handley let go a tirade that Cuthbert found entertaining, though unnecessary because he merely lacked appetite at that particular moment.

'And in this particular company,' Handley said. 'Look at him, my one and only sly-eyed eldest son. He's left-handed, born under the sign of Pisces, and has no lobes to his ears. Could anyone be more marked by the devil than that?'

'Leave him alone,' said his mother. 'Give him time to settle down.'

'He can take as long as he likes,' Handley said, getting back to his meat, 'as long as he works in the meantime. The trouble is, he shows a sad inclination to mysticism, and there's nothing makes you more bone-idle or treacherous.'

'It was your idea to get me trained as a priest,' Cuthbert shouted.

'There was nothing wrong with that, until you gave it up. It's part of a priest's job to be mystical. The bishop might not like it, but they allow it. But you're no longer a priest, so stop acting and behaving like one. And stow the bloody mysticism! We have a perfectly good way of life here, for the twenty souls in our community. It's hard-working, happy, co-operative, and totally unproductive. But all you do is use it as a convenient hostel, drifting around between sleeping and eating—not that I see you do either, come to think of it—wrapped in a haze of self-defeating mysticism that threatens to take up all of us in a cloud of smoke. Don't think I haven't got you weighed up. You'll find yourself in a factory one of these days, working for your living.'

As he sat through the dregs of the night, and more than compensated for his gorge-block at dinner, he did indeed consider it easy to drop his senses into a sort of trance, though in a more uncertain moment he wondered whether this wasn't the onset of a softening brain.

He could sit down, go into emptiness, and not wake from it till hours had passed, without even having been asleep. Or he could daydream, have visions, project himself, reach three distinct modes of disassociation with no effort. For a long time he imagined these states of human sensory breadth as more or less available to everybody, and when he realised they might not be he loathed himself for being different, the effect of which was to make him intolerant of everyone else.

Chapter Four

Rainspots fell as he crossed the yard and made his way between two caravans. The encampment slept, soothed by its futile work of the day, resting from the complex interaction of human relationships that such close living entailed.

He came back and leaned outside the kitchen door. Would he, after recovering his strength, get into the real world again? Having failed at college he not only hadn't 'got on' but he hadn't even been close to the ladder on which he could begin ascending. By going wrong he'd wounded himself. He couldn't believe anybody else had done it. If he accepted that he'd have been closer to being a Christian, and so wouldn't have fouled his chances at college in any case.

And yet, was he turning into a materialist, one of those narrow-minded, one-dimensional, all guts and no spirit, earth and no sky, lobotomised Neanderthal creatures like Frank Dawley who wallowed in the glory of his few months' fighting in Algeria as if he was the poor man's Lawrence of Arabia?

It was essential to get things straight in his own mind—unless you wanted to be sucked in by this community so that you didn't know what sort of a person you were anymore.

A drift of fresh air revived him, and reminded him how tired he was. Even the month of May could give you pneumonia if you came out at night in pyjamas and slippers. Eric Bloodaxe the bulldog stirred its bulk by the gate—but a shape moved near the caravans, and he stood for it to come closer, unpleasantly surprised at his fear.

'On the prowl?' Mandy said.

'Can't my dear sister sleep, either?'

She leaned by the caravan wall. 'Does it look like it, Brother Rat? My bloody husband sleeps like a sack of coal somebody's dropped and left behind after nicking it from a railway wagon. He doesn't sleep: he dies—and takes all my sleep with him. It's impossible to be in the same bed with the unfeeling swine. It's his mother's fault. No wonder she laughed when he got married. That was the only wedding present we got, and as far as I know it didn't even crack her junk-shop face. I suppose she'd laugh on the other side though if we got divorced and I sent him creeping back to her.'

'You'd better have the baby first.'

'That's not for another three boring months.'

The moon made its light available again, and he looked at her face. He remembered hauling her as a baby in the pram with Adam and Richard to the village for their sweet ration. Afterwards they roamed fields and woods to see what they could plunder. Their family was in a perpetual state of destitution because Handley did nothing but paint day and night, a lone and frenzied figure up in his attic, wrapped in coats and scarves when the cold got too much of a grip around the windows. They lived on national assistance, sickness benefit, charity, relief, begging letters, the dole, and what they could loot from the surrounding countryside. And now that Handley sold his paintings at prices which made him rich beyond the dreams of his expectations, they thought he was miserly by refusing to hand over the money to which his new-found fortune entitled them.

As children they had done their bit to keep the family going. When chased by farmer or gardener they maintained a compact group around the pram, from which blonde, plump Mandy either joined in the general panic and screamed with fear, or stayed locked in her own private baby-world and laughed divinely at the worst it could do to her. And now she was a pregnant eighteen-year-old slut. 'Don't you think of your husband at a time like this?'

She laughed. 'If I was planning to kill him, I suppose I would. But I'm not—yet. There's a hard stone inside me first that's got to grind its way through the floor. When that's over I can start living again.'

'What do you think you're doing now?'

'Since you ask, I'm multiplying. When Dad thought this house would be big enough for the community he reckoned without me. I'll have at least a litter.'

Shameless and fetching, he thought, base and lecherous when she's not too heavy to walk. The sway gives her away when her belly's up, and the predatory shoulder-slope when she's empty and ready. 'Father's a great Christian. He'll feed any number of mouths.'

'He's a mean old rattlebag,' she cried.

'Not so loud. He'll hear you.'

'Are you frightened of him, as well? Everybody is. I must be the only one who isn't. I tell him twenty times a day how mean he is. His brain's pickled in vinegar and his heart's clogged with salt. I can understand how he can sleep at night, but I don't see how he can wake up in the morning.'

'He's brittle with good living,' he said. 'A well-charged magneto who lords it over us with all the authority of unexplainable drive and power—and the fact that his hands are on the cash.'

She clutched her stomach. 'That's the third bloody time.'

'What is?'

'I don't know. That's what woke me in the first place.' She straightened, and smiled. 'We'd all like to see the back of him. Give us a fag.'

'I haven't got any.'

'You're even meaner than he is.' She took a packet from her padded and flowered dressing gown. 'If he popped off one day to the South Seas who'd take his place?'

He lit a cigarette. 'Who knows?'

'As long as it's not you. I'd rather die.'

'I thought you were too generous to think that far ahead.'

She groaned. 'Either I've eaten too much, or my appendix has burst.'

'Take a pill.'

'I'll need at least forty to get a few winks before daylight.'

He couldn't resist speaking his favourite interior thought, having often noticed that deciding not to say something was merely the first stage to letting it out. 'It'd be such joy to see the last of father that there's no point in thinking about what would happen afterwards. You'd never do anything if you considered the consequences.'

'You certainly don't think about getting pregnant when you're humping around on a bed with a man,' she said.

An owl sang its nightsong over the caravans, such a cool rhythmical warbling that they couldn't but listen. She bent down, then straightened and turned her pale full face as if to see where the moon had gone. 'If this keeps on I'll have a miscarriage.'

'It'll get out so easily you won't know it's happened,' he said lightly.

'I tried to get rid of it when I knew I was preggers. But nothing bloody worked.'

'Some loathsome member of this community could have given you an address, I expect.'

There was a movement on the higher ground of lawns and fruit trees at the back of the house. Whoever it was had been only a few yards from their conversation, hidden in the thin alleyway dividing the caravans. Cuthbert felt a chill, knowing himself to be a coward, otherwise he wouldn't make so many plans.

'I heard you,' Handley shouted, coming down the steps. 'You pair of plotting nightbirds.'

Cuthbert backed away, smiling so that his father might believe his remarks had been merely a joke, crossed by one of defiant friendliness in case Handley hadn't really heard and was only bluffing—which he often was.

Mandy clutched her belly, and Cuthbert was proud of her quick though dramatic response in trying to divert her father's wrath. 'It's getting out,' she said, pools of sweat breaking from her face.

Handley stood in his dressing gown, looking from one to the other. 'Neither of us could sleep,' Cuthbert informed him.

'I can't hold it,' Mandy said. Between spasms she felt light enough to drift away bodily in the blue air despite her stony weight. It was a sensation of great happiness in which her past returned in one delicious moment, as if every minute of it had been a golden paradise that she'd always wanted to bring back but had never succeeded in till now, when it was totally unexpected and twice as sweet for almost reappearing.

Another spasm struck, and blacked it out. Two faces looked at her, made exaggeratedly clear because of the pain. She lost control of her life so utterly that she was both pleased and frightened by it. Her father's sharp chisel nose, and his thin lined face bent down, eyes burning through to her in sympathy. He should have been named Oswald, she thought, a laugh even in her pain. Oswald the Chiking Viking. Cuthbert's own clear eyes also looked, but knew nothing, as if he were still too young at twenty-five to tell himself what he did not want to know because he would be afraid when he found out.

Handley pushed him roughly aside. 'You bloody fool,' he said, putting an arm around her. 'Can't you see she's having a miscarriage? Let's get her into the house.'

Chapter Five

Dawley could not sleep. He'd drunk too much brandy and got the heartburn. Or maybe the livid globe of the moon was reaching the dark corners of his heart at last, scooping away that mystery of peace in which he might have found rest.

He stood by the caravan window and pulled on his trousers. Sure enough, the moon was there, queen of the thick white night for all to see, high above the chestnut trees of the opposite field. His belt was too tight at the waist, which came from Myra's rich soups and Russian salads, jellied chicken buried in cream, baked potatoes, medium-done steaks, and heavy breakfasts of the sort he hadn't eaten when working in the factory three years ago. English country walks didn't slake flesh off like treks through the valleys and deserts of Algeria. He remembered that lean and mindless state of continual travelling, when staring blankly at a map in the evening was the nearest you got to intellectual refreshment.

Printed matter rained into the community, but in the wilderness there'd been nothing but agonising foodless days, a flycrawl and pencil-scratch across a piece of coloured paper called a map, in memory more real than the actual fabulous land his feet had plodded through. It was a marvellous time.

A wailing bitch-howl flew from the moon's full face. He wanted to boot the dog out of existence for being as restless as himself. When the scream came again it wasn't from Eric Bloodaxe but some poor wracked person in the house, and it startled him even more. He'd almost got used to the oppressive tranquillity of the last few weeks. Certainly, if you had two quiet days in the Handley household you began to worry that it would go on forever, though the others acted as if it had never happened in their lives before.

Myra created a kingdom of ease and plenty. She drove to the markets of Hitchin and Bedford, and came back with a car-load of baskets and bottles and boxes and crates, their son Mark strapped high in his chair beside her, watching rabbits run before them on the country lanes. The house prospered in its mildness, set for a warm summer and a comfortable year, which Frank felt the need of in spite of its dullness, because it was only a few months since he had left the perilous sands and hills of Algeria.

Fetching Nancy and the kids from Nottingham hadn't turned out as he'd expected, but he'd enjoyed the train ride, the usual thrill of going north again. At St Pancras he went by the ticket man to the waiting train—coiling upshoots of grey steam between each carriage.

Passing a stretch of the M1 beyond Hendon the train was overtaking every car on it. Factory walls of Vauxhall and SKF at Luton slid past. A solitary man walked across some tips, seen as William Posters, that indefatigable fugitive from Dawley's past who was nowadays turning more into a ghost and floating further from him than ever.

Rich fields and soil showed the great wealth of England. Pylons rose and fell in their lines, laced up a couple of woods and a crest of rising ground. More farms, rich land, empty roads now that the motorway had sucked off traffic. Crossing the Trent he thought that in middle age one turned to the past so as to arm oneself against what was left of the future.

He was almost sorry to leave the soothing train. The man of action is drawn deeper into rest than most. On a bus through town to the estate he noticed how the centre was splitting into car parks and one-way streets, dead acres and blocks of flats covering old houses now down and gone forever. It gave him a feeling that, in tune with his own travels and actions, the rest of the world had not lived either in vain or idleness. His favourite birthplace and city had done things for itself, though he didn't suppose that those who had stayed thought about it in the same comfortable nostalgic way that he did going through on the bus.

The black slum-zones remained, factories and gasometers, crippled churches and decrepit schools. Handley had offered the Rambler, expecting him to bring Nancy and the kids back on the same day with their belongings tied to the roofrack, as if she would leave job, give up house, and snap ties like a nomad who'd been a few days there instead of all her twenty-eight years. Handley sounded as unrealistic as ever, yet the impossible happened. She severed her woven bonds and was on her way back with Dawley in a week. He was locked in the shock of speed, the flowering of unexpected decisiveness that stopped him knowing what he finally felt about it. He could only be mystified, until calmness of heart returned that would make things plain. In the meantime he preferred to think (in his male and blinkered way, he told himself later when the whole thing got smashed) that Nancy loved him, and did not want to live alone with the kids.

Having wife and girlfriend in the same house he could sleep with neither openly, but visited one or the other in secret—whenever the good mood took him, and if it coincided with the convenience and desire of the woman herself. He kept separate from Myra and Nancy by occupying the caravan. He thought he was in love with both, and this disorientated him, proving something he already knew: that there was no ideal way of existence. Such split love was like having his feet on two different lifeboats in the middle of a stormy sea and far from land. But he liked it, and thought that was how life should be.

It was good being in a community, as long as there were enough women to go round. With the coming of Cuthbert this was no longer the case. Not that Frank was jealous of his women—there was so much trust in the air that no one cared one way or the other. Neither was he aware of anyone being jealous: what harm would it do if he was robbed of either of them, even if he did love both? A fair proof of love was the ability to lose it like a man when it was taken from you, and the only way to enjoy it was to get all you could while you could.

Cuthbert did not seem to fit in, and Handley plainly thought the same, though spoilt his case by shouting it loud and clear, for it was fatal to let Cuthbert know that you hated his guts. It paid to say nothing, and lead him to believe you were the strong silent type who might quietly bash his face in if he ever stepped too far out of line.

The mellow notes of early nightingales sounded in the lilac trees of the upper terrace. He stood with rolled-up shirt sleeves, and a cool breeze played over his skin. He saw Handley by the kitchen door. 'What's going on? You look as if your liver's on the blink.'

'Mandy's miscarrying. Enid and the doctor's with her. She's got moonbeams in her belly.'

Frank lit two fags and gave him one. 'She's been taking life easy.'

'Her heart's not in it, though, and who can blame her with that milk-brain of a husband? I should never have let them get married, but what can you do if they're set on it?' his sharp pallid features were screwed with anguish as Mandy's screams burst from an overhead window.

'Not much,' Dawley admitted.

'It's that doctor,' he went on. 'She was bleeding a few days ago, and when she asked if she ought to go to bed, he laughed in his jolly old English avuncular fashion and said, "Oh no, just carry on as usual and get plenty of exercise, because you're young and healthy and as strong as a horse." What can you do with a murderer like that except take him out to sea and drop him from a helicopter? He's up there now trying to stop her bleeding to death, but when this lot's over I wouldn't go to him again even if my arm was hanging off. He's the sort that rants against abortion but goes on killing foetuses by the dozen whenever he gets the chance—not to mention people.'

'She's not lost it yet,' said Frank. 'Maybe she won't.' It was the wrong thing to say, but what was right at such a time?

Handley didn't think much of it. At the moment he was a pessimist, though when all was going well he was the most optimistic person in the world. 'It tears my guts. First John killed himself, and now Mandy's losing her baby. There's too much death. I hate death.' He said it as if there were some connection between the two catastrophes, which made Dawley wonder if he were using it to work himself into a state where life became interesting as well as insupportable, so that he could get back into his painting.

They strolled towards the boundary wall, and Dawley looked at the façade of the house. 'I didn't know you'd put Mandy in Uncle John's old room.'

'I didn't. Myra gave up hers. It's more convenient. She certainly takes the weight of the world on her shoulders. I often wonder if we're worth it, the ton of work she puts in. Still, I never was one to feel guilty when somebody does me a favour. That's not my line, though

I'd like her to know I appreciate it. But telling somebody isn't enough. There has to be more to it than that.'

'You slept with her last night,' said Frank. 'I hope that put the idea across to her.'

Handley jumped. In spite of the lax rules of community-living he didn't like to make more turmoil than he himself would want to put up with. It was hard to drop your life-long habits when everyone was watching. If he got rid of them at all he'd rather it were in secret, so as to give them most effect, but that would be going against the spirit of the community, so he was split two ways, which was better than the usual six. 'You're a right bastard. But you're wrong.' There was a pause. 'Anyway, what makes you think I did?'

Frank didn't know whether to believe him or not. 'Same as tonight. Couldn't get my head down. Copped you sneaking out of the house with your tail between your legs. Never saw anyone with such a hang-dog look.'

Handley felt it was his turn to laugh. 'Let me know if it gets too much for you.'

'I don't possess anyone.'

'You will, when they possess you.'

'I suppose it is a way of two people staying glued if they can't bear to lose each other,' Dawley said.

'It's inhuman not to be jealous,' said Handley, 'I would be—especially of somebody like Myra. You sound as if you enjoy her—as a woman, like.'

Dawley wouldn't answer. He usually did, but why tell everyone? In his gloating, Handley was pushing it, taking the unwritten rules of freedom too much to heart. Dawley wondered what he'd say if he knew someone had been sleeping with Enid which, by the law of jungle-averages, might have happened.

'The trouble is,' Handley confessed, 'I don't really enjoy it unless the woman does. If I try too hard the woman often doesn't. It's love that makes 'em come, not effort—sparking both of you off at the right time. Then, again, if a woman don't make it, it's no good either of you feeling guilty over it. I knew a chap who used to apologise if he didn't bring his girlfriend off. She had a nervous breakdown. Best thing is not to let them see you worry. Just care for them, as much as you do for yourself. I cottoned on to it when I got married, I suppose. The first act of civilisation is to get married. I've got seven kids, so what else can I say?' He smoothed down his moustache, and grinned, as if he were a young man again.

Mandy was quieter. The house had settled to sleep under the veil of their subdued talk. 'It's also the most uncivilised act possible,' Handley snapped, changing his mind. 'The one social law that stops the progress of humanity dead in its tracks.'

'Where does kicking against it get us,' Frank said wryly, 'except into this weird little set-up that we call a community?'

He was disappointed at not seeing Dawley's face. Was he also full of nails about it? We've all got our reasons for being here. It wasn't that he didn't trust Dawley, just that he didn't know how conscious he was of the ramifications of his altered existence.

'It would be nice to know what living like this is doing to us,' Dawley wondered.

Handley saw that he might be in danger of underestimating him—another pitfall of community life: 'We'll find out when it begins to fall apart.' Perhaps, in the obscurity beyond any immediate concern for Mandy's suffering, they saw something that might contribute to the community's smash up.

Handley had a vision of Cuthbert's face at dinner, of his smile in fact at any time during the last month or so. The truth of what it had been trying to say, and at the same time to hide, came on him now. If there was anyone in the establishment (he preferred that word to 'community') who wanted to break things up, it was Cuthbert. One false move on his part, Handley decided, and he'd get booted out. 'Did you say there was a light in John's room?'

Dawley wondered what the long silence had been for. 'There still is. I thought Mandy was in it.'

During the few moments of peace Dawley had an unrealistic and irrational wish for it to reign forever. But it was not possible, especially when Handley strode aggressively towards the house, his eyes burning and lips set tight, on his way to tackle Cuthbert who was malingering in the forbidden territory of John's memorial room.

Chapter Six

The house was like a hornets' nest, and Cuthbert wanted to cut off. He turned the handle and went into the room that had been fitted as a shrine to Uncle John, arranged precisely like his den in the far-off scorched-down house of Lincolnshire.

There were the same shelves of books, and on a wall were pinned Algerian maps, while along another were colourful sheets of RAF topographical charts covering South Vietnam. Under these was a single bed, and then an altar of radio equipment that hadn't been switched on since it was set up.

He wondered which knob to turn for sound, as another shattering cry of pain shot up from Mandy somewhere below, followed by a heartburst of guilt and sympathy from her husband Ralph. The padded earphones muffled a shout from Handley, and a lugubrious howl by Eric Bloodaxe. He heard no more—and knew how it was that insane and epileptic John had clung to life and sensibility in this zoo-den for so long.

The light held him in its circle, head and hands outlined against the complicated façade of transmitter-receiver. His slender fingers reached across the desk for a pencil pad, as if to switch on, tune-in, take down a message. But he covered the paper in rounds and squares: getting words by morse or voice was not meant for the sane and jittery like him. The animal world was blocked off under the twin clamps of padded earphones. He felt safe. No one could ever tell anything that he would see sense in. Neither God nor father nor friend nor teacher with knowledge or authority could impart useful advice. He who sought good counsel only advertised his weakness. He who took messages and signs as having any relevance to himself merely showed his helplessness before the ways of the cruel and fully designing world.

Handley thought that no one came into this room without his permission, for he alone had the key. But Cuthbert borrowed it for a day and got another made. He liked it here. Even though John hadn't lived between these particular bricks his spirit nevertheless seemed to have spread peace within. John had never been placid, as his suicide on the boat at Dover proved, but maybe this congenial aura was a last gift to the family, in which Cuthbert was able to rest from a world that he couldn't tolerate either.

In the old days Uncle John had shaken his head over adolescent Cuthbert, for John's gentle eyes were hurt at his unnecessary obstinacy. He had wistfully pronounced him to be politically ineducable—not like the others, who drank in his anarchistic and humane socialism with a greedy suspect interest. Cuthbert had always despised rules and principles, and before leaving Oxford he had formulated it thus: never listen or learn; never take advice; never work; never fall in love. You would then live a full and satisfying life. Allow yourself no way out. Hold these precepts like a magazine of musket balls for a last-ditch defence of your true and basic integrity, and you will need neither loyalty nor friends. To be an everything-man you had to be a never-man and a no-man, an impermeable, invulnerable, impenetrable nothing-man living solely on the meat of your own life and nobody else's.

Spinning the tuning-dial of John's lit-up radio, he smiled at the news broadcasts. Various Peoples' Armies were struggling in swamp and jungle, trains crashed and aeroplanes dug holes in the earth, a newly-launched battleship ran against a sandbank, a factory had doubled its futile output of unnecessary goods, a horse had puffed its guts to rags and won some race for a chinless wonder, the Prime Minister had spoken about containing Communism as if it were a foetus you could fasten into a jar, and another copper had been murdered trying to prevent a smash and grab of somebody else's money. He laughed between the earphones, fingers gripping the morse keys as if to prevent himself rolling on the floor at the inanity of the world.

All one heard from the radio, or read in newspapers, was a continual stream of hilarious jokes. If you did not laugh your mind was diseased. Your sense of humour had gone reesty. Books, bulletins, articles were the comics of mankind. Uncle John's mistake had been to search for meaning in it, fit signs and symbols into a pattern and give them a significance they could never have—except to a madman. No wonder he did himself in.

Handley kept the power-leads connected, as if John might reappear and once more get stuck into an ethereal square-search for messages from God which were meant, of course, for him alone. So Cuthbert threw a few switches, waited for the valves to warm up their orange and purple filaments, and had a half-kilowatt transmitter at his wilful disposal. Instead of listening to what the bloody-minded world was broadcasting in all its prejudice and tyranny, he had only to connect the microphone to give it a piece of his own mind.

For weeks he'd speculated on the kind of radio programme he'd run, between going on the air and getting tracked down by slow-moving post-office direction-finding vans. Instead of a sustained obscene assault on one particular channel of misinformation, perhaps he'd play the hit-and-run pirate on several frequencies, popping up here and there saying 'God is dead, long live God', while the announcer paused between lies to get breath.

Or maybe in a parched voice of the soul he'd put on the hellfire ravings of a priest—developed at college with the help of a tape-recorder—whose prophecies would tremble their way to the marrow of any listener ready for his master's voice.

Perhaps, finally, he'd do nothing except dwell on what he'd do, and Radio Cuthbert from Unholy Island would stay a joke in the far-off corners of his megalomaniac veins. Ideas were more potent, and amusing, when you never put them into action. Action ruined them, took all spirit from a noble idea, brought it into the gutter of reality. To act was to share, and to share was to damage your integrity.

With the transmitter fully warm he kept his hand on the morse key, so that a long continuous squeak cut through both ears and was, he supposed, shooting across the sky, close enough to the BBC medium wave to make people reach for their knobs to shake off the interference.

There was a smell of camphor from John's last suit hung behind the door, lovingly pressed by Myra because she thought him the saintliest of creatures after he had gone to Algeria and pulled her lover like a hot chestnut from the fires of revolution and civil war. This demented act of rescue did her little good because Frank Dawley was sleeping with his true and proper wife whom he'd cajoled out of the security of her Nottingham council house to come and live with him.

It was the world's most experimental mix-up, the Achilles heel of benighted Handleyville. Now and again Dawley slept with Myra, but his wife didn't know. She seemed a bit hazy about what went on, though perhaps she knew everything and was nursing her time for the jump. Dawley was too dim to notice, and that was a fact.

What Dawley didn't know, and never would unless Cuthbert blurted it forth in order to shatter him, was that Cuthbert had passed a few nights with his wife. She wasn't that good, but he'd serviced her—and himself—nevertheless. Maybe Dawley wouldn't care, but if he did, it was one more thumb-tack in the coffin of the community.

The family house in Lincolnshire had killed Uncle John, and this community was emasculating his father. There was nothing to choose between them as far as Cuthbert could see. Only prisoners are obliged to make choices, and those who were out of touch with their subconscious, and in thrall to the demands of the tight society in which they lived. Once you realised that nothing was sacred you no longer had to make up your mind about anything. No choices were left. The world was yours when you wouldn't care whether you had it or not. To want nothing was to get everything—in time. The only defeat you could possibly be landed with would be if what you eventually got caused any sort of surprise. That would be humiliation, if you hadn't seen it coming. But it would be presumptuous to try and decide beforehand what it was that might surprise you. That would be a devious form of choice, and therefore to be shunned.

A box of John's cigarettes lay by the morse key, in case he came back craving a smoke with the same intensity as he'd done during his four years as a prisoner of the Japanese. Cuthbert puffed one slowly, trying not to inhale or cough. A score had already been purloined on other nights, but Handley had not lifted the lid to check—during his daily visits to change the calendar and see that the clock above the transmitter was fully wound.

The silence saddened him, but he stuck to it like hunger. If you want something out of life be careful what you hope it is in case you ever get it. He opened the window and leaned out, pressing his fingers on the sill as if to support himself against the rabid noises of life from below. He felt such pity and love for Mandy that tears wetted the flesh of his cheeks, and he ached for daylight so that she might be better.

He'd believe in God if only she could stop screaming. He couldn't bear it when she cried again, because her agony was his, just as, at certain times during his stay at college, she had shared her wealth with him. Living in such a hard-up or tight-fisted family he could never decide where she got such money, but neither did he think to ask in his picture postcards of thanks. And now as he winced at her cries he only wondered about the impulse that caused her to send those occasional few pounds to her elder, no-good, cloistered brother. The rest of the family forgot him for months at a time, and he never blamed anybody for that, but loved Mandy for her sweet sacrifices that allowed him to buy unpriestly comforts in the town, so that on his penniless return to the dark towers of college he fervently hoped she had stolen the money from their father—otherwise he would feel too guilty to enjoy the next lot that came.

It was the one unblemished piece of generosity that had ever been bestowed on him, and he was grateful that it had come from Mandy, and not from someone he had grown to hate. He wanted to tear the night out of the sky for her, and remake tomorrow with a sweep of his arms. But the stubborn stars held on, glittering studs keeping the black cloth down. Mandy's great attempt to get away from the paralysing Handley dragnet had landed her with that blood-filled vampire Ralph, a failed country gentleman who was only good for the bright prospect of sponging off his rich parents. Since his marriage they had disowned him anyway, so that Handley had to take him in.

He shut the window and turned to the room, a wan and shabby memorial that made him think of smashing it to bits. A tin-chest tool-kit under the table had a stout hammer in it—but violence wasn't Cuthbert's way. It was a sure method of having no permanent effect. Leave such dark avenues to senseless Dawley, he thought, for whom brute force towards others was only an attempt to keep his own dead spirit alive.

The tempting hammer was balanced on the radio set, but he knew that he would lose all power of speculating on violence if he used it. It would be a bad bargain, to give up so much and achieve so little for a few lead-heavy blows of the hammer. But he went as far as he dare to the brink by rubbing the steel head slowly down his cheek and feeling the flat cold surface pressing into his flesh.

John had used the tools to make bookshelves, and keep his radio gear in good order. Cuthbert lifted a tray of nails and screws and brackets, brass hinges and fuses and small rolls of copper wire, and underneath was a large cigar box covered with an impressive label, a picture of a multi-chimneyed tobacco factory. Above it was an olive-skinned, green-eyed, smooth-haired young woman wearing a plain collarless common labouring shirt, her smooth thin lips meticulously engraved. He pulled down the hundred-watt Anglepoise for more light.

Who was she, with such a noble and sensible face? Did she work in the cigar factory, or did she own it? Since the cigars were Cuban he could make a case for both, but he wasn't really interested in that. He was entranced by her face, the faint lines going from the mouth which showed that certain facets of life occasionally worried her. She had a sense of humour, though was not smiling at the moment. Faces he passed on the street or glimpsed behind a car wheel on country lanes floated or jerked by so that he could only feel contempt or pity for such utter lack of expression and inner life. But here was a small picture, a mere part of the cigar-label pageantry, and it fascinated him to the extent that he felt sorry for his own unworthiness.

The only way he could get closer to this woman of the cigar box was to prise open the lid and hope to find another good Havana inside, to sit a further half hour smoking it, and gloat on her inadequate though enticing portrait. Not that he believed she'd ever been real, yet her vulnerable improbability looked at him, her eyes fixed on the deepest inlays of his soul, a stare which affected him so deeply that he could not even think of anything cynical by which to turn it aside.

He could no longer take the picture in. It went dead on him. Wanting the promised cigar, he tried to lift the lid, but the small chromed nail held firm in the wood, and he searched the radio operator's bric-à-brac for a knife. He forced it open, and the overhead lamp flooded the sharp grey line of the barrel, the curved trigger-guard, the rounded corrugated butt of a heavy revolver. Circling it, like torpedo-shaped sleeping tablets, were six rounds of ammunition. Along one side was the last cigar waiting to be smoked.

He stared, unable to believe, stricken at the picture of it. He now remembered the woman on the lid as if she had been real. His glazed look went to both in turn. Would this woman have made John happy? He laughed at the thought. It couldn't have been the gun John blew his brains out with, for the police had nicked that. Maybe it was a twin, for John had certainly left it here, or hidden it where Handley had found it and returned it to the shrine. Cuthbert felt sick at a sudden uprush of love and death: he sensed danger—returning childhood mingled with smells of shit—the bite of knowing that decisions came from sources totally outside oneself. The change and destruction they brought might be more powerful than any man could withstand.

The fixed monochromatic picture of the woman made him smile, and the steel flesh of the gun brought down sweat. His finger itched towards it, touched the barrel and shot back as if it were new from a blacksmith's fire. But heat was in his fingers, not the gun, and to someone thrown out of theological college, fire was more important than metal, because fire is alive and metal is dead, and if metal does come alive it is only through fire.

There was little hope of peace when Handley strode away from Dawley. A thunderclap of curses came from John's room, followed by a crash of glass, as if a head had been used to break a window. He couldn't make out the actual words of recrimination, and when something plopped at his feet he saw it was a cigar that had hardly been smoked.

Mandy's bellowing scream was followed by a smack of fist on flesh. The moon covered itself with cloud to hide from Handley's petulance and Cuthbert's shallow taunting. Dawley felt he would be able to sleep if he went in now. He picked up the cigar that had survived the long fall, and tasted the first sweet lungful of Cuban tobacco. John's room darkened and, after a final door slam, all was quiet.

Cuthbert came downstairs with Uncle John's revolver in his pocket.

Chapter Seven

He weighed five thousand tons, not feathers but concrete—the weight of weights when it came to scales. He'd have got up in spite of it, but there was an ant sleeping on top of the five thousand tons, which made such a difference that he couldn't shift a limb, not a hair, not a fingernail. He loathed that slumbering ant which stopped him moving.

Yet he didn't want to get up. Time went quickly. When you were out of bed it went slowly because you were expected to do things. He could not get up because he liked lying there, though the sensation of staying in bed was edging slightly towards pain. Whether this far-off ache was due to the weight on him, or because his moral fibre was out of control, he did not know. He was too tired to find out.

Last night he'd been starving-hungry, and thought of the delicious breakfast he'd have when he got up—knowing that when he did he might be too idle to eat. But feeling ravenous had made him think of his past life, so he didn't mind it at all.

A blur of sun made a slit at the curtains. If they were drawn back it would flood in, warming the carpet for flies to play on. He would sweat then, unable to throw back the blankets. These irritating thoughts lessened the five thousands tons of concrete on top of him. Maybe the ant would jump off.

At the same time, and perhaps because of this weight, he took pleasure in his helplessness, a fair indulgence when living in a community. What else was such a place for? The disadvantages were otherwise so great they could never outweigh the shame that a man with pride must feel at being here.

A black cloth-like bluebottle woke from the ceiling and made towards him like a rocket pulled by the sun. It touched his right temple, picked up the ant from the concrete, and flew away, a morning bout of nature that seemed all it could do at the moment.

He smiled at the decrease of weight. The door snapped open, kicked against the wall where a knob-dent had already been worn. Mandy came in with his breakfast tray. 'You idle bed-rat. When are you going to get up?'

It was two weeks since her miscarriage and, he was glad to see, it hadn't left a mark on her. She was thinner than before her pregnancy, which might not be saying much, since she was almost plump again instead of merely gross. Mandy's glory was her long straight hair, tied with a purple ribbon and swaying down her well-padded back.

At eighteen her face had lost that live pale marble of early youth, though the newly sallow look gave her a more attractive waywardness. She was continually forced into brash assertions of independence so as to bring out that pure sense of her own dignity which all during childhood she had been unable to show in such a large family. And now this community stunt, she thought, had thrown her back to square one, forcing her once more to open her mouth loud every time she wanted something.

In spite of his five thousand tons Cuthbert was able to turn his head and smile. 'It's nice to be awakened by such a charming sister. Did Ralph roll on top of you last night and forget to get off till daybreak?'

She stood over him, lovable, beautiful and foul-mouthed: 'I'll tip this hot coffee over you if you don't stop calling Ralph, you bone-idle two-faced queer.'

'I suppose anybody is queer,' he said, 'if they don't go to bed with you. But I'm your brother, remember? Dad wouldn't like it. And he's your father. He'd be jealous. I know what goes on between you.'

She set the tray on his bedside table. He'd gone so far into the sludge of his mind there was nothing left to be angry about. 'You'd better get up. The meeting begins in half an hour. Dad says if you aren't there they'll come up and lob you out of the window. You're such a rotten bastard you'd burst when you hit the ground, even if you fell on soil. Or you'd dent one of the caravans with your dead weight. Be a pity. Cost a bob or two, them caravans did.'

The more she wanted to rile him the viler her accent got. She could put on a posh tone with no effort at all, speak speech in fact so purely demure that no one would guess her true base lingo. But she brutalised her tongue to remind him how he used to talk, and still wanted to from time to time but didn't for fear of giving himself away. Often he'd curse his luck at being born in England instead of France or Spain where, he'd heard, a beggar's accent could be the same as the king's. At college he'd choked back any trace of picturesque dialect or voluble argot, though when he'd perfected his aural neutrality and could expatiate with fair surety without giving himself away he discovered to his delight that if in an argument he switched into rabid and aggressive slang his opponents, where once they had been contemptuous of his voice, now became wary and impressed by it. They knew his self-assurance in their language and habits, but they could never be at all confident in his.

'Sweetness and light,' he said, pouring coffee.

She stood by the door. 'Myra set your breakfast out, not me. I only brought it up to please her. She don't want any trouble. I don't know why, though. It's liver and chops to this family. We'd starve without it. When there's no more trouble we'll pack our cardboard suitcases and go our separate ways. If she wants to get rid of us, all she's got to do is bring about a state of peace. The place 'ud empty in two minutes. Maybe that's what she's aiming at. I wouldn't blame her. I bet she rues the day she let our lot in.'

'You're too rational,' he said, spreading butter over the toast, his mouth full of bacon. 'I don't like you in that mood. You forgot the newspapers, by the way.'

'They didn't come. There's a strike on.'

A twitch in his knee almost jerked the coffee over. 'What are the lousy bone-idle improvident working-class shirkers downing tools for this time? It's shameful. When my National Theocracy gets in you can say goodbye to strikes. They'll be working double time at the incense factories, and building cathedrals in every street.'

'Roger and Richard,' she said, to needle him more, 'know the man who led the walk out. They even sent money to his strike committee.'

'They're on strife,' he mused, cutting up his egg, 'not strike. That's what it is. They've got no god left, and they get bored. I understand. Well, why are you standing there? Why aren't you downstairs pushing that vacuum cleaner around in your useless way? Or are you on strife, too?'

The pips of her eyes seemed to split two ways: 'One night, when you're asleep, I'm going to come up here and cut you into little bits. You're so dead from the scrotum up you wouldn't know till it was too late. You're just a sponging marauder living off everybody's good nature. You always have been and always will be. I hope I'm wrong, but I know I'm not. We all know where you go for hours at a time. You go to Uncle John's room. I expect you've got a corpse up there that you're sucking the blood out of and wanking off at.'

He appealed to her in an amicable voice: 'Get me some more coffee. I can't do with less than a quart in the morning.'

'You don't deserve it.'

He leaned on his pillow, and bellowed in a voice no one would suspect in him, so that the bedrail shook: 'Get out then, you useless slut, and leave me alone. They can hold their meeting without me.'

The skin on the left part of her forehead, and towards the bridge of her nose, wrinkled in a charming manner. It showed him that she was disturbed, and didn't know how to act. It marked the edge of her tolerance, the beginning of vulnerability. It was nice to know she had limits, that there was a point at which her shame and pride (and even modesty) came out. As a very small girl her skin had wrinkled at this position when anyone indulged in undue spite or injustice towards her, and it was always the prelude to tantrums or tears. But now she simply walked away, and it almost made him feel sorry for her.

As the door closed he leapt out of bed, the five-thousand-ton-weight of sloth dissolved by Mandy's humanity in deigning to quarrel with him. He would go to the meeting, in spite of misgivings as to why it had been called. He put on a black collarless shirt over his vest, and fished a pair of old flannels from the bottom of the wardrobe. This garb was sure to ripple their communal equanimity, though he saw only innocence in it, especially when he wrapped a red cravat around his neck. One didn't want to go too far and leave everything black. As for the rule that one should not lounge in Uncle John's room in case its sanctity was blasted by too much common breath, such ordinances could only come from God—either direct, or through His Chosen Representative On Earth, he decided, moving the gun to another hiding-place.

Chapter Eight

Cuthbert shuffled in wearing carpet slippers. 'Morning, everybody,' he said genially, a fair imitation of his father. Then he touched Mandy affectionately on the shoulder, and took a seat as far from his father as he could get.

She pushed her brother's hand off as he went by along the wall. 'I hear you stopped my papers this morning,' he said.

Richard turned: 'And those of a few million others. We helped. Let's not claim too much. The final decisions are always in the hands of the workers.'

'The bishop didn't get his *Times*,' Handley called above the chatter, halfway through his first cigarette of the day.

Seeing both windows open, Cuthbert complained of the cold. Handley looked at him scornfully: 'Put a coat on, if you're nesh.'

Dawley passed a cigarette to Nancy, his wife. She took it, and allowed him to light it for her, but sat stiff and quiet, being too shy or uncaring to take much part in these gatherings. To say what she thought before all and sundry had never appealed to her. In fact she just couldn't do it in front of people she hardly knew, so merely sat there and tried to look interested. But her silence at meetings had passed beyond them and into her life with Dawley, and so he could never tell what she was thinking, even when they were in bed and as close as they would ever get. She'd turn morose or sharp if he tried to talk to her about the way they lived now. The passion of their getting back together had come and gone in a few days.

The *au pair* girls, Maria and Catalina, appeared with trays of coffee cups. 'Ask them to close the window,' said Cuthbert.

Enid wanted to do it, and get on with the meeting, but Handley pushed her down with his left hand: 'We'll vote on it'—unwilling to let Cuthbert off with an easy victory, even on such a small matter as this. Cuthbert noticed how smooth and cynical he looked, as on every occasion when he took to the vote-meter.

'Say yes—those who want the windows open.' Handley put three spoons of sugar into his tiny cup of black coffee—like a real Turk, Enid noted. The vote-meter had been rigged up soon after Cuthbert's arrival, and on the floor by each chair was a button that could be pressed whenever a motion was put, buttons so hidden it was impossible to say who assented and who did not. On the wall behind Handley was a huge clockface, a circle with ten divisions, so that if two members voted for a proposal the needle swung over that number of segments, and on the rare occasions of unanimity it turned full circle. Agreement was reached if six of the ten parts were covered.

Handley was proud of his democratic installation, but Cuthbert suspected it was fixed in his father's favour, suggesting at each session that everyone sit in a different place to the one they had held before, especially Handley, since Cuthbert believed that his foot-button had several times the lighting-power of any other. The proposal had been defeated, as any would while Handley kept his present seat. But even if the gadget did not cheat it seemed an insult to the more subtle mechanics of the human make-up, a typical innovation of his father who fell for any modern contraption that came along. Cuthbert thought that one day, when his father was in town, he'd call an electrician and have the wires checked.

Seven segments filled with light. He had lost. No one had ever yet defeated Handley on that device, nor ever would, for he played it like a master—as if he were God in heaven, though Cuthbert reflected that he hadn't thrown in his hand at theology just to be kept in place by this ten-bob Yahweh facing him through two lines of faces.

Dawley had voted with his father, and so had his wife Nancy who always did because it was the easiest way out. He'd have to get rid of her, which wouldn't be difficult because she was obviously unhappy in the community. Her eternal silence at meetings was proof of that. All he had to do was drop the hint that Dawley was going to bed now and again with Myra, and she'd be off to Nottingham by next morning's train.

Ralph was placed between Adam and Myra, a small transistor in his coat pocket, from which a thin cord went up to his left ear like a deaf-aid connection. It filled his brain with pop music, and even when his eyes weren't closed there was a far-off look about him. He put a hand in his pocket to change stations when a news broadcast threatened to bring him half-way back to reality.

By such means he fobbed off the horror of living with the Handleys and escaped the malignant tremors passing around the table at meeting times. Personalities festered at cross purposes, and he was sensitised to all their different wavelengths at the same time—hence the teat-plug jammed into his ear in an effort to deflect them. He stayed sane by this appliance but, as Handley often observed, only at the cost of becoming barmy, which someone as congenitally crackers as Ralph wouldn't in any case notice.

He was so involved in changing stations that he forgot to move his foot from the vote-meter, and a segment of the clock dial stayed lit up. Handley was pleased to see he'd voted for him, though knew Ralph always said yes to everything so as to be left in peace.

Music spread like an occupying army to all points of the brain, bringing it under swift and complete submission. Yet despite this totality of control there was a separate and conscious part of Ralph that kept clear of music, a sharply defined zone of his otherwise reeling and flooded intelligence which told him that if he went on hating Handley (though without ever saying so) Handley would sooner or later do something to get rid of him. In fact he may right now be preparing to do just that. Why ever did I pick an artist for a father-in-law? Any man in an ordinary occupation would be far too tired at night, or bent on pleasure at the weekend, to give me such threatening attention, he erroneously thought—since Handley radiated more energy when he wasn't working than when he was.

The community idea was fine because it created an area wherein Ralph could exist. He did what duties were set for him, mealtimes turned up regularly, and there was always warmth and fodder in the kitchen. He had all the benefits of a great mother without having one to nag at him whenever he put his face inside the door. When there was no work to do for the community, his solitary well-built figure stooped as he walked across the fields, as if going through the undergrowth of a dense forest.

Everything was on hand to make life perfect, and the community would have been splendid had it not been for the unsuitability of most people in it. But that was no fault of his, and when Handley's spite against him for having married his daughter had been calmed by the passing of time, maybe he would suggest new people for the community, both to stop it dying, and to outvote the present members whom he would be glad to see walking away from it.

What Handley took as Ralph's vacant stare, caused by too much deadbeat drum-and-tonic pounding in, was really the pleasant conflict of clear thinking against the opposition of the music. But he didn't know this, and was angered by Ralph being cut off from what was about to be discussed.

He swallowed more coffee to take the waves of blue cigar smoke into his stomach. Between one painting and the next he pondered on ways to get rid of Ralph, which seemed vital if he weren't to eat his own liver for the rest of his life.

In the idealism that set the community going (in fact it had come together by accident) it was decided that there should be no constitution—or set of rules. Handley came to see this as an absolutely harebrained state of affairs, even though to an outsider the community seemed harmonious enough. But that hypothetical swine of an outsider, Handley argued with himself in his studio the night before, has not, and never will have, anything to do with the community. He felt the need of a constitution because it was impossible to expel any member without one. To try and get them voted out on his sole recommendation was too risky, and might split the whole system. Also, Ralph was married to his favourite daughter Mandy, and if he were to be expelled it would have to be by her connivance, which at the present rate of progress would be a long time coming.

Meanwhile, to give Ralph no inkling of his possible fate, Handley would push his quarrel with Cuthbert to the limits of civilised decency. He grinned at how the phrase fitted in with the sophisticated terms of the community. While he appeared to be savagely involved with

Cuthbert he could sort out his moves to get Ralph either on to the psychiatrist's scrap-heap or back at his mother's tit.

But nothing was simple and straightforward, not even violence and change, because to force his fiery unpredictable daughter and her husband into the wilderness would be to destroy the community. Handley was enough of a socialist to believe in the power of the family, as well as enough of an artist to get on his knees before it now and again.

They were still drinking coffee, as if wanting to be even more awake for this particular meeting. The sky was clear outside, and Cuthbert felt drawn to lie on his back in some field and look into that flay-mouthed pit of widening mild blue. Meetings bored him—apart from the novelty of the first few minutes, after which he dwelt on how to turn his favourite obsession into a long-term policy, and pursue it to a favourable but acrimonious end.

He saw Dawley as the central pillar of the establishment, and realised that if he could get rid of him then he, Cuthbert Handley, would take control with firm but flamboyant ease. In order to deceive Dawley as to his true purpose he would engage in a deadly duel with his father, and while everyone watched this mummers' bitter fight for the seasons of the world, Cuthbert would do what he could to destroy Dawley. Everything must be done thus, as far as Cuthbert was concerned: chased into coal and cornfield, through street or tunnel, forest or mud-swamp even if it took as long as death to get there, otherwise how could you ever reach what you wanted?

He caught Dawley looking at him, and smiled. Dawley lifted his hand to signal that he had seen. There was something about him that mystified Cuthbert, which may have been why he was so dead set on getting rid of him. Cuthbert wanted to dispense with mystery, because his soul had been poisoned by it. It had been pumped into him for years, scorching the most vulnerable part of his youth.

He had seen through it, however, and undergone all forms of repudiation, but now sensed phenomena in Dawley which disturbed him just as much. There was a depth of purpose in Dawley's face, which recalled his original antagonism at the idea of being threatened by a mystery which had been artificially created in order to oppress and enslave the spirit of the people. Whatever troubled you in youth never vanished. It recurred, as he now found. Mystery was a threat, whether political or religious, and would not let you live, nor ever allow you to consider what riches of the world were at your disposal. He knew that Dawley had to be taken seriously. Mysteries had to be thrust behind him like Satan. They took you out of yourself and so could not be ignored, otherwise their power multiplied.

Cuthbert felt some affinity with Dawley, but believed he could match him for power. He had spent years training to be a priest, while Dawley got his supposed authority from his time in the desert, which was said to have given him experience and wisdom. But this was yet to be proved, and Dawley had no pull over him, except that which forced him into the irritating position of having to think about him at all.

Dawley's hand fell, and Cuthbert's smile drifted. They felt friendly enough at that moment, as two people often do who are together in similar areas of thought, and imagine themselves to be alone in it.

Richard had detected their animosity, and hoped it was nothing serious. At these meetings he would find out whether any half-concealed trouble was likely to threaten the existence of the commune. Even in Lincolnshire, when the family had reigned, he had done the same, and the community didn't feel as staid and safe as the family had in those days. The change of den meant that his father was no longer in proper control. He didn't own the house or pay rent for it, and so felt insecure in his position—though he put in a generous amount towards running the community.

The family, as it were, had almost doubled in number, and was called a community. Its lack of organisation was attractive, yet any believer in guerrilla warfare and revolution must know—as his brother Adam said yesterday—that organisation and intelligence lie at the bed-rock of any society. The easygoing almost chaotic everyday flowing along of the community denied the clear and founding principles on which they worked. They were left alone to indulge themselves in a sort of controlled disorder for as long as they liked each day, and this was its great advantage. Yet Richard was uneasy, for even in the days of Uncle John there had been enough rigidity of life to make them feel that their work and the way they lived were fundamentally connected.

But Adam also told him (they shared a room, and talked late into the night), that they must learn to look on the community as a test of adaptability—as befitted theoreticians of guerrilla warfare and addicts of the Handley way of life. They must recognise the needs of their father, who was an artist. If frequent changes of place and creed were called for by his internal motor, then they must put up with it. The artist always came before family, or community, or state—even the best of states.

Handley suffered enough: Adam and Richard acknowledged it. They had only to observe some of the pictures he occasionally let them see. Hadn't their mother accepted this policy when she said that she liked the community because it gave Handley something to do when he wasn't painting? They wouldn't be so plain about this patriarchal attitude, but saw that to be more subtle might be unjust to Handley as a breadwinning artist.

Uncle John had said that they who believed in altering the social and productive forces of the earth must also honour their father and their mother. Adam tried to explain this heart-exploding paradox by seeing that John had made it because he never wanted them to go to extremes in their behaviour if ever it came to guerrilla warfare. In England, the *foco* of guerrilla warfare was to be the family.

Apart from military history, small-arms manuals, and strategical texts, Adam's favourite reading was the works of Edgar Allan Poe. Because he had never been able to explain this, nor indeed wanted to, it seemed perfectly natural to him, one being a counterweight to the other. There were times, of course, when the undercurrents common to both the House of Usher and that of Handley appeared to be working in the same direction, and this he sensed, and tried to steer clear of while feeling helpless against it.

John's Biblical exhortation to honour thy father and thy mother gave assistance in the right direction while lending an equal weight to John's fervent lit-eyed Christ-like advocation of class warfare. Adam had always seen John as noble simply because he did not know any other word for it. He once asked him why he told them to respect their parents, and John answered: 'Because they suffer. If a person does not suffer, he does not exist. Without suffering you lack imagination, intellect, endurance, and that persistent kindness to others which might eventually turn you into a civilised person.'

To go deeply into the maxims of Uncle John made Adam uneasy. Now and again he went up to gaze at the priceless relics of his life. He had once met Cuthbert coming down from the room, and they had passed in silence. Adam thought that perhaps he had something in common with his elder brother Cuthbert after all, which opened new feelings in him while at the same time making him wary. He also wondered why Handley had stopped them visiting John's room, and sensed it might be because he wanted—after all—to diminish the effect of his teaching on them. The idea was so appalling that he couldn't believe it.

Handley looked at him. Adam folded his thoughts away and smiled. Handley was about to start the meeting. They were ready to listen, and join in.

Chapter Nine

'The only thing that's absolutely necessary, and therefore compulsory, in this community,' Handley began, 'is that everybody above the age of eighteen attend these meetings.'

'Hear, hear,' said Adam.

'I don't think that's too much to ask,' he went on, 'considering the advantages it gives. Of course, there are one or two dead-heads who would prefer not to, though I don't know where else they'd like to be. Probably nowhere, since if they don't have any interest in this set-up, maybe they'd rather be off the world altogether.'

'Anyhow, it's only once a month,' he continued, 'and if whoever I'm referring to—and they know who it is—can sit still on their arses for long enough, they might not find it so boring. But if, on the other hand, this disillusionment with the ideals of the community becomes more general, then we'll release them from their misery, meaning that we'll restrict these meetings to half a dozen people whose hearts are in it. The project might lose some of its pristine democratic qualities, but no one can blame me for that. At least I wouldn't have the discouraging ob of talking to vacant faces.'

They listened. Nothing was what it seemed. No words were what they were spelled out to be. Words did not come out of the grave of a dictionary but were a voluble extension of the flesh in this organisation, a reality of mystification, not a means to an end but a way to a means to deceive anyone regarding what the end might finally be.

Even Cuthbert and Ralph, who took such jibes as aimed at themselves, listened carefully, which made Handley feel better. The sound of Paul playing with the lawnmower, and the lazy good-natured growl of Eric Bloodaxe pawing his breakfast bones around the kennel, came from outside.

'And if it does happen'—Handley spoke slowly so as to make his words cadenced and telling—'that some of you are no longer compelled to come to these gatherings, that does not mean that you'll stop being members of the community.'

Cuthbert stood, and looked squarely down the table: 'Of course it damn well does.'

Myra touched his arm, foreseeing a session of futile bickering which would only delay business and set them against each other even more. 'Anything like that would have to be unanimous.'

He smiled. 'Naturally. That's why I got the vote-meter installed.'

'If our views coincided we wouldn't need that medieval trick,' Cuthbert snapped. 'Nobody's ever got the better of that tombola of human souls except yourself.'

'How do you know it'd be unanimous?' Handley grinned. 'You might even win.'

'He stays,' Enid called, 'so get that daft idea out of your head.'

Just as Handley assumed all statements to be to his benefit, so he sided immediately with anything that went against him directly. He both agreed with everything, and disagreed with everything, but only so that he could go on towards getting his own way without anyone trying to stop him—a tactic they had long grown to recognise, however, so that by now it was almost ineffective, though Handley wasn't aware of it. 'Who said anything about him going? He's got nothing better to do except think I'm getting at him. A bit of work would solve his problem. Which brings me to this month's creative occupations. He can get some of his mystical and muscular talent to bear on the garden.'

If he disagreed, a vote would be called, and Cuthbert could think of no way to avoid defeat, so Handley had his first effective win of the day. 'And you, Brother Ralph, can snap that transistorised turd out of your left tab-hole and do a bit of poaching instead of just poaching on everybody's good nature and eating us out of house and home. Don't bring the same old milk-does, but see if you can't rustle something tasty from the Gould Estate. Round up a few dozen pheasants' eggs. A couple of them peacocks strutting around. Use your imagination a bit. Adam can go with you. That way you won't end up in a farmer's parlour drinking malt whisky and bewailing your fascist landowning family that chucked you out last year.'

'You don't need to be insulting about it,' Ralph glowered.

'I do it,' Handley said, 'because it's the only thing that brings you back to life. The trouble is he's suffering from a permanent overdose of prime bloody beef.'

A huge cliff of white chalk crumbled over Ralph, and his mouth, full of foul dust, moved into the shape of all letters of the alphabet, as if he were going to weep but didn't know how to begin. He controlled these convulsive movements and prevented himself falling into a bottomless pit.

Mandy noticed his pale face, and the sweat on his chin. 'Leave him alone,' she called to her father. 'He's done nothing to you.' She felt her husband's hand, and with the other he turned the music up as high as he could without disturbing them.

'All able-bodied children,' Handley rolled on, 'will wash the cars and caravans, while Myra, Nancy, Mandy and my own fair Enid will carry on running the house.'

Myra made a wry face. The fate of provider and top worker in the establishment swamped her natural tendency to think. Wondering about the future was out of the question, for looking after so many people deadened the mind. Such fervent dedication held the real problems down like a lid on a vat of steam. But as an intelligent person she felt a growing pressure to deal with the basic course of her life. She could not say clearly what her problems were, but hoped that when they made themselves plain they would produce their own solutions. It seemed that the community had been formed so as to draw out problems that might otherwise have lain dormant all her life, but would help her to know herself more when they were opened out. At the moment she did not want to feel so influenced by something which she had not totally conceived herself.

Enid scowled at Handley's directive, changing to a smile when she saw Myra notice it. She did not—Enid said to herself—intend waiting hand and foot on a pack of bone-idle men for the rest of her life. At times the community seemed no more than a trick to bring the Court of Baghdad to England's green and pleasant land.

Handley had picked up her thoughts: 'Nobody can moan about the breadwinning side of things. We pull in a few dozen rabbits and plunder the odd field, so we're fattening up nicely, especially Cuthbert. He had a haircut last week, and we were surprised to see how fat he'd got at the back of the neck. Once upon a time he was so thin he only farted twice a day. Now you have to be careful not to get too close.'

'If you're trying to drive me away,' Cuthbert sneered, 'you won't succeed. You won't ever break my calmness with that sort of boorish talk.'

'You've got such presence of mind,' said Handley, 'that you're dead from the chin up and the neck down. I've seen icy people like you before, but I never thought I'd have the bad luck or foul judgment to breed one.'

'I bred it into myself,' said Cuthbert, 'so as not to be ground down by you.'

'I'm glad you're coming out of your sock,' Handley said. 'Most of the time you're not with us. You're over the hills and far away.'

'I'm communing with my precious and immortal psyche, if you want to know,' he mocked.

The ash fell from his father's cigar. 'You haven't got a psyche. It's just one big powder-burn.'

'You're becoming grotesque and ludicrous by the cancer of conceit that's destroying you.'

'Leave each other alone,' Enid said, while Dawley stared and the others sighed. 'Both of you make me sick.'

'If I stay here much longer,' Handley said with relish, 'I'll strangle that preacher. I'll get ulcers. I'm more relaxed in a London traffic jam than in this place. How can any artist exist in such a death trap?'

Cuthbert regretted having set his father off. A few years must rush by before he'd win any clash of words with him, but he had a good try: 'It's a pity you aren't thirty years older, then maybe you could find a nice cosy railway station to die in!'

Handley fixed him: 'And it's a pity you're not thirty years younger, then you might never have been born!'

'What about the meeting?' Enid spoke softly and slowly. 'Or shall we let somebody else have a say?'

Such a threatening mood in her could not be ignored, but he was amiable at having got the last word with Cuthbert. 'Well then, Adam, Richard and Frank can pursue their tactical studies in subversion. Use the 2½-inch map and put groups of ten men in every wood and coppice in the county. Given the normal number of police, and troops in barracks, devise an insurrectionary exercise for taking control of all communications and public buildings. And don't forget the power stations, like you did last time. Have a mortar for each five sections—120 millimetre. They've got the range. Any gunnery snags, come to me.'

Richard made notes. 'I've a 6-inch plan of the town, to work out the urban stuff. That's always the tricky bit. We're still writing that manual of "The Complete Street Fighter". Adam put in a couple of days last week in the British Museum, getting quotes for us to look over.'

'I've got two copies of the latest *Manual on Infantry Tactics*,' Handley said. 'Only just published. John's army contacts are still working for us. The red-hot bits are on fighting in built-up areas. We'll make a special pamphlet of that. The rest ain't much cop—except the parts on radio communications.'

'These Army manuals are written for idiots,' Dawley said. 'Two hundred pages can be packed into a dozen.'

'I thought of sending one copy to the Soviet Embassy,' Handley put in, 'in case the "Infantry in Nuclear War" stuff will be useful. It'd be breaking the official secrets act, but I'd do anything to foul up the idea of the nation-state. Pity nobody in Russia sends out any Red Army crap. Disloyalty to the state is the highest form of respect for the individual. If everybody thought so we might get somewhere.'

Dawley stood up, and interrupted him. 'I heard an interesting thing the other day from the Military Academy in Jerusalem. They were trying to find out who'd make the best jungle guerrilla fighter. All known data was shaken into a computer, such as character studies from various armies, place of birth, historical details, physical endurance, localities, etc. It turned out that the best bloke would be a young nineteen-year-old brought up in London, or any industrial sprawl—though not a coastal city. His quick thinking, sense of direction, cunning, guts, and artful dodgery against the forces of law and order (or counter-insurgency force) stick that label on him.'

'No surprise to me,' Handley said. 'I knew we were on the right track. It's part of the struggle that's been neglected. What do you think about that stuff from the Police College on crowd control I got for you?'

'Worth a bob or two,' Dawley said.

'In the meantime,' Handley continued, 'I want to talk about the subject of a constitution. There's bin plenty of argument to say we don't need one. Some of the best came from me, I admit, but the way I look at it now is that a constitution will give more freedom to the community. How can one be free unless there are rules? A community without a constitution is like a bird without wings. It can't even get off the ground.'

What would take a normal being like Cuthbert a day to figure out came in a complete plan to Handley between one brush stroke and the next, and that was what made him so dangerous to the community. Maybe there was no place in it for an artist. 'We've done very well without a constitution so far, but I suppose you're getting bored and want something to chew on. The community would slip from benevolent anarchism to a state of absolute despotism in two flat weeks.'

Handley was disingenuous and amicable. 'I won't force anything. It would be voted in—or not, as the case may be.'

A long set-to between father and son could only end in one of them leaving, and that would be the time, Dawley thought, for going into action and getting more say over what happened in the community. Meanwhile, he could sit back and watch.

'I'm not sure whether that sort of proposal can be put forward at all,' Myra said. 'And it's far too serious to be over and done with in one session.'

'I don't agree with it,' said Ralph, who saw change as a menace wherever it came from. Such a feeling had tormented him from the beginning. Face to face with the whole Handley clan he'd never been able to let out any part of the true personality which he felt shifting around somewhere below his consciousness. The fact that he was trying to get to his personality proved to him that he actually had one, which was enough as far as he was concerned, though to others it was an issue still in the balance. At twenty-six, he assumed some fulfilment was about due, and saw tranquillity of mind as the way in which it would come about. And now, having only just learned to manage his meat and sleep in a community without rules, Handley was threatening an innovation which would turn his protective devices upside down, so that he'd have to learn how to survive all over again.

Handley, tired of a smooth-running community, missed the excitement of earlier days. Order was a threat to him, and only chaos brought security. By his craving for peace at any price Ralph could deduce this—while not really understanding it. He was young enough to believe that a quiet life was the one thing of value, while Handley, having lived most of his years in strife and penury, was too glad to throw it off now that he was threatened with the medio crity of it. Even during the worst periods of anarchy and deprivation Handley had never wanted peace. It had been a vague dream whose realisation was viewed as an atrophy of the spirit. In any case what peace was ever peace? There was only a void filled by the violent hugger-mugger of everyday life, in which his own black dog would never leave him be.

His desire to put the shadowy basis of a constitution firmly on paper leapt up because it seemed necessary to keep Cuthbert in his place. Noble Anarchy was too easy: he needed the simmering violence of order. Most of the others were against a constitution being slipped edgeways into the system, so today he'd merely circulate the idea, hoping that next time it might not be looked on so unfavourably. 'There's one final thing,' he said. 'A fortnight from now we shall have Maricarmen Frontera-Mayol with us.'

Cuthbert marvelled at his quick change of topic:

'Who's she?'

'A Spanish woman,' said Dawley, 'an anarchist not long out of prison.'

'What's she coming for?'

'If you'd bothered to attend the last meeting you'd know,' said Handley tartly. 'We must have a constitution, otherwise the whole bloody ship'll be on the rocks in another six months.'

Dawley broke in, before Handley got going on his son: 'Maricarmen was Shelley Jones' girlfriend. He was with me running guns into Algeria, and he died there. I promised him I'd contact her, so the community is inviting her to stay for a while.'

'She'll bring Shelley's trunk,' Richard said, 'full of notebooks which he kept over the years. They should contain interesting revolutionary writings.'

'A grim notion,' said Cuthbert.

'I've yet to see an idea that appeals to you,' said his father. 'Anyway, I want you to go to Dover and meet her. Look after her as if she's a queen. Make sure the immigration police, who do their vile work in the name of every good citizen of this island, don't treat her like the low-down weasels they are themselves.'

'I can't schlep all that way,' said Cuthbert, not wanting to let his father know that he did in fact enjoy travelling. 'It'll take a whole day.'

'You'll go,' said Handley, menacingly.

'If you insist.'

'Or you'll be out on your bloody neck.'

'It's the easiest thing in the world to set you off,' Enid said.

'Contention is meat and drink to him,' said Cuthbert. 'He doesn't care about anybody but himself.'

'That's not true,' Handley said, his voice dispirited but calm. 'There are some accusations I resent so much I can't even get angry. I don't like the way you go on about me. It's not that I can't take it, but I sometimes think you forget all the good things I've done, and the help I've given you out of the goodness of my heart. I don't mind admitting: it makes me sad. You were like a miracle to me when you were born. I loved you more than you'll ever know. You loved me, as well. We went everywhere together. You sat in my studio for hours, and painted to your heart's content. I've always done the best for you, and I want you to know it, and I want everybody else to know it. I don't have anything against you, and in spite of this bickering that goes on most of the time I have every regard for you both as a person and as my eldest son. I just want you to know that.'

Handley was sincere. Their judgments told them that no man could be more so, and they were not easy to deceive in that respect. Cuthbert, while listening to his reasoned voice, had turned white with apprehension. He was filled with a sense of dread, yet he too, somewhere, had been glad of his father's words. But he didn't trust any phrase of them, though he knew he would be the loser if he didn't.

'All right. I'll go to Dover and fetch her.'

'Good lad,' Handley smiled. 'I just wanted you to know I cared.'

Or do I? he wondered. I thought I'd got a community on my hands, and find it's a monster. I feed it a bit of my flesh and blood every day, but it still threatens to eat us up.

The sky was brightening outside, and he felt like a walk. 'Let's get back to work,' he said, 'if there's nothing more to say.'

And there wasn't, for the moment.

Chapter Ten

The steamship trunk was a jig-saw of hotel and liner labels, some faded, others half torn off and in part scuffed through. Shelley had used the trunk, a log book of his meanderings over the world. The fat-faced surly man at the weighbase stuck on one more ticket—Port Bou and Paris Nord—and she opened her purse for the money. With its rusty lock it had been all winter in her mother's damp house, a cloth spread over it like a table. Her brother's record player blared out jazz on the frozen bulk of Shelley's profoundest thoughts.

Back from prison she found that the music had not been hot enough to hold back rust and decay. Catalonian rain had tainted its corners—though an early spring had dried them and left mapstains as part of the fading labels.

Dawley's letter held an open ticket to England. He seemed unwilling to give long explanations, only mentioning the community in which he lived, and asking her to bring the trunk which Shelley had talked about in Algeria.

To queue for and cajole a passport was a blight on her anarchist soul. Begging for the right to leave your country, and permission to enter another, was a bleak tyranny. She was twenty-eight, and during the last ten years had been twice out of Spain with false papers—once on foot over the snow into France. She was followed, and would be pulled back into prison at the first move. The Fascists treated you like a cripple. She filled in dozens of forms so as to take up domestic work in England, with the family of a famous painter whose triplicate letter in Spanish and English was shown at all the offices she waited in.

The passport was her book of servitude. On the train back from Barcelona to her home village, huddled in a corner of the shaking carriage like an animal that did not know which lair to flee to after the tight-lock of prison had been opened, she had been tempted to throw it into the heavily racing river below. The idea was overwhelming, but she pressed teeth and lips so hard that an elderly woman sitting opposite thought she was a mad person just out of the *manicomio*. The effort brought her close to fainting, in the smoke and steam heat, with rain-water sliding zigzag down the glass. Oak groves rising up the valley pinned her into herself.

The sky was churning with rain and more rain, the train shaking as if it would throw her into it. Two years of prison would take much time going from her spirit, and the passport was necessary if she were to survive and get to England. She gripped it tight, for fear it would fly of its own will on to the stony soil, and wear away under mouldering rain.

She loved Shelley as if he were alive and was to meet her next week in Sitges—as he'd done in former days. No love was ever lost. It buried itself into you, and could not disappear so that you didn't feel it any more. He was that rare person who'd been able to love her as much as he was capable of loving himself, so she lived now with the smarting memory of his tenderness. They had regarded each other as equals, and the feeling that linked them was like that of brother and sister, but without the built-in destructiveness of sibling rivalry.

The simplicities and complexities had been there from the beginning. Perhaps belonging to different countries meant something after all. She did not know why, but ease with him had become such a stable fact that she felt all people could learn to treat each other in the same way, so that the world might gradually save itself by creating its own utopia. Only the patience and the will were lacking. From childhood she had grown with the principles of mutual self-help, had been taught to work for universal sisterhood and brotherhood—equality, labour, abundance, and happiness. Her father had died in one of Franco's prisons when she was six.

But the reality of society kicked such beliefs out of you, or eroded them by the fact of its monolithic presence. Or it turned its back on them. It did not matter. Civilisation—if that was the name for it—could be swept away in ten minutes, and if you were destroyed with it, you had no more problems. But if you survived, and others with you, perhaps only then could you build the new society in which you had always believed.

But society was stronger than you thought. Its nihilist underworld could never be contained or tamed. Society was modelled on its meanest jungle, and turned a blind eye to it. The checks and balances knitted themselves together, forming a locked mass of great strength, that could hardly be ripped apart.

She had walked up the Rambla and into the Plaza de Cataluña wondering: 'How can I change it?' It had been tried so many times. The foreign tourists came and went. It was a new thing. They also would try to stop you, no doubt, because they wanted the old Spain, the old world. They loved the butchery and torment of bullfights, these pink-faced unthinking tourists.

You had to try. She had thought so a long time before meeting Shelley, and believed more strongly after being in prison. But nothing was simple any more. Shelley had attempted it, and been killed. It was her belief that he'd never wanted to go into Algeria and fight for the FLN. His attachment to violence, though sincere, was sentimental. He had his weaknesses. His principles and inclinations were never finally formulated. His philosophy was ruptured at the base of the tree. In the beginning was the Word, and in the end was Action, he used to say. He had talked about destroying the property of the oppressors, whereas other left-wing parties wanted to preserve the buildings of their oppressors so that they could inherit them for their own ends—in the name of the people, of course. A genuine revolutionary party would not only open the gaols, but would blow them up and build no more.

He talked, he argued, he intrigued, but never shot or bombed directly. If others did it, in order to bring about a society based on equality and justice, he was always willing to help as a line-of-communications or logistics man. The possibilities of giving actual assistance to revolution or civil war were not numerous, so he had run guns from Tangier over the Atlas Mountains to the edge of the Sahara desert. On one such delivery he had Frank Dawley as his co-driver.

Shelley had not come back, but had done something entirely out of character by continuing into Algeria and fighting for the National Liberation Front.

Their affection for each other enabled her to form correct conclusions. If Shelley had been the typical man who made love regardless and then vanished into the safety of himself or joined his male friends at the nearest bar or cafe, and if her feelings had been those of a woman who accepted this with inner resentment but without complaint, then her senses may not have led her to such plain truth. She may not have cared that he was dead, not gone on feeling an unrelenting sexual want for him month after month, which concealed what was truly happening, and only slowly drew her numbed brain towards the final, bitter fact of their parting.

Dawley, with the same ideas, forced him into Algeria at gunpoint. There was no other explanation. There were many such hardliners who talked about equality of people and the redistribution of the earth's necessities—but they were monsters who did not believe in real freedom, in real love, in real women. Locked in the prison of their deprived hearts, they could not even know how much they fought against themselves. They believed in the power of the gun over the individual, till finally it was the gun that wielded them. Power did not corrupt such people, but reduced them utterly to an inhuman bit of steel called a trigger. It did this as surely as if they allowed tradition and society to crush them into a man with nothing more to his emotional credit than a stick of bone and gristle called a penis. It defiled them. They enjoyed it.

Dawley was as responsible for Shelley's death as if he had murdered him deliberately for his own twisted purpose. He had accepted the way of violence, and let go the reins of humanity. She had often talked it over with Shelley, and though her arguments had had sufficient effect on his reason, they had never got through to his dreams.

All she had to do was confront Dawley and, if he were as guilty as she knew him to be, indulge for the first time in the violence she had always tried to talk Shelley out of. There were some people in the world who killed in the name of innocence and purity, and they called it love of humanity or Revolution. Their feelings of innocence increased the more they were taken up by the force of their own unquestioning violence, and those whom they couldn't kill they corrupted instead. They had to be killed, therefore, so as to save the innocent they came daily into contact with. Such people had nothing to do with socialism.

Dawley was this sort of person, and his innocence was a menace to the good people of the world. Her own life's love had been destroyed because of it, and so it would be the most perfect justice to kill him.

The choice was not easy, and she didn't know where it would lead, or even whether she could do it, but as the train stopped at the frontier station and she stepped down from the high carriage, she knew that her made-up mind ought not to be altered. It was a new way of making a decision, with her heart instead of her head, and though this method was too much of a novelty for her to feel easy about it, she nevertheless sensed it to be a sort of letting go because it was something that she wanted with all her soul to happen.

She moved as if in a dream, as people do when they believe their minds are made up. That was the only way to act if the dream were to come true. She waited in the large hall for her trunk and other luggage to be brought to the customs counter by a porter. To anyone but herself and, for various reasons, to Mr Handley and Dawley, the trunk was valueless, but through its formidable presence Shelley seemed to be telling her that she had made the right decision. She was happy at the moment to stay in her dream, to take refuge in it. No one knew of the dream that was in her except herself and therein, she thought, lay its strength.

It was difficult to get a trunk and suitcases such a distance through Europe, travelling at full speed towards Paris. The trunk contained Shelley's belongings: a lightweight suit and a few shirts, several pipes and an unopened tin of Raleigh tobacco. But the few dozen notebooks, which she had been too locked in her grief to read, took up most space, and formed the deadly leaden weight that porters shied from—showing great regard for their limbs and sinews till she offered them fifty *pesetas* to take it out of train or taxi and hump it bodily through its next stage.

She had registered its contents, as careful and anxious as if Shelley's actual body were inside that she was for some weird reason taking to England. His soul was in those notebooks that he had pleasurably and laboriously written in during the years they had known each other. She did not know where his actual flesh and blood body was, though hoped that Dawley, his fellow-revolutionary and travelling companion, would tell her when she met him in England, describe the place and put it on the map in such detail that one day she would set off for Algeria, to find it and bury him properly, when Dawley was dead.

Chapter Eleven

The raw sky made Cuthbert feel hungry. Purple clouds were clawing their way from nowhere to nowhere. Some were in rags, trying to climb over one another. The expressive English summer held a faint uneasy smell of decay.

He pandered to the fragmentation of his mental state by strolling among the traffic islands around Victoria Station. The day felt so heavy after a sleepless night that even the onset of afternoon didn't bring the usual sharpening of his faculties.

The widespread brick warrens of south London looked squalid and cosy. Would the towers of flat-dwellings blow over in a wind? The train cut through rows of small houses rubbed with the burnt cork of industrialism. Food and fruit and gaudy clothes made a patchwork snake in the street-market below. Backyards and slanting chimneys went on forever.

This, he thought, unable to leave the window and read his *Times*, is where the English would have stopped the Germans in 1940. Twenty Stalingrads. Even Hitler hadn't got such nerve or stomach so early on. Patriotism would have caught on like television. Cunning forms of self-immolation would have enabled them to 'take one with you—even two'. The good old expendable working class would, in its generosity, have bled itself to death—at least so my father asserts, though he's a bit old-fashioned where history is concerned.

Better to save their souls by the God of Heaven than smash their bodies by the God of War. The train ran over a putrid stream, a factory near by, then a sports stadium, then modern factories and fewer but neater houses, a football field, rubbish tips, factories, more backyards, a mildewed shed, a patch of earth, cuttings and tunnels, birch trees, barbed wire, huts, swamps, squalor again. Orpington. A fire blazed on the banks of a cutting. Hop poles. Thank God we're out of it. Smoke in the sky.

He enjoyed the slight burn of sun on a far-off patch of field. It brought the dazzling emerald closer than the dull hedges broken now and again by blades of scruffy chalk. If he opened the window he'd throw his dregs of tea on to it, but drank it instead, and went back to his first-class carriage, empty because he'd scattered newspapers over the seat space, and the sunlight came right across. He was glad to be alone, hating to wonder why people on English railways didn't talk to each other.

Being away from the family, he felt a man of the world: Handley had put enough cash in his pocket for him not to appear mean and give the community a bad name to Maricarmen. Tall, fair-haired, chisel-nosed Cuthbert with the sardonic mouth and pale forehead had faint lines around his light blue eyes that gave an impression of uncertainty to anyone who got a close look. He'd noticed this defect while shaving, but his physical presence and quick speech rarely allowed anyone to see it. He wore an old grey suit, a black shirt and his clergyman's collar.

People in England made way for a parson. Even the most noxious middle-class atheists were finally deferential if you looked at them with the authority of ruthless and magnanimous sympathy. People might nail you with their sordid problems, but he had learned to deal with them in such a way that his victim would never again confide his or her troubles to a parson. He twitched his nostrils so that they moved more than his lips, and while this alarmed those who were timid, it enraged others who had more spirit. It separated the goats from the sheep.

'My dear fellow,' he intoned, 'I'm sad to hear your mother died today. Or was it yesterday? Well, you really should know, shouldn't you? It *is* a trying time. My own father died last week, and I'll never forget it. Or was it the week before? Have a cigarette, and don't think about it. What? You can't smoke at such a time? They're very good. Not at all expensive. Anyway, it's on the Church. You might as well get something out of it. Just back from the funeral? How shattering. I can't tell you how moved I am that you should turn to me at such a time. I shall do all I can to help. It's my job. Sure you won't have one? It's an unusual kind. Do you listen to religious broadcasting on the BBC? You should. A great lift in the early morning, though not, I might say, as great as you might get from these innocent-looking cigarettes. Calm yourself. If you don't smoke, you don't smoke. Far be it from me to force you. Hope you don't mind if I have one? Your mother was ninety-seven! They say that those who die of old age become flowers in God's garden. Isn't that a beautiful thought? It is for me, anyhow, though I haven't just lost my mother. Am I drunk, did you say? You should be ashamed of yourself, bursting into tears like that just because your vile old mother cracked out and you can't bear to live alone at sixty. You're a disgrace to the human race. Hey, don't get rough. I may wear a dog-collar but I've still got enough muscle to bash your face in. Get your hands off me or I'll call the police and tell them you're soliciting, you queer-eyed gett. For Christ's sake let me get away from this raving maniac!'

The ticket-collector looked in, heard his melodious bawling and dragged the door to because you can't disturb a parson rehearsing his sermon. It sounded so fiery that the bloody fool might turn like a holy lion and rend him if he insisted on bothering about such earthbound items as tickets. Just as well, thought Cuthbert, who only paid second-class when wearing his dog-collar.

'Oh yes,' he would say, 'you're quite right. I'm so absent-minded these days, with parish affairs in such a tangle. I'll have to find the right compartment. Wouldn't do to spend too much of the parish funds on a business visit to raise money for the new scouts hall. I may stay? How very kind of you. It's a delight to find some goodness in the world. Only five minutes before we get in? Oh dear, I simply must finish this report on juvenile delinquency.'

Once nearly a priest, always a priest. A woman gave him five pounds when in a similar quandary: 'Please take it,' she said, 'for your church.' Such a nice young curate. While discussing the ethics of his possible acceptance the ticket-collector quietly withdrew. That train, unique in his memory, had been on the Norfolk run, and with an hour of the afternoon still left, the rhythmical convenient clack of the wheels hid the rustlings and whispered nothings of the forty-year-old woman whose half-buried dreams took her by merciless surprise and guilt and pleasure. Later at her house (husband on business and kiddies at boarding-school) he discarded his priestly habit entirely, and passed two days with his partner that she ought not to forget either.

He paced the platform at Dover Marine, and took out the photo of Maricarmen—who didn't look the type for anything of that sort. The way to the quayside was marked by an enormous composite war memorial, of a soldier with a rifle and bayonet pointing his deadly gear towards any tourists (especially German) who might come to this country with anything but goodwill in their hearts and hard currency in their pockets. The forlorn figures had been erected and left there as a warning to the incoming hordes whose forefathers had shot and blown to bits them and a million others.

There was time to spare for a quick look around the group. With those sharp eyes inherited from Handley he saw that such statuary was, in truth, fit only for the rubbish tip. The soldier (to the right of the sailor) was in full Great War rig of helmet and rifle, pouches and boots, looked daxed or drunk. The two were held or half sheltered by a bare-breasted woman who seemed to represent Mother England or some such tosh. She'd got wings as if to fly (should it be necessary) from the common warriors if they got funny ideas. The soldier looked under-sized, as if he belonged to one of those battalions of runts and midgets nicknamed Bantams by taller specimens, the fierce scouring of the slums let loose at the Germans when all else had failed and something—whatever it was—still needed to be done. Mostly, of course, it ended in several hundred poor wretches dead or howling in the mud—which was considered better than having them stay on the streets at home getting their hands on the property of the better-off. Cuthbert wondered what the young Germans thought of it when they came through. Trust the old country to be so welcoming.

He walked into the customs sheds. 'I'm to meet one of my domestic staff from Spain,' he said briskly to a slate-eyed passport official of his own age. 'Mind if I wander along? Might spot her coming down the gangway. Be no end of a help. Wouldn't like her to take the wrong turning at an awkward moment!'

The man smiled. 'That's all right.' He was going to add 'sir', but decided not to, a slightly disrespectful omission that made him feel better, and added pleasantly: 'Go and wait on the left.'

Cuthbert set off beyond the specified point, on to the actual quay, where the ship was bumping into its berth. Seagulls peeled off strips of sky as they slid over the sheds and water. Uncle John's last sight of earth must have been this, before the addle-brained fool went to heaven. He'd opened his suitcase, wind scattering papers up among the seagulls, took out a monstrous revolver, and put it into his mouth. The last hunger of life. The real bite of a starving man. A final look showed gulls flying over Dover Beach, before the armies of the night rushed in.

What else can you do when you've sensed too much, and can't take any more? Maybe it wasn't such a lot he'd seen. One man's much may be another man's little, but it makes no difference in the end.

Suicide is the final act of infantilism, he thought, by those who are still so close to the womb they think they can double back into it when they can't go on. Such a memory spoiled the solid view he'd always had of himself, wondering why Maricarmen had been booked via the fraught place of Dover. Maybe Handley had machined it, to put him at the mercy of a dark omen which would rattle him if he tried to win her on the way home. Yet he sensed that his weak point was the belief that everything Handley did was conscious and calculated. It needn't be so at all, and he would rather have had anyone for a father than an artist, though there was nothing to do but learn how to live with it.

He took a pipe out, and a rubber tobacco pouch, part of his parson's kit that he loathed but had trained himself to work convincingly. He rattled around his pockets for the stubby box of matches, and the policeman walked by without returning his friendly nod. He lit up, but let it fade as the first passengers trod curiously down the gangplank.

He watched Maricarmen carry two suitcases along the quay without struggling, thinking it just as well that she was strong. He caught her up at the passport counter, heard her explaining with an American accent that someone was coming to meet her, and so introduced himself.

Letters were shown, and they allowed her through. One bridge crossed, he thought, silent as they walked to the custom sheds, even false words blocked for the first time in his life. She opened her cases, and the trunk that the porter set down. The customs man slid his hands between the books and papers as if, to warm his frozen self, he was putting them up the skirt of a beautiful woman—a look of distaste at being landed with such a job.

'A lot of papers.'

'I may study while I'm here.'

He opened a book called *Warfare in the Enemy's Rear.*

'Politics and history,' she said.

He flipped through it, as if the title suggested an esoteric treatise on sodomy. 'All these notebooks yours?' he asked, disappointed that it wasn't.

'Yes.'

Cuthbert stepped in, but he made a chalkmark on the lid and walked away, leaving them to close it. The bland official atmosphere of England's well-guarded gates had no effect on her, as it had on a few of the English returning from their holidays who could not yet show the confidence that having had it so good for so long should have given them.

She was far from revealing whatever there was to hide, carrying herself with an air of Iberian dignity that made everyone around her seem physically warped. She had high cheekbones, and long black hair smoothed back from her forehead, but there the resemblance to a typical flamenco dancer ended. Her face was pale and thin, her nose small. There wasn't much beauty, he decided, but her pride shook his heart. She was tall, and her eyes had that look of sensibility that does not draw pity from anyone, though they are able instantly to see the marks of suffering in others. She wore a light grey overcoat none too heavy for the gusty day.

He was wary of getting too close for fear he wouldn't see her properly, yet wanted to be nearer so that people would know they were together. He enjoyed them looking, and wondering what a young parson had to do with such a woman. He wished he hadn't donned his dog-collar before leaving home—touching the small of her back to point their direction along the platform.

A porter had gone on with her luggage. 'It's not far to London,' Cuthbert said. 'A couple of hours. We'll get a taxi across town, and another train from St Pancras.'

'I seem to have been travelling for ever,' she said. 'It's a good feeling, though.'

He opened the carriage door. 'You'll get there soon. England lies before you like a land of dreams!'

He paid her porter five shillings—rather less than he should have done—and got a dark look at his white collar before the man pocketed the coins and walked away. He regretted his meanness, which gave the wrong impression before this new and striking acquisition to the community. His hands were trembling as he pulled out his pipe and tobacco.

Chapter Twelve

The carriage was full and stuffy—a light rain gusting along the foot of the cliffs, grey window-flashes of the sea as they threaded several tunnels.

He wondered what she was thinking, knowing that if he couldn't guess with the sharpened intuition of fresh acquaintance it would be far more difficult in the future. His priestly bent of mind could only get at somebody's thoughts by hearing them speak: having nothing on which to frame questions did not inspire him to use his imagination and make up something which, though colourful, might not be accurate. He thought too much of himself to want anything but the truth.

They sat quiet. At the dimness of each tunnel, glad to be leaving the locality of Uncle John's death, he looked at the illuminated vision of her face in the window, while she sat by his side with unfeeling blankness after a twenty-four-hour spirit-shaking journey from Barcelona. He was nagged by the feeling that he'd seen her before, and he couldn't fathom where.

The precious trunk was in the van, that heavy and sole reason why she had been sent for. As soon as Dawley and his father had their hands on the notebooks they'd kick her out—providing such humanitarian revolutionaries could contrive to get her pregnant and arrange for six-foot snow drifts to surround the house. He saw through their game all right. To fill up John's museum and shrine they wanted the word-picture of Shelley Jones' revolutionary soul fixed into a glass case.

But first they would put every last phrase and statement under the glare of their gritty logic, work on it like medieval alchemists to transmute the raw wires of ordinary metal into the purest gold of future example. Handley was running a country, not a community, and needed an historical museum to justify it. His first martyr was Uncle John, and a second had come along like a windfall in Shelley Jones. He wondered who was lined up for the third.

They wouldn't admit this, would swear to inviting Maricarmen for reasons of international solidarity, and affection for poor Shelley who had died fighting for the downtrodden inhabitants of the Third World. She would need a place to rest in and recover from her ordeal. If the first reason for enticing her to England was icy and heartless, the second was poisonous with sentimentality.

But he also wondered about Maricarmen's motive for coming to this island and latching on to the Handley roundabout. Some solid plan existed beneath the pronounced swell of her breasts—more visible now that her coat was open. The idea of bringing the notebooks hadn't been made till she accepted their invitation and had applied for a passport. The High Command of Dawley, Albert, Richard and Adam had made a chart of STEPS TOWARDS INVEIGLING MARICARMEN INTO ENGLAND and pinned it on the wall, filling in a coloured square every time a certain move had been accomplished. Well, not quite, but he was sure it would have been if they'd thought of it. He would struggle single-handed to protect this strange and unique woman beside him.

She was tired, but wondered what it would be like fulfilling her expected role—until she showed her true purpose for going there. Shelley's last letter had been posted from Tangier, and she knew one paragraph by heart: 'There's this Englishman coming south for a little tourism (gunrunning) beyond the mountains. He's hard, and as solid as a rock—especially in the head, I reckon. But he's the right meat, because this kind of travelling can be tough. We'll be back in ten days, and if he turns out well, we could do more sight-seeing later. He seems ideal for the job, a Limey worker who claims he's not long out of a factory. Providing he can read and write (and I think he can) we should make a good team. There is something about his eyes, a sort of abstract grey, but I can't decide whether such empty hardness will be better or worse for us. But since we don't intend shacking up, but only making this one trial run together, it doesn't much matter.'

Being an atheist she could not speak to the dead. So they were separated forever. Death proved and finalised her atheism. They had once lived in Malaga for three months, shared a cold and barrenly furnished flat on a cobbled street that led to a bald piece of rising ground behind the city called El Egido, into which were built many gypsy caves. The flat was so cold that some nights they would take food and wine and eat with the gypsies, the poorest of the poor who had been hounded and murdered by fascists during the Civil War.

Or they would go to Vicente's bar in town and drink Amontillado at one of the wooden tables, talking for hours, playing Ludo and Checkers. The walls of the cafe were decorated with pictures of the Knight of the Rueful Countenance, showing his pathetic visage as he sat undiscouraged under the broken windmill sail. They grew warm with *vino y tapas*, and the flat seemed no longer desolate when they went back to it.

Walking through the square before the illuminated cathedral at midnight they saw a tree with tiny green leaves just breaking out of bud, points so livid and infinitesimal that it looked as if a cloud of green fireflies was resting on all the tips of the branches before taking off into the dark blue sky towards Africa.

The curtain of death came over her memories, and a row of faces made up the safety-curtain of her mind. She didn't know where she was. A young man gazed out of the window with such a forlorn expression that she wondered if he too were thinking about death. A tight-lipped, severe, thin-faced woman looked into a book, while the man beside her was asleep. Another man tried to get a glimpse of her, but turned away when she met the gaze. They seemed a very far-sighted nation with such empty eyes.

Cuthbert took her to the dining carriage for tea, and they faced each other. Away from home he made it a rule to eat whenever food was available. You never knew where your next meal was coming from in this shifting world of frivolous uncertainties. If he were on his own he would eat and drink as if some invisible person were threatening to snatch the cup and plate away, but with Maricarmen so close the second and civilised Cuthbert took control.

She wondered why he put on such a smile as soon as they sat down, but he wasn't aware of having altered his lips. She seemed to be in a land where people did not speak. Being exhausted after a journey was no excuse. Perhaps they simply had nothing to say.

Cuthbert had always seen silence as slightly ridiculous, unless it was used as a weapon—when you had to make sure it didn't look like a fit of sulking. Pouring tea for them both, he used it as a way of getting her to talk about herself. Some people thought it bad manners to be silent with another face near by, and you rarely had long to wait before they spoke.

But now, such ploys were blown away like dry leaves in a gale. He was aching to talk to her but wasn't able to. The irrational was taking its revenge on the rational. He thought of pouring tea over his hand in order to force something out, but the spout veered towards a cup.

She pulled the soggy cake from its cellophane wrapper and broke it in two. The attractive sight of her appetite cured him of a temptation to reach out and take her hand, though he tried hard not to stare at her. If they were destined to live the first hours of their meeting without much conversation, so be it. He respected himself, and also her. It occurred to him that they were weighing each other up.

'I don't smoke much,' she said, but taking one. Warmth and food had softened that haughty and beautiful façade. She took off her coat. He looked at her as he lit the cigarette. Her eyes, engrossed in the flame, were almond-shaped and turned down slightly towards high cheekbones. When she sat back he wondered what she saw, what her eyes showed, what range, ocean, road, cell. He frightened himself by speaking when he had no intention of it. He couldn't afford such gestures if he wasn't to lose faith in his own shaky strength. Yet one could not go on believing for ever in the power-politics of the unspoken word.

In the taxi crossing London she said: 'Mr Handley didn't mention that his son was a priest.'

'I'm not. I almost was one, but I didn't finish the course.'

'Why do you wear that collar?'

'As a disguise, when I go out and face the world.'

She laughed, in a throaty uninhibited way and he did not know whether to be glad at amusing her, or resentful at being mocked. Maybe she often showed off a ready sense of humour at another's expense, with an attractive, almost sexual laugh which he began to see as the only vulnerable part of her that was likely to be revealed till you knew her better. To her, the fact that he wore a priest's collar when he had no right to showed that she'd have no difficulty luring him into her cause against Dawley when the time came.

She dipped her head to glimpse the Houses of Parliament. 'Is that what you call "the cradle of democracy"?'

'The cradle of democracy is the coffin of religion,' he said. 'Though I suppose it's not a bad idea to have one.'

'Most countries do,' she said contemptuously. 'Heaps of stone to keep people in their places.'

He wanted to laugh at such socialist rubbish, having had too much of a bellyful from birth. 'There's a certain sort of beauty,' he said, 'in such vast spaces being covered and enclosed by so much stone. You have to think about the shape of the inside, and the roof over it showing the limits of men's ideas and ideals. Space wrenched from the elements to prove that you can't have civilisation without religion.'

'Landscape,' she said, as the taxi swung into Trafalgar Square, 'that's my idea of beauty. Earth, space. I suppose that's what drew me to Shelley. He liked it as well. Not cities and buildings. Cities eat up beauty, buildings digest it. After being in prison I never want to enter any again. I like Gaudi's cathedral in Barcelona because workmen are still there, cursing and shouting. When they've gone and it has doors and windows I won't go near it. A finished church imprisons the soul as well as the body. But I went to Gaudi's temple with Shelley. He was interested in unusual buildings.'

'Didn't he want to blow them up?'

'Only the ugly ones.'

'I thought he was a Communist?'

'He was many things. No real Communist is a simple man.'

He was irrevocably naïve. She didn't show the respect for his priest's collar that he was used to. That old subconscious was getting too big for its boots. He'd been relying on a falsehood to give him confidence. 'How old are you?', she asked.

'Twenty-five.'

Her wry expression put him back into the world of non-talk. The complexities in her were as deep and varied as those within himself, and he would have to learn how to handle them. Honest and forthright in her opinions, he didn't know how to counter her scorn, which may still be the main part of her. His active suspicion created lurid pictures. She was honest only in the way lively and attractive people could afford to be. In the lit-up dusk of Charing Cross Road she lost some of her classical Iberian beauty. What was it made her seem so reliable except his own dishonesty of soul?—which meant she was not.

The one thing in life, he mused, but with a shade of regret and sadness because Maricarmen sat warmly beside him, is to be dishonourable, ungrateful and plain wicked. Not in order to benefit oneself—that would be merely selfish—or to do harm to others—that would be simply vicious—but as a clean way of living, in other words to live by the naked law having the rest of the world exist for your especial benefit. Only in this way could one be anti-bourgeois and anti-life, and eventually move in all humility towards God.

The main thing is to give every rotten action a false label, to call it either bourgeois reactionary wickedness (in the name of the Revolution which you didn't believe in) or Red Communist Bolshevik wickedness (in the name of the Good Christian Capitalist Western Freedom-loving way of life which you could never believe in, either). Pretend to the way of life that you act vilely in the name of. Be a man of no principles—that change every day. Only in this way will you extend the limits of your horizon and retain your integrity in the pitted face of all systems. Teach yourself not to care, and do it quickly. He'd tell this to anyone foolish enough to ask for advice while his white collar was on. It is essential for survival to retain the complexity of your nature. And to a man of principle integrity and survival were the same thing.

'People are often broader in spirit than you think.'

'I know,' he answered, vulnerable in spite of what he thought, and unable to dislike her for making him feel so, in case his vulnerability one day turned into love. 'I'm glad you came to England.'

'Why is that?'

'I don't know yet. It's good you're here, that's all.'

At the station he saw to the unloading of Shelley's trunk. The fact that he felt elated could mean nothing to her who made him feel so—not yet, anyway. He imagined every man experienced something like love in her presence, but that she didn't know much about such things herself. The trunk should be draped with a hammer-and-sickle flag, and flanked by a Red Guard of Honour as it went into the station. She looked at it too, studiously and sad, as if the same thought occurred to her. It's going home, he smiled, to its final resting-place: the spiritual incinerator of a half-baked museum.

Sitting opposite her in the train, he knew where he had seen her before. He remembered the cigar box in Uncle John's room, and through the orange and white lights of London's outskirts saw again the impressive labels on its lid, with the picture of a multi-chimneyed tobacco factory, and the crude engraved portrait of the olive-skinned, green-eyed, smooth-haired woman wearing a plain collarless common shirt with a low neck. Her lips were smooth and thin, and the meticulous details fitted perfectly the real features of Maricarmen, whose face softened when her eyes closed from exhaustion.

Chapter Thirteen

Handley thought that to paint the soul of England you had first to paint the soul of Europe.

What shape the soul should take he wasn't sure about. What colour the heart, what composition the mind, had yet to be transmuted into real paint and colour, pain and choler. It was no use relying on inspiration. You mixed the paint with your sweat of fear, perspiration of labour, blood of vision, and let the energy take the hindmost or the rindpest as your heart expanded, chose for you, and finally took over.

Stop and start, trial and error, he painted them all from the very beginning: emanations from the swamps of the dead in France and Belgium, poppy dung, Brecht music, German swamp songs, Elgar's sewer-tunes, sadistic misery, cock-eyed teutonic intelligence, Ophelia in the mud of Passchendaele, Lady Morphine of Vimy Ridge, the Howling Crone of Hill 60, the Angel of Mons. Roses, the Lions and the Donkeys of the Somme: those flowers of the bowels still blooming in Picardy, hectares harrowed and sown and perpetuated in the bone and blood of all countries, the final international fraternisation of the battlefield where the corpses of the world unite because they had nothing to lose but their lives.

Handley's large hut in the back of the garden served well as a studio, as far from the dog and bird noises of England as he could get. He slammed up a window to breathe fresh air, yet despite its advantages wished he still had the attic of his Lincolnshire house, where he could stand at an open window and contemplate throwing himself to his death if the painting didn't go well. Thinking about suicide cleared the head.

Large sketch-books were full, drawings of landscapes in pencil and charcoal blocked by statistics and notes. Cartoons abounded, geopolitic maps and scrawls and crossings out, Piccasso and Haushoffer, enormous motorways traversing saps and wire and dugouts and a thousand inter-denominational faces fixed in the pavé of the road leading to the front—those sacred spokes leading to the axel-hub of death.

He threw the book across the room. Inspiration drove him to work, to keep out the cut of its fangs—or it left him a while to belly-crawl off to pastures new. He walked up and down.

The unsettled wetness of summer weather, with its air of fecundity that had often inspired him in Lincolnshire, made for restlessness here, and gave a leg-ache that wouldn't let him stand in one place. He burned to go, but didn't know where. He longed to settle down into tranquil happiness, but didn't know how. He wanted to work, but couldn't.

Birds of summer sang in the trees. The house was busy. The grocer's van was unloading by the back door. Bourgeois placid life was running its accustomed course. Life had to be lived, one way or another. You called it 'bourgeoise' if it went on too long and started to rot your soul. They'd lived in Lincolnshire twenty years, and here in this place less than one, but already the gangrene was eating him in vital places. The only thing left was a career of crime, or to sleep till better feelings came.

He regretted not having gone to fetch Maricarmen from Dover, but he'd wanted Cuthbert out of the house so that they could bring in a constitution. Cuthbert's voice would have gone against him, so he'd sacrificed a pleasant trip through London, and a possible visit to Lady Ritmeester. After an hour's speech a near unanimous vote at the meeting had brought in a constitution, declaring Albert Handley to be president of the community, with the power of veto on any decision. Let Cuthbert unravel himself from that one. There was no point in not being clear about it. Any room for doubt and you're being unfair to the rest of them. One must never shirk responsibility. At least there was that much satisfaction in life.

If one doesn't face problems one might just as well go out and get a job as a milkman—which didn't sound a bad scheme to him, though not at the moment. In the old days, when he'd got no money, such an idea would never have entered his mind, but he was so bored he'd consider anything. Even manipulating the community held no further fascination now that he'd won control of it, though he'd yet to see Cuthbert's face when he got to know, and sit back to watch his futile machinations as he tried to alter the course of history. He couldn't, and that was the joy of it. As long as you lived from day to day the filthy claws of time couldn't get at you. Courage was all you needed.

Enid strode across the lawn from the house, and came up the garden steps towards his refuge and resting-place. Wind blew strands of her fair hair about, the most wayward being tucked ruthlessly into place as she pushed open the door.

So, he thought, standing by his half-finished picture, my long-wedded wife is going to make me eat wood for what I just did at the meeting. The ascent made her breathless. It's summer, she thought. If it were spring I'd finish him off for what he did. He gave a finely chiselled smile that he hoped would not infuriate her, while knowing for certain that it would.

She stood by the door, holding it shut. 'Why did you do it?'

There was no use denying it. 'If a man can't be boss of his own house, who can?' he said lightly, hoping she would appreciate his jest.

'It was running very well. We were happy—after our fashions, but you have to become President of the Handley Democratic Republic. You wanted to spite Cuthbert, but it's a ridiculous way for a grown man to carry on.'

He picked up a palette knife, as if about to carve his initials on his chest: 'Under Cuthbert,' he said, 'it would have gone Fascist. Or he'd have had us wallowing in Primitive Christian Nihilism in no time. He's got no political sense whatsoever. He's just interested in destroying the community. He as good as told me.'

She liked being in his studio, because not only was it so much part of him, but it often calmed her to be there, since it had all the tools and bric-à-brac, talent and smell of him, that he'd accumulated over twenty odd years. It meant as much to her as to him, those stacks of canvasses, paint and turps, paper and bits of old board, books and reproductions gone pale and shabby from flies and sunshine.

'Give me a cigarette,' she said.

It was her life as well as his, but now for the first time she realised that really it was only him and not her. In a sense he had everything and she had nothing—apart from him and the family, and herself, which was supposed to be everything but wasn't.

He lit a cigarette, and a long thin cigar for himself.

'If the community can't hold together in spite of what Cuthbert can do against it,' she said, 'it doesn't deserve to survive.'

'It's got to be protected,' he said, 'and that's my job. It should be yours as well, but it seems you're leaving it all to me. I owe it to Myra to look after it.'

'The knight in shining armour,' she jeered, swinging back. 'You're a bloody hypocrite right to the depths of your soul. That's all that's in you: hypocrisy, oceans of it, and the worst thing is that you love it because it stops you seeing anything. It's blinded you in both bloody eyes!'

But she spoke as if every word injured her and not him. She stopped by a collage called 'The Angel of Mons'—a big old trench map he'd picked up in a junk shop, covered with photographs of soldiers ripped out of her family album and cut up—without asking. Sunset and blood colours smeared it at various angles—chaos around the eye of a cyclone, at which the only conflict was a matter of life and death. It was sharp and precise at the centre, and calm. All his paintings managed to be so much like himself that she didn't know where he ended and the paintings began, a feeling which rubbed her to the bone.

'You set your son on to me,' he said, quietly enough. 'It takes us back to the house of bloody Cadmus. It really is about time I slung my hook and packed this farce in. I'm tired of it. It's eating me away. It's hungry, that man-eating mouth you set loose inside me. Call it off, for God's sake, before I become hollow and drop down dead like a pack of dust.'

To leave her and go would do him no good, to give into that dream that he dreamed every day, because to wilfully get it would be like a child having a great toy it had always wanted. He'd enjoy it for ten minutes and then wonder where the real and only life had gone. He knew more than Dawley about things like that.

'Can I sit down, Albert?'

He pulled up a chair and one for himself, and placed them by the unlit stove. He was often afraid he'd gone too far in their arguments, but when he found he hadn't he started in again.

'It used to be so good between us,' she said.

He tried to sound honest and reasonable. 'It was all right. But we starved often enough so that the kids could eat. That wasn't so good.'

'I know. But we lived in our own house in Lincolnshire. We were on our own. I know this community idea is working, but it's not the same, Albert. I still think how much better it used to be.'

He was calm about it. 'John put paid to our life in Lincolnshire. He burned the house down.'

'I wish you'd never met *him*.'

He jumped. 'John was my brother.'

'You know who I mean. Dawley. He was the beginning of our troubles.'

'I never thought of it like that.'

'You never do. But if we hadn't got to know him, John wouldn't have had the hair-brained idea of going off to Algeria to pull him out of that war. He wouldn't have set the house on fire as a parting gift.'

'He would still have been a sick man,' Handley said. 'Bad in the head.'

'But good in the heart. He'd still have been alive.'

'You worked it out too bloody pat.'

'It's true, though,' she said patiently.

'I suppose you brooded on it long and good about Dawley?'

'It occurred to me, Albert.'

'In one blinding moment?'

'Yes, Albert.'

'Because he's my friend?'

'Oh don't be daft.'

'This is all I need: somebody to turn me against my friends.'

'That's not my idea, Albert.'

'What is, then? I expect you're still working it out.'

He walked to the window. 'Your honesty appals me. It'll be the death of me. And don't keep saying Albert like that. When you do I know you're up to no good.'

She stood, flushed red. 'The only time you have a good word for me is when I tell you there's something to eat on the table, or when you want me to open my legs at night.'

'What else can I do? I've got to do this painting. It brings the money in.'

'Money! You never used to say that. You thought you hadn't got enough on your shoulders with a wife and seven children so you had to take on this community as well. But I know why you did it.'

'Do you?'

'Yes, I do.'

'Tell me, then.'

'You want me to?'

'Get on with it.'

'To be close to Myra, that's why. You made it out you were full of high principles, wanting to find a new way of life, make a pattern for others and a framework for yourself, and all that bloody rubbish, but you can't fool me. I'd rather you got caught up in politics than this. I know you're in love with her.'

He trembled with rage at her accuracy. Subtlety was never one of his strong points, and so he'd always underestimated hers—out of laziness mostly, because he didn't doubt his own ability to be subtle with those he thought too clever for him.

'It's nothing but an old man's folly,' she shouted, 'I should have known it would come to this. You'd send us all to the wall for a single flick of your randy tail. You disgust me. Oh I can take it, to a certain extent. And I have done these last months, but now and again it gets too much.'

Her agitation shook him to the marrow. He picked up a brush, worked it round a mustard-glass of red paint. He threw the whole lot like a hand grenade—smash through the window, leaving a comet-tail of paint behind. He had lost the ability to quarrel, the art of give-and-take, the humanity of living repartee that was full of love even when steeped in hate. He felt like a rock about to be finally loosened from the sandgrip and swept away. There was a point at which you must shift and flee, and now that the time had come he was unable to do anything. He must get away from her, because if he only breathed, or lit a cigarette, or put food in his mouth, it was to spite her. If he went on living she thought it was only to spite her. Yet to walk away would be the final injustice also—to spite her. Even if he was prepared to commit this injustice he would still be unable to walk away. He was beginning to feel that his spirit was broken.

'You can't answer me because you're tongue-tied by your own black guilt,' she went on. 'But I'm not asking you to be guilty. That's not what I want at all.'

According to the ritual this was the moment for her voice to soften, and start to blame herself, and Handley felt it was time either to walk away or kiss her. The idea of the community had been fine, as he told her now, to try and extend the limits of the family with a few select friends, and not for the reason she imagined. He had no wish to turn it into a graveyard of crushed desires, neither for her nor for him nor for anybody. It was a good scheme that could still succeed, and he was determined to go on trying, if he could get the necessary co-operation. Even if he didn't he would continue working for the commune, because he realised it was in their best interests, and that was the only thing that mattered as far as he was concerned.

'You're not at a meeting now,' she said wryly, an impatient wave. 'You'll have me cheering in a bit. Or crying. I don't know which.'

He laughed, all blackness gone, easy again, and no one knew the reason. He kissed her, and they went down the garden path to see if Myra had finished making lunch. They had gone up the garden path hand in hand many years ago, and had been walking up and down it continually since, and neither of them knew how to get off it.

Chapter Fourteen

Richard waited in the front garden for the children to come from school.

His parents had been shouting at each other in the studio, but calm had now settled on the house. Handley needed such bust-ups to crumble the clogged energy that kept him from painting, and it was plain that his mother also thrived on arguments, for he noted how carefree she became afterwards. Such quarrels made his life a misery.

A warm humidity rose from the fields, almost as sweet in its smell as on the hillside in Lincolnshire. The road outside the gate was quiet, and the field behind the paddock lush and snug, safe and untouchable, eternally green, enticing alike for cattle and children—the land on the other side of the fence, beyond the realm of this incestuous bailiwick in which he was beginning to loose faith.

He wished Uncle John were alive, for he had radiated not only spiritual authority, but shown actual example on how you should accept it, as if he were living under some form of divine guidance. It was different now that he had gone, and committee meetings had taken the heart out of any satisfying life. The richness had left it, and he continually asked himself if it could ever be brought back.

Engrossed in revolutionary tactics and all manner of civil discord he compared the matrimonial antagonism of the family that had bred him to the social and political animosity of people in general; wondered, as he leaned on the gate, whether Handley would have been so obsessed with revolutionary strife if he hadn't been an artist with a wife and seven kids. Children provided him with resentment—against society which made his life so hard because he wanted to live as an artist.

Richard didn't think his father was eaten up by class conflict, at least not more than was healthy in such a country. He was too well off to justify such rancour, and too absorbed in his painting to be bothered. It channelled his spleen from the warping prison of the family in which he lived, yet he could not exist without his wife and children, and loved them so much he felt desperately fettered by their need of him and his of them. Combined with the occasional black frustrations of his art, this made it necessary for him to indulge to an infinite degree in the passionate pastime of revolution.

Richard had worked this out, and it worried him. Encouraged all his life to study revolution and rebellion it was natural that it should one day turn him against this indoctrination. Nothing stood still. You either learned, or you died. It was an ever-fascinating theme, and he had the sort of mind which led him to see the end of it. What better weapon had been put into his hands than the long training already received?

Paul, Rachel, Janet and Simon got off the bus. Simon Dawley was fuming and kicking. His short white bristle-hair seemed about to turn the same beetroot pink as his face because Janet had taken his marbles and would not give them back, held her lips tight as if the sky were about to fall down on her. A cool wind scattered them towards the gate.

Paul Handley put his arms round Simon. 'Don't cry. She'll give 'em up.'

'Finding's keeping.' Janet was rigid with possession.

'It's not, you know,' said Paul, with his fifteen-year-old gravity.

'They're mine,' she maintained.

'No, they're not,' said Simon, who did not know how to right an injustice except by bursting into tears, or punching somebody. And when he saw that hitting out would not be tolerated it looked as if he were willing his head to burst. Paul turned to Rachel: 'Get the marbles, and give 'em to him.'

Dark-haired Rachel walked up to cringing Janet, thumped her soundly on the back, and prised open her hand. 'Thanks,' she said.

'He's my brother,' Janet cried in her rage, as if that gave her a right to be mean to him.

'They were his marbles,' said Paul. 'He got them with his spending money.'

'He's still my brother, you rotten Handleys,' said Janet Dawley.

'Well, you ought to treat him like a brother,' said Paul quietly.

'We're not rotten,' said Rachel Handley, 'so don't say it. It's not right.' They sorted out their differences in a reasonably short time, considering they were human beings. Paul opened the gate and they filed, with a ravening afternoon hunger, into the kitchen for bread-and-butter and milk.

Richard played his part in the system that Handley had created, and carried on working even when he no longer felt that satisfying ray of faith from Uncle John's time. He had spent weeks with Adam listening out on VHF radios to the county police patrol frequencies, noting all call-signs, deducing the number of cars, and drawing a cloured map to show the operations area of each group. In this way he could tell at any hour where the various cars were, and get news even before it reached the newspapers or police courts.

He wondered whether Handley wasn't trying to mould him into a new Uncle John, for any change of role in the household never came about by decree, but always by a slow unwitting half-conscious acceptance of something only fate could have turned you on to. Though feeling this strongly, he had enough moral fibre not to be put off by it, but what really made him uneasy was that Handley seemed to be welding them into one single generation, denying them the differences in age and outlook due to some need for safety and security in himself.

The idea alarmed him, not so much for his father, as for himself and the others. It was the most basic threat to the young community so far —and also a danger to the existence of the family, to which the normal troubles of the community discussed at meetings were nothing. These suspicions occurred to him while watching the children quarrelling their way from the bus. It came while the cool wind blew downhill from the opposite field, and brought the smell of damp herbage into his senses, making him momentarily a child, and lighting his brain as if he'd been smoking pot. He knew then what his father was up to, not by reason, but by an almost religious instinct that, five minutes later, he felt ashamed of.

They came out with their bread and butter—Paul, Rachel, Janet and

Simon: the Handleys and the Dawleys, fair and dark, young and growing-up. Paul leaned against the Rambler, hands in jean pockets, the last bread fast in his mouth. Fair thin hair came evenly over his forehead and his grey eyes stared in front. At thirteen he had been set to govern the younger children, a responsibility which in no way put him out, for he had a gift of tact and strength that no other Handley had.

He grinned, as if his job were finished for the day, whistling a secret and tuneless tune to himself as he led them into the garage for the after-school talk which it was Richard's daily duty to give.

They placed a bench by a wall marked with map-like stains from the fumes of exhaust pipes. The cars were outside, and they sat away from the wind and any stray noise that might interfere with the anti-lesson.

'Stop whistling, Paul, and listen to me.'

'Has Cuthbert come back with that Spanish woman yet?' he wanted to know.

Richard smiled. 'Why are you so interested in it?'

'We just are. We can't wait to get a peep at somebody new.'

He wondered why the children were so bored, with such a variable set of people perpetually around. The atmosphere of the community was usually one of flux and impending change, of activity and rumour, yet when this heady atmosphere relaxed, and life threatened to subside into calm orderliness, everyone grew restless and moody. The children got it sooner than the others. 'They'll be here this evening.'

'Before we go to bed?' asked Rachel, with such curiosity in her voice that he almost caught it himself.

'Depends on the trains. But forget it for the next half hour. When you got to school this morning what hymns did you sing?'

'Horrid,' Janet said. 'I hate hymns.'

'I hate *her* as well,' giggled Simon Dawley.

'Oh for God's sake,' wailed Rachel.

'Tell me which ones you sang, Janet.' Hating things did not look good, when you considered that hatred made an even deeper impression than what you liked. It was positively bad that she was so virulent. Indifference was safer to work on.

'I just sing other words to them,' Paul said. 'It's fun.'

'I used to do that,' said Richard, 'but the teacher could lip-read, so I got caught out. It's safer to mouth the words but make no sound.'

'That's what I do,' said Janet.

'I like hymns,' said Simon. 'I can sing loud. And if I mek a mistake, nobody knows.'

'What number hymn was it?' Richard persisted.

Nobody could remember. Maybe they wouldn't say which one it was in case they'd noticed more than was necessary. Simon Dawley spoke up. 'All things bright and beautiful . . .'

Richard reached into a tool box and took out a hymn-book, flipping quickly to the right page. He read the hymn as a piece of verse.

'It's nice, though,' said Rachel.

'That's because it rhymes and has a strong rhythm,' he explained. 'But you have to look through, to what the words mean. Take the bit about the rich man in his castle and the poor man at his gate. The God who made that up was invented by the people who live in the castle. It was written to keep the man at the gate from getting inside.'

'They chuck boiling oil on 'em when they scramble up the walls,' said Simon.

'It don't stop 'em, though,' Paul said. 'When they get in they kill the barons and set fire to the castle. They don't have to pay rent for the fields then.'

'While things are bright and beautiful for some,' said Richard, when the talk rambled on, 'they are not so cheery for others. I don't expect the Smith children who go to your school without overcoats and with only plimsolls on their feet in winter feel it's like that.'

'That's because their dad's idle,' said Janet. 'He's no good.'

'He's allus in the pub,' Rachel giggled.

'But we have to ask ourselves *why* he drinks,' Richard said quietly.

'He likes it,' Simon suggested.

Richard tried again, when they stopped laughing. 'Why does he like it, do you think?'

'It's lovely,' said Simon. 'Dad gen me some beer once, and I liked it. So he don't gi' me any no more now.'

'You was sick,' said Janet.

'It's all right to sing hymns,' Richard went on. 'You might even enjoy letting yourselves go. But I want you to know what the words signify.'

'They mean what they say,' said Simon, scraping his boot along the concrete.

'They do,' said Richard, 'but people don't even know that much. They think they mean something else.'

Simon grunted. 'I know what they mean, though.'

He was the most promising child of the group, in spite of being a Dawley. Or maybe it was because of that. He hoped not, but there was no point of going into it. Simon was an entity on his own. He doubted few things at the moment, so one couldn't press the anti-lessons too far, but let his school-teachers do it, so that when he turned from their indoctrination he would do it with a useful sort of finality. Handled carefully, it would certainly not be a kindness to let him loose on the world.

At the same time it hurt Richard to regard him like this. For all his knowing remarks he seemed an unprotected bundle, lively but vulnerable, a child to be looked after even more than the others—not something regarded with favour by this egalitarian community. He followed its rules nevertheless, but made the anti-lessons easy and humorous half-hours for the children.

The idea of them had started after Handley looked through Paul's notebook one day, and read from his Scripture jottings that: 'The Jews fought the Romans because they were forced to pay taxes.' The words rankled, and later he read in Rachel's history book that 'the Jews in medieval England were all money-lenders.' In the first case Handley was rabid because the statement was untrue, since the conflict between the Romans and the Jews, as far as he understood it, was one between paganism and monotheism. In the second place nothing seemed to have been told to the children about why many of the Jews in England, before their expulsion, became money-lenders.

When he wrote to the headmaster politely pointing out these anti-Semitic tendencies in his educational system, he received an irate reply telling him in effect to mind his own business. They had children of every race in his school, and it was nonsense to accuse him of racialism.

Handley went back to his pen and informed the headmaster that his own opinion was different, and that he knew racial prejudice when he saw it, and that furthermore he would take care to see that his children weren't poisoned by it. He'd give them a talk every day on the lies they were told at school, and thought all parents ought to do the same if they valued their children's minds.

There was no reply to this, but certainly Handley hadn't since then seen anything similarly offensive in his children's notebooks—though the talks had been kept up just the same to deal with what other lies and false information English schools still disseminated.

'We'll leave the hymns for the moment,' Richard said, 'and get back to where we left off yesterday. If you remember you told me about a film at school on life in Spain. I'll tell you something about the history of this place, and how it's governed at the present day.'

Chapter Fifteen

The moon was in disparate parts of the car while crossing the yard to reach the sky. Adam felt crazy till he realised he was drunk, so pulled deep breaths into him for the alcoholic daze to wear off.

Eric Bloodaxe, that ancient bulldog and probably best friend of the Handleys, snored loudly in the kennel, dragging its overfed body across the coconut-matted floor to avoid troublesome dreams leaping from the dark imaginary trees above its head. Ever alert, it gave a growling throaty bark when Adam slammed the car door, then went back to those dreams which it had long regarded as more interesting than real life.

Adam was sober at the wheel, though the two-ton car became frighteningly light when it went along the lanes above sixty. But he stayed cool, as he'd been trained all his life to do, open windows bringing smells of grass and fresh soil against his cheeks. Headlights lit the lane that cats and rabbits crossed at their peril, and he kept a safe speed in spite of too much sherry since teatime.

He pushed on the radio to hear the final bars of a magnificent symphony. It was always like that, and to avoid endless unnecessary clapping he switched off and drove with only the engine to lull his thoughts. He'd grumbled at having to fetch Cuthbert and Maricarmen from the station, but much good it had done him. He'd have preferred staying in the warmth and light, drinking wine, and playing liar-dice or laryngitis-brag with Frank and Nancy Dawley.

But it was no use complaining about the things you were asked to do while living in a community, where what you did was supposed to be for the good of everybody else. He'd rather go and chop down the gibbet on Hangman's Hill, to strike at the emblem of oppression so that American tourists couldn't take photos of it anymore with their friends standing underneath to send back home. The Handleys had spent days over maps and timetables working out the gibbet's disappearance with a thoroughness that would have been totally successful, except that a gang from London beat them to it, drove it off sticking from the back of a van—as one eye-rubbing farmer witnessed it.

Cuthbert took off his parson's collar as he stepped on to the platform, being too well known to wear it near home, the tip sticking from his pocket as he turned to help Maricarmen. Adam went forward to take the cases.

'My brother,' Cuthbert told her, 'will drive us to the house.' Adam took a soft hand offered, and would have expected it to be warmer judging by her face in the shadow of the station lamps. He was always uneasy when introduced to someone, but this time he was intrigued as well, and envious of Cuthbert who had already spent a few hours with her.

They stowed the trunk and cases in, and set off along the lanes in silence. Adam saw Cuthbert as a man of experience because, as the eldest son, he had been pushed while still a raw youth to schools and college. The rest of them hadn't expected to go, for after the effort of getting Cuthbert out, no more resources had been left. But now that there was money in the family it wasn't the case anymore, and nothing need stop either him or Richard going to university—a thought which had lately occurred to them both.

Handley was waiting on the lit-up doorstep. Eric Bloodaxe barked its welcome, shortlived as it slid back kennelwards when Handley's boot made the usual half-loving gesture. Dawley stood in his shirt-sleeves, arms folded, and came over to help get the trunk down. Maricarmen, surprised at no greeting, thought them more like a gang of efficient railway porters, but when her things were stacked near the back door Handley held out his hand: 'You've met my sons. I'm their father. And this is Frank Dawley.'

Lights were on in upstairs windows, and others glowed from the caravans. She looked at Dawley, but did not shake his hand, unwilling to waste observations in the half light, merely noting his strong head and short greying hair, and powerful but harmless stance which gave no clue to the personality he was supposed to have.

Handley led her into the house. 'We put off supper till you came. I hope you managed to sleep on the train.'

He was fazed by her silence, but put it down to exhaustion after her trip, and meeting strange people. She followed Myra upstairs to the room got ready, and ten minutes later came into the dining-room. She wore a white blouse, dark skirt, brooch at the throat, and held her head high as she walked to a chair, placing a bottle of Fundador brandy on the table.

'That's not necessary,' Handley said, 'though it's beautifully polite!'

She'd been safe on boat or train, locked in the actual journey and cut off from people packed around her, but now she felt isolated, and it put an added touchiness and pride into her face, which caused those who noticed it to speculate on how she would get on in the commune. Handley, with a small ironic smile, was curious as to who would fall in love with her first. His smirk dropped when she turned and wondered what it was for. He poured wine: 'All I want to say is: welcome to Maricarmen. But we're hungry, and she's tired, so I suggest we get down to eating before any of us drop in a dead faint.'

She looked at the scalding and meaty soup, asking who made it. 'It's one of mine,' said Enid.

'Do the men cook?'

Handley's head jerked up: 'We have study groups going, and do work in the garage. I paint all the time. There are one or two idle bastards among us, but we pull our weight—by and large.'

Ralph looked over his soup, wondering whether he could afford to ignore this slight on his honour. To let it go would disarm Handley sooner than any other reaction.

'If the tin-hat fits, watch out for shrapnel,' Handley called.

'Oh stop it,' Enid said.

Ralph decided to copy Cuthbert who, for the moment, was unaware that his father was getting at him. 'But cooking, and washing up, and looking after children, and things like that?' Maricarmen kept on.

Handley decided that if anyone did fall in love with her it wouldn't be him. She'd only just arrived and was already getting the boot in.

Cuthbert saw that she'd immediately put her hand on the weak spot of their society, a point which he'd never thought of. Myra saw the danger: 'Enid and I look after the domestic side. It works well, and we're willing.'

'I'm not bloody-well willing, though,' Mandy called. 'We're glad there's another woman in the place to set to and give us a hand.'

Cuthbert was amazed at how danger to the Handley machine was immediately deflected by its hidden wheels within wheels. It moved into action with such precision that the threat itself was clumsy and Neanderthal by comparison. 'I thought three women were enough,' he said, too much struck by Maricarmen to see her standing by a stove or sink all day.

'She'll want a rest first,' Handley put in, for once in agreement with his firstborn son. 'Then we'll go through those notebooks of Shelley's to see what revolutionary wisdom we can get from between the lines.'

'I've not read them,' Maricarmen explained. 'They were put into the trunk by Shelley, and I couldn't bear to look at them. I just kept them safe, expecting him to come back for them. I wouldn't want him to think I'd been prying into his personal papers. He was very easy-going, and very proud at the same time.'

She felt a devastating loneliness, wondering why she was among these people. It was impossible to remember much of her journey, as if she'd been spirited here by magic. The lights were too bright, and she thought they'd arranged to have the greatest glare over where she sat.

'We won't look at them if you think we've no right,' Handley said, delicately, 'or if it would upset you in any way. Relax for a few weeks, and then see how you feel.'

Myra fetched in a huge joint on a platter, which she put before Handley to carve. 'It's good of you to make it easy for me,' Maricarmen said.

Like hell it is, Cuthbert thought.

It was a floating world she lived in. The more she wandered the more settled she felt. Three months in one place and she began to feel rootless. Her head swam and she became dizzy, as if there were nothing to hang on to. Movement was stability. When she was on the move she didn't notice the spinning of the earth. She could be happy and confident on her own firm level.

But having to stay in one place made her cling to the world for fear of falling off. She'd once changed her address every week for almost a year, delivering street-fighting pamphlets to underground workers groups, and felt absolutely cool and normal. It was easy to merge with the crowd, and one man who took the inflammable tracts from her was so shocked at seeing this ordinary young woman handling such firing-squad material that he sweated about it three nights running, and even wondered why he had joined the revolutionary movement.

Surrounded by the strange people of this extended family who, through Dawley, had some remote connection to Shelley, she felt able to control and even enjoy the situation. With them, she could be herself, so was indeed at home. And her tiredness from the journey had diminished now that there was food inside her.

Her observations were not analytical, merely her customary musings out of which useful truths often came. Because of this born ability to be herself she didn't suspect that they in turn were wary of her, and that she might be at a disadvantage when set among people who, like the Handley's, found it even easier to be themselves. She noticed this, but only vaguely, because she was invariably ready to see good in people rather than anything else—and always condemned them more harshly afterwards if they didn't come up to her expectations.

To appear straightforward was a sure way of putting people on their guard once they thought you were doing so. Though not sensing this sudden alertness among them, especially in Cuthbert and his father, she did have the perspicacity to detect a slight change of attitude as she sat at the table.

Dawley was observing her in a cleverly unobtrusive way. This was as it should be, for he after all was her reason for travelling to England. Another aspect of being herself was that her set purpose would never falter—of finding out how he had tricked Shelley to a sure death in Algeria, and then pay him back in kind.

While the ways and means of it unrolled, she would be careful of him, knowing from experience in the organisation to which she had belonged in Spain, in the years before meeting Shelley, that when a man who happened to be her lover was taken to prison, or escaped to permanent exile in France or South America, the person to show love to her afterwards was often the man's best friend. And it was just as usual, in that sort of life, for her to be drawn strongly to him, for the casual reshuffle of love worked in as immutable a way as any social cohesion.

And Dawley was the last man in the world she would want as a lover, or even as a friend. To say that he was the sort of intelligent man who kept all power to himself only because he was selfish, and that he was therefore his own worst enemy, would be to underestimate his qualities, especially if he were an enemy of yours. She had seen this aspect in many men, for they usually ended, if they could, by making an enemy out of her, even if only to take the pressure off themselves. She had a firm belief in first impressions, and clung to them even when the initially accurate vision receded into a more general picture.

But outside her sense of mission regarding Dawley, was a feeling of well-being and happiness, and the certainty—as more food and wine was set before her and conversation spread in a friendly way—that she had reached a peaceful haven of sympathetic people whom she in turn liked and understood and, in some comforting way, was understood by, not in the style of old comrades but, weirder still, as if she were some distant cousin who had just come in from Gibraltar.

They were foreign and strange, yet because of these qualities, and not in spite of them, they were close to her. Was it only during this first meeting that she would feel such a thing?

Chapter Sixteen

Day after day he bent close to the intricate colour and detail of the large-scale maps of the Algerian wilderness that covered the caravan table, trying to equate their contours and empty areas to the actual journey made on the ground.

Between reality and the pretty picture, memory posed its special problems when it came to fusing both into dull deadbeat words. What picture ever agreed with reality? Reality was one and indivisible, and the representative fraction of Dawley's split mind as he gazed at his maps—more detailed and expressive by far than those used on the trek itself—showed little sign of coming together and recreating the vanished though recent past.

He was in England, and safe, and the war was over, and his memories had no clarity though they still, somewhere, had meaning. Having more or less marked out the course of his footslog from the Moroccan frontier to the Khabylie Mountains near the northern coast, and re-knit a daily account of what happened, much of it was nevertheless inaccurate because he felt that his recollections were not to be trusted, and possibly never would be.

Knowing that reality and the past were so bound up that they could not be brought back, created a larger drier desert in himself than the scorching sand and stone he had walked over. It made him see that, returned to the safety of England's green and truly pleasant dead land, he did not know with any surety why he had gone to fight for the rebels in Algeria.

True, out of a sense of idealism, and to help the down-trodden of the world after a lifetime believing that the international socialist brotherhood of man could cure the evils and inefficiencies of capitalist-imperialism, he had agreed to join Shelley Jones in driving a lorry of guns to the frontier beyond Tafilalet—a practical action that could never be confused with any dream.

After a successful ambush, he persuaded Shelley to go on to the war in Algeria. Shelley knew his limitations, and did not care to enter the battle zone. But Dawley, drunk on the tactical superiority of the fighting, and the intoxicating though diminishing noise of their own gunfire, forced him to embark on the most stupid enterprise it was possible to concoct.

They struggled across desert and rocks and mountain ranges, hunted and hunting, half dead from sickness, hunger and thirst, yet somehow recuperating and surviving. Each day the sky altered, from darkness through scorching heat to darkness. Even now, it came back real enough when he descended down into the dream to think about it. During a night attack, Shelley was wounded in the foot, and died of gangrene a week later.

Maricarmen hadn't come to England so that the Handleys could comb Shelley's notebooks for aphorisms on revolution. They, after all, were ten-a-penny compared to the rarity of action. Who could say what the notebooks contained, anyway? Shelley had never been one for writing his great notions down, but usually spouted them to whoever was near by. His friendship with Shelley had been deep enough for him to laugh at the more impractical ideas. Maricarmen had another sort of friendship with him, and he saw that she had come to find out exactly how it was that Shelley had decided against his usual and better judgment to go into a country that was at war. Frank felt that the revolution had really come home to roost, and he was uneasy.

Later that night, when they went back to the caravan, Nancy sat opposite with her knitting, while he tried to scribble a few notes out of himself. The kids were tucked into their sleeping places, dead to the world after a day roaming the woods for cowslips and birds' eggs.

His thoughts floated, idle and infertile, and because he was tired, and in a way content, he waited for them to tell him something new.

'I can't stand this life any longer,' Nancy said, pausing in her needlework.

He looked up.

'What's wrong with it?'

'I want a home of my own, that's what's wrong with it. I don't like living on top of other people.' She was knitting a jumper for Simon, having bought a Fair Isle pattern from the store in the village, one of those fly-blown pamphlets paled by the sun that you see all over the country, with an illustration of a kid on the envelope already wearing it, the sort of smiling nipper that never was except in Nancy's mind.

'I want to live in private, not public,' she said. 'Nor in a caravan, either. It's like when I was a girl and lived in a slummy street, everybody sitting on their door-steps and shouting across to everybody else. I was glad when we went to the housing estate.'

'You can't compare this to a slum.'

The clicking needles showed off her mood. As if he needed them! She had a lot to say, and didn't relish the fact that he was making her say it. He was sly as well as idle these days, and such people can't love. 'Perhaps not. But I'd like us to be more on our own.'

'I wouldn't want to,' he said. 'This is a good way to live.'

'Where does that bleddy leave *me*, then?' she demanded.

'If we can't agree, there's not much point in things.'

'If you'd agree with me,' she answered, 'we'd be all right. Depends which way you look at it, don't it?'

'I expect it does.'

She was not prepared for it to stay like that, though she didn't doubt he would have been. 'I'm going back to Nottingham, then.'

'Oh ye'? Gonna get rooms?'

'Not bleddy likely. I kept the house on.'

He hadn't known about that. 'You just came down for a holiday, like?'

They sat at the table, with a pot of tea between them—which he had made. 'I've got two kids to think about, and I know I can't rely on you to do anything. You've been back months and you haven't even got a job yet.'

'It's not so important.'

'It is for me,' she said.

'There's plenty of others to sweat in factories. I've done my share.'

'Twelve years isn't a fair share. And where's the money going to come from?'

He saw the lines already at her mouth, the hard-bitch determination to do nothing that wasn't approved of in TV adverts and the *Daily Retch.* To her there was nought else to do but the done thing, to knuckle under and get back to it and pull your weight and feed the hungry mouths in the handpainted nest—mostly for the benefit of bastards who'd faint at the smell of an oil-rag, or who couldn't even mend a fuse. He felt an ugly mood in him, and held it back. 'Are you short of money? I'll solve that problem if you are.'

'You wouldn't have talked like that in the old days,' she shrugged. He'd be an old man if he stayed here much longer, doing something he was never cut out for. But he was shifting and unreliable. He'd left her once, and would do it again, so she might as well get it in first.

'Times change,' he said.

'I don't think so.'

'Well I change, then.'

He'd done the wrong thing going to see her in Nottingham after coming back. He couldn't think why he'd done it now, except out of curiosity, and a wish to look at the children. But it was a useless waste, because even if they'd missed him they were used to him having vanished by then. Such a thoughtless return had ruined everything, and now it was being done again—by Nancy this time—so he had to do his bit and not make it look too easy: 'Can't you stick with things for a while? What about all the love you told me you had?'

He wouldn't have said that a year ago, either. He felt a wave of self-dislike, yet at the same time knew he hadn't come back from Algeria to get caught in this.

'Maybe it's gone so deep I can't get to it,' she said, 'But I know what would be best for the kids.'

'They're happy here.'

They were, too.

'They'll be happier in Nottingham, even though I'll have to go to work. It'll be more real for them up there.'

More real! Good God! Wasn't it real everywhere? But there was no moving her. Nor did he want to, finally. He was aware of being unjust in his indifference, but there was nothing he could do about it. He'd known for weeks it wasn't working out.

'I'll pack tomorrow,' she said. 'And if you want to follow on, you can. But don't leave it too late. Things have a way of altering for good. I'm only thirty, don't forget.'

'I won't go back to work in a factory,' he said quietly. 'Not till I've tried something else.'

'What, though?'

'I'm not sure yet.'

'Well, you ought to be. You liked the factory at one time. That's all you know how to do, anyway.'

'Do you think that's a good life?'

'I don't know. But I've worked as a bus conductress, and that wasn't exactly fun. And I sweated in a stocking factory from fifteen, till I married you. I've done my share, and I know I'll have to go on doing it—all my bloody life.'

So Nancy left. Nobody could persuade her not to, and they all missed her when she went, which made him feel quite bad about it. In fact he didn't realise how much she and the children meant to him till afterwards.

A final set-to at the station showed that she knew Myra's son Mark was his child, and that her pride would not let her live so close to them. He couldn't blame her for it, and it was as clean a way of parting as he could think of. He did wonder though what vile gett had thought fit to tell her. It was strange, he brooded on his way back from the station, how she'd made up his mind for him, instead of it being the other way round.

Chapter Seventeen

Ralph Spilsby regarded himself as an honourable man, but since marrying Mandy he had lived on his in-laws and earned no money at all. He therefore computed to the best of his ability, being honourable, how much in cash he owed the Handley community, hoping one fine day to pay every shilling back.

The fact that he was in their debt, yet went on living with them, tormented him from time to time, though Handley to his credit did not remind him of it, nor tell him to get a job, any more frequently than he did to a member of his own family. But Ralph kept his calculations, and waited with fierce patience for the day when one of his rich aunts would die and leave him a fortune.

He came to live with the Handleys because he'd married Mandy. But also he valued the priceless silence of the countryside. When even those sounds were pushed into the background, all remaining noises were his own, and in the middle of the day, with the kids at school and Handley in his studio, it was indeed peaceful around the compound. Dawley's wife Nancy had left the community and taken their two kids, so even that made things quieter.

A calm life to Ralph meant hearing no other noises but his own, for then the silences belonged totally to him. He wanted infinite space and emptiness in all directions, that he could fill with his own speech and movement, shapes and colours. He had an active imagination, and sat alone like a king, quiescent in his benign selfishness, which was his one pure reason for having been born, and the nearest he ever got to real happiness. He thought it was this craving for peace and silence that made him an honourable man.

He got up from his log in the paddock, and talked inwardly with himself while burning yesterday's paper-rubbish from the house. Maricarmen came through the gate. 'I thought everyone was taking a nap,' she said.

'I can't rest at the moment.' He raked stray bits of paper closer to the fire. 'I prefer to sleep at night.'

'Do you like being in this community?'

'I can't live anywhere else, so I have to,' he said, kicking a pile of school exercise books into the flame.

'You're honest. Why not?'

'My wife's here. I have shelter. That's a good reason to like it. And I eat good food.'

'Do you agree with their ideas?'

'I don't have to,' he smiled.

She sat on the log. 'If you have pride you do.

'What does anyone want with that?' he laughed—uneasily.

'Aren't you a man?'

'A gentleman,' he said firmly, and she was afraid of the violence in his voice, 'who has all the pride he needs. I believe in doing as little harm as possible to my fellow-men, and living as quietly as I can.'

'That means you consider yourself one of the elite, living off those who do real work.'

A smile disguised his face. 'There's a lot of unemployment in the country. It would be unjust of me to take somebody else's job.'

'With a socialist system there'd be work for everybody.'

'I suppose there would be a lot of pushing around,' he said. 'Who do you live off?'

'I've worked since I was sixteen. I've picked olives off the ground, or harvested oranges, and have done domestic work in hotels. I've worked in prison. I've worked in the textile factories of Sabadell. I'm not a stranger to it.' She was angry with him.

A bag of broken plastic toys swept into flame, and they moved from searing heat. 'Those who don't work,' she said, 'should have no food. In a democratic system a steel-worker and a coalminer would have ten votes on the electoral roll because they are what Shelley used to call "primary producers".'

'What about doctors and teachers?'

'They're important, too.'

'Everybody is important,' he said. 'Your beliefs and Dawley's are similar: ruthless justice. Two of a kind. To me all people are equal.'

Her eyes were full of scorn. 'I don't understand that sort of equality.'

Large drops of rain were spitting on to the fire. They watched it, drawn by its noise and little puffs of vapour. Grass and earth sent up a heavy smell of pungent soil. The rain seemed weightier than the steely needles of water that fell among the olive trees behind her village at home. The soil here soaked up water, whereas there it ran into gullies and fed the Ebro, unmistakable in its purpose.

Ralph wanted to go into the house where it was dry and there'd be fresh hot tea to drink, but he couldn't move or run while Maricarmen stood there. Her thin blouse was quickly soaked, the upper part of her breasts showing pink through the material. Noting the colour and shape, he blushed and looked towards the hedge.

She smiled at his stupid embarrassment, and didn't think Dawley would turn away so readily. Nor would Handley, who often stared at her either as an artist, or with the brazenness of an older man.

She walked to the house. Everyone agreed that she and Dawley would get on well together, but so far she had avoided him so successfully that she thought he was deliberately keeping out of her way, which only proved how guilty he felt because of what he had done to Shelley. This made her more determined to settle him for his crime. Yet she must have proof. Her sense of justice required it. To kill for a good reason was still murder. If society killed for a bad reason, it was justice. Yet where was the difference if you had no belief in the so-called rights of the State?

On the other hand, to kill someone when you had proof of his guilt was also an act of revenge. Was that better for your conscience than an act of passion? Society carried out these acts of revenge all the time, and in her name who had never sanctioned it. And yet why should she imitate a society she despised? It confused and worried her. But the fact that she had to kill Dawley kept her calm, though she couldn't do so till she had proper evidence on which to convict him. If she didn't find enough proof to back up her intuition, which could only mean that he was innocent, then she would go quietly back to political work in Spain.

She went to help in the kitchen. Enid, stirring a huge pan of sauce on the stove, turned at the noise of the door: 'You got caught in the rain. I'd change if I were you.'

'It's nothing.'

'You won't say that if you get pneumonia. I'll lend you a blouse if you haven't got a clean one. We're about the same size in front.'

They looked after her as if she were some delicate flower who might perish in their hideous climate, not knowing how bad Spanish weather could be, how she'd often been caught in snow and rain on journeys that none in this house might survive. Such persistent solicitousness affronted her pride, yet out of natural politeness she said nothing, and went up to change.

In her room she rubbed herself dry. Her only other brassiere was still damp, so she put on a vest and clean blouse. Suddenly tired and tempted to lie down, she wondered whether such lethargy hadn't come on her since seeing the person she had decided to kill, a state of somnolence in which the act would resolve itself without any effort at all.

She looked at the grey light of the window, rain hammering the glass, full blown trees creaking in the garden. Who wouldn't be sleepy with such a green and deadly landscape? Who wouldn't act in it?

A dozen cups and saucers had been set out over the formica-topped table, and two-year-old Mark looked on gravely from his highchair as Myra clattered a spoon into each saucer. 'He's an intelligent child,' Maricarmen said.

'They are, at his age.'

She liked Myra, though they had made little contact so far. She sat down, but feeling livelier in face of such activity, and the high wattage bulbs radiating in the large kitchen. At the slightest sign of dim weather, or hours before dusk, even if it was bright outside, every houselight was turned on. In Spain one small bulb sufficed for a whole thrifty family, and here the continual waste made her uneasy. 'Who is Mark's father?' she asked, not finally clear on who belonged to whom.

'Frank. I had Mark in Tangier just after he went off with Shelley. Whose did you think he was?' she asked, seeing an expression on her face as if a needle had been stuck into her.

'I thought maybe he was Handley's. It's a strange house.

Myra took a cake tin out of the cupboard. 'It is if you're a stranger to it.'

'I mean,' said Maricarmen, 'it's very normal in one way because all the women stay in the kitchen, while the men do their own work. It's not what I'd call a liberal community—the men plotting revolution and equality, and the women kept at their traditional labour.'

Myra laid pieces of cake on a platter, and cut bread for sandwiches. This girl was saying what went continually through her own mind. 'There isn't too much to do. It's shared between Enid, myself, Mandy and the two *au pair* girls. It's mechanised. Ralph and Cuthbert, as well as Albert now and again, take care of the garden and garage chores.'

'It's the principle of the system,' Maricarmen went on.

Myra was interested to know how she would alter it.

'I'm not sure.'

'There you are, then.'

At that, she was stung to reply: 'Everyone over eighteen, male or female, should do a day's work in the kitchen. That would include Mr Handley, who may be an artist, but even an artist has to eat.'

Myra laughed. 'Let's talk to Enid, then we can put our new system forward at the next meeting. You're living in the house, so you can vote, and that'll make four of us. It's a pity Nancy left, because she'd have been with us. But if Mandy can talk Ralph to our side that will be five. Cuthbert might back us for devilment if he sees his father's against it. That'll be six-four. We may do it.' She was surprised at her optimism, and renewed energy at the thought of breaking the usual flaccid routine. Mark clattered his spoon against the highchair tray, and made a noise as if asking for cake—which was passed to him in a plastic dish.

'It'll be interesting to see if they really believe in equality,' Maricarmen said. 'But don't say anything till the day of the meeting, then perhaps it'll come as such a shock that no one will oppose it!'

Myra was dubious. 'You've had experience at this sort of thing.'

'Of what?' Enid came in from the hall with a bowl of cooking apples, which she set on the table and began to peel for sauce. Myra went through the plan, elaborating each stage with Maricarmen, who began to help Enid.

'I've been in it so long,' Enid said, 'that I'd die if I ever got out of it.

But I'm only forty-odd so I can always start a new life. It'll certainly be new for Albert if we pull it off.'

'Pull what off?' Handley demanded, coming in from the garden, trousers and jacket smeared with paint. Even his face was pocked with colour.

Enid stood to pour his tea. 'Just one of those little domestic issues that bore you to death.'

He sat down, and held up both hands which were also caked with paint: 'I've always been a dirty worker. It's just that I forget myself. Splash, splash, splash.' He stretched his legs towards the Aga. 'Any biscuits? I get a ravenous appetite, being the breadwinner.'

'You look as if you paint houses, not pictures,' Myra said, mixing eggs for a custard.

'Thank God it is pictures.' Handley lifted his cup for more tea. 'We'd be on bread and jam if it was houses.'

'Some people are happy with bread and jam,' said Enid.

Handley sneered—but good-naturedly. 'They stick together longer.

'What's wrong with that?'

'Too many flies on 'em.' He laughed into his empty teacup. 'I get thirsty.'

She filled it. 'Choke.'

'How are you enjoying life in the commune?' he asked Maricarmen.

She put out her finger, and Mark gripped it. 'It's restful, but I'd better start work sometime.'

'If you want to make yourself useful, it's up to you.'

Enid put the finished apples into a cauldron and set them on the stove. 'She is already.'

He reached for the cake platter. 'That's fair, then.'

'We all work in this house,' said Mandy, just coming in. 'Except you. You just splash paint about.'

'How's my lovely nubile daughter?' he asked, always able to forgive her taunts—unless they were a prelude to wanting money.

'Your Dad's an artist,' Enid said sharply, whose ire rose whenever Handley went soft over his daughter. 'So have a bit of bloody respect for his work.'

Mandy had no fear of her father, but went into sullen silence at any outburst from her mother—who was never above a sudden stinging slap across the face.

'I'm full of tea,' Handley said, 'and sweet things to eat, and my family is in its usual state of mutual antagonism, so I think I'll get to my solitary studio and work till I drop. Goodbye all. Don't heave on your plots and ploys while I'm away.'

There was no response when he went out.

Chapter Eighteen

Ralph sheltered in the garage till the rain stopped, then went back to the paddock with another huge plastic bag of waste for burning. He disliked the flames consuming what he tipped from these sacks. What fire took, it never gave back. And so much squandering frightened him. He hated it, almost as if it were a direct threat to himself. He had two wishes in life—one was to be fabulously rich, and the other was to exist on as little as possible, using the barest amount of the world's goods to keep himself breathing. In that way he would be secure. He smiled at the living mass of contradictions that seethed in him—so much useful rubbish that he would not throw away and burn.

Out of the bag came unused drawing paper, efficient boxes, half-finished exercise books, plastic bottles and containers, decorative tins, useful bits of pencil, broken gadgets and toys of all sorts that ought to be fixed—though there was no one to spend time and talent repairing them, and he wasn't able to do it himself. It was indeed an extravagant house, he thought, tipping a further bag into the embers.

He strolled across the paddock. The air was warm and heavy—sweetened milk to him after the utilitarian rain. Brambles proliferated, and doubled the thickness of the hedge. Across the angle of the far corner was a slit-trench ten feet long and several deep, a parapet thrown in front from excavated soil. Dawley had dug it for the children to play Viet Cong in, and Ralph recalled him a couple of months ago in wellingtons, wielding spade and pick, the sleeves of his shirt rolled up. It was a neat trench, revetted with boards, a few inches of muddy water in the bottom from recent rains adding to its realism. The children had enjoyed it at first, firing two-two air-rifles at a line of target tins stuck in the ground thirty yards away, but recently they had lost interest.

Coming back at another angle towards the still burning fire Ralph saw a small grey-brown object lying between clumps of grass. It was a baby hedgehog, and he picked it up. A few feet away were pieces of prickle-covered skin, the remains of the mother.

His mind only acted with speed when a sentimental issue was involved. The catastrophe to the hedgehog family unrolled with heart-rending immediacy. A few nights ago, with Mandy curled beside him in their narrow bed, and the rest of the house in equally dark pits of sleep, he was roused by a high-pitched shriek, as if a fox had caught hold of a cat and were tearing it to shreds. The noise went on and on, and the sweat of terror poured from his arms and legs, soaking his pyjamas. He wanted to go down for the shotgun, but sleepiness and inanition prevented him.

Holding the small frightened hedgehog in the palm of his hand, he knew now what the noise had been. A fox had got into the garden, found the hedgehogs and prised them open. The screams came from the mother who tried to protect her young, before she also was killed and eaten. He knew that hedgehogs, even when rolled into a ball, were not well defended against foxes. The small one in his hand had escaped the massacre.

He hated the savagery of foxes. There were tears in his eyes when, putting the hedgehog back on to the ground, it made its way cautiously towards the piece of skin that had belonged to the mother. Hedgehogs were gentle and harmless, the gardener's friend who ate noxious insects and slugs. It was too young even to know how to roll itself into a ball. He walked back towards the fire, cursing fox-like animals who preyed on helpless and innocent creatures. The thought of such cruelty in the world put him into agonising despair. Then he was cheered by the fact that one hedgehog of the family had survived.

He couldn't leave it alone, and after raking the fire went back to where he had put it down. A huge bottle-green blowfly had settled on to its ear, and two more flew away when he picked it up. Its spikes pricked his hand, and it made as round a ball as possible, but the cool dark skin of its feet and head were nevertheless visible.

By the kitchen door he set down a saucer of custard. To his delight it unfolded and pulled itself to the rim with its short legs. It began to suck, and enjoyed it so much that it climbed completely into the saucer, sat in the custard, and lapped till it was gone.

Ralph told himself that hedgehogs died in captivity—if for example he made a nest in the garage—so he took it back to the middle of the paddock where he had found it. It burrowed into a clump of grass, as if glad to be home.

On his way to the garden he saw Maricarmen and Dawley walk through the gate and on to the road. It was difficult to know who was talking, but he assumed it to be Dawley because Maricarmen's head was lowered, as if intent on listening. Perhaps she had asked a question that needed a lot of explaining.

Smoke from the paddock fire drifted in, and Frank wondered why Ralph burned rubbish only on days when wind was blowing back to the house and yard. He closed the window—and his sweat dropping on the top map distorted mountain contours north-west of Laghouat. Standing away, he sharpened a pencil. There was a hesitant knock, and even before opening the door, he knew who it was, and called for her to come in.

She looked at the maps. 'Are you still thinking about Algeria?'

'I must get it out of my system.'

Her dark hair was wet, but she'd tied it lankly behind with a piece of ribbon. 'It sounds clean and clinical. Isn't it too important to get rid of so easily?'

'It turned my hair grey,' he smiled. And tore up my confidence, he added to himself.

Her brown eyes looked, and he couldn't meet them. He wanted to spit. They were cow-like eyes—but they burned nevertheless. 'What was so unusual about your adventure?'

She was questioning him for some deep reason, and he sensed that she hadn't intended him to see this. There was a warmth inside her that would not let her be casual. He decided to be on his guard. 'I died, but somehow got my strength back.'

'But you didn't die.'

He couldn't mistake her tone of wishing that he had. 'There were enough bombs flying, but my name wasn't on them. It isn't easy to tell what happened.'

'Are you writing a book?'

'It'll fill one, certainly.'

He lit cigarettes for them both. She was surprised by it, and accepted. He found it hard to meet such knowing eyes, such softly arrogant eyes that finally knew no right or wrong. But he was glad she had no fear of him, that she appraised him and talked on a level of fair equality. He hadn't often met it in Englishwomen.

She was weighing him up, too, wondering how much cunning there was behind those grey eyes. Cunning was the diplomacy of the powerless—or was it the unintelligent? So was it weariness or sloth? She stood by the door, as tall as he was and looking at him with a friendly smile—which he didn't trust. Lack of trust made him feel middle-aged, but it occurred to him that for some people to be middle-aged is to be grown up at last.

He was pale, his face was thin, his spirit plain. She told herself there wasn't so much mental substance inside him that everyone supposed. Maybe Algeria had sucked out his spark of life, but if so he could never have been strong.

'When you've finished what you're writing I'd like to read it.'

He leaned against the table. 'I'm doing it in the community's time, so it'll belong to all of us. I don't know what there'll be of value in it. What's anyone's life worth?'

'Who can say, till they're dead?'

'True'—thinking that his life wouldn't cost much at the moment.

'Are you glad you came out of Algeria alive?'

'When I was there I never thought about it.'

'That made you indestructible.'

'Did it?'

'I wonder what was in Shelley's mind?'

He reached for an ash-tray they could both use. 'I never wondered about dying. It's not part of my nature. But Shelley always assumed he would get out alive. He was confident.'

'And you weren't?'

'I told you, I didn't think much about it.'

'And now you're safe and sound?'

He grimaced, not liking the talk. 'I suppose you think it would have rounded things off very well if I'd caught a mortar shell and got blown to bits. I didn't, and for my sins I'm still alive and kicking. Look,' he said before she could say something else, for it was plain she had plenty on her mind, 'I've been cooped up all day. Let's walk down the road.'

She nodded, and Ralph saw them go through the yard.

'We need some wind and sun to dry the fields'—knowing that one day he would have to think about dying. He noticed her loose breasts, and found them attractive. She was a beautiful woman, and he wanted her to take his arm as they walked. Her nearness told him how pleasant it would be to make love to her, as if it would give back some of the life-blood he needed. He wanted to go to bed with every young woman he saw these days, and wondered how much closer you could get to lack of back-bone than that.

'I think you must have been a good factory worker,' she said, when they were passing the village shop. 'Nobody should stop doing what they are good at.'

'I can't return to that.' He thought that as soon as he found a woman who didn't want to get him back into a factory he'd marry her.

He was straightforward in his answers, and she pitied him for his honesty. An honest person took too long getting to know themselves. Shelley said as much, and she could see how right he'd been. Maybe it was this doggedness in Dawley that had snared Shelley into Algeria. Such people were dangerous, and it had been Shelley's bad luck to fall in with him. She was momentarily alarmed at wondering whether she wasn't being trapped by it. 'What will you do, then?'

'Drift for the rest of my life. Once you begin, it's hard to stop.' But he didn't know why he was living in the community, either. Nancy had jacked it in, and so ought he. He should never have left Nottingham in the first place. Surely it was better to stay where you were born, to go from womb to grave in the same town, with one woman, and work that never altered, so that life could be empty, really empty, and go by in a flash, get itself and you over with. He didn't believe it, but had to say so to convince himself that he didn't. Birth was a prison and death was a prison, but life needn't be.

She stepped from him to avoid a pool of water. 'So going to Algeria was just one phase of your drifting?'

He wanted to dodge her sharp questions, but he could only give straight answers. He'd never been much of a liar. 'There were political motives, and the only person who could prove it is Shelley.'

He felt her stiffen, and wished he hadn't spoken so brutally. Shelley's death would be raw in her forever.

'I wonder what he'd say if he were alive?'

'That you can't live on memories,' he said sharply, beginning to see that something was wrong.

'He'd like being here. It's a pity the three of us were never together.'

'And John,' he said, 'with Handley and Adam and Richard. Even Ralph and Cuthbert. The eight of us might have had a lot to tell each other!'

Her smile, more than words, put him in his place. 'You don't think much of women.'

They passed the school and watercress beds, leaving the houses. He led her along a footpath and into the Gould Estate, a route ascending between two dark patches of wood. The air was so heavy she could hardly breathe.

'Depends who they are'—glad to get her away from unhealthy recollections about Shelley.

'The three you left out of your list are all intelligent enough to understand politics. I thought Spanish society was dominated by the male, but it's as bad in England.'

He had no defence. She had caught him squarely. 'You're right. But they never talk to me.'

'How many of them have you been to bed with?'

A minute went before he was able to answer. 'Mandy, once. Then I lived with Myra nearly a year.'

'Don't you live with her now?'

'In a way. When there's something in the air that we can't stand we fly to each other. Maybe that's love.'

'Is that why your wife left?'

'One of the reasons. It'd be useless going into all that.'

'I suppose that's why Nancy left, then, because you wouldn't go into anything.'

'I think you may be right,' he said.

She was curious and persistent. 'Have you ever been to bed with Enid?'

He didn't like her asking questions about his sex life as if she were a mate of his in the army. 'No,' he told her.

'Isn't she attractive enough for you?'

'She's gorgeous, really, but she doesn't like me. Maybe she thinks I want to disrupt things. In any case, Handley wouldn't want it.'

She folded her arms across her chest. 'You mean she's his property?'

'She belongs to herself.' They were silent for a few paces. 'I wouldn't make love to my friend's wife.'

'Don't you believe in free love?'

They turned on to a sunken lane, and a sheep with full udders wanted to get out of their way by crossing the ruts, but they were so deep it got trapped in the mud. Dawley went to it slowly, its blue and vacant eyes nailed helplessly as his grip tightened. She watched him. He straightened his legs and lifted it with much more strength than she thought he had, walking through the mud and setting it down in the open field. It stood, then walked along the hedge, following them for a while. 'I don't believe in free love,' he said, still out of breath.

'Why not?'

'I've never seen anybody else who does. Let's talk politics—it's more interesting.'

'This *is* politics.'

'Do *you* believe in free love?'

'Yes. But I'm careful about it. I don't like to hurt people.'

They stopped by a stile, and he touched her arm. 'It's going to rain again. We'd better turn back.' He couldn't take his hand away, and gripped her flesh, hoping she would come towards him.

'How did you persuade Shelley to go into Algeria?'

He held her close, but not to kiss, not feeling love, but glad of her ample warmth spreading over his body. He whispered, afraid of the words: 'I pointed a gun at him.'

She drew away. '*Entonces?*'

'He accepted it. As fate, I suppose. I didn't frighten him with the gun. He wasn't afraid of me. He just used me and the gun in my hand to make up his mind for him.'

'You liar.'

'I don't lie. The fact that he died is eating me away. I'm guilty of his death. I'm dying because of it. I loved Shelley. I've told nobody. You're the one I shouldn't tell because you're in love with him still.'

She walked back across the field, and he followed. 'I made him stop playing politics and act,' he said. 'But I was the one who was acting. I'd have given my life to save him, but I couldn't. It's never like that. I was wounded later, but I didn't die. I wanted to, but I couldn't.'

'He never played politics,' she said. 'He did a lot in Spain, at great risk.'

Tears were on his cheeks like acid. His lungs were contused and burning. 'It's a nightmare with me. It goes on day and night. It gets worse.' He wanted to crawl into the middle of a wood, and rot painlessly to death.

She walked quickly. 'Stop it.'

'I hadn't started to live until that happened,' he shouted. He caught her up and pulled her close. 'I don't expect to be forgiven.'

'You won't be.' She regretted her words in case her hatred gave him comfort, only wishing she had a gun to kill him now.

'We talked about you. You might have done the same thing. He told me you both believed in revolution to the point of being willing to go to war for it.'

She was silent.

Shelley had only hinted as much, but he felt the need to defend himself, not being utterly craven with guilt. They walked without talking, and when he took her warm hand she did not draw it away. But she could see no hope for him.

Chapter Nineteen

The hedgehog made its way from the paddock, through the garden, and up to the back door, where Ralph found it two days later lying in the saucer from which it had eaten the custard. He had been looking for it.

Brought up on a farm, he didn't know whether this was the reason for the hedgehog coming back to him. His own slow nature burned with sympathy where such a creature was concerned. He was in touch with animals. As for people, that was another matter.

After his mother, Mandy was his longest involvement. He loved her but, being shy and not talkative, didn't know whether she loved him. Sometimes he was sure she did. At other times he was certain that she did not. Real love meant someone who loved him all the time, no matter what he did or in what state he was, giving continual ease, security, and total independence. He knew it was a ridiculous ideal, yet couldn't help hankering after it. But Mandy was volatile, and he was moody, she wanting an unattainable sort of real manly love, and he craving something which he had never got from his mother.

Now and again their expectations met half-way, and they could love for a few hours, or even a day or two, until both suddenly realised that life was bitter because they were only half-way towards what they wanted. And then the antagonism of disappointment tore them apart—which was happening at the moment.

He picked up the hedgehog, well defended against the world by its own prickly nature. Its face was not entirely covered by its attitude of self-defence. He noticed a small yellow and white area behind its ears, and realised with pity and horror that they were maggot-cases laid there by blowflies while it had been unprotected in the paddock. They had burrowed in, and put their eggs there, all their consciousness in the grip of nature.

With his fingernail he scraped a few of the cases away. There was a box in the garage, in which the children had once kept a white mouse. But the mouse had escaped, so he bent down at the edge of the paddock to fill the empty box with choice dock-leaves and juicy grass. He put the inert hedgehog inside, then set it in a cool far-corner of the garage.

He stood, unable to move for some minutes because he had a terrible feeling that the hedgehog was going to die, and that nothing he could do would save it. The savagery of the world came down with full black force as he put his hand among the grass to reassure the innocent creature that it was not alone.

It seemed obvious now that he should have brought the hedgehog into the protection of the garage when he had found it two days ago. It had occurred to him instinctively to do so at the time, but then the voice of reason told him that such animals die in captivity, and he had obeyed this stupid precept rather than his own common sense. In that vital time the blowflies had laid their eggs.

This is the animal world, he mused, asking himself if the human part was any better. In many ways it was not, and the great question as to why this was so hammered in his head. He got bits of cold bacon from the kitchen and put them in the hedgehog's box, stooping to see if it would eat. The feet scratched as it unwound itself, and its small nose came out. It ruminatively sucked at a piece of fat, then went back into its domain, either sensing that he was there, or giving in to the more immediate deathly presence inside itself that it couldn't now shake off. But Ralph took it out bodily and held it in his hand, stroked its sharp bristles till it unwound and stood on his palm with its webbed feet. Then he put it back.

All evening he was silent, saying nothing at dinner, not even listening to the transistor radio carried in his pocket. He was thinking of the hedgehog and its fate, as if it were some creature or even person with a soul whom he had known since birth and been in love with, or as if it were a child of his own, and perhaps in some way as if the animal were himself.

Next day he picked up the hedgehog and saw that the maggots had hatched. When he stroked it, and it opened for him, he felt its belly gone cold and damp. He got a saucer of water and disinfectant, and with a piece of cotton-wool tried to swab the maggots away in a last effort to save its life.

We are so helpless, he thought, because as he rubbed maggots off, others came out of its ears, small and white. The solution of dettol had no effect, and even disturbed the animal, who only wanted to die in peace.

Maggots were coming from its mouth. When he lifted its head they were pullulating at its throat. Its soul was being eaten away, its body consumed from within. He wept at such cruelty to an innocuous animal, his heart feeling as if it were being wrenched from his body.

There was nothing left but to put it back in the box. It coughed, its lungs full. His dettol had driven the maggots deeper inside, prodding them to greater industry. It rolled into as tight a ball as possible to escape their gnawing. He covered it with grass and leaves.

At midnight he was in bed with Mandy. Her hand touched his face in the dark. 'What are you crying for?'

'I rescued a hedgehog from the paddock a few days ago, and I think it's dying.'

She kissed him. 'You are a great soft thing. That's why I love you, I suppose.'

'Why do the innocent suffer so much?'

'It's only an animal,' she said softly. 'Don't cry, love. You make me want to.'

'I can't help it,' he said, fobbing his tears back. 'We are born into the world without meaning, and we die without reason!'

'Oh stop it,' she wailed, 'or I'll kill you!' She put her arms around him, and tears poured from her eyes: 'Don't remind me. All I know is that I love you.'

He drew her soft body to him, until a great heat was generated between them. 'Don't worry,' she wept. 'And please don't cry.'

In the morning he went to look at the hedgehog, even before breakfast. He opened the garage door quietly, as if afraid to wake it. Pulling the leaves and grass back he found it was dead, the maggots busier now that all resistance had stopped. His tears were hot and bitter, and he tormented himself by thinking that if he had taken the hedgehog into shelter on the first day then it would not have been attacked by the flies. It seemed incontrovertible, and there was no way out.

He lifted the wooden box with the dried vegetation and put the hedgehog back inside, then took it to the paddock. He left it there while he collected all the wastepaper from the house. He made a great heap at the place of fire in the corner of the paddock and put the box, with the dead hedgehog and all its maggots, on top. Then he lit it from four sides, and watched the smoke and flames rise, till the whole mound was burnt to ash. He pushed the unburnt paper towards the centre to make sure not one maggot escaped, but it did not curb his black despair. The heat was so intense that the hairs on the back of his hands were singed.

'Talk to me,' Mandy said on the bus coming back from Bedford.

'I'm talking to you,' he said hoarsely.

'Say something, though.'

'What do you want me to say?'

'You haven't said anything for days. What's making you so speechless and black? It can't be that hedgehog.'

The top deck of the bus was empty and they sat in front. They'd been shopping, and to the pictures to see a coloured mind-emptying extravaganza about the Wild West in which Ralph had flinched and squeezed her hand cruelly every time an Indian was shot.

'I'm all right,' he said, feeling sorry for her at having to put up with someone like him. He'd been taught never to speak unless he had something to say, consequently he didn't know how to say anything at all. This maxim of his upbringing wasn't necessarily a bad one, but what was interesting was that he took it so seriously.

She fretted over his silence, knowing that an educated person thought a great deal, and so ought to say something. His only fault was in not sharing his mind with others. If an educated man was inarticulate he was either selfish or cruel, but she saw him, because he was her husband, as simply damaged by his early life. Information was fed into him but he held it inside as his method of keeping a grip on life. Ideas churned in his head, but he would not let them out because he did not know how to introduce them to whoever might listen. Someone with a giant pair of invincible scissors had cut his communication tubes. Handley unjustly considered him a 'dumb ox', but only she knew Ralph, and the madness which his irrepressible melancholy led him into.

He saw a pond when the bus stopped, with ducks on it, and chickens standing between its banks and the door of a slate-roofed stone house. Such a rough and peaceful scene took some of the anguish out of his soul.

The bus moved, and he remembered the man who had been watching him from the corner of the paddock where the enormous bramble hedge reached towards the children's play trench that Dawley had dug.

This man, whom he'd never met, blocked out the good sky of a moment before, dropping him into a sort of grass cellar with four high hedges around. The man's face, which took on an uncanny featureless power as it played in his memory, suddenly overwhelmed him. A pain stabbed into his bowels, and the noise which rushed from his mouth was like the last roar of a trapped bull before it disappears under the bog.

She wanted to hide her head, get under the seat, kill him, run off the bus, leave forever. But she could only stay fixed, put a hand on his hand, grip the rail and stare at the road in front. His great bellow broke down into a dog-wail, and then stopped.

The conductor stood at the top of the stairs: 'What's going on?'

Ralph's face was bloodily flushed, but frozen into stillness, and he didn't turn round. Mandy smiled:

'It's all right. He's only practising!'

'I'm being followed, these days,' Ralph said casually, when they were left alone. The face had grinned, huge and important, not so close as to be intimidating, nor so distinct to be seen as either good or evil, but it was a peculiar memory to trundle over the earth at such a time. Had it come to him only because he was underground, in the mines of grass and brambles, among galleries of pungent soil? And if it had, wasn't it time he struggled up to daylight and proper life again?

'What do you mean, followed?' she frowned, the inward sweat of his fit no longer trying to kill her.

'Followed.'

She understood none of it. 'Who by?'

'Somebody. Just followed.'

'It can't be,' she said, frightened. 'Nobody wants to follow you.'

He smiled, all-knowing, trying to puzzle her. 'How do you know?'

'Stop it,' she cried. 'It's stupid.'

He was alarming her even more than when he roared out, and her tears were sharper to him than the vision of the observing man. 'Maybe I was wrong. It was probably somebody walking across the field who stopped to look over into the paddock. I won't mention it again.'

His willingness to be nice made her happy. 'You are silly. Mention it if you want to. I ask you to talk to me, and when you do I say I don't want to hear it. Tell me. I don't mind. That's what we mean to each other.'

But he wouldn't be drawn. He was wary. She was waiting for him with daggers. The heavy trees hanging over the lane were freckled with green infant leaves, blue spots of sky just able to show through when they came to a bend. 'I hope the summer's good,' she said, 'because it's certainly been a difficult year so far, getting this bloody community going, then me having a miscarriage. Do you hope I get preggers again?'

'You know I do, though I'd like to get out of the clutches of the community before it happens.'

'We need money, and jobs.'

He squeezed her hand too hard for it to be affection. 'We'll get it.'

She pulled away. 'Listen, no stealing father's paintings, and trying to sell them like you did in Lincolnshire. Next time he'll get you ten years in the nick.'

He was silent for a moment, gritting his teeth. 'I haven't stolen anything for months.'

She sighed heavily, the good mood going. 'Just leave things alone.'

Not wanting to upset her, he counted the raindrops that kicked against the window, watched how they joined forces before streaming down the glass. 'A blue van passed the house three times yesterday.'

'Was your mother in it?'

'I'm tired,' he said. 'I can't wake up properly in the morning.'

'You're mother's got a powder blue mini-van, but she's in Lincolnshire.'

'There was a policeman in this one,' he said. 'On the lookout.'

She kept up a normal response: 'Don't worry, love. They aren't after you.'

There was a shine of superiority in his deep brown eyes, then a glint of reproach, ending in infinite regret that he had married such an uneducated slut. 'You don't understand.'

I chose him, she thought, looking at him with a tender smile, not him me. When I first saw him I wanted him to love me, and he fucked me nicely because he's big and slow, and tried to care because he thought he wasn't able to. If he'd picked me I suppose I might have got a better deal because then his mother would have been on our side and given us some of her money, which would have made him happier. But I'd rather make the choice myself and get a dud, than be chosen by any bloody man like I was a slave, even if he did turn out to be better than Ralph.

'We'll get away from it all,' she said. 'Just you and me. Find a cottage and live on our own. Then if I have a baby it'll be marvellous because nobody from the house will get their hands on it. We'll be happy, and you won't think people are trailing you. You'll be your old self again.'

'What is my old self?' he asked mournfully.

'You'll know when it happens, you big daft thing.'

'I'll get some money so that we can buy a cottage.'

'I'd like that,' she said, happy that he'd spoken more in half an hour than for a whole week.

'Everytime that mini-van passed it had a different number-plate.'

She pulled her coat tight to keep out the cold. 'It couldn't have been the same car, then.'

'I recognised the driver. He must have altered the number before passing the house. It's easy. I once changed it on my mother's car—from an old car in the barn that we didn't use anymore—and she didn't notice till the policeman stopped her because her brake lights weren't working. He let her off because he knew her. Or he knew my father, who sends him a bottle of whisky every Christmas.'

'You'll get pneumonia if you don't shut up,' she said. 'You're always playing them rotten tricks.'

'Why do you think it is?' he asked sadly.

'How do I know if you don't?' she sulked.

'I'm asking you. But nobody can give me a good answer. People aren't sympathetic. I ask your mother what's wrong with the world, and she tells me to wash the dishes. I ask Cuthbert and he tells me with a leer to believe in God. I ask your father, and he tells me to give him back the circle I cut from the painting I stole. I ask Dawley, and he tells me that if I get a job in a factory all my problems will be solved. Richard and Adam invite me to a game of guerilla warfare on their maps. At the moment they've got a General Strike going, and they're working out schemes of deployment with all the army units in England.'

'They play around like kids,' she said.

'And when I ask you, you just tell me to shut up.'

'It's a shame Uncle John isn't here anymore.'

'He committed suicide,' he said, helping her down from the step. His large hulking form went in front, trailing a hand behind whose fingers she held. They walked along the village street, he in the same self-protective forward hunch, Mandy much smaller though no mean presence by his side. What was he trying to protect in himself by this loping stance? Sometimes it was worse, and he walked like a man who had just recovered from bronchitis. It had got really bad in the last few weeks. He was trying to hold something into himself which he couldn't live without—an illness, a weakness, even maybe a secret strength that he couldn't bear anyone to know existed. She was glad of the silence on their walk to the house.

The trouble is, he thought, I don't know myself, and so I don't exist. And if I don't exist, others don't exist either, so how can they know me, or even see me, and how can I know them, or see them? They don't see me, so first I've got to make them see me. What can I do to make them see me?

Chapter Twenty

The longer she delayed opening Shelley's trunk and taking out the notebooks, the more afraid she became to do so. It lay under the bed, and the key was part of a bunch on the dressing-table by the window. They were warm from the sun when she picked them up. She put them down again, and finished dressing. Someone knocked at her door.

'*Quien es?*'

'Enid.'

'Come in.'

'I'm driving to Hitchin market. Do you want to help?'

'All right. I won't be long.'

Enid sat on the bed. Her long hair was snaked up into a pile, and her face was remarkably unlined for a woman of over forty. 'How do you like being with us?'

'Time drifts by. I'm not sure I like being in England, but it's nice here.' She sprinkled perfume from a bottle of Maderas de Oriente on her neck and under the arms, where Enid saw demure sprouts of black hair. She put on a sweater.

'You're very attractive. You'll have to find a boyfriend.'

'That's not so easy. Do you have one?'

Enid laughed. 'I've been too busy bringing up children.'

'You should look for one.' She took her shoulder bag, and lifted the trunk keys to bring them with her, but thought Enid might see it as a gesture of mistrust against the community, so left them where they were. 'Does Albert have girl friends?'

'Not as far as I know.' Enid was ready to go. 'At least I've never caught him at it. Neither of us has ever had many friends of any sort.' They stood close, and Maricarmen came forward. The kiss was brief on the dry skin, and they rested a few moments, arms on shoulders, a warmth of tranquillity and understanding. In sensing the youthfulness of Maricarmen's body Enid realised how much more alive she might become if she got to know a younger man. 'Stay as long as you like,' she said, pressing Maricarmen's warm hands. Her own fingers were cold, and she enjoyed such contact.

Ralph watched them get into the Rambler. He had been up since early morning, but Mandy stayed in bed, exhausted by his menacing fluctuating moods of the last few days—though they had lifted slightly since the turgid mechanism of his mind had decided to *do something*.

He knew that every move depended on personal, spiritual energy. The only problem left in the world was how to stop going mad when that energy withdrew from you. If he felt ill, either in the stomach or the soul, he did not even have the strength to go to a doctor, or talk to anyone about it. But energy always lurked somewhere in the chaos of his mind, though it rarely turned into action. That which stayed was not energy at all. But when he acted without thought it never occurred to him to think he was energetic, and so it did not help to console him for all the times when he'd been listless and without hope.

The two women drove away, and he walked towards the back door with a large plastic bag folded neatly under his arm. How is it possible, he wondered, to stop what you are going to do if you are going to do it?'

Cuthbert, sauntering down from the garden, watched from between the rose bushes. Ralph was a difficult bird to fathom, he decided. What could you make of a grown man who walked around the house with wet cheeks because, in the natural order of things, a hedgehog had died?

He plucked a budding rose to pieces, and thought that if Ralph had gone into the house intent on stealing something, one ought to find out what it was. No doubt Ralph would bungle it. Somebody would see him, kick his shins and raise an outcry. Or would they? Mandy was deep in her daytime dreams. Dawley was re-sweating his Algerian skylark. Richard and Adam were moving pins on maps. Myra was in the vegetable garden plucking early peas.

He began to shake at the idea of him upstairs looting John's stuff. It was no use thinking he wouldn't dare. Nothing was sacred to a founder-member of Kleptomaniacs Anonymous. Ralph had all the stupidity of an intelligent thief. He'd nick anything.

Cuthbert leapt down the steps, went in through the kitchen, then silently upstairs in his plimsolls, listening at every door. Mandy was snoring, and there was silence in all the rooms but Maricarmen's. Ear at the keyhole, a great deal of paper material was being stuffed into the plastic bag. A lid fell to. A bunch of keys jangled.

His brain revelled in such information. He went downstairs and out again. Eric Bloodaxe tried to grab his ankle, wrathful perhaps at not having challenged him on the way in. Cuthbert casually shot back his foot and pushed the dog into its kennel.

Among the rose bushes, his heart beat hard. Ralph was helping himself to Shelley's archives. Three people at least would bury him alive for it—Dawley, his father, and Maricarmen. And since Ralph was considered by the community to be the champion waste-burner of the Home Counties, Cuthbert had no doubt what he intended to do with such combustible material.

From behind the bushes he watched him walk to the garage with the plastic bag slung heavily over his shoulder. A moment later he came out with his two-two air rifle and strolled up the steps towards the paddock, trying to keep himself erect and proud, and make as complete a changeover as possible from cat-burglar to landowner. The community had bought an extra air rifle so that he could go on daily patrol to keep the pigeons off the peas and beans. His aim had improved, and since the death of his pet hedgehog he had scared two birds.

Cuthbert nipped along the path, and hid by the far side of the house. Ralph greeted Myra in the garden, his offer to help with the vegetables altruistically refused. In the garage Cuthbert saw half a dozen identical plastic bags lined along the wall. By opening each he found the notebook cargo he was after. It was a long time since he had done so much shifting and carrying, and he'd forgotten how one sweated.

Myra laid the bucket of peas on the kitchen floor, and made coffee at the Aga. The smell of it drifted to the caravan, and after taking a cup to Mandy she found Dawley sitting at the table waiting for his. She brought Mark down—who'd been looked after by Adam and Richard, and clutched a piece of old map which he crisscrossed with pencil.

Dawley took his son on his knee: 'How's my old Mark, then? What've you been up to?'

He dropped the map and pencil and began walking up his father's chest, held by each hand. 'I was going to bring your coffee,' Myra said.

'It's all right. I like to drink it in the bosom of my family.'

'Which one? You have so many. Or you had before Nancy left. Have you heard from her?'

He put Mark on the floor and held Myra, kissing her gently. 'I've only got one now. I love you and Mark, and that's about it. Things come plain at last. Nancy's making her own way, and I'm making mine.'

Mark crawled between their feet and, hands pinching his flesh at the calves, stood between them. 'He heard me,' Dawley said. 'He knows how I feel.'

'He knows you're his father.' She held Dawley—not wanting him to let her go. 'You work too hard. Give yourself a rest.'

'What's rest? Idleness. Death. Boredom. Gives you time to think. I even feel lazy doing the so-called work I do.'

'You're getting too thin.'

'That never harmed anybody.' He drank his coffee black, without sugar. 'Some for you?'

'Please.'

He poured milk for Mark, and sat at the table with him on his knee: 'Don't splash it all down me. Put it just there. Come on, open your little soup-box.'

'Why don't you sleep with me at night?' Myra asked. The direct question sounded strange coming from the shy woman he knew her to be. But it was what he liked about her. On the day when they first met, she had been the one most direct in the approaches. It was a big reason for loving her, and still was. It simplified life, and made the sexual part so obvious that you were free to get to the greater complications underneath. 'I want to,' he answered, 'but I go dead for weeks at a time.'

'Is it because Maricarmen's here?'

He laughed. 'I could never be in love with her.'

'That's not what I mean,' she said.

'I don't know why I haven't been to you. Waiting to see how I felt maybe. But my love for you doesn't change.'

'I suppose you've been waiting for half a hint—as Mandy puts it. We all go dead from time to time, but it's still pleasant to have someone in bed with you.'

Mark was looking at them intently, and Frank steadied his cup when the milk was about to spill. 'I've been wrapped up in myself. I can't see the straight-edge of life any more.'

She smiled. 'Who *can*? But things have a way of realigning themselves without too much worry or thought. As long as you talk about them—with somebody else.'

He set Mark's empty cup on the table. 'I tell myself the same, but it goes on and on, inside my head and won't come out.' He put Mark on the floor, who crawled to his map and pencil. 'I'd like to go to bed with you right now.'

'We'll have to wait till tonight.'

He filled a mug with coffee, went out and up the path into the studio.

'Do you want a brandy?' Handley offered.

'Can't take it these days. Tastes like razor blades. How's the painting?'

'All of a splash. I'm trying to expand my consciousness, to fight away the fear of death. Now that I'm over forty I'm beginning to remember my dreams again. Maybe the break-through is coming.'

Frank sat on a box to look at the canvas.

'I'm trying to paint the world moving closer to the sun,' Handley said, swigging his coffee noisily. 'But must it pass through the eye of a needle to get to it? Be blasted by a nuclear explosion, for example, to reach its good warmth? See all the green of that primeval forest? I dreamed it last night. And those figures? Dreamed them as well. Adam and Eve are in paradise, with the Bomb going up on the horizon. Time has no meaning when that happens. Maybe the earth shouldn't move closer to the sun. Perhaps its survival depends on it being equidistant from the sun and the moon—spiritually I mean. A shift of polarity and we're all for that high jump, and nobody can leap as high as to clear that cloud. The colours are coming about right.

They'll blind everybody. If you want to see the world in its true colours you've got to be colour-blind. That's how I paint. I know nothing about colour. Or I don't allow myself to. To know is to kill. Naturally, I know everything. But I don't trust anything, so I always start from the beginning. Everything fresh, vivid in juxtaposition—all that crap. If you've got the form and the imagination, the colour will look after itself. The colour's in your own soul. Paint Jerusalem on the end of your nose.'

'What do you think about the future?' Dawley asked.

He put down his mug, and laughed. 'I'm an artist. I've got no future. Life is short: here for a minute and gone tomorrow. I paint till I croak. It's my nature. You go on and on doing your work, and keeping out of mischief as much as possible.'

'What do you call mischief?'

'Making people unhappy. I hate that.'

'I know,' Dawley said.

'I know you do, old chuff. Otherwise I wouldn't tell you. If you didn't know it there'd be no point telling you.'

Dawley was interested. 'You mean you can't teach people anything?'

'More or less. They only learn by experience. When the oppressed start to rebel it's because they've got no food, or because they've just seen their brother shot. They don't have to be told to rebel. By the time somebody comes along and says you've nothing to lose but your chains they know it. Experience had already told them. If nobody tried to rouse them they'd rouse themselves, and do it more effectively than if they'd never been got at by your middle-class socialists who only want to guide them in a great big circle, into becoming the same as they were before . . .'

'Why do you encourage Richard and Adam in revolutionary studies, then?'

'Because when the downtrodden realise they're oppressed and start to rise there'll be one or two people around to show them what to do. That'll be useful—technically and tactically. But they don't need to be told what's really what.'

'Do you think art and literature are useless, then?'

'Bollocks, no. They keep the world from committing suicide. But to say that the brush or pen is mightier than the sword—well, that's not true. When was the pen so contemptible that it had to compete with the sword? I assume the pen to be a noble instrument, like the brush for painting.'

Dawley was more receptive to other people's opinions than he used to be. And yet, maybe because he was older and his own views had ossified, he found most of them irrelevant. Handley was an exception because he jig-sawed everything into his work, and what he said seemed to have significance.

Frank stood. 'I'll go back to my maps and notebooks.'

'And I'll finish this canvas,' Handley said, 'as long as there isn't an earthquake.'

'I'll try to hold it off if I feel it coming,' Frank called as he went out.

'That's what friends are for,' Handley shouted after him.

Chapter Twenty-one

Cuthbert, wearing a pale blue shirt open at the neck, leaned against the wall, drinking his coffee in the sun.

'Are you still stuck in your past?' he called at Dawley walking down from his father's studio.

Frank noticed how relaxed he looked, as if he had smelled blood. 'For the time being. It does seem important. I don't know why.'

'Mine's not,' Cuthbert said, with the certainty that covered an abyss.

'That's because you haven't got much.'

Dawley walked towards his caravan and Cuthbert followed: 'The past is dead—or ought to be. Look at the big glossy attractive future! All our life is there, the unborn and the what-will-be—which is bound to be better than the miserable fucked-up existence of here and right now.'

He sounds like his father. Even looks like him: straight nose, and the mouth edging a bit that way. If he grew a moustache and lost weight you'd hardly know the difference, though he doesn't have the same talent or resilience. Handley at his age knew exactly what he wanted. Maybe it's not so good being an artist's son, especially one who's made money. 'Come in for more coffee,' he told him when they were at the caravan.

It's as well he's writing a book, Cuthbert thought, otherwise there wouldn't be much to him. He's the hollowest person I've seen—as if all his pathetic life's been sucked away.

Ralph struggled from the garage with a plastic sack of rubbish, going up the steps to light the day's bonfire. Frank faced Cuthbert across the table. 'Ever been interested in politics?'

'Mysticism's more my line,' he answered flippantly.

'Some begin with mysticism and end in politics. Others begin with politics and end in mysticism. Depends where you start. Most don't begin or end anywhere.'

'What I believe,' Cuthbert said, 'is that people need something to believe in, a symbol they can look up to.'

He didn't say anything that wasn't seriously considered first—a trait Dawley respected. Still, though he might have a stiff upper lip, he did observe that it trembled from time to time. 'You mean it's what *you* want?'

'Not really. I'd like to help people to believe. When they lose their faith in God they start to believe in themselves, which they can't stand so they latch on to some monstrous industrial corporation or political organisation, or a combination of both, presided over by a squawling demagogue who leads them into the evil of their own bleak fantasies.'

'The only salvation,' Dawley said, 'is that which benefits everybody. Communism is still the greatest moral force of the age, whatever its faults, in that it helps those who try to set themselves at the beginning of individual spiritual development. They never had a chance of it before because they were too busy getting their bread. Underprivileged people in underdeveloped countries are fighting for the opportunity to pull themselves up—not by their own bootlaces, because most of them don't have boots—to a level where they can get enough to eat and wear. Instead of trying to do it through the feudal or capitalist jungle they do it with the Marxist philosophy of spiritual salvation. They want food, shelter, and the social machinery to give them the basic necessities of civilised respect.'

Cuthbert lifted his head from his hands. 'I hear you had a hard time in Algeria. What made you go in the first place?'

'A heavy question. I worked in a factory from the age of fifteen to twenty-seven. Got married, had kids. Stuck in the domestic rut till I couldn't stand it any more. I had a sense of grievance which, as luck would have it, developed into a sense of protest. They hated me in the factory, some of the men and all of the management. Troublemaker. Shop-steward of Tory journalists. So I left, the only thing to do if I didn't want to get killed in my car, or die of a disease nobody ever heard of. Do you know what a factory's like?'

'I've never work in one.'

'I did twelve years, and I was still a young man. I'm thirty now, though I feel older. When I heard in those days of anyone signing on for twelve years with the army it seemed as if they were giving their lives away. I liked the factory, and fitted in because I worked hard, not having the conscience to skive. That's more boring than work. I was also a good union man, went to all the meetings, collected dues, gave out notices and circulars, helped to organise stoppages, and read books on trade-union history. I fostered discontent whenever I thought it had a chance. But I was inconsistent, because while believing in Revolution, I worked hard on peace work. Though the gaffers were glad to get rid of me when I left, they also knew they'd lost a good worker who set an example. A group of us would down tools at the drop of a hat, but when we worked we more than made up for it. Agitation for better conditions, and the extra few bob now and again, is the oil that keeps the machine running, and the more enlightened bosses knew this, and didn't panic. But I saw the split more and more clearly till I was falling apart, and had to get out before I went off my head.

'Perhaps the industrial life wasn't for me. The protest I developed may be part of my basic temperament for all I know. So I joined up with a guerilla army which, when it's got the country it's fighting for, will begin building the same industrial society which I was forced to escape from after twelve years.

'Yet working in a factory, in a country that has no manufactured goods—and assuming that socialism is the system by which the goods would be shared out in such an initial shortage—would be different to sweating in a capitalist state whereby you support an entire class of idle bastards on your back.'

'It must be difficult to keep your faith.'

'It's not my faith that's in danger,' Dawley said, 'as long as I spread my intelligence wide enough to understand all possible realities. I suppose there's something about myself I want to find.' Ash dropped from his cigarette. 'But people who try to "find themselves" only want to get back to what they were before whatever it was came along and blasted them out of it—not in fact to change their life, but simply to return to their real and possibly undamaged selves. In military terms it's called the "indirect approach"—never meeting something head-on because it only strengthens the obstacle you're up against, in spite of all the force you bring to bear. In fact the more force you use the firmer the obstacle becomes. So you go a roundabout way to overcome it, no matter how much time and distance and energy is involved, so as to meet it on your own time and terms.'

For someone who wasn't a talker, a person who came from the 'grunt and thump' level of society (as he'd hear it put so charmingly at college) he keeps it up very well, Cuthbert thought.

A fine fat missel-thrush strutted across the window-sill, its whole breast speckled, as if it were a sparrow that had found a leopard skin and put it on to appear brave. It pecked at the wood, and flew away. 'There are too many second-class citizens in the world,' said Dawley.

'Only God is a first-class citizen.' Cuthbert stood by the door, watching smoke rise from the paddock, more directly into the sky because of a slight shifting in the wind. 'We need a God in the name of good to look after us and stop us killing each other.'

'He's not made much of a job of it so far.'

'God is a reflection of man. He is good only when men are good.'

'Men are good when they are persuaded to be by a socialist system of ethics,' Dawley said. 'You talk as if men are guilty. They're not. They just can't help themselves. So they have to be shown themselves right to the bone, and given a pattern to live by which they can respect and understand.'

'I've not noticed much good from the communist system so far.'

'It's hardly been going sixty years. Yours has been here two thousand—and look what a mess it's made.' But Dawley felt friendly towards him in spite of his worn-out views. 'When I was in Algeria,' he said, coffee steam mingling with smoke from his cigarette, 'I saw a man in the desert eating a snake. He belonged to some wandering sect. I'd been on the run for days, after a big balls-up of an attack on a French base, a forlorn hope that was only done to relieve pressure somewhere else, or maybe to influence peace talks at Evian—no bloody less. I was delirious and half dead, and wondered later whether I hadn't imagined the whole thing. But I hadn't.

'There were a few scruffy palm trees and a tent or two, and nomads pulling water for their camels. I was dying of thirst, and hoped to get some. I couldn't have cared less, either, because there wasn't much life in me. You get beyond it after a while. It's quite a revelation to have gone that far towards an absolute end. You're sinking into peace yet you're still doing something about saving yourself.

'My shirt was like fire, but even that feeling went when I heard the music and edged through the crowd to see what was happening. I'd heard no music for months, and it soothed my aches and pains. Dusk was coming on, and my will to live was at its height. Maybe I was born at that time of the day. My parents are dead and they never told me. An old bloke was playing the pipe. A middle-aged man with a bad-tempered face moved his head from side to side in time to the music, and a young chap beat a drum.

'At the feet of the middle-aged man was a damp sack, and when the music reached a certain pitch he bent down and took out a live snake. After playing with it for a while he began to roar and tremble, his yellow eyes bulging. The people drew back, but they couldn't stop watching, as if he was a demon who'd show them what they were made of.

'The speeded-up music helped him to keep the mad intensity of his vision. He needed all his strength, because he was actually fighting with the snake. It was fat and strong, about a yard long, and he was trying to subdue it, to get the energy and strength out of it. He was after its life. He was quick and knew how to fight, otherwise it would have buried its fangs in him a dozen times. He must have been immune to to the venom, and a bite that did get through only increased his strength and cunning. He was determined to kill the snake.

'There was worse to come. When the snake was almost done for he began to bite it. My guts turned to water. The nomads must have known what he was after. They groaned, as if the world was coming to an end. As his teeth ripped at the snake, which had done no man any harm, after all, I felt he was biting me. The music stopped, and this made it worse. It was horrible. All that the world meant, or had grown away from, was in this. I forced myself closer. It needed more push and courage to keep looking than it did to face bombs and bullets. I was dying with the snake, yet I was killing it myself. I was being bitten. I was struggling, and biting. I hardly thought about whether the man was brave or cruel, mad or benevolent, a wizard or a fool. He'd ripped my heart out.

'The sky was milk-white and turning pink, but dead and empty. No help could come from that quarter. The gravel underfoot was cooling from the heat of the day. The camels nosed around us as if nothing were happening. I didn't know whether to kill the man or kill myself. That was my moment of truth. If I'd been what I saw myself as—a true revolutionary who believed in rationality and progress—I would have killed him. I'd got a gun and ammunition. But I couldn't move. He was tearing at the earth's heart, and by watching I was approving of it. I was not only a revolutionary, but a human being, with whatever that implies.

'There was a movement on the edge of the crowd. Two other FLN men came up, who weren't hypnotised by it like me. They saw it as disgusting, and humiliating for all those fighting to create a just society. One of the men drew his gun and poured bullets into the snake-eater.

'It was the death of the swamp in me. He'd done the right thing. I even thought so at the time. And his action had been a reproach to me—though he didn't see it like that. I hadn't been able to shoot the man. I was a foreigner. I was me, and my principles didn't allow me to kill a man who was doing what in some primeval way he had to do. That was my excuse, though I had already killed people for less. But I failed, and knew at last that because there are things I can feel, there are things that I can't do. I was dying and awake in the same egg.

'I collapsed. Apart from my absolute exhaustion, the knot of the world slashed by bullets had shattered me. I was ill in every corner of my body and spirit, maybe for weeks. I don't know. I can't piece the days together. There are gaps. The sun ate the moon, but both were diseased. My solidity shifted. I'm another person. No, that's not true: I'm the same. Everyone has a greater breadth than he or she imagines.

'Bullets broke everything. If the man hadn't arrived, and the show had ended as it was meant to, I might have been less affected. It would have worked itself out. But looking back, and I'm still forced to much of the time, it was the most crucial thing about the desert.

'I stayed a few more months, till I was wounded and could do no more. It was like living in a dream, though the fighting was clear enough. It amazes me that I survived, but because it went by in a dream I was protected. The dead snake kept me safe. I was more in sympathy with it than anything else. I shouldn't have been, but I was. I was closer to my own soul at the same time, closer to the soul of man than I had ever been. I accepted it. I still accept it. I wasn't frightened enough to start shooting. The snake had been killed, but it still lived. The man was killed but he still lives. I still live. The earth is eternal. The soul of man has roots which go deeper than Marxism—only a fool wouldn't think so—but Marxism can give it an honourable coat, something to cover the broken human spirit with.'

What had haunted him, he told Cuthbert, was the face of the man eating the snake, showing the sanest and most pitiable eyes he had ever seen. Each pore of his skin was corroded, eating himself, and whoever his eyes turned on. It was less painful to look at the snake he was eating. The face, at the moment before turning to the snake, was one of pain, desperation, self-loathing, panic, fear, awe, the terror of letting go and, finally, courage.

He saw the face later when Handley's brother John found him in Algeria. On the final night when they were making their way down the hillside to a waiting boat that would take them to a ship out at sea, John had run back up the rocky slope with the intention of staying behind. He didn't want to go—out and back to England—but Dawley had subdued him and forced him to the beach. In the dim light of a torch he had seen the same multiplicity of expressions on John's face as had been on the snake-eater's in the desert before he turned to consume the snake.

Chapter Twenty-two

A ginger-haired youth of eighteen, with a checked and gaudy shirt showing under his open jacket, got out of the car with Enid and Maricarmen. He had freckles and bright grey eyes, a narrow forehead, and the smooth skin of a well though not overfed face. He looked around nervously but, standing in the yard, seemed confident that things would ultimately be all right. To threatening belly-shuffles from Eric Bloodaxe he leaned his rucksack against the kitchen wall, and returning to the car he freed two basket-loads of groceries.

'This is Dean,' Enid said, when Dawley and Cuthbert approached. 'He helped us get the stuff to the car park in Hitchin. He was coming in this direction, so we gave him a lift.'

'Hi, there!' said Dean, a hand held out in a friendly manner.

Cuthbert ignored it. 'Are you American, then?'

'No, siree! Just a bit of old Limey down from Nottingham, on my way to hitch-up with some of the lads in London. They've got a grotty pad in the Earls Court.' His language was a prattle of false American and raw Nottingham and, undiscouraged by Cuthbert's glacial stare, he turned to Dawley—who saw no reason not to greet him properly, though he hardly touched the hand when he shook it.

Maricarmen, struggling across the yard with a box, wondered why there was so much smoke in the paddock. 'Dean can stay to lunch,' Enid said defensively. 'He's been a great help.'

The provisions were quickly got from car to kitchen, where Myra stowed them into their various store-places. Dean stayed in the sun, sitting on the ground with his back to the wall, eating an apple filched from one of the baskets. 'What did you say your name was?' Dawley asked.

'Dean W. Posters,' he said readily, 'as my old man named me. But for shit's sake don't ask what the W stands for or I'll have to tell you it means William—Billy for short—though I allus use Dean 'cause it suits me better.'

Frank crushed an impulse to laugh. 'Are you on the move?'

'Since last week. Decided to hop it. Get out of the mill race. Threadin' bobbins was never my idea of the good life.'

'What is?'

He threw the apple-core as far as it would go. It wasn't far, because soft arms showed below the rolled sleeves. It hit the side of the Rambler, however, and left its mark there. 'Wain't know till I find it, will I? Don't even want to find it. The good life's in looking for it, you know.'

Frank stamped his cigarette. 'I can smell cooking.'

They washed hands at the kitchen sink, then collected their stew and went into the dining-room. Ralph, Maricarmen and Enid were already eating. Cuthbert sauntered in, and Richard and Adam came from upstairs.

'Where's Mandy?' Handley said.

'In bed,' Ralph told him.

Handley left his steaming plate and ran three at a time up the stairs. 'Leave her be, for God's sake,' Enid shouted. 'He'll get ulcers one day if he don't stop disturbing his mealtimes for a thing like that.'

'Or we'll get them,' Dawley said.

'What have you been burning, Ralph?' Cuthbert asked, unmoved by the disturbance. If his father wanted ulcers who was he to stop him?

'Rubbish,' Ralph said with a faint flush. 'I'm clearing the garage.'

'Make sure it is rubbish,' Cuthbert said. 'Once it's burnt you can't bring it back.'

Ralph stood, as if he would reach over to Cuthbert and stifle him. 'What are you trying to accuse me of, you unfrocked priest?'

Frank looked at Ralph. 'Sit down and eat.'

'He's got too much on his conscience,' said Cuthbert, spearing a carrot from his soup. 'Otherwise he wouldn't get so hot under the collar.'

'Another word from you,' Enid said, 'and you'll be outside.'

Dean's head was bent to his stew. Frantic shouting came from upstairs. A door slammed, and Handley walked back into the room, breathless but smiling. 'The princess will descend in a few minutes.'

'Lovely,' Dean said, his plate empty.

'Who the bloody hell are you?' Handley demanded, noticing him for the first time.

He stood, as if to be polite. 'Dean William Posters. I'm on my way to the Smoke.'

'He helped us with the provisions at the market,' Enid said, 'so we asked him to come and have a plate of stew.'

Handley sat, breaking his slab of brown bread into chunks before dipping. 'Can you poach?' he asked. 'Not eggs—rabbits.'

'No.'

'Where you from?'

'Nottingham.'

'So's Frank. Rare old place. And you can't poach?'

Dean helped himself to more stew from the huge tureen. 'I was two years threadin' bobbins in a lace factory, and then I thought: this is no bleedin' life for me. Too much like 'ard work.' The more he ate the more his Nottingham accent came back.

'You're at the right house,' Handley said, 'if you don't like work'—looking meaningfully around. 'What put *you* off?'

'I'd done enough. I'm eighteen, and I left school at fifteen. So I thought I'd get on the move, see what I could make, hitch to Turkey, maybe India. I hear blokes do.'

'What about money?' Cuthbert asked.

'I'll peddle,' Dean leered.

'Peddle?'

'Hash. Mary-Jane. Scrubbers bristles. Holy Smokes. Make plenty of gravy.'

'So that's what William Posters has come to,' Handley grinned. 'I wouldn't have thought it, would you, Frank?'

'Young kids get up to anything,' he said.

'What did your parents say when they heard you were going off like that?' Enid wanted to know.

'Mam cried a minute. Dad thought it was natural. Didn't like me giving up my job, though. Saw a dazzling career in boobin-threadin', Dad did. A job to him is a sort of paradise. Dad was young before the war, and allus talked about what life was like without a job. He thieved for a while and got shoved inside. Then he thieved again and was on the run. All through the war he was on the run. Used to make a joke about Bill Posters being prosecuted, and the bastard even named me William as a joke, so's I'd carry the name on. But I'm not Bill bloody Posters. If I go on the run it's at my own fair speed. Speed, see?' he laughed, mouth full of food.

Handley smiled. 'You'd better watch it. Peddle hash and you'll run faster than your old man ever did. I don't suppose blue seas and olive groves will feel much better than the good old slums when you've got a dozen Turkish coppers on your tail.'

'Life's different now,' Dean said confidently, 'to what it was in the old days. Easier.'

'I wouldn't bank on that,' said Handley.

'It is. I skived all I could at the factory. Blokes tried to get me to join a union but I said my old man was in one and it never got him anywhere. Why should I join a union when I could skive? I had to join, though. Threatened to bash my nut.'

'What does your old man do now?' Dawley asked.

'Poor bastard ain't good for much,' said Dean. 'Had bronchial pneumonia last winter. Reckon he'll croak one of these days. Works at the Raleigh sweeping up rammel. Poor old Dad. No future for him. He's not above fifty. Had it too hard all his life.'

'Don't cry,' said Enid, seeing he was about to. 'It wasn't your fault.'

'I know,' he wept, 'but I'm sorry for the poor lousy bastard.'

'Maybe you should have stayed at home then,' said Handley, 'and looked after him. Give him some more stew, Myra. That'll stop his blawting.'

Maricarmen looked on with absolute contempt.

'Any road up,' Dean said, reaching for the bread-platter, 'it wain't happen to me, you can bet.'

'As long as your old man don't feel sorry for himself,' Dawley said.

'I don't think he does any more. He did at one time. Sees it's no good. But he thinks a lot. That's why I left. I couldn't stand it. You've only got to look at Dad and you can tell he's had a hard life. The misery on his clock makes you wonder what you've done to make him like that. And you can see he's thinking the same. So I'm steering clear.'

It was impossible not to believe him, which was a good reason for changing the subject. Handley turned to Maricarmen: 'I was wondering when we could have a look at Shelley's notebooks. I don't want to hurry you. I'm a master of patience when necessary, but it might do us good to read some stirring revolutionary stuff. We need a new tone to inspire our decadent pedestrian souls.'

She looked at her plate while he spoke. 'Maybe after the next meeting.'

'That's in a fortnight,' Handley said.

'I didn't know I'd stumbled into a nest of Reds,' Dean observed.

'If you don't like it,' said Handley, 'it's bloody easy to stumble out again.'

'I was only talking,' Dean said in a wheedling tone. 'Just talking, you know.'

'There's one thing,' Maricarmen said. 'I think Maria and Catalina should have a vote on the committee like the rest of us. They're full-time working members of the community, even though they are *au pair* girls.'

'That's ridiculous,' Cuthbert exclaimed. 'They don't know enough English to understand what's being said.'

'They do,' Maricarmen told him. 'I've been speaking to them.'

Handley didn't like it either, but knew he'd have to agree if he expected her to hand over Shelley's papers. 'She has a point,' Enid said. 'They do more work than some people I could mention.'

'Where are they today, then?' asked Cuthbert.

'In London,' said Myra, collecting empty plates. 'It's their day off.'

'The first for a fortnight,' said Enid.

'There's a whiff of conspiracy here,' Handley joked. 'I'll adjust the vote-meter so that it registers the proper number of ayes and noes.'

'We'll do it on a show of hands,' Enid decided. 'It's simpler, as well as cheaper.'

'That's the end of the secret ballot, then,' Handley grinned.

Two huge apple crumbles and a bowl of custard were placed on the table. Mandy came into the room wearing her padded and flowered dressing gown. 'Am I too late for stew?'

Ralph smiled, and beckoned. She stood close to Dean: 'What's this?'

He looked up with a wide smile, his small teeth so even that Handley wondered if they were false. 'Hey up, duck! My name's Dean. You look nice!'

'Another sponger,' she said, walking over to Ralph, whose face had turned purple at Dean's insolent remarks to his lady wife. She kissed Ralph, and went into the kitchen to get some food.

'Everybody'll have full voting rights,' Handley said, 'including Eric Bloodaxe. He can sit on the floor. One bark for yes, and two barks for no. We'll soon train 'im.'

'It's no joke,' Enid snapped.

Handley stood, leaving half his dessert. 'Maria and Catalina can vote at the next meeting, then. And on the evening of the same day we read Shelley's notebooks.'

Enid smiled significantly at Maricarmen, and Frank wondered what secret plans they had devised for the rest of them.

Chapter Twenty-three

After each meal Handley went to his studio, and everyone thought he was working. They got on with their chores and duties, and grumbled while the days and hours passed, but thought it worthwhile because it allowed the great man to do his immortal painting.

These attitudes sifted through. He brooded too much on the forces that kept him going. It was good that he worked well for a time, but when it went on as if the peace would last forever he felt empty and irritable. If he laboured well, everyone concerned about him with such calm efficiency that he didn't notice it, he felt that nobody cared whether he lived or died.

In his sketchbook he drew a clock, with hands over its eyes, and a huge mouth from which blood ran. The community worked by the clock: every piece of machinery was in place and doing its job, and the only result was that time passed and nothing happened. The peace was killing, but he realised that when he thought this, something violent and heart-wrenching was on its way. Yet even this couldn't be guaranteed. You were in the hands of fate. What you expected was what you hoped for, a wish never to be granted except in such a back-handed fashion that it knocked you flat.

He paced up and down, from easel to door, from the bookcase to a small table in the corner with an electric kettle and cups on it, and paused at a shaving mirror nailed on the wall. His face looked more tormented than usual, and he could find no response except to fart and stroll across to the door and lift his cap from a hook, put it on, and resume walking up and down.

It was months since he'd seen Daphne Ritmeester, but feeling empty he had no desire to visit anybody. He wasn't in love with her. He muttered that he didn't even fall in love any more, and whatever he told himself, true or not, he believed at the time the words went uncontrollably through his head. I have a full life of work to get done, he hoped, plugging in the kettle for the sake of something to do. Love is a form of self-destruction, a kind of slow suicide, a full-time occupation that pulls you away from your central self—though I wouldn't mind a bit of it right now, because it can be useful in hauling you clear when your middle starts to eat you up. Still, it's a bitter sort of get-out, expensive and time-consuming.

He pondered how refreshing it would be to pack a tent and hide himself in some impenetrable wood or other. You can't run away. Or can you? He felt in the grip of fluxes, fevers and frenzies, and to calm himself began composing a begging letter, maybe practising for when he was on his uppers again. The good thing about life was that nothing was certain, which was a thought to keep him going.

He threw his dip-pen at the door, then screwed up the paper and ate it. His heart wasn't in it. Maybe he never would have to write such things again. The kettle boiled and he filled the pot, thinking to drink himself into a colander.

After the first cup, supped vacantly while looking at a couple of squabbling rooks by the window, he went to his sketch-pad and roughed out notes for a large new picture.

It was Enid's turn to do the washing, and sheets from the machine had been hung up to air on a line from garage to back door. She'd thought it would stay fine, but at the moment it didn't look good. A thunderstorm might clear the air.

It had been hard work most of the day, which reminded her how difficult things had become compared to life at their burned-down house in Lincolnshire. She had taken to the community like a duck to water, as far as Albert could see—which was not far. She'd nevertheless found it interesting to live in such a way, and useful in that it opened doors wide to her discontent. Maybe it would have come anyway—with age.

She was discontented, though not unhappy—a state which made her feel light-headed and confused so that she didn't, as it were, know which way to turn. She used to expect all the days of her life to be the same, but now the end of a day was like the end of an era, so that tomorrow was bound to be different. Nothing was settled anymore.

She looked on Handley as a cancer-producing agent, having decided that in some unreasonable underhand way he had ruined her life, while at the same time she'd made certain that he had, so as one day to blame him for it and ruin him back. Such marriages must surely be made in heaven.

Handley sensed it, too, for they touched on it in their arguments. 'We'll go down together when we go,' he'd said, the white devil of mockery in him. 'A handsome though ageing couple, you going left into a door marked HERS, and me going right through a slot labelled MINE—to have our shock treatment. The hallmark of a successful marriage is how many volts it can take before it's blasted apart, how much current to make the common united cinder fit to be exhibited in any church or townhall as the apotheosis of holy moonstruck matrimony. Raise the voltage, sling in the amps and slap down the ohms, and sooner or later the equilibrium will split at its strongest point while the weaknesses remain uncharred to become the strengths of another day.'

Love with a capital L she thought, watching him spit. We loved each other so well at the beginning it was bound to come to this. If a man can't let you blame him for ruining your life he just doesn't love you. And the fact that he doesn't love you proves that he ruined your life, and will go on ruining it for as long as you try to put it back together again.

She knelt by a herbaceous border and tried to calm herself by pulling up weeds, but they snapped half-way because she could never get at the roots. In any case they were weak except at the roots. When I was young I was naïve, she thought, full of love and hope, and help for others but mostly for him, and now after seven kids I'm middle-aged and he doesn't want me any more. So how can he deny he's ruined my life? But he goes on denying it only so that he can ruin it more, because though he's an artist he's the most callow man alive. He knows nothing about me in particular or women in general, or human beings at all.

Even if he wasn't an artist it would be the same, because the Handley in him goes deeper than the painter he's turned into.

When we were young and had no money and lots of kids to feed we'd get depressed and hold hands and shed tears at our common troubles, console each other at our plight and he'd kiss and make love and promise to try and sell a painting and write another dozen begging letters to bring some money in.

But now he thinks he's rich, and there's not a bit of tenderness left for me. He doesn't even see me anymore. His tears dried up long ago if ever they were there in the first place, which I doubt because I think he only shed them so as to get deeper into my spirit and start to destroy it by the hatred he has for everybody—not only me.

There wasn't much work to do, and maybe that was the trouble. There were more willing hands than necessary, as well as dishwashers, vacuum-cleaners, washing-machines: a fully automated house run by as many people as if there were no gadgets at all. It was Handley's little plaything of a community, the modern doll's house of the selfish man complete with furniture and more people to play around with. The only sensible member of it was Dawley's wife Nancy, who'd left as soon as she saw what was going on.

She went in and took off her apron, then came out again. Dean was inside the Rambler, lying along the back seat reading a comic. He lifted an idle hand as she went by, and blew her a kiss. Not much had been said about him staying on. Some were for it, others not, so he glued himself to the place as a sort of watchman-gatekeeper till a proper decision was made. He was already firm friends with Maria and Catalina, who were said, among other things, to be teaching him Spanish.

She opened Handley's door without knocking, stepped inside and closed it. He sensed her presence, but went on mixing colours, and attentively applying paint to the large canvas pinned before him. She wondered how long he'd go on ignoring her.

He turned, jacket off and shirt open, a piece of rope holding up his paint-smeared trousers. 'I love you,' he said, but staying where he was. 'I love you, Enid, more than I've ever loved anybody or anything. You're the one great fabulous love of my life. I always loved you, and I always will. You're handsome, beautiful, passionate, and violent. In other words: marvellous—all I could ever wish for. But don't disturb me, sweetheart, because I've got a fantastic painting to do, and I've just begun it, the best thing I've ever started. So I'll see you later, if you don't mind.'

She was latched to the floor with anger at the cool machine-like injustice of his ploy. By the look on her face Handley realised that he'd wasted his breath. There were times when she wanted to make love but was too clogged with frustration to start it, and so a quarrel was the only way to get through to them both. Sometimes it worked. Sometimes it didn't. Sometimes he was too soured to move when it came to the point, but when it did the trick they were calm and loving afterwards as if they were seventeen again. He felt like going to bed with her, in fact, being often most randy when working well, but he was determined to get to the bones of his painting first.

'Are you too dead-ignorant to say anything?'

He looked surprised at her opening move of attack, as if only half knowing what she meant.

'We live together,' she said, coming close to the table, 'but we don't ever get five minutes to talk. That suits you, doesn't it, because as long as you can be at your paints, you're happy. But I'm just one of the domestics in this set-up. I exist like a robot, and if I didn't say anything you'd never speak a civilised word to me again.'

He was uneasy because he sensed some truth in what she said, so he levelled his voice skilfully to appear reasonable. Such hypocrisy cut into her sharply, for she knew how he wallowed in his deceptions. 'We often talk,' he said. 'And there's Myra and Maricarmen. The place is full of people to talk to.'

'I hate you.'

His control snapped at the venom in her, as she had known it would. 'You hate me, do you? Did you hear that?' he said, as if everyone were listening at the window. 'She hates me! If only you'd said so when we first met. I'd have known then that you loved me. Fancy telling me now, after so long. I didn't know you cared!'

'I hate you.'

'Oh God,' he groaned. 'You say it every month. Tell me something new.'

'You don't know me,' she cried. 'We've never met. You won't meet me. Your shell's too hard. You're stuck fast in your own concrete shelter.'

'I do love you,' he answered. 'I've said it till my stomach's full of holes. I know you'd like it if we spent all the time looking babies in one another's eyes, but all I want just now is to get on with this painting.'

'Do it then,' she screamed.

'I can't.'

'Well, don't blame me. You blame anybody but yourself.'

He wiped the paint off his hands with a turps rag, a gesture he knew would annoy her because it meant he didn't expect to paint any more that day, and that it was her fault. 'We've got seven kids,' he said. 'The eldest is twenty-five, yet we go on shouting like thirty year olds! Can't we calm down a bit?'

'You want old age? I'm still a young woman, as far as I'm concerned. You've got money but you hardly ever take me to London. Oh no, you go on your own, and God knows what you get up to.'

'What the hell do you think?'

'I've heard tales. There's more than one poison-pen letter writer in this village. They go down to shop in the West End, and spot you up to your antics. They can't wait to report back.'

'I'll kill the bastards!' he said. 'I'm absolutely innocent. You know how hard I work. I slave at it too much to take time off having affairs.'

'You expect me to believe that? What would you do if I bloody well carried on?'

'You want to know?' he raved. 'I'd kill him. And if he got away I'd search him out from the seven corners of the earth with a double-barrelled blunderbuss and blow his bollocks off one by one.'

'If ever a man walked in the spitten-image of injustice, that man's you.'

He relaxed, as if they'd reached the end of round one.

At night when they slept together they seemed to eat each other up in their dreams. The peaceful life of the community had failed to wean them from the attractions of a rough and tumble life. What they said they wanted was absolute order and calm, but they wouldn't admit that what the consciousness craves is often what the subconscious doesn't allow it to have. To get what they wanted meant settling the hash of their subconscious—and what self-respecting subconscious would ever allow that done to it?

'Sit down,' he said, approaching her. 'I'll make some more tea, just for the two of us, and put a good drop of Irish whiskey in.'

She sat. 'Don't touch me.'

'I want you to be happy,' he said tenderly.

'You haven't acted like it this last couple of years.'

He plugged in the hotplate, and reached for the bottle. 'I thought you were happy here. I tried to create a paradise but it's turned into a medieval slum. Apart from the house there's two caravans, the garage, tool-sheds, coal-stores, three cars, a greenhouse, a wendy hut, two spare lavatories, and a leaking sauna-cabin. Talk about the back-to-backs of the affluent society. I sometimes think I'd be happier in a remote cottage with a bog outside and oil lamps hanging from the ceiling, with a plain wood stove that fills the kitchen with smoke every time you want a warm.'

'It sounds marvellous,' she said. 'We'd have a garden though, and there'd be a wood where we'd go for kindling and bluebells and blackberries.'

'You're right,' he said regretfully. 'This community can't work. Not for me, anyway. The trouble is I've got my family mixed up in it. If I was on my own I'd have more of a chance. But I'm too bound up with you and the kids to be on my own. And if I've got to choose between the family and the community I suppose I'd pick the family. You can't beat it for the homely and profitable suffering it keeps you stuffed up with!'

While she reflected on this he washed two mugs at the sink, then poured a good flow of whisky in each, and strong tea after it.

'You've always wanted to be free of the family,' she said. 'You never stop hoping you'll come back from Town one day and find we've been the victims of some madman with a machine-gun.'

'I'm only human,' he said calmly, putting the mugs down. 'Of course I've often thought that. I'm honest: I admit it. But twice as many times I've told myself how much I love you. God knows, if anything happened to you or the kids I'd die of misery in a fortnight.'

'You don't know me,' she jeered. 'If you did you'd control yourself, and not say such things about wishing me and the kids dead. I'm not the hard woman you think I am. I may look it because you've made me that way, but I'm not. I can't stand the way you're always trying to kick me down.'

Of her many accusations, the one that he didn't know her galled him most. It filled his brain with razor-blades. It brought out the worst in him, so that both of them were soon lost in the mists of spite—further from each other than ever.

'When I want comfort,' she said, walking around his table, a movement which made him nervous, 'you don't give it to me.'

'How can I,' he shouted, 'while you're ripping my guts out? You're a shark. You want to bite people.' He took a gulp of fortified tea and wallowed in false, lying counter-accusation, knowing it to be so but swinging out joyfully like an ape over the trees: 'You want to eat people. So you're worse than a shark because you're a shark out of choice and not just because you've got to survive. You're a killer shark, and I can't live near it anymore.'

I must stop, he thought, at the sight of her face poised for retaliation. It seemed thinner in the midst of battle, but at the same time less lined and tired. I mustn't give in to spite, he told himself, his heart suspended while the mechanics of self-preservation worked out a suitable reply in her breast. I must never give in to spite. I've got too much of it, like everything else. But leave spite out of it. I don't want her to turn into a bitter cabbage with mad eyes and a slit mouth.

She spoke in a quiet voice. 'You'd stand there forever, wouldn't you? You'd leave me to rot and die before wondering how I was feeling.'

'Drink your tea, love.'

'You're paralytic,' she said, 'paralysed by your own weakness.'

'Old spirit-breaker.' He laughed drily, sweating under his emptiness, picking up his brush and making a great letter X across the painting he'd so far done. 'Does that make you happy? I'll sacrifice that to you, because I know that's what you want, old spirit-breaker!'

'If that's so,' she smiled calmly, placated slightly by his Handley-like gesture of love, 'your spirit isn't up to much. But then, it never has been.'

'Well,' he went on, 'you *can* break it there's no denying. I'm human, even though I am an artist. But you can only do it as far as you are concerned. You can't smash it so finally that no one can come up and pulverize it again in their particular way. That's love, though. Your spirit can be knocked up a hundred times without it being forever. And if you do smash it, it would only mean I'd be shut of you. But maybe you're only trying to get rid of me. Nobody can blame you for that. I'd be free of you as well, don't forget!'

She listened to him going on. He was vile, and neglected her for his so-called art, but now and again if she prodded him hard enough in the right places she got him to talk, even if it was the worst sort of wordy flow that cut her in all the wrong places—though more truth came out than when they were sitting politely around the table with the others.

'I'm a painter,' he was saying, while she drank her tea. 'How do you think I became a painter?'

'To get away from me.'

'To express all those pains I suffered and got no sympathy for. I hoped that the world would get the sympathy and understanding that I didn't get.'

She laughed. 'It's these woolly epigrams I can't stand. You look so pompous, like a parson who's had to chop his pulpit up for firewood.'

'You're a frigid castrating bitch,' he said, before he could bite his tongue off.

Both of them thought this was a lie, which was something that united them, but Enid, in the fury of quarrelling, chose to believe that he was serious in what he said. So she had to reply in kind: 'That's because you're impotent. Everybody thinks that because we've got seven kids you strut around with a permanent hard-on. What a mistake they make! And you wouldn't tell 'em otherwise.'

'I didn't mean it in that way,' he said, 'though it's interesting to hear what you think, you one-track-minded bitch. We've always fucked well, and you know it.'

'You say so. Oh yes, I know, sometimes we have, but with you, you just about get me going when you've finished. I have my orgasm and you think that's that.'

How did I get this far in? 'If you don't like it,' he said, pouring more tea, 'if you suffer so much, why don't you go? Take the kids if you like, but go. You're free. Go on, take all the money to live on if you like. Take everything. I'm generous. Leave me a tent, that's all. I'll survive. I don't want to go on ruining your life any longer. It's a crime against civilisation. I never wanted to ruin anybody's life.'

'You're so selfish,' she cried, her voice packed hard and ready to break, 'that you don't know when you're making somebody suffer. And as soon as I let you know it, because I love you, after all, you tell me to get out. You want to chuck me and the kids in so that you can look for a young girl to marry and start a new life with.'

'No!' He wailed—his eyes wild, as if about to go into an epileptic fit. He grabbed his head, pressing to squeeze his whole vision out of existence. He closed his eyes because he couldn't bear to look at anything. The space he stood in was blocked off from him even though he opened his eyes, and the whole room of the hut was locked in the wide spaces of his own head. He could not get out of it.

'Now you want to frighten me,' she called. 'You'll try any rotten trick.'

He'd scared himself more, and was ashamed that he should be so goaded by her taunts. He stood, breathless and pale, looking across at the table. It's a war of attrition. The flower of one's manhood perishes in it. Why do we do it? How did we get locked into it? He wanted to weep, but couldn't. Not even when she'd gone would he be able to weep. There's no victory, only an occasional armistice to allow us to renew our strength, a pulling back of the battle lines for a bit of reconstruction. The losses are too great for us to get much from such blood-letting. There's no hope of being buoyed up to the skies by victory in this sixty-year war. 'I'm worn to the bone,' he admitted.

Soothe his wounded heart, patch up his deepest gashes, get his arm in a sling, a shade on his eye. Put a cap on his head at an even cockier angle than before, and send him back into the matrimonial barrage.

'I'm sorry,' he said, holding her in his arms. It was too soon to try and kiss her, though he managed one on her forehead. She remained stiff against him, but he was roused by the closeness of her body. 'I know you've had a hard life, though God knows, you look young enough for it.'

'You've done your best to pull me down,' she said, her hot breath against him, 'and keep me in my place.'

'We've lived,' he said. 'What else do you want? And what's more, we're still living. Very well, too.'

'As long as I eat three times a day you don't care.'

He felt the quarrel priming up for another take-off, but all his energy was sapped, his body a hollow tube, his mouth dry, his eyes tinderous. 'I don't want to hurt you. I don't mean what I say. I don't own any of it. As Job said: "God destroyeth the perfect and the wicked." Which am I? You tell me. I can't.'

'It's a pity you can't,' she said. 'You're like a volcano. You spew for the sake of spewing. Why do you say such things, if you don't mean them?'

'Because I don't want to burst. I've got to say something. How can I mean what I say when it comes out like that?'

'If you lie at such a time I don't see when you can ever tell the truth.' But she gave his hand a friendly squeeze.

'Don't you? I do. Let me tell you why, and get it straight. I mean what I say when I say something in a tender and loving voice. That's the only time. All else is wind and piss, hot air and jelly-bile. I'm sorry about it then.'

She pulled her hand free, and walked towards the window: 'What a child you are!'

He could see her smile, though her back was to him: 'Why don't you cut your wrists and stop bothering me?' he shouted. 'I take you into my heart and it means nothing to you. A child, eh? Is that how you've seen me all these years while we've been struggling through the mud of this matrimonial Passchendaele? As for you, I suppose you're still looking for a daddy—a great big cuddly daddy for his little baby girl!'

She swung round, and rushed at him. 'You vicious lousy rotten gett!'

Her white bare arm swept the table like an iron bar, and what she missed because it was too near the middle she reached over for and picked up piece by piece to throw at him with all her strength. The cup with the dregs of tea bounced from his mutilated canvas, a steel ruler spun like a scythe, a stone he'd found in his younger days on some isolated beach flew by his head and smashed the window neatly. A jotting pad winged his face, and a jam jar full of nails and thumb tacks travelled over like a shrapnel bomb.

He watched her with a sardonic smile, and dodged as best he could, feeling the beating rhythm of his heart slowing down. 'Go on,' he said when she paused. 'Smash everything. If I had the strength I'd help you.'

'Stop laughing.'

'Oh, I know, you're serious.'

She reached a large bottle of spirits and hurled it as a final effort. It turned many times in flight, and smashed against the glowing hotplate accidentally left on from tea-making. It exploded like a Molotov

Cocktail. Flames crept gleefully along the floor, and Handley side-stepped calmly when they threatened his shoes. They edged up the wall.

'You'd better save yourself,' he said. 'You'd think I belonged to a family of arsonists. I'm staying here because I've had enough.' He folded his arms on his chest and stood still.

'Albert,' she said, 'let's put it out.'

'Let my forty paintings burn,' he said magnanimously. 'And me with them.'

'You're still trying to torment me,' she screamed. 'When will you stop? What have I done to be treated so vilely by you? If only you'd treat me like a human being at least.'

'I'll die,' he said. 'A one-man holocaust.'

'Please!'

He reached for the fire extinguisher, knocked the top, and sprayed the flame with powder till it subsided. Scorch marks showed on the wall. It smouldered, and they coughed as they talked. 'Does that satisfy you?' he said, kissing her on the lips.

Her hot tongue was in his mouth. Her legs opened and curled around him. 'Only one thing satisfies me.'

It was already rampant, and he pushed it against her. 'You know how I love you,' he said, his hand over her breasts and pressing them hard in the way she liked.

'You only say you love me,' she said, 'when you want to have me.'

He wanted to strangle her, but the impulse went when he realised the cost of resuming their quarrel. But he was afraid that murder would brew up one day between them. He unbuttoned her blouse, while she let down her skirt. Half-way to the cot-bed in the corner of the hut she began pulling at his trousers. They hadn't made love for days, so the pot had had time to boil. He loathed her. He loved her—so sublimely that the loathing didn't matter. He could drown it any day.

Chapter Twenty-four

Handley stood up to open the session: 'It seems to me—because I'm not blind—that certain power blocs are forming in this community, which between them will deaden the life of all future meetings. It'll come down to the stupid brute strength of party politics, which are anathema in a true democracy. Innovation may be possible, but real human progress will be out of the question.'

Thirteen people sat along both sides of the table, and a snap vote had already decided that no one could occupy the head or foot, so he moved next to Maria, the tallest of the *au pair* girls with blue-black hair and sultry eyes, who felt uneasy that he was so close, and wanted to move away.

'There's been an immovable power bloc at these meetings ever since they began,' Enid said, 'and that's been you. Maybe we will end up with two sides, but that'll be better than being manipulated like puppets.'

'It's been fair give and take,' he said.

Myra stood. 'I'll explain what we want. There are a few of us who believe it's time that the domestic work was divided equally between the men and women.'

Her slight pause enabled Handley to snap into argument: 'And who's going to give me a hand with my painting? Who'll work with Frank on his book? There'll be no lack of volunteers, I expect, to help

Cuthbert to do damn-all, or to muck in with Dean and his pot-smoking.'

'That's not the point,' Enid said. 'This place is nothing but a holiday camp for those with a penis. Otherwise it's shopping, or sewing, or washing, or cooking or cleaning. I'm not doing any more unless the men share—and as a duty, not a bit of skylarking when they want exercise or a change of scenery to make them feel good. So if you don't help, we stop work altogether, and you can live off tinned food and wear paper shirts—or however you want it.'

'This is the most uncivilised notion I ever heard of,' said Handley. 'Don't *you* think so?' he called to Dean, set between Enid and Maricarmen.

'You'll get no change out of sponger,' Mandy laughed. 'If he doesn't vote with us he won't get another crust.'

'He'll feel that bloody road under his feet if he does,' said Handley.

Dean knew he shouldn't smile, but was unable to do anything else to save face. His narrow eyes had no smile in them, only a desire to explain to Handley the truth about his position. He disliked all of them except Enid, but couldn't say so because the idea of pushing on to the Smoke didn't seem so good compared to the lotus-ease of this slack mob. He cunningly kept silent, knowing she would stick up for him.

'He votes how he likes,' she said to Handley, 'so stop badgering him. It's wonderful how nasty you can get when you think somebody might be trying to take your power away.'

'How will you arrange the work?'

'I've planned it already,' Myra said. 'There are twelve of us, so three can be on duty every day. That means you work one day in four, which isn't so bad. It should be feasible, with good will all round.'

'There are thirteen of us,' he pointed out.

'Dean's not part of the schedule,' Enid told him, 'being the general caretaker and errand-runner. He'll have plenty to do, don't worry.'

'He's stunned with drugs most of the time,' Handley said. 'All he's fit for is sleeping in the car like a dog, on a bow-wow trip to the bone factory. I've noticed Cuthbert's not above a little pull at the old weed now and again. Nor is Mandy. Oh yes, I've seen you at it. I know you think I'm a tight-arsed reactionary, but your brains'll get softer than they are already if you keep on with it. You should have more sense than to drag that crap into your lungs. I'll tell you another thing: if anybody in the village gets a whiff of it you'll have the bloody constabulary down on us like a pack of elephants. And if it spreads at the rate it's going, this house will be belching it from the chimneys for everybody to flake out at.'

'It relaxes you,' said Mandy. 'Why don't you take some? There'd be more peace in the house.'

There was a glint in Handley's eyes. He had diverted them from the main issue—though this was serious enough. 'I'm proposing,' he said, 'that we put it to the vote: do we allow drugs on the premises, or not?'

'It's a matter of free will,' Myra said. 'If they want to smoke pot there's no harm in it.'

'If I'm honest with myself,' Handley said, 'I agree with you. But you're the official householder on this compound, and if the coppers find grass and such stuff they'll get you in court.'

'He's right,' Dawley said.

'I smoked it in Tangier,' Myra told them, 'though I didn't let it get a grip. It's a stupid law that says you can't smoke it, and the general policy of the community is, as I've always understood it, that such rules aren't to be taken notice of. The good laws of society might be necessary from time to time, but not those that try to tell us what we can and can't do with our own minds and bodies.'

'Hear, hear,' said Richard.

'I had a smoke the other night,' Enid told them, 'but it gave me stomach ache.'

Ralph came in with the coffee.

'I expect he has, as well,' said Handley.

He smiled. 'Often. I smuggled it when I was on my world trip three years ago.'

'Everybody smokes it now and again,' said Adam.

'You too?' Handley demanded.

'Not much. But I have. Haven't we, Richard?'

Richard reached for a cup of coffee. 'We had a smoke-in with Maria and Catalina last night, in the Operations Room.'

'That's why they're always so bloody dopey then,' said Handley. 'I expect you mix a bit with Eric Bloodaxe's food. He has been a bit quiet lately.'

'It's an idea,' said Cuthbert.

'You keep off him,' Handley shouted angrily. 'That dog's as innocent as driven snow.'

'In Malaga,' said Maricarmen, 'there are vendors on every corner selling it. It comes from Morocco, just over the water. It's the peoples' opium though. I hate it.'

Handley lit a cigar. His plan was broken. 'Don't think you shock me. But don't go smoking it in the shop or pub. I don't mind us being had up for poaching or any other honest to God escapade. We can handle that. But the bastards are red hot on this stuff.'

'About this domestic issue,' said Enid. 'Who's in favour of work being shared equally as a duty between men and women?'

Handley stood. 'Before we go through with this farce, let me say something else. With thirteen pair of hands there'll be more people than there's work for. So on the grounds of general economy I think we won't be needing the help of Maria and Catalina'—believing that if he could get them sacked before the vote was taken the women might not have a majority.

'If they go,' said Myra gently, 'you'll work one day in three instead of one in four, because we'll still win by a small margin.'

He sat down. 'A bit of good old healthy ballot-rigging has been going on, has it?'

Enid, Myra, Mandy, Ralph, Maricarmen, Dean, Maria and Catalina voted in favour. Handley, Cuthbert, Dawley, Adam and Richard cast against—a majority no one could gainsay.

'This is the end of peace,' said Handley, before walking out of the room. 'I don't expect I shall ever paint another picture!'

Everyone was so excited about the new regime that Shelley's notebooks were forgotten. Handley had remembered them, but thought they could stay where they were. Who knew what other bright ideas they might give Maricarmen?

Chapter Twenty-five

Dean strolled across the yard and sat by Dawley in a friendly unassuming manner. He lit a cigarette, so that the sweet vegetable pungency of pot flowed from between his lips in pale blue shades. He didn't even smoke it properly, Frank saw, who had done so when he was wounded in Algeria, and it was the closest he could get to anaesthetic. If he inhaled to his toe-nails it would come out the colour of steel, but when he went on to do so Dawley saw that he wasn't such a novice after all.

Had William Posters ever been one? His children certainly were brought up on the art of survival. 'You've found quite a resting-place here.'

Dean's eyes turned on him in the half darkness: 'I like it. People help each other. That's good.'

'You smoke that a lot?'

'While I've got it. I invested my post office dough in it before I kicked Nottingham. I gen Cuth some this morning, and he's bin stoned all day. He's a good bloke, Reverend Cuth is. Says it's changed 'is life!'

Dawley laughed. 'He's having you on. He's not new to it. Smoked it at his college.'

'You want a bit of the old straw?'

'No thanks. I'm not bleeding to death. Why don't you read a book or two? There's plenty in the house.'

'Girlie mags?'

It might be a big change if young Bill Posters read a few things. 'Good books. Go and look.'

'I'm travelling,' Dean said. 'I learn a lot from that. My old man says he's allus wanted to travel.'

'He was too busy running away,' Frank said. 'You always get back to the same place.'

Dean laughed, and took another long pull. A few minutes passed before he could answer. 'Ask me in five years whether you do or not.'

He liked his open, ignorant and generous nature. 'I expect we'll bump into each other somewhere in Nottingham.'

'Not me,' Dean said, dreamily confident, his words meandering out. 'I'll never see that Dracula-castle again.'

'What makes you so sure?'

'I'm moving.' A minute went by. 'Moving, I tell you.'

Frank threw his fag-end towards the setting sun. 'You're sitting still, at the moment.'

A few minutes of peace passed.

'I'm still moving, though.'

It was no use arguing. Only smoke was moving, and that was a fact. He was too young to reason with. And when he was old enough he'd be too set in his ways. He hadn't had time to get frightened yet. Frank hoped he never would, felt enough of the old Bill Posters in himself to know all about the man on the run from his own spirit and the world that wanted to crush it. It was a perpetual motion of the heart, until the mechanism seized up.

'What you goin' ter do?' Dean asked.

The question startled him because he often asked it himself. 'Stay here for the time being. It's a good place to recover in.'

'What from?'

'Too much running. I'm trying to get out of the same old track and circle.'

'I'm in a circle now, and can't get out. Floating. Moving. Flying, I tell you.'

'That stuff'll kill you,' Dawley said. His words were wasted, and he was tempted to ask for a puff. 'You'll get softening of the brain. It drugs people who might ask awkward questions.'

'I'm coming back to life.'

'Wearing off, is it?'

He stretched himself on the ground. 'I'm me, now.'

'Enjoy your kip,' Dawley said. 'But don't stay long or you'll get pneumonia.'

Not too stoned to ignore the advice, Dean stood up and rubbed his eyes as if he'd been asleep ten hours. 'Go into the caravan and use the bunk,' Dawley said.

'Where are you going?'

'Across to the house.'

Dawley strolled to the steps and leaned against Handley's darkened studio backing on to the paddock. Not smoking or moving, he looked up the slight rise of land towards the skyline and pale stars. An elderberry bush veiled him from the gate, a bush that had proliferated so much since spring that he decided to come and saw it down next morning.

A muted noise drifted from the kitchen, but it was quiet where he was, a necessary peace as long as it didn't mean sloth or idleness. At thirty he felt old enough to be Dean's father—and found the coincidence of the name with his favourite working-class mythological character amusing. Even the William was prominent in it, William Posters Junior who, right from the start, would put up with none of the crap and had slung his hook at so early an age that he would do little damage to himself or others.

Was the world changing after all? Not much. But he felt that he had altered a bit in the three years since leaving home and factory, a short enough period when he looked back on it, though he didn't doubt that time's laws would make his Algerian trip similarly brief when he tried to recall it from the future of ten years ahead. Part of his life was coming to an end, and not knowing how or exactly when almost frightened him in the warm evening air: he was worried about the future, as any self-respecting man ought to be.

Two people walked up the path. He'd been so deep in his problems that they were too close for him to announce himself, and after their first words it seemed rather late to do so.

'When can you get it?'

He was shielded by the bush, as long as he didn't move. He had learned to keep still in the desert.

'Any time,' Cuthbert drawled. 'Why didn't you bring one from Spain? You could have.'

She spoke in a quieter tone, as if afraid someone might listen. 'I didn't want it in my luggage. If the customs find a gun in your case you're in trouble.'

'When do you want it?'

'Whenever you can get it,' she said, and in his animal-like immobility Frank sensed her tone had become more urgent. She didn't want Cuthbert to see how anxious she was. But he spoke the question that Dawley wanted to ask: 'Why do you want it?'

'To take to Spain. It will be useful there.'

Cuthbert pulled on a cigarette, the glow hidden by his hand. 'Why did you come to England?' he asked suddenly.

'To get Shelley's papers to a place where they'd be safe.' Dawley wanted to join the talk and his heart beat faster. She turned to a bush and broke off a twig, cracked it to pieces as if it were an insect. Her hand nearly touched his face.

'Uncle John had a revolver and half a dozen bullets. I know where they are. But when you take it to Spain, for God's sake be careful. I don't want you to get caught.'

'Don't be silly.'

'I'd perish if anything happened to you.'

There was a rustle of clothes as they kissed. 'I can take care of myself. I've done it often.'

Cuthbert's laugh was the nearest he could get to expressing concern for her and love for himself in the same breath. 'Perhaps I'll go with you.'

'What for?'

Dawley caught the suspicion. Nobody trusted Cuthbert, but they all had different motives. 'To save you doing anything foolish.'

'I won't. I'm an ordinary person with everyday desires—as Shelley used to say.'

He clicked his tongue, irritated at her old boyfriend coming into the talk, even though he was dead. 'If I'm with you, you won't get into danger.'

'I don't let people make plans for me.'

His loud laugh startled Dawley. 'You're a lone wolf, and so am I! One lone wolf attracted to another. We'll have to get married!'

'Why? Don't you like being a lone wolf?' Dawley imagined her smile.

'I'm willing to give up a lot.'

'Get me the gun,' she said.

'What do you want it for?'

'To kill someone. What do you usually do with a gun?'

'Who?'

'I was joking,' she said. 'I don't trust anyone who has no sense of humour.'

'I don't trust anyone who has. Which cuts both ways.'

'I like you.'

'It's a dry night,' he said. 'Let's go into the paddock.'

They stood with their bodies pressed together, and Dawley heard her heavy breathing above that of Cuthbert's.

He moved silently, getting the stiffness out of his legs as he walked towards the house. Who, of all people in the community, was she planning to kill? Maybe she did want to take it back to Spain. There were many uses for guns there. With Franco's fascist regime they were a way of defending oneself, the only vote that meant anything. He couldn't argue against such reason.

But why didn't she ask for it openly at the next meeting? If her case was well put, there were enough of them on the revolutionary side for her to get a good majority. But she had asked Cuthbert to hand it over without anyone knowing, and Cuthbert was so cock-happy about his new girlfriend (whatever that meant in the fevered state of the community) that he'd do anything. For all his tight-lipped wisdom he was a bit of a fool at heart. The cynical had to be protected from themselves.

He paced up and down, from the front gate to the steps, and the thought of Maricarmen with a gun and ammunition frightened him. Luckily, her desire was no longer a secret. He would talk to Handley, who might be able to get all fire-arms under the hatches before Cuthbert looked for the gun.

Chapter Twenty-six

Washed plates lined the rack, and scoured pans were hooked on the wall. The duty roster of the new domestic regime had been drawn up in large plain letters and pinned on the notice-board. To avoid strife Myra had sorted them according to their tolerance for each other.

'My second day's stint since the New Order,' Handley said, 'one more sweep and I'll have done.'

Dawley sat down. 'You seem to be managing.'

'I'm not one for complaining, once the rope's around my gullet. Drudgery helps me to think about my painting. It's even improved since this lark started.'

'Any coffee?'

'Make some. And wash your cup after. It may be a fair system but I still don't like the way it was done.'

Frank plugged in the kettle. 'Hoisted on your own democratic principles.'

'We'll have to get rid of you-know-bloody-who, before she thinks up another bundle of mischief. She's an attractive woman, but I just don't trust her. In fact there's nobody I can trust except you, and Richard and Adam. As for Cuthbert, he's on pot, he's fallen for Maricarmen, and he's my eldest son. There's too much stacked against him.'

Frank set out two mugs for coffee. 'I was up at the paddock for a quiet smoke, and heard him and Maricarmen talking. Do you have a gun in the house?'

'Gun? Look, I might not trust him but it doesn't mean I want to kill him.'

'Maricarmen's on at him to get one. Wants to take it back to Spain.'

'I've got a horror of guns,' Handley said, 'since John died.'

'Why do you keep so many in the house?'

'What do you mean?'

'You said you had a sten, a rifle, and a few shot-guns.'

'That was only a bit of a joke on our part. John came back from the war with a couple of revolvers, it's true. I kept one in my room, and let him hug the other. I wish I hadn't, because he took it to Algeria, and killed himself with it. Which makes me responsible for his death.'

'If I hadn't gone there, and he hadn't had the blameless idea of coming to get me out of it, he'd have still been safe,' Frank said.

Albert took his hand, and held it for a moment. 'It's good of you to share it, but I hope you aren't regretting your time in Algeria.'

'I don't know. If John could be here now I'd rather not have gone. It's terrible for a good man to get killed, and for somebody like you to lose a brother. I'm a different person to what I was a couple of years ago. The older you get the more there is to regret. I change, but at the same time I stay young. What's the use of time passing if it doesn't improve you? Wasted life. If you stay the same you've got no sense. I regret the killing I took part in. It seems as if I wasn't responsible at the time. I'd give everything to go back and to do the right thing.'

'What's the point?'

'It's the only way for self-centred bastards like me to learn. Yet maybe if I had my live over again I'd do the same thing.'

'We've got to stop this bloody gun nonsense, though,' said Handley, 'or Cuthbert will have *his* regrets as well, and God knows what effect it would have on somebody like him. John's other gun is stowed in his toolbox.'

Dawley asked how safe it was. Handley put down his cup. 'You think . . . ?'

'I expect he roams around.'

He was stricken at the thought, which he knew was true enough: 'I love Cuthbert like a son, almost, but he makes me sweat at times. I saw him once in John's room, and kicked him out of it. But I'll move the gun in the morning. I'll forestall him.'

Dawley hoped he would do it now, though didn't say so. He saw no point in needlessly alarming him.

Myra was in bed, the light still on. She took off her glasses and put the book down. He glanced at Mark, whose cot was in the small dressing room opening off from theirs. His mouth and closed eyes were peaceful, but his brow suddenly wrinkled, as if some deep dream were passing there like a fish through water. Dawley loved him more than his other two, glad he'd got back from Algeria if only for him. Yet glancing through the door at Myra he didn't know who he loved most. His child seemed too vulnerable, as if all the peril of the world had passed from himself to Mark, and he desperately wanted Mark to be safe, felt a biting need for the years to go quickly so that he would grow into a man and be able to hold his own. There were so many pitfalls, and Frank knew that the dangers never receded, no matter how strong a person was. He couldn't bear the thought of anything painful happening to his son, or indeed to anyone he loved, as he looked again at Myra—who had been looking at him so engrossed in their son and wondering when he was going to turn back to her. She smiled: 'At least we've produced something together!'

'He's beautiful,' he said, going into their room and sitting at the end of the bed. 'But I'm so full of fear for him. It's daft, I know. I can almost see why people believe in God: they'd do anything to put such anxiety behind them.'

'You're a violent person,' she said, 'to think that so much can threaten your son.'

'Fearful,' he admitted. 'My spirit's gone, and peace with it. Danger and violence have their own peace. How does one get it back?'

'You need a long, tranquil life,' she said.

'Will I ever get it?' he wondered, closing the door to Mark's room.

'Only with me.' She lifted her hand, and he went closer to hold it. He undressed slowly, and pulled the bedclothes back, getting in naked beside her. She had the most beautiful eyes, yet only took off her glasses in bed. Nipples showed through her pink silken nightdress.

'Take it off, so that I can feel your skin against me.'

She did so quickly, and then embraced him: 'I've always loved you so much.'

'There's nothing else that means anything.'

She wanted to say: When will you get a divorce from Nancy so that we can be married—but she was a proud person who treated others as being as free as she had always hoped to be, and so didn't speak. She suspected that this was part of her conditioning in a man's world, not something out of her own basic nature, and so would ask him when the time came, whatever she thought. 'What do you think you'll do?'

It wasn't the right time for such a question, but he slowed down the speed of his desire, to do the right thing and tie it to her own. 'I don't know about the future. I want to finish my book, first.'

She was pleased at hearing him call it a book for the first time. 'I was reading George's book this evening,' she said, 'and thought that perhaps his publisher would like to see yours when it's finished. He's got that sort of list. He likes revolutionary literature from young working-class men!'

'Is that his name for it? And how many of us does he think there are? Anyway, it's not a book yet. When I've finished you'll have to tell me what you think. Make sure it's all ship-shape and grammatical. I haven't felt like a young working man for a long while, though I expect I could slot back into it if I had to.'

'You won't need to,' she said. 'All I want is for you to be happy.'

He craved a smoke, but knew she didn't like it in the bedroom because of Mark. 'If I stop living from day to day I might be able to see some distance ahead. Then I'll know what I want to do, though finally I don't know what happiness is. A necessary illusion, maybe.'

'We're unhappy so that we'll know when we're happy,' she said, wondering whether he wasn't too locked up in himself to ever give her anything at all.

He smiled, and kissed her. 'We've got enough to eat, and we aren't being bombed, so we ought to feel happy. But I can't while such atrocities are going on in the world. I'm happy now and again though, in spite of myself. Life would be insupportable otherwise. I sometimes think: to hell with the world! Why should it make me miserable? But that's weakness. I'm so weak I can't stand my own bloody weakness.'

'That might turn out to be your strength,' she said, pushing the clothes back so that she could see his body. It seemed ridiculous that only their heads were visible, as if they were some form of transmuted life, not whole and to be seen even by each other when making love. He lay facing her, and she stroked his flattened stomach. 'Why do you worry about everything?'

His gloomy preoccupations were an area in which she seemed powerless to help, and she wanted to cure him, bring his whole person back to herself and Mark. 'It's more than mere worry,' he said. 'I feel pity and fear and hope for Mark, and for you, and so can't help extending it to everybody else. While they are threatened, you two are threatened, and I can't stand that.'

She lay on her back, her head turned to him, kissing the wrist of the hand that touched her short dark hair where it met the pillow. 'We have to look after ourselves, then do what we can for others. It's all part of the human pattern.'

Was there any point in arguing? If he agreed they might make love sooner. Now that he was no longer in danger he was becoming civilised. Her hand roamed down his stomach until his penis became alive. When he kissed her the rest of the world vanished. 'This is happiness,' he said, thinking that when he loved he was most at rest.

Her breasts pressed into him: 'I want another baby.'

They were both so ready that he was in her without guidance. There was no greater happiness, at the moment.

Chapter Twenty-seven

It nagged at him all night long, invaded his dreams through the sort of sleep that gave no rest. Towards dawn Enid said that if he didn't stop scraping around like a rat in a trap he could go off to his own bed in the studio. Finally, he slept a couple of hours, though the gnawing fact of getting John's lethal pistol under lock and key woke him sharply at eight.

In his dressing gown, and without that vital first swig of coffee, he went on to the landing and up the stairs. The unreal den of his dead brother's room made the world real again. Its creation was an act of lunacy that pulled him with a soiled almost sexual immediacy back down the years and on to the landscape of childhood. Not that life in the small Staffordshire town had been all sunshine and lollipops. He spat in the firegrate: far bloody from it. His mother was forty when he was born, his father fifty, and they'd died within a year of each other when he was twenty-five, having given him the benefit of their dry hearts if nothing else.

His father, a small-time builder, had gone bankrupt just in time to retire, a hard old man who'd forced him out to work as soon as it was legal. The word 'legal' had been his ever-loving word: it was legal to do that, or it wasn't legal. He used it so often he'd stoop to any illegality he could get away with—a bald-headed man of middle height with grey eyes so piercing that people never took him seriously.

When Handley went to work at fourteen he had no time for his father. He didn't hate him. He just wanted to get out of his way, remembering him as a miserable creature, though it was no good feeling sorry for him, because while you did he'd kick you so hard you wouldn't get up for ten minutes. Handley slipped out one day and didn't see him till the lid was fastened on his coffin. His parents hadn't even loved each other, so how could they have been expected to love their children?

He had been particularly unobservant of his parents because they were so hard on him, which might explain why he was able to jettison their influence so painlessly. Later, the emptiness he found in rooting around the distant corners of his anguished mind drove him to painting—not in an attempt to discover himself, but to create a world in which it wasn't necessary to do so.

He sat on the swivel chair by the radio table, and suddenly felt afraid of this replica-room and the touchingly placed paraphernalia that had belonged to John who had never lived in it. John had burned down his real room in the Lincolnshire house, having meant it should no longer exist after he'd set off for Algeria. His suicide dated from that mad act—unable to live anywhere but in the room he could no longer go back to. So why perpetuate his memory with this homely shrine? Don't we trust ourselves to remember him? By keeping the room intact he was celebrating death, not John, because he distrusted his loving memories of him.

He walked to the window. He opened the curtains. Across the road, between two houses, were emerald meadows, and a glinting sluggish stream. John wouldn't have liked such scenery. He loved the wolds of Lincolnshire.

No one had loved him more than Handley. He was his one and only elder brother, that last real line that connected him to far-off Staffordshire. This mocked-up signals cabin, this faked hermit's cave, this phoney remembrance centre, had nothing to do with it. When you created your own ghosts there was little you could do to get rid of them.

He shook his head. The cigarette tasted foul before coffee and bread-and-butter. By the radio he lifted trays of nails and screws, a spirit-level and calipers, plumb-line and a pedometer, though John hardly ever walked, depth-gauge and spanners—his brother's beloved gear without which life would have been even emptier. Man must have his tools, his toys of reality, aids to tame the world yet keep it at a distance, and not get too enmeshed in its despondencies.

The cigar-box lid was held down by small tacks. From the radio-operator's odds and ends on the desk he took a one-bladed pen-knife, and forced it open. He swung the powerful lamp to it. There was nothing inside, and no amount of light could fill it. He felt a fool before turning angry. It was hard to move. He was rabid. The sweat came, as he let the lid fall. With a gun loose, the community was a death-trap.

He switched off the lamp, went over and closed the curtains. A shade of day still came in, light which didn't seem safe any longer. He sat on the bed and wondered what to do. His nature was to exaggerate everything, scare himself with the possibilities of disaster. The others thought that his bark was worse than his bite, and that he could never hold back what was on his mind, so for the moment he would say nothing, and hope to get some advantage from not letting Cuthbert know he'd found out about the gun.

He closed the door quietly. There was no reason to lock it anymore. Back in his room he dressed rapidly: underwear, a pair of corduroys, an old white shirt without the collar, waistcoat. Hunger would consume his chest-wall unless he got a mouthful soon.

Dawley had been up since seven to give Paul and Rachel their breakfasts and send them to school. He was glad of a day off from his Algerian travels, waiting in any case to read Shelley's notebooks and get a few quotations to light up his reasons for going there in the first place. The abortive attack on Laghouat, and his encounter with the snake-eaters, had no time scale joining them together. The days were bruised and broken from each other, so what better way of poulticing the narrative than by a few earnest observations from Shelley's truly revolutionary soul?

Handley was stubbled around the chin: 'It's flown. Where is he?'

'He got up to do some gardening.'

'Gardening? Cuthbert?'

He put a plate of scrambled eggs before him. 'With Dean. They're planting pot in a corner of the paddock, clearing the virgin lands for home consumption. It's a dirty business, really.'

Handley sat with head bowed, then looked up and began eating: 'A drug-crazed maniac with a gun! I should never have let him into the community.'

'You couldn't keep your own son out. Maybe he didn't take it. There are plenty of others. Ralph, for instance. Who knows?

Handley poured more coffee. 'I bloody well do. A father knows more about his son than he does about himself. I may be a mystery to myself, but I brought Cuthbert up from unconsciousness. I watched every gesture as it came out. He's got a wayward and villainous nature—though God knows where he gets it, because it's not from Enid, and it ain't me. It's something totally different. But he was always delighted to exaggerate my bad traits, mimicking me behind my back in the hope I'd fall into a pit and get swallowed whole. What have I done to make him like that? I was so taken up by my painting that I had no time except to clout him when he cheeked his mother. It's his way of getting his own back, I suppose. What a curse the family is. Where's the bread and butter?'

'We're trying to solve that problem by this community,' said Frank, passing it, 'though we won't feel the effect for twenty years.'

'It's just an idea for middle-aged people,' Handley said, 'this community. The young ones don't want it, and won't see the need of it till their own kids are grown up—by which time it's too late, like it is with me. Cuthbert's trying his best to ruin it. Ralph and Mandy want a nice little cottage thatched with daisies and buttercups so's they can be all lovey-dovey in their pervy way. Adam and Richard are just a couple of lazy bastards pounding out revolutionary ideas in a permanently non-revolutionary society in order to avoid working. That's not hearsay, it's realistic. It's costing me three hundred pounds a month to run this community, apart from what Myra puts in, so you can see what a bargain it is. It's not that I'm worried about being ruined, but at least a man might expect peace at such a price. I want to get on with my work. That's a natural desire, ain't it? Domestic life is society's secret weapon to stifle the artist. I've never had peace in my life, not with seven kids, but at least I don't want a disaster with that bloody gun on the loose. The idea of killing never appealed to me, especially when it comes too close to my own skin.'

Dawley always knew that Handley only let his sons play at revolution so that he could get on with his painting. If revolution ever became so real that he had no electric light or couldn't get razor-blades he'd be the first to turn against it. He wanted to paint just as most people wanted to work and live in peace, and as an artist he really did represent mankind in that respect. Volatile and unpredictable as he was, he still loved his family and tried to look after them, and if there was injustice on a larger scale he was the sort who would get up and do something about it. There was no doubt about that.

'I must have that gun back,' he said, 'and put it in a safe place where nobody can find it.'

Dawley set plates and cups in racks of the dish-washing machine: 'Ask Cuthbert point-blank what he's done with it.'

'He'd laugh in my face.'

Frank thought for a while. 'Why don't we call a meeting and read Shelley's notebooks? It'll break the ice, and might throw a hint on where the gun is. I don't like the thought of it being on the loose, either.'

Handley was puzzled. 'It's a zany idea, though I suppose it can't harm anybody.'

'The indirect approach,' Frank said. 'Uproar in the East, strike in the West. Everyone will be at their ease, lulled by interest in the notebooks. That'll be the time to pop the question.'

'It's too subtle,' Handley said, 'though it's better than nothing. I'd almost forgotten about the notebooks. It is time we had a look. Do you think there'll be much good in them?'

'You never know.'

Handley went to his studio, and Frank cleaned the kitchen. Not only would he use the material of Shelley's notebooks to pad out his narrative, but he needed to shore up his revolutionary enthusiasm, to point the difference between the true fighter for the freedom of the underprivileged, and that of a simple mercenary soldier who was paid for his actions by the excitement he got from it.

He was beginning to wonder whether it had been no more than a great screen to conceal his real feelings from himself and others. Only peace brought out the truth—which led him to see that Handley's attitude might easily be the right one.

Chapter Twenty-eight

Dean would follow Enid anywhere, beat down thistles even with his hands in order to be alone and out of the house with her at the same time.

But he wasn't making a trail, as in the picture painted by his self-esteem. He was walking behind, and letting her scythe the high thistles with a piece of stick, and tread them flat with her shoes. His own first version was still agreeable, as he watched her straight back, strong confident hips, and long hair only a few feet in front. He was never at ease in the house, even at meal-times. The family either did not like him, or thought him worthless because he was young and had no money.

Being among enemies he hated the house, and detested anyone who thought he did not matter. It was impossible to brush off such insults. By showing he didn't matter they were trying to get at him. He regarded himself as the most important person in the world, so they were wrong to think him insignificant, and insulting to let him know that they felt it.

The person who didn't treat him like a maggot was the one who mattered most in the community. Enid led him deeper into the paddock, wading through thistles, beyond the iris of any roving eye, trying to find the football that Paul had kicked this way—the second lost in a month. She wanted a stroll, and used it as an excuse. She'd seen

Dean already wandering, and when he spied her, he followed. It was like having a dog, especially since he didn't say much. It was strange to be with someone so silent, a young man younger than her eldest son. What did he want to follow her for? The question led her to wonder why she allowed him to. She supposed he needed to be near someone, even if only a few paces behind like a dog. He was so young he had the harmlessness of another woman.

'You wain't find anything,' he said. 'I expect the birds eat the footballs in half an hour. They love rubber.'

'It was leather.'

The hot sun's warmth was pleasant on top of her head and against her bare arms. She sat on the tree trunk felled across the corner, Dean a few feet away looking at her. She wondered sadly what he saw, while quite clear what she saw herself. The open weather of summer released the vitality of her soul. It was her time of well-being, so she was pleased when Dean said: 'You look good in the sun. It suits you.'

'How can you tell?' He had thought about her, anyway, though it was impossible not to tease him, he was so much a little dog. Even his face was like one, his low forehead, earnest eyes, small mouth, curly hair.

'I can tell.'

'But why?' Her further question put a shade of irritation over his features. Then they cleared as he said with a smile: 'Blonde women allus like the sun.'

It was amazing how, no matter what she saw, he saw himself as her equal, as one man to her woman. His remark warned her to take him seriously, but it was difficult because he took himself so seriously.

'Come and sit down here.'

He hesitated. When she tried to accept him as a grown-up, he distrusted her, because he had been fervently hoping she would do so. But he sat down, her offer being too good to miss, since you never knew what it might lead to. 'I'd like to live where there's sun all the time,' she said. 'But I don't suppose I ever shall.'

He pulled a piece of dusty bark from the tree. 'You ought to go on holiday.'

'I've got too much to do. Albert'd never want to.'

'On your own.'

He reached into his shirt pocket, and took out a loose cigarette that looked as if it had been through the last wash. 'Want a drag?'

'It'd knock me into a three-cornered stupor.'

He had a relaxed smile—which became a laugh, showing teeth discoloured but still whole. Lighting up, he blew smoke towards her.

'It smells nice,' she said. 'But don't waste it on me.'

He had been sober and nervous with her, and now wanted to relax by inhaling his lousy weed. Instead of fighting his way through such a mood he was taking a short cut. His stiff shyness had seemed slightly menacing, so in a way she was glad. A few minutes ago he'd seen her as someone she'd imagined she couldn't be any more to such a young man—which was more worrying than disturbing—though not much of either. She didn't know whether it was these thoughts or the pleasure of the warm sun that made her smile.

He caught the movement of her lips. 'Now you're laughin' at me'—the hard sullenness going as he puffed on the cigarette. 'You're the only one I like, in this place.'

'You're sharp,' she said, knowing she'd always been easy with people who had nothing to lose, and needed pulling up from the bottom—maybe like Albert in the early days.

'If it worn't for you they'd chuck me out.'

'They might not. We aren't that bad.' There was a quite fundamental shyness about him, she noticed, which made her wonder what he was getting at. He was like a child still, wheedling at her—as if wanting everything because he didn't yet know what exactly it was that he wanted. He would deliberately continue to want everything so that when he did decide what it was there'd at least be a chance of getting it. The groundwork would have been done. But she thought all young people were like that. It wouldn't be fair to give him too black a mark for it.

'Have a puff o' this,' he offered, as if the smoke were making him generous. 'You've got to have it sooner or later.'

She pushed his hand away. 'I don't like it.' Yet she was tempted, and he saw that she was, which satisfied him for the moment. 'You're turning everybody on with it. Why is that?'

'I just offer it 'cause I'm friendly. Anyway, they ask for it. I like to be friendly with everybody.'

He was sad, so undiscriminating and unprotected that she wondered how long it would last, whether he would grow up and become wary before it did him permanent harm. 'What if they don't like you?'

'I step aside.' He almost sang it, as if he'd used the phrase many times. But he wasn't so unconscious of his desires, for he made a clumsy movement to get hold of her wrist. 'I like you more than anybody. I've liked you ever since I saw you at the market trying to lift them baskets.'

She was frozen, so he drew his hand away without having to be told—which she hadn't meant him to, because there was obviously no harm in it. It was a gesture anybody could make, especially Dean, with his all-embracing friendliness which was difficult to be offended by. She wanted to reassure him by taking *his* hand, but didn't, suddenly knowing why she had stiffened in the first place.

'It's just that I love you,' he said, decisive now that she appeared uncertain. 'You're a real woman.'

She laughed at his earnestness, especially since his words could have no meaning. 'I'm married. I've got seven kids.'

He pressed the cigarette between his finger-ends, and threw it towards the corner of the paddock. 'You're beautiful.'

'You're a kid.'

'I'm not. I had a woman when I was fourteen.' It wasn't hard to believe. He had that furtiveness and persistence, and an underlying ineradicable self-confidence that stopped at nothing—a forceful attraction that few women might want to resist. He wasn't ugly, either, when a look came into his eyes that told him he might be getting somewhere. 'You want to get the most out of life while it lasts,' he said.

'What makes you think I'm not?'

He knocked his heels rhythmically against wood. 'I don't reckon anybody could enjoy life in this set-up.'

She never questioned it. Enjoyment hadn't been much of a problem. She liked life now and again. Who didn't? Hard times couldn't crush everything out of you. Albert had always been as good as he was able, and no doubt the same went for her. There were times when she wished she hadn't had so many kids, and moments when she could have done with none at all, but now she wouldn't want to be without them. And then this kid of eighteen comes along and makes her think she might not be enjoying life! What a cheek!

Yet he was right. She was forty-three, and the fact that the many years of life still to be lived would go on in the same old bickering way made her so depressed that often in bed at night the tears poured down her face. If her life didn't change it would come to an end—an unbearable thought.

'I can read it in your face,' he said, a renewal of charm on seeing that he had made her think.

It was amazing how the tricks with which people fought each other in marriage were there almost from the cradle. No girl would be lucky who married Dean. 'I'll get back and see how things are at the house. Mandy's cooking lunch—assisted by Frank. I keep an eye on them just in case.'

'I thought you liked being in the sun?'

'I do,' she smiled, feeling so much older and superior, 'I only enjoy it because I know it's got to stop.'

'You ought to travel south.'

'I'm not going anywhere. Come on.' She wanted him to lead a way through the thistles, because her legs were sore from them, but he was suddenly holding her, his lips on her cheeks. She was amazed at the strength of his arms when they went around her. He was as demanding as a baby in its primal urges, and his confidence foolishly led him to believe that she needed him with similar intensity, though for some reason he was afraid or unable to say so.

He was trying to force a knee between her thighs, and at the same time get at her lips. The fact that she wanted to hold him, but couldn't because his grip was too firm, gave her the strength to unravel him. He lost balance, and she pushed him so that his whole body went sprawling among the thistles.

Chapter Twenty-nine

Burning Shelley's notebooks made up for the hedgehog's death, though tears still plunged from Ralph's eyes, and his heart broke all over again, when he thought about it. But there was some consolation in those final black fumes that cleansed the world of paper and ink. Madness is a song that you cannot control.

When life was bearable, it wrought such change in him that people took notice. His timeless self-contained floating filled Handley with suspicion. An unhappy face suddenly at peace with the world threatened the equilbrium of Cuthbert's stomach. The pleasant alteration in her husband gave Mandy some happiness back, for she soon took such contentment in him as his normal behaviour.

But she never knew when he wasn't going to find a dead snail and flip his soul about that, and it was more painful expecting him to go off again than it had been waiting for him to recover from previous devastations. Yet at the moment of getting his reason back she was grateful at the unknowing goodness of the world.

Ralph latched the hose to the kitchen tap and, clad in Wellington boots, with the spurting nozzle in one hand and a huge sponge in the other, began swilling the Ford Rambler. Dean, by way of reinforcing Eric Bloodaxe as guardian of the gate, slept on the back seat as water combed its way up and down the closed windows. After its washing

Ralph would dry and polish it, a pleasant task that would take him as far as lunch.

Because nobody yet knew of his atrocious deed in burning the notebooks his fingers were itching for another kleptomaniac performance, but at the moment there was no significant item to send him purloining by back door or bedroom window. The stasis was intolerable, as if the earth were softening under his feet.

He leaned against the tailgate, pressing on his sponge. Water ran down the shining metal. The only final pleasure to Ralph would be a mind in which no mental sensations could make any mark. He had noticed that when on the point of attaining this difficult state one of the Handley mob was bound to sense it, and maliciously smash the oncoming mood of bliss before he could even taste it. From far back he had put up with something similar from his parents. Life was so constructed that you could never escape. It had sharp teeth, and all-round vision. Sanity was in being left alone, but Ralph also knew, though he rarely admitted it, that this was impossible. It confused and worried him that no one had yet discovered the burning of the notebooks. Such a vacuum brewed up a feeling of moral uncertainty which, if it were left too long, would make him feel guilty. And the guilt of an undiscovered crime was worse than that which came after being condemned for one.

Not that guilt of any sort was close enough to worry him. When Handley smiled from the kitchen door he was not put out, but faced it, as he always did, and as he had been brought up to do. Still, smiles and a pleasant word from Handley were not the best things for his peace of mind. Sharp words and insults steeled him, and those he could usually resist.

Handley switched off the tap and, when the hose dried up, took Ralph firmly by the elbow: 'Let's go for a stroll before lunch. It'll give us an appetite. The rain can swill the car down later.'

Ralph agreed, so as not to appear intimidated. They walked on to the road, father and son-in-law of equal height, though Ralph was bulkier, an unusual sight of them together. Ralph had a sick feeling that Handley might be forcing him out for a walk so as to question him about the notebooks. He was well aware that Handley may have discovered the loss but kept it quiet while trying to trace them.

'How do you feel these days?' Handley asked.

'I had a headache this morning.'

'Regarding the community, I mean?'

'All right,' Ralph answered guardedly.

'I suppose it bothers you, not having much work to do?'

'Not really.'

'It would me,' Handley said. 'But then, I'm working-class—to use a common middle-class expression—while your parents are rich Lincolnshire farmers who made so much money they spent a lot of it training you how to be idle without going mad.'

Ralph stopped worrying, since Handley was insulting his father and mother instead of him. They passed the shop, where dumpy Mrs Harrod, Myra's char when her husband was alive, gave Handley a baleful stare as she walked by with a basket of cornflakes and tinned carrots. Handley and his clan had not only spoiled Myra and ruined her house, they had also given the village a bad name. He was a well-known painter who had been on TV—once—and had his photo in the papers, but he didn't act like a gentleman. When he'd first come to the village the local publican thought him an ex-poacher who had won a fortune on the pools.

'Idle people get into mischief,' he went on. 'Their feet itch. They can't sleep at night.'

'Do you think I'm idle?' Ralph asked, mildly.

'Not *bone*-idle.' They passed the church. 'You're willing but, like most members of the community, except me, you don't have enough to do. That'll be its undoing, I fear.'

'We work more now on domestic chores,' Ralph said.

'Getting you down? Well, it is me, as well, but don't worry: the more it does the sooner you reach bottom and shoot up again. If it goes on much longer though I think I'll get flu.'

Ralph's dislike of his father-in-law was so intense that it gave him the alarming feeling that Handley was almost human after all. Sensing it now, he had more reason than ever to beware of these little confidences which could lead to an onslaught impossible to resist.

After the watercress beds Handley took a path going left, where the stream widened and turned into a long shallow lake whose northern bank was reedily indistinct. Hills rose on either side. In front was a wood, and to the right, a little beyond it, was Gould House, whose tall chimney-stacks were just visible above the dark green. He paused by a wooden gate through which they were not supposed to go. The lake was blue, as if the clear sky had fallen in it, and a pair of swans floated placidly at the far end. 'England's a beautiful country,' he said, 'when you don't think about it.'

Ralph nodded, following through and closing the gate. 'I need fresh air now and again,' Handley said, 'to stop that paint scarring my lungs. When I was a kid my mother thought I was going consumptive, but my natural talent for life soon scotched that one. I was bone-fit when I joined the army, not like some of the knock-kneed pigeon-chested boss-eyed flat-footed blokes straight out of the dole queue. God knows what they thought they were going to fight for, but a lot of 'em went willingly enough, bless 'em!'

They passed a wooden jetty and boat house, a rowing boat moored inside. 'I'll have his trout one day. Good for breakfast. Plus a couple of rabbits for lunch, and a few pheasants for supper.'

Ralph walked by his side when the path allowed, and wondered what he was getting at with his irrelevant chatter.

'They were called up to fight for land-owning bastards like Gould.' He spat a green shoot of grass. 'But I suppose they had to fight because the Germans would have been worse if they'd got here. Not that I believe in violence any more,' he said, taking a flat stone from his pocket and idly skimming it—but with swift force—at a rabbit that bolted from behind a tussock of grass and made for the bushes.

The rabbit ran right into it, and was stunned. Handley took it by the legs, slamming the blade of his hand against the back of its neck. 'I wasn't a gunner in the artillery for fuck-nothing,' he gloated, pushing the dead animal inside his coat. 'We all learn a bit in life, even if it's only how to get meat for the pot now and again.'

Ralph was enraged, blood swamping his temples. The vile act had only taken a few seconds. Its sheer unthinking speed made it impossible to interrupt and tell Handley not to do it.

'What's the matter?' he demanded, seeing him pale, immobile and furious.

'You shouldn't have done that,' he stammered.

'It was too good to miss.'

There were tears on his cheeks. 'We aren't so poor that we have to come poaching.'

'You don't like seeing animals killed,' Handley scoffed, 'is that it?

They all are, you know. I've seen you clearing your plateful of meat three times a day for months on end, and you don't blubber about it then.'

Ralph's look of bewilderment and pity for all human and animal kind changed to one of horror at the justice of the argument. Handley softened at his distress: 'Don't worry. It didn't know what got it. If we all die as quick there'll be nothing to complain about. And to tell you the truth, I didn't think I had a chance in hell of hitting it.'

'But you threw the stone.'

'By instinct. I didn't mean to kill.'

They walked back the way they had come. 'I hate violence.'

Handley stopped, gripped Ralph's arm, and stared directly into his yellowy-brown eyes. He eats so much he's turning liverish. 'Do you? Are you sure you do?'

'I do,' Ralph said, so that anyone but Handley would believe him.

'What have you done with that Smith and Wesson pea-shooter that you took from the cigar box in John's room?'

Ralph did not know whether to feel relieved that he wasn't being questioned about Shelley's papers, or shocked at being accused not only of what he hadn't stolen but of something that he might have laid hands on had he known about it. The resulting fusion of expressions puzzled Handley, who nevertheless repeated his question in blunter terms: 'Where's that gun, you thieving magpie?'

'I don't know what you mean,' he protested, to the jutting face smelling of aftershave and strong cigars.

'You'd better get it back, or it'll come up at the next meeting, and you'll be thrown out of the community. You'll starve then.'

'I haven't got it,' Ralph shouted, so that Handley began to think he really hadn't, though he knew better than to trust his cries of innocence. Neither of them noticed Mr Gould, the owner of the land on which they were trespassing, come up till he was barely a hundred yards away. He was a tall spare fair-haired man of sixty with a small mouth, narrow watery blue eyes, and a long chin. Ralph was embarrassed and wanted to walk away, but couldn't because he didn't care to be impolite.

'Good morning, Handley,' Gould said sharply.

'Morning, Gould,' Handley said.

He knocked a briar aside with his stick. 'Out for a stroll on such a fine day?'

Handley looked him in the eye. 'Who can say it'll last?'

'Still painting pictures?' Gould had heard about him from his butler, but hadn't met him before, though he'd seen him several times from a distance. It was good to have an artist in the village.

'They keep rolling off,' Handley said amiably. 'Do you want to buy one? It's a good hedge against inflation, though I can see you wouldn't want one for that reason with such a nice slice of good old England under your heels.'

Gould laughed in a relaxed manner. 'I'll call in one day to have a look.'

'Any time,' Handley said. 'You might see something you like. Drop by. No formality—really.'

'I see you have one of my rabbits?'

'Knocked it down with a stone. It tried to eat my bootlaces, and I couldn't have that.'

'They're vermin. Impossible to get rid of. The farmers complain and try to exterminate them.'

'Rabbits are a multiplication table.' Handley turned to Ralph: 'This is my son-in-law. I was showing him the landscape. Very pretty around here.'

Gould nodded to Ralph, as if thinking he was hardly worth it. 'Still, must get back,' Handley said.

'Close the gate then, there's a good man.'

Handley and Ralph went on. 'Not a bad stick,' Handley said. 'He did well in the War, so I hear. Lost his whole battalion at Cassino. There were only sixty of 'em, though. The other five hundred went sick the day before the attack.'

Ralph spoke bitterly, and the serious tone of it surprised Handley. 'You've no respect for anybody.'

'That's as maybe,' Handley snapped back, 'but you can tell me where that gun is. Remember?'

'I don't know,' Ralph wailed, and before he could dodge it Handley felt a hard blow on the shoulder which almost pushed him down.

I should have known better, he thought later, than trust a man who has the doctrine of non-violence festering away in his heart. Timid and mild, he had a gorilla lurking inside, and not very deep in at that.

Ralph came up for a second lunge, but Handley had steadied himself, and dodged it easily, so that his large form lumbered by. In self-defence, though he wasn't hurt, Handley thought he'd better do something, so put his foot in a sort of kick, and caused him to trip in his clumsy Wellingtons. Ralph didn't fall at once, only ran more quickly because of it, which took him towards the bank of the lake. Handley saw what would happen and, with swift and compassionate energy, leapt at his flailing arm, and pulled him round so that he fell into the grass only a foot short of the water.

Ralph brushed mud and grass from his trousers. 'I'm sorry,' he said morosely.

'So you didn't take that gun?'

'No.'

'That leaves only one person.'

'I expect it's Cuthbert,' Ralph said when they reached the gate. He held it, and closed it after they had passed.

'What makes you say so?' If Ralph didn't claim the credit for a robbery, his suspicions as to who had done it could be worth something.

'I'm not sure. I'll find out, if you like.'

'Can I trust you?' Handley said, feeling a new respect for his erring son-in-law because he wasn't shy of a fight if driven too far.

'I won't mention it to the others. I'll see what I can do.'

Handley, though uneasy, would take on any ally to help him find that wandering firearm. When danger threatened he was a man who still had the ability to trust his senses.

Chapter Thirty

Handley went into the paddock for a stroll because he didn't know where to put the next stroke of paint. The mass, the shape, the theme and the colour were slipping out of his hindsight.

It was no simple situation, he knew—padding through the thistles smoking a cigar. If somebody had told him a month ago he'd be worrying about John's missing side-arm it would have been laughable, but right now he wanted to get far from the house because, being the prime voice and mover in it, it seemed that whoever had the gun was only waiting for an opportunity to level it at his head and splash his brains against the nearest wall.

He'd always believed it good and necessary to live with his own full-blown unique ideas, and fatal to go by anybody elses. Yet this limitation had made him rancorous and self-opinionated, and showed off notions that he did have in a poor light, at the moment curtailing any imaginative ideas as to where the stolen gun might be.

It was like living in a state of war, and no artist (nor any man, either) could give of his talented best in such conditions. Only he, and whoever had the gun, knew that this war existed. The others still lived in a blessed zone of peace, and while he wished them luck for it, knew it couldn't last much longer.

He walked along the paddock hedge. Brambles sent tentacles into the grass and thistles, so he thought he'd come with the clippers later and rake them back. Such work kept his muscles hard at a time when they might be of use.

Regretting his scarcity of ideas at how to get the gun from Cuthbert, or discover who otherwise had it, he knew at the same time that hugging things to himself might not be the wrong tack for him. His instinct hadn't let him down yet. He needed infinite patience, and to keep his nerve while the peril developed, so as to wander slowly around the house and grounds, mulling over everything in the surety that some clue or solution would come to him. He was old enough and sly enough to try this way, though he was far from easy living under the menace of it.

Dawley's slit-trench, long neglected by the children, had soily water in the deepest part, and grass had grown on the parapet thrown in front. A few yards behind, concealed by tall thistles, lay a space that had recently been flattened. Someone had cut back the brambles, pulled them free, and dragged enough of them out by the roots to reach soft grass underneath. The briars had been clipped at wide parts of the creepers, so it was not the work of a child. What's more, the cuts were pale, and no more than a few days old.

It was an efficiently cleared and well-hidden love nest. Standing in it, and judging by the flattened area, whoever used it had done so in the last day or two. It was strange to find such a nest in any compound inhabited by him and his family. Weren't there enough dry and comfortable beds in house, caravans, or garage-flat? Not for this clandestine bit of sexual knockabout, evidently.

He wondered if it had been constructed by Cuthbert for his liaison with Maricarmen. He had the strength to cut the briars, and also the inclination, since he seemed to be in love to the fatuous extent of promising to supply her with a gun. Yet why such secrecy, unless the gun had already changed hands? If they were in love it seemed only in order to make war—on him, on the house, on the community. Life suddenly felt short and savage, a bit of string with both ends going nowhere.

His lingering fear came back. He laughed at it, for he'd always known that life had no meaning beyond the thick fence of his family and the spreading avenues of his painting. All the interest in violent revolution was only a wayward hope of blasting down whatever hemmed him in. He wouldn't know what to do if suddenly set free, so lived with the fact that there was no way out, forgetting it most of the time so that he could work and not go crazy.

He got on his knees, no call to do so except instinct, which was reason enough. He looked more closely at the grass, and then into the stumps of briar on either side. He swore, and drew his hand back when a thorn stuck in his finger, the pain pushing a dome of blood after it. He liked to bleed, though not too much, and pressed it into the cuff of his white shirt.

He picked a cigarette-end from under the briar, not an ordinary nub, but one so small it had been smoked to the bone. The plot thickens, he thought, like chicken soup with barley. Cuthbert smokes pot, but he wouldn't be doing it out here with Maricarmen because she's too much of a straight-laced revolutionist to let him. Her knickers would catch fire at the merest whiff of it.

So who was Dean's lady-friend? Who had driven him to fashion out his love-pad with the utmost cunning of his squirrel-brain? When there was a mystery to be solved Handley lost his sense of humour, as if the only way to get to the bottom of it were through the swamp of his self-esteem.

Who indeed would lay here with Dean, that scrag-end of a William Posters who had stumbled so unerringly on a cushy billet? He sucked blood from his finger, and walked away more thoughtfully than when he'd come.

It was obvious that the two large platters of *hors d'oeuvres* for lunch should have a centre column of salami, with black olives and spring onions spread to left and right. What other art was left to a woman? It got more like Mrs Beeton every day.

Salads were made with lettuces pulled out of the garden. Dishes of potato, cheese cubes, tomatoes and cucumber were laced with mayonnaise. For the main course there was veal in the oven, and water was heating on the Aga for rice. Fruit salads were fortified with muscatel—helped down by double cream for dessert.

It wasn't a special day, just her turn on the new domestic schedule, and Myra was nothing if not conscientious, intelligent and imaginative, working with a free hand because Dean was amusing Mark by playing the car radio.

The new arrangement had simply increased her discontent, the slight let-up giving her a glimmer of wider freedom. She even began to regret that the community was lodged in her house, for if it had been at somebody else's she could have walked away without deflating it completely. Yet she couldn't gainsay that this style of life had grown on her, and it was impossible to imagine what her existence would be without it.

Why were all arguments good, even the bad ones? Domestic slavery had palled, but at the beginning, when there was a real sense of community among them, she hadn't noticed it. Now she sensed the silences that lay so thick around, people pairing off, and secrets brewing up.

Maybe the conflicts that had brought them together were healing, or going underground, which meant that it was settling down and not, as she feared, in danger of blowing apart. She was fundamentally pessimistic, but hid it by a generosity that made everyone think they could not do without her. The pessimism remained—the inability to make up her mind—but the work she did was doubly blessed in that it benefited her even more than the others.

She was reluctant to investigate too far, yet saw it as a miracle that the community had held together so long, being a marriage of such disparate characters. But she believed in it still, and would do her best to keep it firm, even if it meant the eternal organising of the kitchen. And if by such speculation she discovered flaws in the mechanics of the community, it was only so that she would be able to stop any rift in time.

It was obvious that Maricarmen had been weeping, and was struggling not to show it. A handkerchief grasped in her hand was no bigger than a marble. Her breasts were gently moving, her blank stare still fixed by some shock. Cuthbert took cutlery and plates from the cupboard to set the dining-room table.

'What is it?' Myra asked, but Maricarmen lifted a platter of food to follow him: 'I'll tell everyone at lunch.'

Myra was puzzled by such a melodramatic pose, wondering whether it could be so serious if they had to wait till lunch to hear. She sent a chute of rice into the water: why had she never before seen how stern and discontented Maricarmen's face could be?

The sky was darkening, as if thunderstorms promised by the radio were about to grumble on the horizon. Maricarmen put two olives on her plate, then chewed at one as if it were a stone. Handley was the first to comment on her distress: 'Is the weather giving you a headache?'

She was silent.

'You might as well tell everybody,' Cuthbert said.

Handley took salami, and pushed it with bread and butter into his mouth. 'Anything bothering you?'

'Give her time to speak,' Enid said. Dean turned to make sure that Mark, perched on his high chair, spooned up his food without spilling it.

Maricarmen stood. 'I was cleaning my room just now, and pulled out Shelley's trunk to vacuum under the bed. It didn't seem heavy, and when I opened it I saw it was almost empty. Someone has stolen the notebooks.'

'If you've been robbed, the community's been robbed.' That was all Handley could say. There was some devil loose, that had taken the gun, and now the precious notebooks. He wanted to stand but didn't think he'd be safe on his feet. He was being pushed under by forces outside his control.

'You've stolen them,' Maricarmen said accusingly, a look of misery on her face. 'You deceived me into bringing them. Shelley wouldn't have been tricked.'

Dawley threw down his knife and fork. Everyone looked in his direction. 'Just because there's one mad dog running loose there's no need to brand everybody.'

'We were going to do research on them,' Adam said, trying to feel the enormous loss of it. 'They'd have been priceless.'

'You talk as if they've been buried or burned,' Handley said. 'But I'll find them if I have to take the house and grounds apart, stick by bloody stone. I'll not touch another bit of paint till they're found. So get plenty of grub down you, because after coffee we're going to form into search parties. We'll leave nothing unturned.'

'I know it's too late,' Maricarmen wept, tears on the soft skin of her cheeks.

Enid stood behind and took her hand. 'They'll be found. Albert would have been a policeman if he hadn't become a painter!'

Ralph felt as if an enormous stone had been lifted from his heart. After suffering a slow-burning attack of asthma and indigestion in the last few days he now, suddenly and miraculously, found the oppression gone. They could spend ten years looking for the notebooks, but all the perverted revolutionary data written in them had gone up in holy smoke to England's blue air.

The rice and veal came, and the news had certainly blighted no appetites. 'We'll find who took them,' Handley said, 'and whoever was bloody responsible will be publicly booted out never to return. By God, I'll know who it is. But as we're on the subject of thievery some light-handed lunatic has nicked the revolver and ammunition from John's room.'

Enid turned pale, and shouted in a frightened voice: 'How long have you known?'

'A while.'

'You should have called the police,' she said. 'Why have you been so tight-lipped about it? Do you want to get us killed?'

'I thought somebody had taken it for a few sporting potshots with bottles in the woods. Or that it had been mislaid and would turn up. But now that the notebooks have been snatched I think things are getting a bit more serious—shall I say? I'm putting one and two together.'

Cuthbert looked on at the ants-nest he had kicked over, worried that Handley would suspect his uncontrollable silence. Giving in to a purely nervous twitch he smiled, then turned his head away too quickly. Dawley, hating the reason behind Cuthbert's smile, saw him as a man without honesty or generosity, a carcass of plot and counter-plot, out to do what damage he could to all and sundry because it was his only form of amusement or feeling.

Then he despised himself for such thoughts, and was angry at Cuthbert for making him have them, aware that he might be no better than Cuthbert if he were thus a prey to his diabolical twists. He had tried to be friendly but it was impossible. His amicable remarks were seen as weakness, for a smile to Cuthbert was an insult that had to be avenged.

Cuthbert surprised Mandy by offering her a cigarette. His look had produced the desired result of hatred and confusion in Dawley—not very difficult since those who were dull and honest, and therefore strong, were easily broken down. But Dawley was the lynchpin of the whole rotten fabric of both family *and* community, so he had a grander fate in store for him than a disdainful turning away of the head. Dawley was the idol of the family now that Uncle John was no longer alive, a guerrilla-fighting idiot who had come to his throne like any upstart king—over the dead body of Myra's husband, of Shelley, and of Uncle John himself. Cuthbert often saw events in such medieval shifts of power.

He had worked out the trio of deaths with Maricarmen, always returning to the fact of how Dawley had 'forced' Shelley into Algeria, so that Shelley had died of gangrene. Once when Dawley was out for a walk he had strolled into the caravan and read the manuscript in which Dawley admitted guilt at Shelley's death. He had not claimed a similar credit with Uncle John—and in truth he couldn't be blamed for it—but Cuthbert had only been interested in Shelley's unnecessary demise, which he whispered to Maricarmen in her room at night, burying his poison into her undying Iberian righteousness.

'If I'd got that gun I'd sell it,' Mandy joked, to whom the disappearance of both gun and papers was of absolutely no importance.

'When I get my hands on it,' Handley said, 'I'll take the bloody thing to the middle of Gould's Lake and drop it where it can't cause any bother.'

'Like King Arthur's sword,' Adam laughed. 'Maybe a hand'll come up and grab it.'

'And fire a few shots,' Richard giggled, 'before pulling it under for good.' They laughed at the joke, as if the deeper the trouble the more light-hearted they became. Maricarmen again doubted the probity of this community she'd been trapped into joining. They gave you refuge, showed what good hearts they had, spouted of ideals to lull you into safety, and even into feeling affection for them—when, without warning, you saw them laugh together as if they were wolves who had drawn you into their den by posing as human beings.

Enid was the only person whom she trusted, and felt something close to love for, yet given the jungle-logic of this house she was the one who should be suspected of stealing the notebooks. It was enough to drive you mad—unless you did quickly what you had come for and then got far away from the place. She would keep silent till they recovered the notebooks. Then she would kill Dawley, and go back to Spain, where life was perhaps better than the chaos around her.

Chapter Thirty-one

It seemed strange to Handley that Cuthbert should volunteer to wash the kitchen floor when he could selfishly leave it for the next day's shift, but he was out of the door and half-way across the yard to look for a bucket in the garage before he could call him back.

The rain had spent itself—after laying pools of water which Cuthbert jumped across so as not to get his slippers soaked. Myra's dead husband George, a man of high standards and much dexterity, had spent a few Saturdays excavating a repair pit in the garage floor, giving the rectangular hole a lid of two neat doors which closed it off completely.

Cuthbert blessed him for it, got into the Morris Traveller parked above, and let down the handbrake. He'd planned on doing it in a leisurely fashion, but also with desperate hurry if necessary. The floor was on a faint slope, and he sweated as the car rolled clear of the trap doors. Half-way out of the garage, he noisily yanked up the handbrake ratchet. They were still too busy in the dining-room, deciding who would search where, to hear him. Minor decisions were swamped in such time-wasting debate that three hundred years would be needed to live a full life under such conditions. Only a guiding brain to give firm orders—even if occasionally the wrong ones—would get any good out of such an organisation.

He pulled up the doors and leapt into the pit, where Shelley's notebooks in a plastic sack had lain since he switched them for a false lot which his brother-in-law had incinerated in the paddock. Poor Ralph, he thought, had lived with the triumph and guilt of having burned them, while still leaving him the means by which to destroy Dawley and the community for good.

The bag seemed heavier than when he'd first dragged it from the garage and let it drop there. He pulled and sweated before it eased up the side. Time was not with him. The discussions in the house might end, and a search party wonder what he was up to. Not that he didn't have a good reason for tidying the garage and 'accessory spaces'—a good phrase, appealing to any community heart—on his duty-day.

His luck held, and the bag was by his feet. He got back into the car, and let it roll right out of the garage. For a full minute it had been unobserved in its suspicious position, and now he pulled on the brake and went back to use more strength on the bag. He didn't fancy himself as a toter of bales and humper of sacks, but had enough muscle in his arms to perform all that was called for.

Using the Morris to cover him from the house, he went across to the caravan, where Dawley had his quarters, and began stuffing the notebooks under the bed. It was difficult to stop them slipping out, there were so many, but soon they stayed hidden—yet not hard to find.

He dropped the sack in a corner of the garage. Picking up the bucket he was supposed to have come for, he ambled to the house, expecting to be met by people setting off in all directions. They hadn't yet finished coffee.

'We were waiting for you,' Handley said. 'You can cast your eyes over my studio. As for the rest of us—the details are all worked out. Maricarmen and Dean don't search anywhere because they don't know the ins and outs like the rest of us.'

She stood by the window, pale, but smiling now, convinced at last that her loss was being taken seriously. Cuthbert wanted to go and hold her, but preferred to be cool till his plans had worked themselves out. Walking back to his accustomed place at the table he folded his arms truculently: 'I'm not rummaging anywhere. Who'll clear up the squalid mess from lunch?'

'What's the matter?' Handley demanded. 'Gone conscientious about your duty-day all of a sudden? Are you trying to hide something?'

His face reddened. 'Why should I join this farce? It's nothing to do with me. I've never known anything so stupid.'

'Listen, you emotional juggernaut,' Handley cried, 'those notebooks have got to be found, not to mention the gun. I expect you to realise that. I suppose you're playing awkward because you think it's a black mark on the community, and that makes your rabbit-heart jump with joy. But Maricarmen is a guest, and she's been robbed, and it's bad for the family if they're not found. Don't you see that?'

Cuthbert sat down, afraid to go on standing for fear his knees would shake. His father seemed absolutely sincere in what he said—as usual. Maricarmen picked up a tray from the dresser and stacked cups and saucers on it: 'I'll stay behind and clear up lunch.'

'All our problems can be tackled and solved,' Handley smiled, 'with a bit of goodwill.'

Cuthbert was becoming uneasy at what he had set going, a feeling of exhilaration and potent terror—held well down for the moment. His father was right. The family honour was at stake, though being his father, and unscrupulous to the end, he touched exactly the nerve to put uncertainties into Cuthbert's scheme of things. His father was rotten, but was nevertheless right. The damned community had blasted them all, and Cuthbert had been trying to destroy it from the beginning because the sort of family he had been born into had set him against it. He might accidentally end by destroying the family as well. Had that been his intention all along? His head spun. Who was to know how deep and far back this terrible corkscrew went?

If he spoke out now, that he had put the notebooks in Dawley's caravan, that he had already given the gun and ammunition to Maricarmen, then peace would return and let them go back to living again. He was strong enough to set the machine in action, but too weak to stop it. Vanity wouldn't let him tell what he had done. He would appear a fool, and be scorned for the rest of his life. He would lose what love Maricarmen had for him if he didn't give everything up. In her, with both strength and weakness, he could live and find himself, something which mattered to him at last. All he had to do was get the gun back before she killed Dawley. 'When do we begin?' he asked.

'That's my son!' Handley called, really happy now that this petty issue of Shelley's lost notebooks was turning out as he wanted it to. Cuthbert waited till no one was in the room except Maricarmen, who stayed to clear up the pots and debris. 'I want that gun back.'

'Be quiet,' she said, 'Mandy will hear you.'

He went into the hall. Mandy was searching the cupboards with a bored air. He went back to the dining-room: 'I want that gun.'

Her mouth was set hard. 'What do you mean?'

'Go and get it for me.'

She set the tray down, and stood before him. 'Why don't you look for the notebooks?'

'I want the gun back.'

She smiled, and kissed him lightly, without an embrace, a mockery of whatever feeling he wanted her to have for him: 'You think they'll find the gun as well? Don't worry. I've put it where nobody can.'

'Are you sure?'

'Of course.'

His manner alerted her when he demanded: 'Where?'

His expression was tense, his voice about to break—she thought—into hysteria or tears. His pale face was not quite clean, as if he had been sweating. 'It's safe,' she said.

'Where is it?'

She had no intention of telling him—stacking plates and cutlery on her tray. He grabbed her arms: 'I want that gun.'

'You're hurting me.'

He knew he was. 'I'll twist your arm off if you don't hand it over.'

'You gave it to me.'

'I want it back.'

She snatched herself from his grip. 'You don't need to be afraid. I told you what it was for.' Her voice was breaking, too.

'I know what you want to do,' he whispered, but not daring to say it. He went silently to the hall and looked into the lounge. Mandy was sitting in an armchair reading a copy of *Nova*, so engrossed that she obviously had no intention of going on with her search. They wouldn't be overheard.

'Why did you give it to me, then?' Maricarmen asked in a normal voice.

'I didn't know till afterwards what you wanted it for.'

She looked at him, her face as he'd seen it in the railway carriage after their meeting at Dover. 'I can't trust you,' she said quietly. 'And you won't trust me. If you loved me you'd trust me.'

'You don't give me the feeling that I can,' he said, knowing it was useless to hide anything from her. 'But I still love you. I always shall.

But I must know where the gun is. Give it back to me. I'll let you have it when you go to Spain.'

'Search your father's studio. Who knows what you'll find there?'

'Nothing,' he snapped, 'and you know it.'

'Who do you think has stolen the notebooks?'

He laughed, and forced out words he'd no intention of saying: 'I expect Ralph burned them on his bonfire.'

'You're lying,' she cried. 'Ralph would never steal anything.'

He hid his smile. 'You think not?'

Her eyes were half closed: 'You know where they are. If you didn't you'd already be searching your father's studio.'

'I don't,' he said. 'But I'm lazy, and don't believe in wasted effort. My father hasn't had anything to do with taking them. He's not that sort of man—whatever else he is. I stayed behind to ask for the gun back.'

'I'm not giving it up.'

The door clicked. 'You two sound as if you're having a lovers' tiff,' Mandy said scornfully. 'Why don't you get married so that you can really fight?'

Maricarmen walked into the kitchen and Cuthbert followed. 'Brew me some coffee while you're at it,' Mandy called. 'Looking for them notebooks has made me as thirsty as a dying camel.'

'Get off your fat arse,' Cuthbert said, 'and make it yourself.'

She came into the kitchen and sat on a stool, saying venomously: 'I'd love to see you get married. Why don't you?'

'Shut up,' he shouted, standing over her with his fist lifted, a terrifying and pleasurable desire to batter her to the end of his strength. But his cowardice got the better of him. There were some things which were too open to do.

Her face looked as if a bottle of crimson ink had been poured into her head. 'Something's burning you,' she sneered, a smile following. 'What have you been up to?'

'Leave her alone,' Maricarmen said. 'Go and search the studio, and leave us together.'

Chapter Thirty-two

Dean felt internally injured on being told not to take part in the search, saw it as a positive slur on his good character. He brooded on what a shame it was that no one trusted such an easygoing person as himself.

He couldn't understand what Handley's motives were, and was shocked that after so many weeks the community still didn't have confidence in him. If Handley had shown that he could trust him Dean would not have considered stealing anything. Since arriving in the community, and imagining he was thought to be as reliable as any other member, he hadn't laid hands on a thing that wasn't his own.

It didn't pay to get humpy, because it stopped you smiling and staying on good terms with the whole wide world around you. But when people didn't trust him there was no telling what he would do.

During his threading-and-bobbing days in the factory he'd been on the best of terms with the women workers, and they liked him because he'd always got a smile and sometimes a fag for them. On slack days he'd go down to the basement where George the mechanic had his workroom of tools and gauges, and talk with him and drink his tea for as long as he thought he wouldn't be missed upstairs. He called him 'Engineer' which made George smile because he'd been a stoker in the navy till he was sunk in the Atlantic and got oil on the chest.

The square room whose benches were lit by long bars of strip lighting seemed separate from the rest of the factory, warm and cosy with pipes running along three of the walls, turning and coiling in and out, elbows and junctions and U-bends carrying their water and power and steam, various dials and clock faces showing pressures and current which George glanced at now and again to see that all was faultlessly running. He was a medium-sized man with a pale face and short hair still black for his age, and a pipe set in his teeth. Even the foul twist he smoked was a comfort to Dean as he took the bacon sandwich that was offered and slowly munched it.

The factory wasn't too unpleasant, seeing as how you had to earn a living, but the foreman didn't trust him, and so trouble was always simmering. Dean was generally hardworking enough never to let it come to a head, while in his wisdom the foreman realised that if he chucked Dean out he might easily get somebody worse, and then have to put up with him because he'd be afraid of getting somebody worse still.

Dean gave in his notice one Friday night and left a week later. Everybody was sorry to see him go, even the foreman, but when a William Posters had to move nothing could stand in his way, because it was his blood that spoke. Admitted, he hadn't yet come far from Nottingham, but it looked like he'd be pushing on soon, away from this community, because the first clear sign that he wasn't trusted had just been given.

He walked upstairs to see what progress there was, thinking he wouldn't like to be in the boots of whoever nicked those notebooks, because a family like this would rend him or her in pieces, even if it turned out to be one of their nearest and dearest—which it surely must.

The only person he liked was Enid, the woman and mother and wife who was so beautiful he was always wanting to tell her he loved her in the hope that she'd let him kiss her. But he was afraid to say too much, or make too many moves, in case he offended her and she too turned against him. You never could tell with such a mob.

Through an open door on the first floor he saw Myra pushing a bed back to the wall. He went one flight up and into the room where Enid was, which belonged to Maricarmen who was arguing downstairs with Cuthbert.

Enid heard him, and closed the cupboard she was looking in.

'Any luck?'

Her face had a worried expression. 'I expect they aren't in the house or anywhere near it.'

'You shouldn't let it bother you.'

'It's bound to, isn't it? Especially the gun.'

'Well, not so much, then.' He looked at her across the bed, thinking that her face had got slightly thinner since first meeting.

'A thing like this could be the end of our community experiment,' she said, sitting down.

'Be a shame if it is.'

She smiled at his unexpected concern. She was touched, and liked him for it. 'I'm always sorry when something breaks up. When my brother-in-law went away and the house caught fire, it was terrible. It turned us into refugees, and I still don't know why it did.'

She felt at the end of her tether, and didn't know what to do. It seemed as if she could only wait for a catastrophe to change her life so completely that whatever happened would be for the better. Things couldn't go on as they were, and that was a fact. She was stuck in the blackest of cul-de-sacs with Albert, worse than it had ever been—and it had been bad at times. Yet the diversion of the notebooks, and the necessity of looking for the gun, had in a strange way lightened her mood. It was this slight sense of relief that made her smile at Dean, and suddenly enjoy seeing him there.

He was a child, really, or only a youth (if she were honest with herself) but the protectiveness she had felt on first seeing him in Hitchin market had turned into something that she could not define.

He was the age of her own children, and she remembered needing to hold them lovingly when they were like him, but not being able to because they wouldn't want it and because it would do them no good. But though it had been impossible with them, it certainly wasn't out of the question with Dean who, after all, was not her own son and so needn't be afraid of it.

'I hope it don't happen,' he said, breaking the silence. 'It's a nice community. I could gather moss in this place, but I don't want to stay much more, or else I'll never leave. I wouldn't a bin here so long if it hadn't a bin for you.'

He went around the bed and sat by her.

'Don't go too soon, then,' she said.

The bed creaked when he put an arm over her shoulder, ice melting in his stomach for fear she'd shrug it away. He didn't know whether to be glad or afraid, but felt no doubt as to what he wanted. 'You ought to come with me. We can travel away together.'

'You're mad,' she told him, but smiling happily.

He laughed softly, as if they were getting into each other's secrets at last. 'I know. But it's great, being mad like that!'

She kissed him lightly on the cheek, and he looked at her, holding himself back. He never had difficulty in believing his luck, but he always saw an end to it. So he looked at her face and kept it in view till she lowered her eyes modestly (that's how it seemed to him, and he was right) and turned her head away. These gestures made her more beautiful to him, vivid features enhanced and increased by all he knew of her: her good ripe age (though she wasn't too old), and her seven children (whom he hoped she wouldn't bring with her), and even her husband (whom he prayed would walk out one day soon and conveniently never come back), and her life and long experience of being a mother (which he wanted turned entirely on to him).

His grey eyes had a powerful animal stare, and she could barely meet them, yet knew it was her own heat that put such intensity into his stare. He was more of a man than she thought, and she wondered how she had got into this situation of him tightly clasping her on the bed. But the heat became greater when she saw him also as even more of a child than he was, and when he eased her down she knew that she was pulling him towards her with just as much passion. His confidence was that of a child, which made his manhood so irresistible that, as it came down, she felt something of what rape must be like.

Dawley had been through the attics and storage rooms with a flashlight and found nothing. He sat in John's old armchair before the altar of radio equipment.

It was a restful place, and he remembered his first encounter with John, on a bleak snow-deep Lincolnshire day after meeting Handley in the village pub and being invited back to the house. Handley was bone-poor in those times, and having enough money to live on nowadays hadn't altered him, because it had come so late in life.

Dawley lived in the same village with Pat Shipley the district nurse, whose door he'd knocked at for a drink of water during his zigzag hitchhike after leaving autumnal Nottingham. Instead of searching

John's room he seemed to be searching himself, remembering that the only thing he didn't do on that far-off Saturday afternoon was tip the table up before saying good-bye. Being the traditional thing, was it a mark of progress that he hadn't done it, or merely a slip of his shattered mind?

He had wandered upstairs at Handley's place looking for the toilet, and by chance opened the door of John's room, seeing a bald-headed thin-lipped man of about forty, illuminated by a desk lamp because the blinds were drawn, sitting with earphones on and fingers tapping at a morse key. John wore a good suit, he noticed, and was shivering as if in a hard stage of malaria. He turned a panicky glare on Frank's intrusion, and swivelled from the radio with a gun in his hand.

He saw him next when he came to get him out of Algeria. Only an insane-idealistic-socialistic-epileptic-Englishman, who weighed the problems of the world as clear and simple, could have done it, who imagined the earth as a battle-ground of good and evil—one of which would eventually reign forever. The good of the world was lost when John lifted the gun to his mouth as the cross-Channel steamer entered the welcoming arms of the breakwater at Dover.

In Algeria John had seen that the pursuit of equality brought nothing but death and suffering. He realised that almost anything was preferable to the annihilation or crippling of people.

No one doubted that he had been the unfortunate and tormented possessor of a finer organism than themselves. He was the person who could bear his calamities least, that rare being whose sensibility was in fact increased by them. Unable to put up with it any longer, he realised that the onset of further agony might make him callous, and therefore alter him to himself and those among whom he lived. He did not allow it to happen.

Dawley had gathered all this from long talks with him in Gibraltar. He thought John's last letter must deal with it, a letter that he was soon to open before the assembled family, part of John's final instructions to him. In the last few weeks he had often felt a need to read it, but would put it off for as long as possible, as John had said he should.

But whatever John proclaimed about the futility of violence, whether they were his dying words or not, Dawley was unable to wipe away the last few years of his existence in order to suddenly believe in them. Such sentiments had no connection with the realities of the earth—

though they made him uneasy nevertheless, as if one day they might have some influence on the raw wound of his soul.

He'd tried to make things good with Nancy and their children, but when he'd walked out on her three years ago he hadn't realised how final a move it had been. Maybe we never do, he thought, until the irrevocable steps of time cement the issue into something dead and gone forever. Nancy had tried to live in the community, but it hadn't been possible. What he'd so thoughtlessly destroyed was not easily rebuilt. He couldn't blame her for it, nor himself, either. If things turned out to be so irredeemable it only proved that he'd had good cause to make the decision in the first place.

Nancy was working as a conductress on the Nottingham buses, and he'd got a letter saying that she'd taken up with her old boyfriend, who was still single and now wanted to marry her. In effect, she asked if she could divorce him for his desertion of her. He should have been happy at her civilised proposal, but it depressed him, made him feel that the world was not as secure as it had been when his options were open. Yet he was strengthened by his closeness to Myra and Mark, an attachment which was now as firm as all the others he had made in his life.

Fatigued, he stretched his arms, and looked along John's books. Among them was a Bible from which the New Testament had been ripped. A verse had been ringed by a dark soft-lead pencil: 'And Solomon said, If he will shew himself a worthy man, there shall not be an hair of him fall to the earth: but if wickedness shall be found in him, he shall die.'

The impression was vivid and profound, and he stood unmoving, his soul blacked out painfully with peace. When his senses reopened he thought of death, and there was less agony in it than in the emptiness. Such ideas were not easy to resist, sitting in John's studio. He recollected that John, in Algeria, at the point of embarkation on a black and turbulent night, had wanted to stay behind, perhaps because he wasn't sure what his future would be. But Dawley fought with his remaining strength to get him down the hill and on to the boat, a struggle which put off only by a week John's final bleak victory.

He sat in a vegetable state, mulling along the lines of circular thought, knowing it was no use searching John's room and hoping to find anything unless he first searched his own heart.

Chapter Thirty-three

Adam read to make certain there'd been no mistake. Having pulled a notebook from under Dawley's bed, and made three ricketty piles on the floor, it was hard to see what all the fuss was for, because there was nothing subversive about these unhallowed slabs of prose.

Skimming the spidery open handwriting, he saw it might have been better if they'd been burned instead of stolen. Each story, sketch, paragraph and page of notes was signed by Shelley Jones, otherwise he'd have thought the books belonged to someone else. There were a few heavily marked quotations from some authority on guerrilla warfare, a clumsy sketch on how to lay explosives under railway sleepers, and one describing a silencer for a pistol, but mostly the writings were lewd, vivid, and humourless pornography that could never have been looked into by Maricarmen—or read by whoever had taken them from the trunk. He felt such awe at being the first to broach their covers that he broke into a giggle.

Richard stood on the step. He was tall and swart, with black curly hair, a year younger than his brother. 'I've had no luck.'

Adam was red at the face. 'I found the golden hoard, that's why—the sacred mysteries, Shelley's notebooks as I live and breathe! I don't think we'll get much out of them.'

'So Dawley did it?'

'Seems so. Can you see Dad anywhere?'

Richard bent his head to look. 'Leaning on the front gate having a pleasant smoke. Shall I get him? I always feel guilty if I disturb an artist in his meditations!'

'We'll need somebody's wisdom to sort this one out.'

'His experience, anyway,' Richard said, going down the steps. Adam opened another notebook. Four men were having a go at each other. On the next page, a group of women. It was abominable. How could a dedicated revolutionary indulge in such horny nonsense? Judging by the names they even belonged to the same family. Maybe Shelley had been preparing a long plain tome on the brotherhood and sisterhood of humanity, believing so much in the harmony of people living together in peace and love that it was necessary to work out every possible permutation of sexual congress in order to see if any snags cropped up. What right had he, Adam, to judge his motives? Either he'd been amusing himself, or his mastabatory musings were simply another twist to his idealism.

The caravan boards creaked under Handley's walk. 'In Dawley's bloody quarters, too. That's awkward.'

'I suppose he needed them to help with the writing of his book.'

'He'd ask for 'em,' said Handley, 'not nick 'em'—taking a ball of string from his pocket and giving it to Richard. 'Tie 'em up and let's get 'em out of here. Neatly though, or they'll slop all over the place.'

'But he must have taken them,' Richard said.

Handley stroked his moustache. 'It's obvious. As plain as day. But anything plain in this gang's fit to baffle old Nick himself.'

'But you'll still get back to the indisputable fact in the end.'

'What's in the books?' Handley asked. 'I'm sure you've had a good look already.'

'Dirty stories,' Richard said. 'They're so filthy they can't even deprave and corrupt. You could call 'em miscellaneous writings—to put a good face on it, but he must have had quite a sexual drive.'

'Got it in the head, like everybody else,' Handley said scornfully. 'There's no point in studying 'em, then?'

'Not much. There's the odd page of revolutionary stuff, but nothing we don't know or couldn't have thought up ourselves. Pornographic trash mostly.'

'Be a bit of a let down for Maricarmen. And Dawley.'

'Maybe he didn't filch them,' Richard admitted. 'There wouldn't be much point.'

'Now you're talking,' Handley responded. 'If you distrust the obvious you'll soon find out who did it, even if it leads you back to the obvious, as aforesaid. What we do now is this, and we do it quick . . .' Nobody was in much of a hurry for action, but they did it nevertheless, because there was nothing else to do.

Cuthbert walked through the yard. Noises were exaggerated in the sultry afternoon: he heard doors and cupboards banging, as if everybody for the first time in the life of the community were finding out what possessions everyone else had, almost as if the initial well-planned step towards common ownership of property within the compound down to the last razor blade and sanitary towel were finally taking place. It was amazing what devious means were needed to attain the simplest objective: you try to destroy the community, and unwittingly put it on the road to such a permanent foundation that it might never dissolve—if the others were but genuine enough to see it, which, being imperfect human beings and not fit for such an exalted form of society, they never would be.

He paused behind the lilac bush, water shaking on to the sleeve of his jacket. His father wasn't sneaking around, so he went along the lawn path to the other side of the house. Looking up the wall to Maricarmen's room, he noticed the window slightly open, and a convenient drainpipe located within a few feet of the ledge. The idea of searching for the gun in her room seemed insane, but his heart beat time to such insanity, and it was only the madness of the venture that gave him the strength to do it.

He gripped the pipe, rubber-soled shoes fastening on to the bricks as he levered himself up, hoping that by the time he got there his mother would have finished and gone elsewhere.

The climb went more quickly than expected, and soon he was level with the window. Nothing ventured, nothing lost, he smiled, breath pounding from stomach to head, legs trembling so that he wondered if they'd last the course. The broad pipe bent towards a bathroom, and it was little trouble to get himself along and reach the ledge. A spot of rain fell, but it was a false alarm, and he smelt the divine odours of damp grass and foliage coming from surrounding fields. It was as though he were about to enter the kingdom of heaven. A car roared along from the direction of the church, but trees hid him from the road.

Both feet lodged so tightly in the brackets of the drainpipe that he wondered if they'd ever snap out again. He heaved himself up till the ledge became his horizon and he could see over it into the room. At first, looking keenly around its four walls, and wanting to believe it was empty, he was about to pull jubilantly in to look for the gun he had foolishly given up.

Two people were lying on the bed. Or, rather, it seemed at first as if it were one person, a single body, a demi-octopus with limbs still faintly writhing as if some noble intrepid warrior had nonchalantly delivered a death blow and gone on his merry unfeeling way.

It was clear that the short curly reddish head belonged to Dean. His bare arse would have been visible in all its narrow extent only if someone had been hanging from the ceiling—which they were not. He thought that the underneath part of the demi-octopus was Myra, or even Maricarmen who had nipped up after he had left her in the kitchen. But the hair was fair, and though the face in its ecstasy was turned away, he knew that it was his mother lying on the bed.

His head descended, an involuntary movement to stop crying out with surprise. He unlatched his feet, and went down at such speed that when he reached the earth he had scorched both hands. The pain was so intense that he wanted to go back into the kitchen for some Burnol, but his head was a junction-box of wild thoughts that spun in circles and lead him nowhere.

His first impulse was to go and tell his father, but impulse with Cuthbert was never a straight road, even in this situation. Don't rely on instinct or intuition, he had often told himself. Never believe in anyone. Never trust those whom you trust absolutely—including yourself. It would be a terrible waste to blurt out his knowledge until it could be turned to some use or other.

He walked up the path and into his father's studio, his face burning almost as intensely as his hands. His heart felt suddenly battered, his veins jammed. The only thing to do when your mother's being humped by a kid of eighteen was give a good laugh and hope she enjoyed it, and that the old man would never know. At the same time he'd do his best to get rid of Dean before it went too far. It was all right trying to smash the community, but he had no wish to see his own family broken.

Still, he had Dean to thank for the fact that he was at last able to see his mother as just another woman. The disadvantage, however, was that it made Cuthbert feel younger than his grown-up spirit could support. It made him feel sick.

Handley had set off the mechanism of this farcical search, though what had initiated things in the first place was too far lost in the backward swamp of timeless events even to bear thinking about. He sat on an upturned box. Handley's bits and pieces were scattered over the table, and in the middle was an ancient two-ounce tobacco tin, the sort Handley kept his gear for tailor-made fags in, which he rolled with one hand—as became an old gunner—when he was in a mellow and contemplative slant of mind. A piece of fossil stood on top, and Cuthbert idly opened the tin to sniff the tobacco, as he'd often done as a child, when Handley offered it to his nose even before he'd been able to prise off the lid himself. It was one of his earliest memories, and he wanted to see if the smell would bring it back.

The tin was jammed tight with thirty neatly folded ten-pound notes, three hundred pounds which his father had left lying there for any pilferer to come across, though the tin was in such an obvious position that no one would think it worth looking into. He wondered why he kept so much cash available, enough to get him to Australia, which would hardly be far enough if he discovered what was going on under his stupid unknowing nose.

He was sorry he'd seen it: one more black secret to carry under his armpit like a plague boil. He wished he had never come home and into this lunatic community. Theological college had been a haven of peace, a past life comparable only to paradise. He felt pity for his father, who had created this hell. Yet everything was bound to be hellish outside an ordered monastic life, and so Handley couldn't be blamed for it. He only created this faction-house so as to escape whatever personal torment burned within him; and Handley often shouted in a light-hearted manner that for an artist any life was hell except during the short periods when he was painting—not knowing that a unique spate of it was brewing up for him.

Chapter Thirty-four

He stood, but said nothing. Maricarmen gave a soft ironic smile, which suggested that maybe his own share of hell was also gathering. 'I haven't wasted my time searching for those bloody notebooks,' he said, 'if that's what you think.'

'So even you won't help me?'

'You got the gun, didn't you?' He lit a marijuana cigarette. 'I hope they've gone for good.' When she came close he offered her a smoke. She refused it as if he were trying to insult her, but held his hand: 'What are you thinking about?'

He had tried to irritate her by passing the cigarette, and now responded to her tenderness by asking: 'Do you love me, then?'

She wouldn't speak, her face embroiled in some far-off world of her own. 'You're the first person I've ever been in love with,' he went on. 'I wasn't thinking, though. I never think. My mind unfreezes now and again from the Ice-Age emptiness it was born into, when something startling happens, but it soon silts up and gets back to its state of comfortable polar ice.'

Her distant mood broke into a normal smile. 'You always say you're not thinking, and then show that you are.'

'If I really began to think I'd tear the world apart! Anyway, if I had told you what I was thinking I'd only have lied.'

'Do you always have to drive somebody mad to make them fall in love with you? I'm not very impressed with that sort of so-called love. You don't love anything or believe in anything. You like to be cruel, that's all.'

'So that you'll love me!' he laughed. 'You guessed right. I feel calm in here. God knows what's going on outside. It's nice to talk before the flood comes in. My father created this place. It's got great peace. He rants against God, and does the most marvellous Old Testament paintings. I don't know who else you've destroyed in your life, my sweet and heavy-breasted Maricarmen with the Iberian eyes and Cantabrian cheekbones—but don't get too bloody close to me!'

'You're the only real person in this community.'

'Thanks. But you'd like to see me at the knackers' yard. I'll walk there on my own one day. You've got to put up with me. Here I am. Something's latched us together that's more than love. Having to tolerate myself is the worst thing.'

He caught the same tone of trapped domestic fury in his voice that he noticed in his father's, and wondered how it could have come so quickly unless he had wanted it to. Maybe it had nothing to do with domesticity at all. He waited for her to speak. It wasn't rare for him to intimidate someone into silence, though he didn't like it when he did. When in doubt, talk. 'If I sit quietly for a minute'—he took a long pull at his cigarette—'I see faint grey smoke drifting between my eyes. I get frightened sometimes, but I don't know what of. A cigarette drives it away. It stops me thinking, and that's what I like.'

She noted his precise movements, the sharpness of his eyes, and the self-satisfied smile when he'd forced her to speak at last. 'All you have to do is to forgive yourself,' she said. 'The mind becomes clearer then.'

'How did you learn to forgive yourself?'

'It came to me in prison. As soon as you have stopped blaming yourself for all your sins, and for what crimes you've still to commit during the rest of your life, then everything becomes easier to bear. An anarchist friend told me that the only gaoler in the world is God, and guilt is the prison he locks us up in. But once you've talked somebody into killing Him for you, you're free. Don't try to kill him yourself, though. It does too much damage. Kill God for somebody else, and let them do the same for you. Isn't that what we're in this community for?'

He was pale. His hand trembled that held the cigarette, so he threw it down and put his foot on it. 'I'd rather believe in God, because finally I belong to the world, and not to myself alone. Maybe I love you because I've always wanted to find someone worse than myself.'

She flinched when she had no intention of it. 'Shelley used to say that belief in God is a cosmic form of self-pity.'

'I believe,' he said, 'because in the end I have to.'

'You're not capable of suffering, that's why.'

'If I suffered it'd be even harder for you to tear me from what I believe: you don't get wisdom from suffering. You only get more faith.' He spat. Such phrases wore him down. They left him foul and dissatisfied. Maybe he had learned a lot by coming to this place, for it was the other side of the coin to his three years at college. It wasn't too late to go back, get readmitted, and stay till he became a priest.

He said something so abruptly that it confirmed his love of God. He didn't know why the command came into his mind, though it seemed absolutely right that it did:

'Give me the gun.'

She took it from her handbag, and pointed it at his face.

Having burned the offending matter it was obvious he'd find nothing while searching the flat over the garage. Every member of the community was scurrying about the property looking for non-existent notebooks, as if an electric shock had gone through them, and it played on his sense of humour. He hadn't felt so positive and well since before the hedgehog died, he thought, with a faint cut of sadness on reminding himself of it.

Now that his kleptomaniac *coup* had been discovered, he wondered how he could let them know—with suitable dramatics, and without bringing any shame on to himself—that the note-books had been fed to the Devil. That could come later, he smiled, as he leaned against the damp whitewash of the wall, though not as blame, for he felt no guilt from it, but as a victory for himself when he gloatingly told them that he'd taken the irreversible step of sending Shelley's revolutionary paraphernalia up in smoke.

Yet there was always something to spoil it. Because nothing was ever perfect for him, nothing short of perfection could cure the corrosion in his heart. The fact was that his own crime was diminished by the theft of the gun. He'd give much to know who'd taken it, and where it was, for then he could fulfil his promise to Handley, who had begged him to look for it, and it would enhance still further his own act of burning the notebooks. Having done something, he wanted to do everything. Who could be satisfied with less when you lived in a community?

He didn't dare search too closely for the gun in case he was seen at it, and suspicion fell on him for having taken the notebooks. Maybe it had been Handley's idea to sow such distrust, and take it off his own sons. By marvelling at such deviousness, he gave more credit than Handley either deserved or wanted.

The garage-flat was daintily furnished. Myra's mother, old Mrs Zimmermann, had stayed in it before she died. He stood by the curtains, and watched Adam searching Dawley's caravans across the yard, observing his movements through the open door. If he'd saved a few pages of Shelley's note-books, even though burned half-way across by scorchmarks, he could have waved them under their noses. He cursed himself for his inability to see into the future.

'We'd better hide them in the garage,' Handley said. Adam had made coffee on Dawley's spirit stove. 'Nobody can be blamed for stealing 'em when they get found there. We can put 'em in the repair pit. I used it once to tighten the exhaust pipe on the Rambler when it came loose.'

Adam was proud of his father's simplicity, which couldn't but be effective. 'We can look for clues on the faces of the others when they're told where they were found,' Richard said.

Handley slammed his mug down. 'What brilliant sons I have! It's a shame Shelley's doodlings weren't more instructive, though. Back to square one, I reckon.'

'There's no such thing as square one for us,' said Richard.

'I don't know what you mean by that,' Handley said, 'but in the meantime let's get rid of this pornographic muck.'

Chapter Thirty-five

Her hand was firm. There was no tremor in her arm.

Nevertheless, he pushed the gun aside: 'You may be a dedicated revolutionary, but I'm a priest.'

'A failed priest,' she mocked, lowering the gun.

'That makes me stronger,' he said softly, 'and if you threaten me again, or otherwise play around, I'll kick you to death. I hate violence when it comes too close, or when it threatens innocent people.'

He reached to take it, but she backed away. 'I've used guns before. I'll shoot.'

She would. His icy lack of fear had gone, and the present real danger made him wonder if she intended to kill him rather than Dawley. All he had to do was explain that the notebooks were in Dawley's caravan, but then she would guess he had put them there, and so might kill him just the same. He followed his usual course of not speaking, of standing in his own easy air of stubbornness that he was too lazy to break through.

She put the gun into her handbag, the brittle stare gone from her eyes. She shook her head slowly. 'You were quite brave.'

'That's brain damage, not courage. You'd have been doing me a favour if you'd blown my head off. One problem less.'

She seemed about to weep. 'You haven't got much fear, so you can't love anybody, either.'

He felt safe again, so decided to be on his guard. Always expect the unexpected. She wondered why he didn't try to get the gun from her, since he'd wanted it so much.

She was mistaken: he hadn't been brave when she put the gun at his face, simply too stunned to react. There was more of his father in him than he supposed, but also much else that he didn't yet know about.

He wouldn't take the gun from her because whatever she did with it would cause the final smash of the community, and he wanted to see what was in her mind. Icy or not, he still had a massive interest in life. He was often troubled at his inability to use this interest for the moral good of himself and others, but the gratification he got from it was sufficient to conceal his uneasiness. He'd always said that until the day came that proved there was more advantage to the world in good than bad, he'd see no reason to alter.

Yet he was already at the mercy of chemical change—without knowing why. And because the reason for it wasn't instantaneously supplied by his intuition he felt suddenly smaller to himself. He smiled, and acknowledged his understanding. The end of the beginning was on him because he saw it as undeniable—looking at Maricarmen who waited for him to speak—that if any good was to be done at all then he would have to take the first step towards doing it. If you perceived something bad you immediately accepted a moral responsibility to make it good. If you didn't, you weren't human. Evil seemed inanimate and could do nothing but stay devilish because it would not move. Good was mobility, perception, life, a desire to move towards evil and overcome it. Evil was an anchored bigotry, and lack of perception. Good was a far-seeing sensibility that could spread everywhere. He knew it wasn't true, but thought one should try to make it so. He loved himself for becoming normal.

He said: 'I still think you ought to give me that gun. It'll be better for all of us, in the end.'

He was aware of self-sacrifice in demanding it, for if she gave it to him no evil would be done, which was good, but then there'd be no smash of this godless and revolutionary community. He began to see the futility of calculating too many moves ahead, knowing that the immediate peril had to be dealt with because that was the only one for which you could take on responsibility.

These speculations calmed him. He felt light of weight, and somehow wise, as if he'd grown older in the last hour and had decided to live up to it.

'Come on, my love,' he said, putting concern and tenderness into his voice. 'Hand it over.'

'I have something to do with it, first.'

'Don't.'

'You're a child,' she said. They were all children, she thought, these easy-going yet close-hearted islanders who only want to be left alone. They hadn't had a civil war or a revolution for three hundred years. They had become rotten with safety.

'I wouldn't be sure,' he said. 'Not that I would mind being a child. A child can grow up, after all. A big advantage, if it can survive.'

'The English are a nation of survivors, and you belong to it with all your heart!'

'Shit!' he cried angrily. 'Don't confuse me with the English! I'm not a bloody Englishman. I'm me, and nobody else. I'm responsible to me and to God alone, not a bloody nation or a bloody king or a bloody queen, or even a bloody party or a bloody president.'

He felt foolish whenever he ceased to be calm, yet he also enjoyed the swing of his own exclamations, as if he were more himself.

'It's an excuse for selfishness.'

'I know I love you,' he said. 'And that's something.'

'I can't feel it from you.' She stood by the door, as far away from him as possible.

'Leave Dawley alone. He's innocent as far as Shelley is concerned. Nobody in my family blamed him for John's death, though I suppose a case could be made out for it by someone like you. Blame fate. Blame God, if you like. Do you think Shelley would want you to blame Frank? Being a sincere revolutionary Shelley must have known that his death was the only possible one. I hate this damned revolution stuff, but even I can see that. After all, Shelley was the educated go-ahead member of the duet, so it's feasible that he manipulated Dawley into the scrimmage of Algeria. Dawley's more passive than you think—as malleable as hell.'

'He hated Shelley,' she said. But she didn't sound convinced, and took the gun from her bag and offered it to him. It was the most beautiful picture he could wish to see. The handle was held towards him, harmlessly, and things were turning out all right at last.

The door rattled, and whoever it was hadn't the patience to fully turn the knob. Then he had, because the force of the opening door hit her in the back, and pushed her forward. She was so much in line with the door that Cuthbert couldn't see who it was. Despite the unexpected blow she kept hold of the gun, then looked with dislike and annoyance at Cuthbert, as if, being in such a hurry to get the gun, it was all his fault.

Ralph had evidently expected to find the place empty, and as he lurched crazily over the threshold, passing Maricarmen in his flight, a box of matches fell from his hand. Something had frightened him, and it wasn't Maricarmen holding a gun, or Cuthbert standing angrily by the centre table. 'What the hell do you want?'

Ralph was gasping from his frantic leap up the steps to the studio. His face was blotched red at the cheeks, lank hair slipping over his forehead. 'They found the notebooks.'

'Shut up,' Cuthbert said. 'Get out of here.'

'Where were they?' she asked, as if barely interested.

'In Dawley's caravan. But they're going to put them in the garage.

'Are you sure?'

'I saw everything.' He had been utterly confused at witnessing the unmistakable bundles carried by Handley and his two sons. He was dropping into madness again. The world swam with maggots in the head and throat and mouth of the dying hedgehog. His brain ached, as if it were going rotten. But he saw it, and believed it, and out of the putrefaction realised that he must have burned the wrong papers, and that they had by some means turned up in Dawley's caravan. Without thinking he'd snatched a large box of kitchen matches and ran to Handley's studio with the intention of setting it on fire and thereby creating a diversion which might give him time to think.

'It was me who stole the notebooks and put them in the caravan.' But for all his calm speech Cuthbert knew he couldn't say anything she'd believe. And he wanted to convince her at last.

'You're lying,' she said, 'as usual'—and ran out of the studio with the gun.

She can't kill Dawley, he told himself, because through his death

Death will live. But he thought it still too early to get down on his knees and pray.

'They've had time to take the place apart brick by brick,' Mandy grumbled, as she lifted the lid of the Aga and set the kettle on. 'If it was money I could understand it. If I saw a thousand quid lying about I'd grab it, but not some dead bloke's notebooks.' She opened a biscuit tin and took out a handful. 'I could do with a lump sum to get a car with. I feel like a burn-up on the M1.'

'Take mine,' Myra suggested, knowing she couldn't go fast in it. Mandy seemed helpless and vulnerable—the sort of young person she read about in the newspapers who was 'in need of care and protection'. She was outspoken, kind, and pretty. She had a faintly split nose, but so subtle that you might not properly notice it for some time. It came down from the short bridge and gave an amiable charm to the rest of her face. Handley always referred to it as a 'saucy little coal-tip nose'.

She smiled at Myra's attempt to turn her from thoughts of a new car. 'That old banger would split in two after ten miles.'

'The Rambler, then.'

'Dad would have a fit. I'd never hear the last of it. The trouble about artists is they're dead mean.'

'What do you call being generous?'

'Somebody who gives all he's got, and doesn't bat an eyelid, even when he goes broke over it.'

Myra poured her tea. 'You always say "he"—why?'

'Men are the ones with money. I don't think it's right, though. That's what's wrong with this set-up. Men run the place, even though we do let them play at keeping house. We voted for 'em to do it, but it only makes 'em think they're more top-dog than ever. They'll be thinking they're as good as we are soon. Why the hell did we help to search for those crumby notebooks? Whatever's in 'em's bound to make things worse for us.'

'I thought they ought to be found: Maricarmen was upset.'

'Yes, she's a fine freedom-loving revolutionary, she is. I expect she can't live unless she's under somebody's thumb. I know all about that, living in this house. I suppose her boyfriend Shelley kept her under his thumb right enough. And now that he's kicked the bucket she's missing it, and wants us to get under the influence of his papers—whatever's in 'em.'

She was like a young mare knocking down the hurdles as she went over them. She lit a cigarette. 'She gets upset about anything. I've never seen such a bloody neurotic. No wonder she's a revolutionary.'

'She's spent time in prison.'

'She's not the only one. Some mope, some don't.'

'That's not a very nice remark,' Myra said.

'I suppose not. You're the only generous person in this roundabout. It's your house, and you chip in plenty of money, as well as do a lot of work. It beats me why you do it, it does.'

Myra thought for a moment. 'Maybe I'm idealistic—which is a way of saying I've found an outlet for my neuroses. I joined this experiment because I wondered if it were possible for a group of people to live together and kill the dead weight of the family.'

'Is it, though?' asked Mandy.

'It's too early to say.'

'What if it got smashed?'

'Why should it?' She spoke guardedly, knowing Mandy was close to the truth. 'We've done well so far. If it gets difficult it's only because we haven't made a bigger community out of it. It's too small. We need more people, and another house. If we could get planning permission we'd build two more dwelling-places on the paddock. We'd have a real kibbutz.'

'They'll never give *us* planning permission,' Mandy said. 'They hate our guts at the council. Anyway, we'd have to get land as well, and farm it.' She was fired with enthusiasm: 'We ought to get lots of animals, have a real farm to live off. We're too idle, really. What's it like being Jewish?'

She coloured slightly as she asked her question. Having lived for a long time in such an un-Jewish atmosphere it was difficult for Myra to clear her thoughts for the serious answer that Mandy deserved. 'If you're Jewish you can never forget that you are Jewish—no matter where you live, or what you might become. It's with you all the time.'

'I suppose it is,' Mandy said sadly. 'You being the only Jewish person here.'

'One can't forget that the Germans killed six million of us just because we were Jewish. Several hundred thousand were children, just like Mark and the other children at this house.'

Mandy bent her head, and tears fell on to her knees. 'I know,' she said. 'Dad told us years ago. But don't tell Ralph, will you? He couldn't stand it.' Misery was a dragon, a great monster that fixed its teeth into her heart till the pain became unbearable. If Ralph went mad because a small animal of the field had died, what would happen if he heard about the Germans murdering so many children—not to mention all the others who'd done nothing to nobody either? 'I expect he already knows about it though, and that's why he can't bear to see a hedgehog die.'

Myra smiled, sorry now to have upset her. 'None of it's your fault.'

'It is,' she sobbed, 'or I wouldn't be crying, would I?'

She comforted her, but one couldn't cut it off in midstream: 'Mark's Jewish, because the son of a Jewish mother is always Jewish, no matter what so-called race or religion the father is. So I'm not alone! Anyway, I feel that we're all the same sort in this house.'

'But don't you ever want to go to synagogue?'

'Sometimes. On the Day of Atonement. That's when all good Jews fast for twenty-four hours—and hope their sins will be forgiven.'

'That's a fine idea,' said Mandy, drying her eyes with the Kleenex Myra gave her. 'But I don't think I could go for even four hours without food. Still, it must be good to be Jewish if it makes you feel different.'

'You think that's good?'

'I reckon so. It's not dull, is it?'

'I suppose it's not when you come across people who are anti-Jewish,' Myra said, hoping to change the topic.

'If somebody got at me because I was Jewish,' Mandy said, 'I'd scratch their eyes out. They'd never do it again to anybody. And if I was a Catholic and somebody called me for it I'd kill them as well. That's the way Dad brought us up. We used to go to school in rags, and when the kids mocked us we slaughtered 'em. Mam's the same way.'

'That's why I call your parents generous,' said Myra.

'Dad's not. He's a mean old swine.'

Myra laughed.

'If it hadn't been for you,' Mandy held her hand, 'this community would never have got off the ground.'

Myra stood and put more water in the kettle. Any minute she expected the others to converge on the kitchen. Food was the one unalterable law of life, which she perfectly understood. Maybe they'd found the notebooks. Handley would avoid blaming anyone if it were possible, unless Cuthbert had had a hand in it. In that case there'd be a bit of a row, before calm wrapped them up once more.

As boiling water steamed into the pot, a clear brick-splitting crack of a noise sounded from somewhere outside, its echoes whipping along the belly of the clouds and throwing a final stab back at the windows. Eric Bloodaxe whined with fear, a chilling heart-cry that went on and on.

'Sounds like a firework,' Mandy said casually.

Myra finished with the tea, but breath pounded in her veins. Handley shouted words which she couldn't quite make out. A scream of rage or pain came from someone.

'Was it a firework?' said Mandy, sensing it was far worse.

'It was a gun,' Myra cried, rushing to the window. She looked out, then turned and ran upstairs to Mark when she heard him waking up.

Chapter Thirty-six

He'd had enough of John's room. There was nothing more to think about, and not much else to say, and no one in any case to say it to. John was dead, and Handley had lost an elder brother, but the spirit of the world had not come to an end because of that. Life was renewable, even when the angels died. It had to be.

He came downstairs, and went out of the front door to get some fresh air. Pink, white and lemon-cloured roses were in full smooth bloom, scenting the heavy afternoon. Their sweetness cloyed at his nostrils.

On such a day the house and compound seemed to have drawn itself into an imperishable cocoon. The air surrounding it was electrified and brittle, as if one flint-spark only was needed to touch it off like a shell-burst. Maybe he was afraid. His lack of energy made him fear the end. His yen to ward off the rest of the world and protect only himself, Myra and Mark, was bad breath to him. It was a poor wish. He'd had it all along yet not been familiar with what it meant. To get rid of such an idea would mean setting off alone to some other country, thereby confirming that his native energy was not so snuffed out as he had felt it to be for a long time. But weren't those days over for everyone?

He wanted to stay alive, but not by allowing any false desires to get the upper hand. You have to be practical, and think of others who depend on you, even when it seems that your spirit has reached the end. Walking into the yard, he noticed someone in the garage.

Richard saw him from the doorway. 'Dawley's coming. He's spotted us.'

Handley was in the repair pit. 'All right,' he said to Adam, who was passing the last pack of notebooks, 'We've just found 'em, and we're getting 'em out.'

'Understood,' Adam said, taking the bundle back.

It was a useless and farcical run-around, and Handley was tired of it. The notebooks had turned up, had been seen to be worthless, and here they were caught in a whirlpool of subterfuge just to save somebody's feelings. He wanted nothing more than to go back to his painting and forget the whole thing.

Dawley came in. 'Any luck?'

'If you can call it that,' Handley said. 'Adam and Richard stumbled on 'em down here. They've had time to read a couple.'

Dawley smiled. He too wanted to get back to work, though he was interested to know how they'd landed in the garage.

'That'll remain a mystery,' said Handley. 'Might as well forget it. No names, no pack drill.'

'They're not worth much,' said Adam, when the last one came out of the pit. 'Shelley may have practised revolution, but he didn't write it. They're only feeble attempts to write dirty stories.' He pulled one from under the string and threw it to Frank, who took it to the entrance where a mirror on the open door reflected a better light.

'Not that I'm against anybody writing pornography,' Handley said, 'as long as it's good. I've done a bit myself, though I didn't call it that. I turned out an album of Goya-esque drawings last year—one of them showed a man's head up a woman's cunt, I remember—cartoons of bodies and faces from all angles. Then this potty little Church of England windbag in Cheshire gets hold of one and writes me a whining letter about corrupting youth, though I suppose he wasn't slow in letting his choirboys see them.'

Frank stopped listening. They were right. It was twisted, fly blown trash—a part of Shelley he'd never known about. Shelley's socialism was fired in action, and presumably ended there. The revolutionary government would have shot him as he walked away from the victory parade. What he wrote in his private notebooks had been for amusement, or to resolve sexual problems which were his alone. He'd delved into a world of dreams and fantasies which weren't latched in any way to valid ideas of human decency. Shelley was a practical man, and not an intellectual, otherwise his writings would have theorised about his realities, and not dealt with such putrid stuff.

'Satisfied?' said Handley.

He handed the book back. Before looking into the garage, where Handley stood, he glanced at the mirror, which reflected enough of the yard for Maricarmen to be seen on the other side of it, standing calm and still, and pointing a gun straight at him.

Chapter Thirty-seven

Cuthbert laughed so long that Ralph, thinking he was going off his head, came close to regaining his own sanity. It seemed to Cuthbert that the worst was about to happen now that Maricarmen had gone off with the gun, and when he stopped laughing Ralph was shocked at the acid smile on his face.

'Don't go after her,' Cuthbert said. 'Stay with me, and escape the slaughter that's about to start. You'll never hear the last of it, and that's a fact.'

'I will,' said Ralph grimly. 'Slaughter won't worry me. When my hedgehog died it was eaten to death by the sort of gnawing life that this community specialises in. If I don't get away it'll eat me as well.'

'Maybe it's finished us off already.'

Ralph came close: 'What did you do with the notebooks?'

'That's easy. When you had them neatly knotted up in the plastic bag I untied it and took them out. The bag you so gleefully confined to the flames contained another sort of old rubbish.'

'You're the worst of them all,' Ralph said. 'Number one maggot that leads the others in, and then works hardest to undermine any sign of life. You'll end by eating yourself, not because there's no one left, but because everyone will get wise to you.'

Cuthbert grinned through his unhappiness: 'There's one born every minute. And the reason Heaven doesn't fold up is that one dies every minute. Even a priest can have his jokes.'

At the first pistol shot Ralph jumped as if the bullet had shattered him. He cried out, and put a hand to his face. No part of Cuthbert's flesh moved. He was pallid, but still sure of himself. To accept his responsibility for it would make him seem naïve before all and sundry, especially Ralph, whom he had always despised. But Cuthbert, in the vital self-criticising space between gunshots, knew himself to be immature because he was afraid of appearing naïve. The only honest way to be unmoved was to admit that he was the cause of Maricarmen running amok.

At the second explosion Ralph sat down by the table, as if the strength of his legs had gone. He once shot a hare with a two-two rifle and saw the hole in its head. There were tears at his eyes as he visualised those grey rings of pulverized human flesh. He lifted his agonised face: 'I took the notebooks from Shelley's trunk under her bed. But I didn't mean this to happen.' Cuthbert was unable to smile at his weakness.

'What the hell did you imagine, then?' he shouted as the third shot went off.

'The future's empty,' Ralph said sadly, as if there had been a time, thought Cuthbert, when he'd expected it to be full. That was the difference between the old days and now. Ralph belonged to the time when a future was said to be possible for everyone. Cuthbert prided himself on knowing that he'd never believed in that sort of Utopian dream. The present day was always a rope around his neck by which he may be hanged before nightfall.

'You mean it's only full when there's mischief in it?' he demanded. 'No one but God can take care of the future for us, and fill it or empty it however He likes. That's my insipid though heartfelt conclusion.'

Ralph's eyes shone, a deep uncertainty struggling to assert itself in a threatening manner. He wondered whether he should kill him, and get it over with. But they were too evenly matched, and he had no more treachery left.

'In a way you're worse than this hotbed of constipated hornets plotting revolution,' Cuthbert went on. 'They're at least trying to go in the right direction. But you're a compost heap of smouldering English virtues just waiting to be touched off by a spark from the Devil. I've got enough of it in me to see it in you, and to know it's the wrong way for anybody to be.'

'I used to think you were different,' Ralph said, drawing a coat sleeve across his eyes, 'but you're a Handley after all. I'm someone who won't ever be tolerated as a human being in a family like this. It just confirms to me that things are like they've always been, and that they'll never alter. All one can do is find a little protected area where nobody can come and spoil it.'

Cuthbert saw him as the common denominator of fear, and he hoped God would protect him—though someone like Ralph would not protect God, except in so far as his own safety was threatened. He lived a life of waking fear, and so his humanity wasn't to be trusted, because, trapped in that fear, the worst injustices could fester roundabout and he wouldn't notice. 'It's not a God you want, but a nanny. The sort of nursery world you're after doesn't exist.'

'It must, though,' Ralph said, more tears falling. 'I don't know what I really want. I'm falling apart, that's all I know.' He leaned against the wall with his head bowed.

At his terrible and disheartened cry Cuthbert became strong. He knew exactly what to do. He put a hand over his shoulder, and felt the sobs that seemed to be breaking Ralph from the inside—just as a black frost breaks up hard soil in the middle of winter. He held his hand. 'Let God take your guilt, and then you'll find peace.'

Ralph nodded, wiping his eyes on one of Handley's clean paint rags as he followed him to the door.

Chapter Thirty-eight

Dawley dropped. Having lived this moment before allowed him to act with a speed which saved his life—as he spun in his crouched position to face her.

Handley screamed—it sounded like a scream, and no one had heard such a noise from him before—but Dawley's brain was so filled up that he caught only a burst of lungs which disturbed him more than the second bullet. The first broke the mirror, and would have killed him if he hadn't leapt forcefully down. Based on the sharpest instinct, it lead to the pause, which followed the strong and vivid sensation of having been through it already.

He hadn't. But the second shot missed. Glass of the mirror cut his face. It burned like ice. From the crouch he ran. Energy which he thought he had lost rammed itself into every fibre and muscle. He hated life because it humiliated him by making him run, and he felt ashamed. But the shame gave him more strength. He ran towards her, but in a wide zigzag, as in any situation when under fire. His skin felt pitted with fear.

Her aim was out, because she didn't know how to offset the sights to his quick movement. When he got close enough to run at her, he turned the offer down because it seemed still too dangerous. It was the sort of opportunity to close-in which often got you killed. He was exhilarated by his own cunning. On his last angular approach, which should have taken him straight at her, he ran by, into the driveway that led to the front of the house. He was alive. If he hadn't been too busy trying to save himself he would have laughed.

She turned, to fire at his back. He zigzagged. He sweated and grunted wanting to run on all fours, but keeping upright, because the speed of it gave less chance of being hit.

Every line of the wall was clear though not so close, detailed like an engraving, rusty and grey in the same eyeful. A daddy-longlegs spider ran out of a crack. He was again bashing his lungs and senses at the limits of his experience. Only a bullet in his back would send him beyond it. There was no cover to lie down or crouch in. He was terrified. He was elated. He smelt soil and rain, pumice and grit, tea leaves and burning paper. He prayed that those by the garage would do something. Vomit was disturbed in his stomach like a cat. He felt too old to live.

In firing at him, she held her back to them. He ran round to the front of the house, and paused under the cover of its far corner, too set on saving himself to feel safe. There was shouting from the yard and garage. He staggered to a further angle of the house.

All was clear. He was alert and intent in case she should appear from any direction. The sky was empty. His hand slid along the smooth warm brick. While he dodged and ran, his wits stayed with him. If he remained still he would be helpless.

So as to get more room to manoeuvre he ran up and on to the lawn behind the house, then came back slowly towards the garage, having completed a circle of it. His thoughts had been pulverised and smashed —his brain rotten, but his body now working to its own good time. He went by the coal sheds and into the yard again, to approach from behind.

Handley, taking cover in the repair pit, saw his chance when Maricarmen turned her back to them.

It was out of the question to chase Dawley. She would not have missed if he hadn't inexplicably dropped a split second before the first well-aimed shot. How had he known it was already travelling, that her finger at that moment pressed his life away? Then he ran, in that hilarious cowardly fashion so that she couldn't aim quickly enough to bring him down. It had seemed easy before she began. Unable and unwilling to move, she decided to stay where she was forever, the gun in her hand and pointing forward, waiting for him to reappear, or to shoot the first person who walked into her sights.

Adam was motioned to her left, by the house. Richard was nodded to the right, along the sheds, while Handley, taking off his shoes, rushed like a nimble and silent cat. He put a sudden steely grip around her so that the gun dropped. He'd not been a real worker since early youth, though his arms drew enough force from the shoulder-blades to hold the burden he had taken on. But the pressure needed to stop her struggling free and picking up the gun was almost more than he had, and he felt a cracking at the heart.

He pulled her to the cover of the caravans, so that no curious passer-by along the road might see. She moaned, and turned passive at this undignified end to her attempt at killing. It had seemed easy during the months she had thought about it, and now that it was over, and she had failed, it again seemed easy, and she even more of a fool at having bungled it. A sort of black fear took hold of her, that her defeat and helplessness would bring down a thousand indignities.

Adam emptied the gun. She had fired three shots. Maybe the others were echoes, or the normal multiplications of fear. Spent and live cases fell from the chambers, and he bent with trembling hands to pick them up.

'Run to my studio,' Handley called to Richard, 'and in the drawer under the left-hand window you'll find an old cigar tin full of bangers left over from last bonfire night. Bring 'em out, and set two or three off, so nobody'll wonder what the noise was.'

Maybe the whole of the county constabulary was already converging from all points on to the house. The shots had certainly gone a dozen miles into his heart and soul, for he was shaking—like a bloody lily, he said afterwards—and asking Maricarmen in a gentle voice to get up and try to walk. The instinct of simple loyalty told him to make sure neither outsiders nor police poked their noses where they ought not to belong. Even though Maricarmen had gone all out for murder he still saw her as one of them. Luckily he and Dawley had enough of the soldier in them to handle it, otherwise it might have been difficult to keep one or two corpses under the doormat.

'Get Enid or Myra to come out of their foxholes,' he told Adam. 'Even Mandy. Anybody. Get going. Quick.' He caught the touch of panic edging into his voice, and told himself to check it.

Dawley, sitting on the steps above the garage, had a good view of the yard. The danger was over, and he lit a cigarette. He'd been in the middle of it. So had they all. Even while running from Maricarmen, he'd felt no panic. Death mattered and he was afraid, but he'd been reasonable all the same. He was undefeated, and cool, but he was close to weeping. If you acted wildly when facing it you let it master you. Not that he tried to be calm. If you had to try you weren't calm, though that was often all you could do. Luckily he had kept cool without knowing it, which was what saved him—that, and knowing what to do.

He sat and smoked, as if after some hard work during the quietest of days. But his senses were fragmented, a feeling as if they were melting into each other. If he stood up he would fall down. Maricarmen had gone into the house with Enid, and Handley came over: 'Let's have a fag.'

He passed one.

'You're a cool bloody customer.'

'Thanks for saving my life,' Dawley said.

'It was mine as well, when I was creeping up on her.'

'Is she all right?'

'She will be.'

'She imagines I'm responsible for Shelley's death.'

Handley sat by his side. 'I feel sorry for her, at the moment.'

'If I'd been killed in Algeria instead of him,' Dawley said, 'Myra could have made out it was his fault for organising the gun-running in the first place. That, too, would have been a lie.'

'You'd better tell it to Maricarmen.'

'I will. If I get the chance.'

Handley threw his cigarette away. 'Tastes like shit. She's got to be told the facts of life. Both you and Shelley knew what you were doing. We'll have a meeting to sort everything out.'

'I'll read John's last letter,' said Dawley, 'that he wrote in Gibraltar, and handed to me as I got on to the plane. I was to read it in six months, he said, or when I thought "circumstances demanded it". That time seems to be about now, I should say.'

Handley agreed so firmly that he laughed. 'Do you think it'll hold us together, or blow us apart?'

'I haven't read it.'

'I won't be able to do another stroke of work till I know what's in it.'

Richard set a handful of fireworks along the front wall. His first match was blown out, so he cupped the second carefully. 'You won't have long to wait,' said Dawley.

The first banger wasn't as loud as a pistol shot, but it brought a cry from Maricarmen who had been given a couple of valium pills and put to bed. Handley felt pity for her. The second and third banger went off, to the amusement of the butcher who was passing by, and paused to watch those mad Handleys playing with fireworks in midsummer.

Chapter Thirty-nine

Handley took the oars down from the rack, and stepped into the boat. 'Don't let's lose any time.'

He held Mandy's hand, and steadied her in. It wasn't the first occasion he'd used the boat, having once found a way of opening the bolted door. He thought Gould might have seen him on the lake from the house, but it hadn't been mentioned when they met. He rowed over the calm water. The fresh smell of it, as the oars dug deeply, so delighted him that he almost forgot why they had come. Mandy sat drowsily in front, trailing her fingers in.

A small sketching case lay on the plank, with a block of cartridge paper, charcoal and pencils inside. He often carried it on his rambles, since it still gave him pleasure to portray with architectural and topographical accuracy exactly what the eye could see. He'd ended the war as a sergeant instructor at gunnery school, elucidating the skills and mysteries of panorama-drawing to artillery recruits.

The large white house was a quarter of a mile away, the view of it more striking because only the glistening slate roofs, one of the gables at the eastern end, and the windows of the top rooms could be seen. He stowed the oars and opened his box, then set the board on his knees to begin sketching.

After the turmoil and danger of the day he revelled in such perfect exercise. His mind loved to work—a worthwhile activity that gave more tranquillity than anything else. Mandy looked about her—trees on one bank, reeds on the other—brushing away a cloud of gnats that annoyed her till she lit a cigarette and drove them off.

'You'd better drop it in,' Handley said, when they were at the middle of the lake. 'But keep your back to the house.'

'I'm not a baby,' she smiled, taking John's revolver and bullets out of her handbag. She held them a few inches underwater, and let them go so that Handley didn't even hear a splash.

'Let's hope we never see it again,' he murmured after a few minutes.

'Back into the bosom of the lake,' she said, 'like in King Arthur and his screwy knights.'

He paused in his work to light a thin cigar, then went on with his drawing. 'I shan't be long.'

'It's all right,' she said drowsily. 'I've got enough fags to keep the gnats off.' An amiable breeze drifted across the lake. 'I like your drawings. Ever since I was a little girl.'

'So you did,' he smiled, holding it up for her. 'I used to draw you pictures to laugh at—remember?'

'I've still got 'em somewhere.'

'I don't know what an artist would do without his family,' he said, getting back to work. 'It's nice when his children appreciate him.' Certainly, he found it easier to talk with them than Enid, a depressing fact when he wanted tranquillity all round. Two people couldn't be at peace, though, when they'd lived so long together. It wasn't in the nature of things, unless their souls went dead. The miracle was that they were still under the same roof, though the continuing cat-and-dog price of it too often put him off his work.

He rowed back to shore, steering into the wooden hut. 'We might still get tea if we hurry,' he said, laying the oars on the rack.

'My handbag's not so heavy now,' she said.

He walked, feeling like a young man, as if all his troubles might be over. He hoped they were, in his moment of light-heartedness, but knew they weren't, and that they could never be. He wasn't an artist for nothing, and an artist realised—or he had no right to call himself one—that trouble was not only the spice of life, but the ingredient that could also dull and ruin it.

Such confusion was part of his gaiety. Uncertainty and levity made him want to sing and dance in the fresh cool air at the end of the afternoon, when the breeze pushed at grass blades and birds flowered the treetops with their noise. No matter what was coming, he was glad to be alive, because Mandy held his arm like the affectionate daughter she was, and under the other arm was the sketch he had made while she'd slid gun and ammunition to the harmless lake-bottom.

The happier you felt the worse it was likely to be when the mood was destroyed, yet such knowledge only made him happier, and allowed him to appreciate it more, so he would at least have been happy to his utmost when the floor fell out of paradise. After the murderous turmoil of the house the day had ended well, so his happiness was not ill-gotten, and may not be held too much against him if a time of reckoning came.

The uncertainty that turned his head, the confusion that made him lighter than air, the relief of the grim day's end, and the satisfaction of his modest drawing on Gould's Lake that reminded him of the juvenile efforts of his early days, made him feel young again. And in real happiness, he thought, no matter how old you are, you always feel young. Not even the future could take that away, as long as you looked on it as a thing of the moment.

Chapter Forty

'This is where we should have started,' he said when he closed the door, 'instead of with Shelley's pathetic bits of pornography.'

'We weren't to know,' said Ralph, taking drawing-pins from the map corners.

'All trace of John must be eliminated, except for the family and personal photographs that can be framed and put on a sideboard, or carried in a wallet till they drop to pieces. Nobody's been to Dover since John died, to cut the grass and put new flowers on his grave, because they've been so obsessed with this potty little inappropriate shrine.'

'I think Handley has been there,' Ralph said justly, crushing the first map into a ball of wastepaper.

'That was only an excuse to get to London and see his mistress,' Cuthbert told him, unplugging aerials and power-points to the transceiver.

To rip all meaningful gear from the four-walled psyche of John's holy room was so grandiose an idea that Ralph was saddened at never having thought of it himself. He could not have done it alone, though, for the power of the individual had its limits, which led him to see, as they went on with their vandalising labours, that maybe there was some virtue in co-operation after all.

Cuthbert was at the door, propping the heavy communications

receiver on his knee to open it. 'Just follow me with the transmitter,' he said sternly.

While the others were busy in the kitchen and dining-room talking of the day's events, and about food for the coming supper, they stepped downstairs and went out of the rarely used front door, avoiding the yard and the predatory sentinel growls of Eric Bloodaxe.

They walked unseen to the far corner of the paddock, where a suitable grave awaited their burdens, a deep place already dug by Dawley as a slit trench for the children to play in, so long neglected that grass grew from the sides and almost obscured it. Cuthbert pulled back an armful, showing a foot of muddy water in the bottom. He heaved the receiver in, a deep thumping splash as it found its final resting-place in the drek.

He was glad now that no one had been killed because of their folly. It needed more to destroy the community than attempted murder. He believed that God would look after them, and stop them veering from the true path—the truest path being where no path existed at all, which was where he wanted to go. Maybe Dawley had discovered this magic and decisive region, and Uncle John was there already. He shivered, and checked himself. There was much to do yet before the community crumbled. Setbacks only seemed to make it stronger.

The transmitter had been set on the grass, and Cuthbert pushed it with his foot so that it hit the receiver already there, and bounced against the soft soil. Part of the lower trench fell in.

Ralph walked across the paddock, as if the dreadful noised burned him, glad to get out of earshot before anyone caught them at their game. Cuthbert followed, back to the house, for the conversion of John's den must be done by the time Handley returned from Gould's Lake.

They worked hurriedly, Ralph's twinges of conscience entirely gone. The rest of the maps came down. All logs and notebooks were crammed into baskets. The desk was cleared, racks dusted and posters destroyed in Cuthbert's excess of self-imposed evangelical uprooting. But he knew he was right, saw himself as the appointed discarder of the play-things of a community that was spiritually at the end of its tether. The false gods must be thrust out if righteous and proper life was to resume its course.

It looked like the sort of bare plain room one let to students or put aside for guests. He gave it a final glance, as if he would never see it again. Then they descended with their last loads and went unobserved to the paddock, to fill in the trench, and burn all incriminating paper, this time with no mistake.

Smoke rose from the declining fire in the paddock, mingling with the damp afternoon air as Handley went in by the kitchen door. Tea was still being served, and Myra was at the stove making Mark's feed. 'Where's Cuthbert?' Handley wanted to know.

'He went upstairs to comfort Maricarmen.'

He poured tea. 'I'm as thirsty as a centipede. She'll need a bit of calming down, I expect. I'm glad he has the necessary human feelings about him, though.'

'That walk took you long enough,' Enid said, coming in from the dining-room.

'I did a sketch while I was about it. Can't have people wondering what I was doing on Gould's Lake. They're a suspicious lot around here.'

'You think of everything.'

He wondered why there was such irony in her voice.

'Nearly everything. I'm sure I wasn't missed.'

'You weren't,' she answered scornfully. It didn't take much, he saw, for a good mood to melt. She went out, and he heard her talk in the dining-room to Dean—whom he couldn't abide these days. He was only waiting for him to go, though there seemed little hope of it unless he was booted out bodily. If he didn't take himself off soon he'd discuss with Cuthbert how it might be done. Everybody was too tolerant of him, especially Enid, who'd gone soft in a rather motherly way. But Handley told himself magnanimously that he was too proud to be vindictive, and went off to the peace of his studio for an hour before dinner.

Her straight dark hair spread to one side, except for a few strands that lay on her pale forehead. She looked at the plain white ceiling, preferring emptiness to the humiliation of seeing other people's faces. There were the marks of tears on her cheeks. She hardly breathed: using as little air as possible would keep out her shame.

Cuthbert sat in a chair by the bed. 'Feeling better?'

It was a meaningless question. 'I'm leaving tomorrow.'

He waited. She was rational again. 'Where are you going?'

'Back to Spain. That direction.' But she spoke in a dead voice, which wrung his heart because he knew there was so much life in her. 'I shan't be taking Shelley's trunk. Myra told me what was in it.'

'Any idea what you'll do?'

'No.'

'One needs to have plans.' His words were irrelevant. To those in distress you only listened.

'It's no good thinking what to do. I'll pack, and go in the morning.'

He bent close and pressed her hand, feeling a response. Any comfort was better than none at a time like this, she told herself, when she had no right to any.

'I'll be going with you,' he said.

'I don't love you.'

He winced, but only inwardly. 'I don't want love. I give it. How can I expect it? Giving it means everything.'

'Don't leave me,' she said.

Not like Shelley, he thought, or the Dawleys of the world. 'Come down to supper.'

'I can't.'

'They want you to. They love you. The community's successful in that respect. They've worked out a way of living that takes in everybody. You've been forgiven for this afternoon. All you have to do is turn up at supper, so that we can make our good-byes.'

'I don't know what to do.'

'Who does?' he wondered.

'I think you do,' she said with a sad, half departed smile. 'I must get up and wash my face.'

Once more he had escaped, though bleached by God's wrath. Mad man, mad woman, mad dog—the many manifestations of one's defective self—year after year they came at him with fang and claw, bullet and fire, rain and snow. What could he do to hold them at bay?

He went to the stove, hardly able to keep on his feet from so much whisky and close air.

Maybe he might after all stay alive and see his son grow up. The coffee-smell freshened him. It wasn't much to want, though in that blinding minute of conflict with Maricarmen he had asked and been given it by something which did not have a name and never could have. He was alive, and wondered why he should feel worse now than at the moment of peril. But the blood ran in such a way, the spirit worked peculiarly, and if the warning came afterwards instead of at the actual time, then perhaps the reason was that he must double his precautions against any such danger ever coming back.

The bulb filament glowed with a piercing question mark and lit the table brilliantly, showing up the half-drunk bottle of whisky. He took John's letter from under the typescript. It was a poor exchange: a wad of paper for a man. John had died when he should have lived. Dawley didn't think suicide was sinful, but would never do it himself because it was even more than a sin. There was no name for it. A man who killed himself had never finished being born. His mental sufferings were those of birth that as a grown man he was still by accident going through. The process overwhelmed him, for which he was to be pitied.

The whisky deadened him, but the coffee cleared away some of the deadness. His thoughts perished. He stood at the door of the caravan and breathed fresh air. It was still light, but dimming at the ruins of the sky which was blue and heavy. He was tired, but as if he would never sleep again, a feeling he'd often known in Algeria after real exhaustion. The evening smelled good, a trace of smoke from the paddock fire. Eric Bloodaxe growled at nothing, his chain scraping along the coconut matting of his kennel. Dawley put John's letter into his trouser pocket and strode across to the house, to kiss Mark goodnight before supper. Nothing perished for ever.

Chapter Forty-one

She didn't know why she married him, but then, who ever did? In fact it was hard to say why she'd done anything, even a few minutes after having done it. So far it hadn't mattered, but now, the fact that she regretted the big as well as the little things was beginning to eat at her liver.

Ralph slept. His huge looming menace, which she knew about from his frequent paranoid moods, didn't frighten her, because her trusting innocence sensed no physical danger. But now, pretending sleep on the bed, curled up and looking peaceful as long as his eyes were shut, he shot out a big homicidal fist when she went close and said it was time to get up. If she hadn't dodged, she'd have been felled to the floor.

So she stood by the window: 'Get up, you vicious slob. You can't lie there all evening.'

A few seconds seemed forever. 'Can't you hear me?' He didn't move. 'I've been married to you over a year and you haven't said ten words. It was the worst thing I did, getting tangled with a dumb pig like you. If this is marriage you can throw it up. I've had enough. Why don't you go back to Mummy and leave me in peace? I'm only twenty and you make me feel sixty. I wish Maricarmen had blown your head off when she was on the rampage. I'd divorce you if I weren't having another rotten baby—though I expect it'll drop out dead the same as the last one. You're so twisted-upside-down you can't make anything stick.'

He opened one eye, and gave it permission to look at her, a dim light of pettish resentment.

'I know you're awake,' she said, before he could close it. 'Let's go downstairs. I want to hear what goes on at supper. Then we can come back and make love. We haven't done it for a week. It ought to be marvellous.'

He opened both eyes. 'Are you really pregnant?'

It had been her favourite ploy since she was sixteen, and such casually dropped news often helped her to get what she wanted. 'I ain't seen a doctor yet, but I know I am.'

'Are you glad?'

'As long as I'm blind drunk when I have it, and push the bastard out alive. It won't make any difference to my life. I'll just leave it with mam and take to the road if it gets on my nerves. Or I'll send the sweet little bundle up to your mother in Lincolnshire, in revenge for palming you off on me. Better still, we can visit your parents for a grand reconciliation so's it'll shit and puke all over their chintzy parlour.'

'Oh stop it,' he said impatiently.

'The only good thing they can do,' she said, 'is drop dead and leave us their money. Then I could get a decent car and go for a long drive. They've always hated my guts, so why should I wish them well?'

'They're all right,' he said gently, knowing she had to have her fit now he'd had his—a pattern he'd frequently observed. 'They're just a bit misguided because they're older.'

'They hate me,' she pouted. 'They told me to my face, so I can't forgive them. Not till they grovel. If people love me I love them, but they hated me from the beginning.'

He put an arm over her shoulder. She was right. 'I'll write a letter in the morning, and tell them you're pregnant. They'll like that.'

Not even in the days before they married had she heard such a sane tone in his voice. When he kissed her lightly on the back of the wrist she began to worry, yet hoped it might last after all. The heady sensation was so intense she thought she was going to faint, a lack of will that convinced her she must be pregnant even though she wasn't absolutely sure.

She fought off the desire to inform him of this uncertainty, in case it had an adverse effect. She was beginning to feel a more complicated person, and wondered if she'd be able to live up to it, and whether he would be able to live up to her if she succeeded.

Handley sat by the vacant stove in his studio, indifferent to the huge half-done painting on the easel. After the happenings of the day he was quite sure Maricarmen would have to go. But there was much about her that he liked because she epitomised the spirit of female violence that could hold an artist in a state of enslaved youth till his dying day. He positively licked his chops over it, especially when thinking of petulant complaining Enid.

Maricarmen had stepped out of the recurring dreams of his life, but, as plain as any man could see, she was hooked by Cuthbert, his one and only freebooting fishy left-handed son with no lobes to his ears. Maybe your eldest son always held the final card of carrying off your own life's dream. Or perhaps it was just a sign of Handley growing up and getting old at last, and a brute sort of revenge from Cuthbert for having brought him into the world. It was a form of continuity he felt like spitting his guts at. But to lose one dream would merely set him free to conjure up another.

He stood, and stretched himself, lit a cigar and poured brandy from a hip-flask, as if determined to lead the good life even in his bachelor studio. The sooner Maricarmen went the better, so that the community could settle down once more. And if Cuthbert left as well, it would be another troublemaker less. Handley sniffed victory if he could get rid of them both, though he would say nothing at supper, and wait for a quiet opportunity to have a word with them in the morning. It would cost him his dream to get shut of Cuthbert, but every victory had its price. He drank to the peaceful months ahead.

Enid took cutlery into the dining-room and laid out thirteen places. Her progress along the table was slow because confusing and impossible notions raced through her mind. However devastating to her peace of heart, she felt already far away from the house she lived in. The uprooting had taken place during the long years she had been most solidly where she was. She hadn't noticed it. The roots had loosened when the roots were firmest, as it was obvious they would, considering the sort of life she had been forced to lead. Maybe she was thinking this so that Dean would not be blamed. There was a difference in their ages—

though not in the intensity of their love—which would put all foul imputations on to her and not him. She must be ready for it.

Life with Handley had been a vivid dream that had suddenly lifted and revealed a state of painful chaos. Her hands trembled, yet the disarray brought fabulous compensations, and the confusion gave her a base of euphoria not felt since the age of sixteen. It was as if seven children and Handley had never existed. Life in its changing cycles, its mysterious circles, was arbitrary in its miracles. She could have gone on getting older, taking the not unfruitful road to middle and old age, but she had changed because her ordinary heart was not so null as circumstances had continuously and relentlessly given out.

She pushed her hair back, and wiped a tear with one of the napkins. Love was the only thing that gave freedom. With love you didn't care any more, and so felt ready for any kind of freedom that love might suggest. Dean came in and set loaves of bread along the table. He smiled at her, too considerate to speak what others might hear, but he laid the the bread down and came to her where they couldn't be seen. 'I love you,' he whispered, kissing her. 'Don't forget to think again about what I asked you.'

She gripped his hand. 'Are you sure?'

His lips pursed, in pain and youthful anger. 'It's got to happen, you know it has. Don't wait too long.'

Enid felt his strong young arms around her and, in spite of the rather hard grip, sensed infinite sweet tenderness in them. The sensation was strange for, instead of her seeming to embrace him like the youth he was, it felt as if she were a small girl being fondled by someone twice her size and age. This impression almost caused her to swoon, so that it was impossible to distrust it.

Chapter Forty-two

Rain descended, dark and heavy, as it often does in war at the end of the day, when the guns have stopped firing, and clouds relax after the awful tension of destruction. Handley stood at the window and relished his thought, a will-o'-the-wisp banality to which rainfall gave the piss of death—he grinned, turning to sit down when the others came in. Richard had unchained Eric Bloodaxe at dusk, and the dog crouched gratefully in a new world of warmth and noise and plenty by Enid's chair. The company was now fourteen, pleasing to whoever felt superstitious.

The meal of cold meat and smoked fish and black bread and salad and sundry wines had gone on for nearly an hour, very little said because the day had made them wolfishly hungry. A cold chicken leg kept Eric quiet. Maricarmen sat by Cuthbert, as if he were the only one in the community on whom she could depend for protection. He put a comforting hand on her shoulder. She didn't look up, but he knew she needed his warmth, for the flesh was cold to the touch through her blouse. He felt her tremble, as if life were coming back in her, which might be necessary, judging by her pale and stony face.

Handley noticed that both she and Cuthbert ate with one hand each, the other two joined under the table. In fact most of the company seemed similarly afflicted, being split more into couples than usual—

except for Handley and Enid, who occasionally looked emptily at each other down the whole length of the table. Dean sat at her left side, he noted, still with that sly and satisfied look on his gullish face, which stayed there even while he butchered a loaf of bread.

Enid had an aura of happiness about her, as if she wanted to smile but daren't risk it in case it chased the happiness away. Or she was afraid someone might see it and wonder why? She wanted to hold Dean's hand, and it was plain a mile off that Dean wanted to touch her, for a vacuous self-important grin gave him away. But they didn't make contact, and this deliciously thwarted desire increased the air of glowing regard between them. Cuthbert felt sorry for them both—for the life sentence, he thought, that seemed in store for them.

Mandy and Ralph were together, and so were Catalina and Richard, and Maria and Adam. Myra was half-way along the table, and Dawley who was next to her had the blue envelope of John's letter conspicuously by his plate. Cuthbert wondered if he had read it already, he looked so wise and smug, or whether his hunched preoccupied pose of a misplaced Chelsea pensioner was fast becoming his normal burnt-out state. You couldn't tell with a man like that, who might be a vegetable one day, and a panther-like murderer the next. He gave an impression of great strength, an immense force that, if it suddenly lost its moral reasoning, could pull him so deeply under that he'd never surface again. Perhaps he didn't have a thought in his head nine-tenths of the time, though Cuthbert readily admitted that the thoughts he did have might conceivably support the dead nine-tenths of him buoyantly enough.

The wind outside grew to such strength that Eric Bloodaxe growled at phantoms thrown by it round the yard. You didn't know how loose the windows were till the bang of the wind got up, Handley mused. The four young children of the community were in bed, and he hoped the racket wouldn't stop them getting a good sound rest. When not on duty at the guns during the war he'd slept through such salvoes it was a wonder the people in his dreams had any eardrums left. Sleep was the source of all strength, he told himself, and children needed it like meat or calcium. He nodded to Dawley while standing to reach for the wine: 'You'd better read that letter, and get it over with.'

Richard lifted a tape-machine from behind the chair, and set it on the table. 'We chose a stormy night right enough.'

'You'll hear me just the same,' Dawley said, taking a clean knife and opening the envelope. He spread the sheets of paper, and began:

'Queen's Hotel, Gibraltar. By the time Dawley reads this letter I'll be speaking from the dead. I imagine your smiles when I say this. Is he mad? you'll ask. Is he really off at last? No, you aren't so ordinary that you will describe me with such words. They say there are no forests in Arabia Deserta, but why are there so many trees in me? I am not mad, but the trees are getting thicker and closer together, so I'll have to die before they stifle me.

'I can picture the scene, and feel I'm sitting at the same long table. Accept me back for a while so that I can tell you my thoughts. Maricarmen will be there, because Frank told me what Shelley had told him. It's natural she should visit you, if only to confirm that Dawley is not to be blamed for Shelley's death. The God of Revolution is an insatiable and jealous God, and drew them both equally into his savage mouth, and the mysterious ways that He moves in are not for anyone to question.

'I'm speaking to you from the dead, so listen to what I say. Do you know where the land of the dead is? Nor do I, though I am there already. But I've had the final experience that you haven't yet come to.

'I am able to go back and forward in time and space, between life and death. I'm sitting in this austere hotel room in Gibraltar. Dark clouds have hung over the Rock all day, and no doubt still do, which makes it as dull and chill as England—in spite of the smell of Spain. I also am with you one English summer's evening several months from now, having achieved the difficult state of being in two places at once, and at different times. I'm with you in life while this is being read. And I'm resting at a distance from you, in my own death. The light shines in both places. I am a man of faith. I love God, and He loves me in spite of everything. We respect each other.

'I've been conscious of this twofold fundamental split all my life. When I was tormented in Singapore twenty years ago I encouraged and developed it so as not to go under from suffering and pain. I survived when others perished. God did not love them enough to send them mad. Even then this ability to create a grand canyon out of the psyche in order to survive wasn't new to me. I used it early in life when my father bullied and beat me. You remember what a foul temper he had, Albert? I protected you from him once, and he hit me on the head with an iron poker that drew blood. But we combined forces, and that was the last time he was ever violent.

'You took me into your home after I got back from the war. Enid and yourself were the angels who saved my life. You provided me with a room in your peaceful Lincolnshire house where I could store my books and assemble my equipment—by which I still contrived to be in two places at once, often to the distress of occasional strangers who stumbled on me while I was at work.

'The state of being in two places at once meant that while my body was fixed to the radio as if I were on a foundering ship and trying to make my SOS heard before the water drowned me, my spirit was out in space among the stars searching for the word of God. Would the new Book of Genesis tap its way like bird noises into my brain from outer space? I waited avidly for it, but it never came—not at least in the way I expected. I learned Hebrew in case it appeared, for it was hard to believe that God would need to change His language.

'It is now midnight, and a ship's hooter is calling from the harbour. In the morning Dawley gets on the plane for London, and he'll take this letter. Before he does I will talk to you about Revolution and War, matters in which I have always had a profound interest. So I must try to make myself clear, to be in one mind, at one place, at the same time.

'Revolution and War have absorbed and obsessed you. The decaying components of the brain and body won't wait, so I write quickly. Revolution means War, and we are *living* people, all of us at this table, so how can we speak the words War and Life in the same breath? Listen to me. Don't despair. Don't condemn me. I am innocent, therefore I will kill myself. Think deeply. Someone is shouting from the street in Spanish.

'If War were a means of preserving life there would be no justification for this letter. But War is a method of acquiring more property, and killing in order to get that property. It is only another way of greed and death. It is not War however if a man has to struggle to save his family or his home—or even himself from imminent destruction. That is self-preservation. In the same holy language, a man who has nothing has a right and a duty to persuade he who has much to share his excess. Can the Prodigal Son become the Good Samaritan?

'It is easy to keep a sense of reality, being so close to my earthly death. Self-preservation means individuals, small groups, tribes at most, a small country perhaps. War, which is organised aggression, needs the resources of a nation and religion to sustain it. Nearly everyone admits this, but are glad nothing can be done about it. We are lazy, and too close to the earth. The men who wield the sword or fire the gun don't get rich. They are hired labourers, because armies maintain their hierarchies and caste structures in order to preserve themselves for future robberies. Those at the top get everything, while those at the bottom receive nothing.

'We know about the vicious war of aggression which calls itself defence, but educated people who should know better connive in this assassination of language so that robbery and murder can begin. The "involvements" in Africa and Asia are terrible for those deliberate victims stricken by these "defenders" from technologically superior nations.

'Noted military writers have commented that War is a continuation of life by other means. It is a conceit as old as Empedocles, but death and maiming of the young, energetic and talented is an insult to life.

'If the dead could speak we would know more about life. Would we know more about the nature of War from those who died by it? Those who do not want to die can say that War is evil. Coward is the most abominable word ever invented. Those who have died are the only ones who have a right to express an opinion. Perhaps they would say that death is good because they have already achieved it, and thus got over the dread of it. But the word "evil" may well sound hollow in such ears, and something far stronger would be spoken by them, because they have nostalgic memories of life when it was good, full of the love and peace which God intended they should have.

'But only the living can speak for the dead, and who of the living can rend the imagination to the extent of telling us what death is like? The act of dying has been many times described, but can anyone make real and pertinent the non-sensation of being actually dead? I am dead, but I cannot do it.

'Until the dead have spoken, those who are living may still find some among them who will say there is virtue in War, who will give out that there is pleasure and excitement in it, talk about the law of the jungle, and the survival of the fittest. There are poverty-stricken spirits who believe that to be a member of a diabolical army dedicated to the destruction of life and property will enrich themselves and their lives. They are always less poverty-stricken than the people they are about to destroy. The people they wish to destroy are nearly always spiritually richer. After they have destroyed them the aggressors can only be spiritually poorer themselves, too spiritually denuded in fact to realise it.

'Show me a patriot, and I will show you a monster of the human race. Patriotism is akin to sex in the head, a sort of spiritual pornography. A patriot ends by killing children, and lives to an honourable old age. He mixes back into society like a fish in water, and society accepts him willingly. I read English newspapers here, and notice how it is rightly deplored when an unfortunate man is knocked on the head in the street for his money and dies from it. The newspapers make an outcry and call for the criminal to be hanged. Yet when the crew of a bomber kills men, women and children, they keep silent or try to justify it. Governments who do not condemn these atrocities are composed of bandits and butchers. The air-crews are pushbutton slaughterers from the stratosphere, who murder in my name. I have never wanted to hurt anyone. Each bomb has my name on it, but if I am dead it won't have, because my name will no longer exist. My guilt is expunged, by suicide. Society has given me no other way.

'I think of Richard and Adam working over their theories of insurrection, sketching out timetables for a *coup d'état*, pinpointing the logic and hopes of Revolution. These are not fantasies. You would have them real. But Civil War is the same as any other war, its motives similar because the end result is death and an exchange of property. A country may fight for self-preservation, to keep out the robbers and butchers, but for no other reason.

'But I took part for many years in your discussions, and my motive was that of revenge against British officers who betrayed me to the Japanese for starting a left-wing news sheet when I was a prisoner in Singapore. For their action they were rewarded by no longer having to do labouring work with their men.

'So my revolutionary fervour arose from a desire for vengeance—to overthrow that system which willingly betrayed me for so little. But revenge belongs to God alone.'

'I'm thinking slowly, so have the patience to hear my sermon. Revolution is a holy cause, and the pursuit of it must go on. But without a sense of God and goodness and justice Revolution is bound to fail. Revolution always has, and always will, only come as an act of God, or after a series of circumstances which must be considered acts of God because no single group of men could have brought them about.

'But still one must train for it like a high priest in his or her apprenticeship. God desires this. Train and purify yourselves for it. Imbue yourselves with skill, patience, and faith, and goodness of heart. By regarding Revolution as religious more than political you can never be robbed of your faith by the shallow and insipid world. There is no such thing as a God that failed. Only you fail. The transient world lives in a dream. It lies on the edge of nightmare yet rarely tips into it—though this century of tears isn't over yet. Only good can negate evil.

'In order to attain and pursue these necessary qualities, Revolution must become the salvation of the individual. There is no contradiction. Revolution is not the normal enslavement of people which we have seen so far. It must mean liberation into mutual good. It must begin in peace and end in peace. A revolution that does not lead to real equality and real freedom is counter-revolution: it takes us back instead of forward. A revolution that is brought about by War and Civil War is likely to destroy freedom. So stop your false pastimes and theoretical pursuits, and instead convert people to the goodness of Revolution by turning it into a religion, but without idols, without figureheads, without suffering and killing, and with no more ritual than that of inspired words that will show all people how to understand and love.

'It is getting light. One side of me is drifting apart from the other. My lucidity is melting. I need a long sleep from which I shall only wake briefly so that Dawley can read this letter. When I kill myself the two sides of me will be so far apart that I'll know they can never come together again.

'You have often asked why I killed myself. These words must

explain it. I am tired and can suffer no more. Someone else must take my guilt and pain. There are many of us, though never enough. I hope I can remove the false influences from my dear and charitable family, having just come from a country where I saw a war being fought with such ferocity that it will bode little good for the future. I hope I am wrong. The world must have had enough of it. I am supposed to be an Englishman, but at the same time we're all foreigners, whether we like it or not, whether we believe it or not. With the elaborate visa of life we are allowed a short stay on earth. The one virtue is to know oneself as a man or woman of the world, and not of one country.

'I want to save you from the perdition of unnecessary bloodshed, of fruitless hope, of futile and useless suffering. Leave your intoxicating, heart-chilling pastimes and seek the more spiritual way. Be like cosmopolitan Children of the Book. If everyone followed the precept—Know thyself—there would surely be no greater Revolution. Don't let the easier road pull you along it. Deny the fervent drudgery that kills whatever god-fearing regard you have for your fellow women and men. Goodbye, until the final meeting of us all.'

Chapter Forty-three

'He's broken my spirit,' Richard said, turning the recorder off.

Handley scratched a match into flame, and relit his cigar. 'You're lucky. It'll be soonest mended.'

A wine bottle tapped at a glass. Wind banged the house, and thunder rumbled over the chimneys. Richard unknowingly drew his head back in the attitude of Handley himself. 'You can tell me that when you've had yours broken.'

'It has been often enough,' Handley said mildly, 'and I expect it will be again.'

Cuthbert shaded his eyes from the light. John's thoughts in some uncanny way accorded with his own. 'I'd like to ask him a few questions, though,' Richard called out.

'Makes sense to me,' Handley said sharply. 'Slide the brandy along.'

'That's because he's your brother,' Adam said. 'We'd still like to talk to him.'

'Wouldn't we all? But that's his strength: we can't. And never could. He had his language: we had ours. And he's had the final say—at a price.' He collected meat scraps and chicken bones, an overspilling platter which he set in front of the dog.

Having read aloud, and done his best to put expression into it, Dawley had missed some of the letter's finer points. He would study it later, because the argument had seemed confused. For what its message of crack-pot God-love might be worth, he would try to sort it out. But first he'd copy it, and give the original to the museum upstairs.

'I'm leaving in the morning,' Maricarmen said, breaking the brief silence.

'I'll be going as well,' Cuthbert told them.

Handley was on his way back to his chair. He was glad, but at the same time regretted it. 'Where to?'

'France. Spain, maybe. Where Maricarmen goes, I'll go.'

Handley envied him—for a moment. 'I'll drive you to London. We'll take the Rambler so's there'll be enough space for your luggage.'

'I'll need money,' Cuthbert said.

'There's a tobacco tin on the table in my studio with a few hundred in it. No, don't take that. That's my secret reserve!' He didn't look at Dean while he said it, but knew his sharp ears took it in. I'll trap him yet. 'We'll call at the bank in town, and get five hundred out. That'll see you right. But don't be too rash with it.'

Dawley was surprised that Cuthbert and Maricarmen had given in so easily, and wondered whether, with the main threat shifted, the community could go on. The shattered spirit did not need peace: with danger pressing like a stone on his veins, he had in fact worked better at his book.

'What do you want to go to London for?' Enid asked, the first words said directly to him that evening.

She hadn't taken in that her eldest son was leaving home, which seemed strange to him. 'To see Teddy Greensleaves about my next show,' he said, though hoping to visit Daphne Ritmeester, after such a hard wearing day. He expected an argument, but she was unusually quiet, and he was glad, because even if he'd no valid excuse for the trip he'd have gone just the same.

She got up to make coffee. 'Dean can help me carry it in.'

'He is a jack-of-all-trades,' Handley said, touching off laughter along the table.

Adam stood: 'Father, may I say something?'

Handley poured more brandy. 'I'm in a good mood. I'll drink myself into a three-cornered pigpen if I'm not careful. John's letter put me into a considerate frame of mind. Makes me realise that life is short. Perhaps I've lost my youth. If so, there's hope I'll paint something yet. It's nice to think, though, that one's sons can become inordinately polite when the occasion arises! Even Cuthbert's getting that way. Maybe it's because he's in love. We all go under in the end. Love is the most extreme form of alienation I know. Or is it marriage?'

'Stop it, Father,' Cuthbert said mildly.

'Don't worry, old son, at what I say. I'm relieved and happy that the day's ended well, and when I'm happy I tend to say the opposite of what I mean because my nerve-ends get a bit painful when they jump.'

Ralph, too easily disturbed by such moods in Handley, twitched his wrist and broke the delicate stem of a wine glass.

'You're not with us,' Handley said. 'You're over the hills and far away.'

'Leave him alone,' Mandy cried, drawing the loose bits together, fearing he would send her unstable husband on another lone trail of mad zigzaggery. 'You're getting as pissed as a newt.'

'You know I'm fond of Ralph,' Handley said. 'We understand each other at last. It's just that so many pots have been getting smashed lately we'll soon be eating off the backs of old envelopes.'

Adam sipped coffee. 'We're thinking of going to university.'

The cigar fell from Handley's mouth and hissed in his coffee, ruining both. 'What's that?'

'We've got our A levels. It should be easy.'

'And if we don't go now, we may be sorry one day,' Richard said.

'So you regret not going to university?' Handley said. 'They're hankering to round off their state education by a final bout of conformity. Nobody with any self-respect has ever been to university, you couple of fat-necked moaners. Don't you know that? You can regret you weren't born to inherit a million acres, or that you haven't won the pools, but for God's sake don't regret not having gone to university. Can't you skive here just as well as there?'

When Handley carried on like this it was easy to score points against him. 'I'm not an artist,' Adam said, 'so of course I'll regret it. I can't live on National Assistance, like you and Mother did, or hang on to your turn-ups forever.'

'You see,' said Richard, 'we think we're wasting our time studying the theory of revolution. As far as you're concerned it's only something that keeps us out of mischief. Yes, we've known that for a long time.

But if we go to a university we can put our revolutionary and working-class contacts to good use in the student movement.'

Handley lit another cigar, and snapped his finger for Dean to bring more coffee. 'You want me to fork out the money and help you through?'

'It would be good if you could,' said Adam.

'My children's wish is my command.'

'Buy me a car, then,' Mandy called out.

While Handley was concocting a suitable reply, which by the workings of his face promised not to take too long, Ralph said, in a reasoned and amiable voice: 'It would be a big mistake, father-in-law, to buy her a car.'

'There's no danger of old tight-fist doing that,' Mandy said, shocked at Ralph going so firmly against her, yet not angry because it seemed another mark of his newly found sanity.

Handley controlled his ire by waiting for Enid to stamp vociferously on Mandy's dearest wish. But she merely looked before her in some embarrassed way that had nothing to do with the present issue. He wondered what great or secret event had taken her over in recent days. He'd go to London in the morning, but resolved to be more attentive to her when he got back. He knew it would be better if he squashed the idea of his trip, but when he was impelled to do something by the compass-pull of his loins, not all the persuading lodestone of both poles could draw him away from it.

Chapter Forty-four

They put their trunk and cases in the big rear space of the Rambler, and leaned close against each other in the back seat without saying a word the whole way to Welwyn.

No speech could touch the galaxy of devastation inside her. Dawley's farewell grip of her hand, and his bereaved immobile face, were still there. She had not spilled his blood, but felt she had killed his revolutionary spirit nevertheless, and because of this could not remember what Shelley looked like any more. The only chance of retrieving something from the wreckage would be if Handley turned the car round and took her back to Dawley. But she was empty and icy, and could ask for nothing. The stiffness of pride and honour had taken over from the heart.

When she touched Cuthbert's hand, it was not out of affection, but to feel skin which had living blood behind it. He sensed the depth of her loss. Its misery spilled over to him. So he responded to her touch, but with casual affection, reasoning that the poison of her recent disasters would slowly spill out—the further they got from the house. And if it came back at times he would be there to guide her through any psychic upset. He was calm and solicitous, and would wait for her to collapse, if she had to, so that he could mend her. By then she might grow to love him. If not he would be satisfied for the privilege of being near. He settled for such conditions because it seemed the only way she could begin to love. She was someone who needed life itself to break her down, and life itself to mend her.

Handley enjoyed driving on empty lanes. He liked handling a car, and he loved painting. He was fond of women, and he relished the countryside. In other words, he felt in a good mood, wearing his new brown suit with collarless shirt and button-up waistcoat, watch chain and ankle boots, cigar and aftershave. He'd even cut his nails the night before. A poor old coney was flat on the road, fur and blood spread-eagled. The machine age was mixed with his bucolic aspirations. His obsession with machines was entangled with a desire for people and slow-motion living, the beautiful raped by the abominable and all in the same body and soul. He fondled machines, angles, emotive forces that he could not see but which functioned under the slightest whim of his will. Maybe if I got this peace of mind I'm always hankering for I wouldn't paint, he thought.

Adam and Richard would also be packing up soon. With four people pulling out he wondered if the community would keep going. Thinking of the future made him so nervous that, coming to the main road, a lorry almost ground him into the tarmac because it was too close and fast behind. A duel of hooters followed, till Handley's powerful engine pulled him out of earshot. Fluent and flowered curses died in his gorge because Maricarmen sat in the back. It began to rain, and traffic was thick on the narrow winding trunk-lane. 'You should have taken the motorway,' Cuthbert suggested.

'It's too dull,' he replied, vision beamed on a huge truck in front that spat black sludge over his windscreen. 'I'll get you there.'

'I'm not worried.'

'You trust your old Dad, eh?' He pressed the brake pedal when the lorry suddenly pulled up. The car skidded slightly. He put the gear in neutral and drew the handbrake on, then reached into the glove box for a hip flask. 'They tell you not to drink and drive, but I can't drive in these conditions unless I have a drink.' He took a swig and passed it back: 'Have a good go. I filled it up last night.'

They drank, and Cuthbert sent it forward. Handley sipped again, just in time before the lorry moved and he slipped into gear to follow it. A police car waved them on. A car was upside down beyond a bend, and an articulated lorry lay on its flank. A wall had crumbled under the impact, and dozens of barrels were scattered among the trees of an orchard. Police were writing in little books, and marking maps, and several people were walking dazedly up and down, as if to get the chill out of their veins, though the day was warm and humid. One man lay in the grass with blood on his face.

He looked in the mirror to check traffic behind, and saw Maricarmen cross herself at the accident. 'It's a battle-field,' he said, hearing a yelp of brakes some way in front. 'You often wonder whether the next car you see's got your name along its bumpers. I feel like an old soldier though where driving's concerned: the longer you survive the more you learn how to.'

Traffic speeded up, and on a straight section Handley overtook the sludge-chucking lorry. 'I hope you'll be all right at home,' Cuthbert said.

'No danger of that.'

'Take care of mother.' The memory of her being loved-up by Dean chilled him—a picture he'd not forget in a hurry. He'd said nothing about it either to Handley or Enid because, after all, they were grown people who had to sort out their own problems. No doubt Dean would be sent on his way, and they'd settle into the old cat-and-dog routine once more. The only thing he was sure of was that his parents loved each other. It was good to have an eternal set-up you could fall back on at moments of insecurity.

'I'll guard her with my life,' Handley told him. 'Why else do you think I'm on earth? I'll look after anybody if they need my help, but she's number one.'

'I'm sorry for the disturbance I caused,' said Maricarmen.

'It's good to have a shake-up now and again,' Handley smiled. 'Anyway, there's no hard feelings in our family—otherwise we wouldn't have lasted five minutes.'

Sucked into the London rush hour, he kept his window shut to avoid lethal gusts of coagulating motor traffic, but then opened it for fresh air to avoid going to sleep, finally cursing the sharp metalised poison that came in and gave him a headache. At half past nine he drew into a parking bay near Covent Garden, convenient for his bank on the Strand. Cuthbert and Maricarmen waited, and when he returned he put an envelope into his son's hand: 'There's fifty ten pound notes. Don't spend it all at once.'

'I feel I'm robbing you.'

Handley lit a cigar. 'You're my son, aren't you?'

'You're generous, that's all I can say.'

'As long as you don't hold it against me. Generosity don't count with your own family.' They walked through the market to a café, and sat down to sandwiches and tea. 'A steamy day,' he said, 'like a cold jungle. Take care of yourselves. Don't get shot, squashed, poisoned, or slung in clink. If you want to pay me back for the five hundred quid just live safely. That'll satisfy me.'

Cuthbert sat opposite his father and Maricarmen, amazed at how one of a pair they seemed, Handley lean like a gypsy, and she a Spanish woman who was bound to thicken to his satisfaction in later years. Such similarities drew them together, all in the same family at last, no matter how farspread they'd be in a few days time. 'We'll stay in town tonight,' he said, 'somewhere around Victoria, and set out for France tomorrow. We'll get off the train at Bayonne, near the Spanish frontier, and talk things over there.'

'I have friends in San Sebastian,' Maricarmen said, 'and in Irun. They'll tell us if there's anything we can do.'

He remembered her crossing herself in the car. 'Nothing violent, I hope?'

'No,' Cuthbert said.

She smiled. 'We'll be all right.'

'You'd better be,' Handley said, 'or I'll come and pull your arses out of it—wherever you are. Still, you're grown up, just like I am—if that means anything—so you can look to your own safety. It's a hell of a world, though, if you want to do something about it. All I ask is that you mull over John's letter.'

Cuthbert finished his tea, and pushed his cup to the middle of the table, as if wanting to be on his way. 'I typed a copy last night. I'll always want it with me.'

'Maybe I'll get it printed,' Handley said. 'A hundred pamphlets. John might like that. Ay, but it's terrible to lose a brother. It's still eating me, and always will, otherwise I'd be dead. All he was suffering from was a regressive return—as they call it—the famous depression of incoming travellers back to this tight little island after a fair sojourn somewhere else. Or maybe he was the man who thinks there's something beyond the womb but discovers there isn't. John always felt like a rat in a trap while he was in England. No wonder he couldn't come back. I hope you don't get the same way when you feel like hiving in again.'

Cuthbert lifted a hand benignly. 'There's no chance of that.'

Handley drove them to a hotel on Ebury Street, and left them alone at last.

Chapter Forty-five

The sun dazzled as he rounded the island by Buckingham Palace. He felt free, caught in the vital pull of London, which he always enjoyed. He swore it wasn't because Cuthbert had gone, but knew that in part it certainly was. Dangerous and smouldering Maricarmen had taken hard-headed Messianic Cuthbert to some mad do-gooding adventure on the slopes of the Pyrenees, and now he hoped for a great peace which would enable him to resume his painting and pull off a few big ideas that were jumping on the trampoline of his mind.

He turned up the Mall towards Piccadilly, going smoothly between traffic. London was hell to get into and out of with a car, but once inside it didn't seem too bad because he knew every one-way back-street and was never at a loss for movement. He thought of Daphne Ritmeester, whom he hadn't seen since their spine-shifting encounter several months ago. In fact he couldn't smell London without the wick-fever coming on, and hoping for a repetition of that midnight potent flash in the middle of the day—which seemed never likely to happen again, at least not by chance.

He went along Dover Street and through Berkeley Square, finding a spare meter almost opposite the gallery. It was only half past ten and he wondered whether Teddy would be in. He was certainly difficult to get by phone, like all other English gaffers and executives. If you phoned before eleven they weren't there yet. Patiently, you went back to your painting and forgot to phone again till twelve, by which time they were out at lunch. So it was no use phoning before three. And if you were too absorbed in your work and didn't ring till four they were already on their way home. Whole days had often passed before he'd pinned someone down. The phone seemed more antiquated than smoke signals, and he found it quicker to make contact simply by driving to London, or writing a letter. They talk about the working man being a skiver, he thought.

The gallery wasn't open, so he walked to Selfridges to search out a present for Enid in case he spent time in Daphne's bed. The midweek store was crowded, and he hated being thrust among so many people, wanting only to get back to the quiet of his paddock and studio. The rhubarb noise burned his ears.

A sweet old English lady with the usual sharp holdall jabbed at him as if to get by. He trod on her foot by way of his own back, and smiled an apology. She bent down to rub the pain out of her toes, and slipped two pair of tights—which she had previously knocked off the counter—into her shoplifter's reticule. She was too low to be seen by television scanners beaming from above, and in any case he'd screened her by his apology. It was well worked out, he thought, getting on his way before he was grabbed as an accomplice.

He bought a tin of cigars from the tobacco section, then an expensive bottle of French scent for Enid. Glad to be in the air, even though it was ninety per cent fumes, he dashed between the cars and towards Teddy's gallery.

It was open, and he walked through an exhibition of huge grey drawings by some gloomy sado-masochistic German who seemed to have been brought up by a mad aunt in a damp cellar on the banks of the Rhine. He went into the inner office without knocking, to find Teddy in a casual embrace with a young man in overalls who looked like one of the window-cleaners. He hurriedly unclasped, a flush spreading over his strawberry face: 'Off you go then, Bill. I'll see you later.'

'All right, guv'nor,' said Bill, walking nonchalantly back to the main part of the gallery.

'I know we have no secrets,' Teddy complained, 'but you ought to knock.'

'I'm sorry,' Handley said, sitting in the leather armchair. 'I was here half an hour since, saw the place shut, and thought you'd gone off to Portugal with all my money.'

'Yours wouldn't get me far,' he laughed, noting how smart Handley looked. 'But you have got some more coming to you. The Tate are asking for a dozen paintings, and they'll do half of them on postcards. Then the Keel Gallery in Zurich wants to put on a big exhibition of contemporary British painters. You're to be the big star. A private gallery in Rome, and one in Venice are getting the hot flushes about you. You're really hitting the jackpot.'

'That's just as well,' Handley said, feeling fashionably dead at the idea of getting more money than was good for his inner life. 'My children are starting to leave home—which is always expensive.'

Teddy, ever hospitable, poured him his customary brandy. 'Too much tranquillity can ruin an artist. Maybe a bit of emotional stir-about will do you good.'

He held up his glass before drinking, not caring to mention the stir-about of the last day or two. 'Any news of Daphne?'

Teddy didn't like anyone referring to Lady Ritmeester by her first name. 'Daphne?'

'Oh piss off! You know who I mean: my glorious proud-arsed patroness with the hair like Sugar Loaf Mountain.'

'Lady Ritmeester? Came in last week and mentioned she was going to the family chateau in France for a while.'

Teddy seemed glad to give out this piece of news, Handley noted, as a little titbit of revenge. 'I'm thwarted in my evil sexual designs. Like you were when I came in. So let's get back to money.'

'Didn't you receive my letter?'

'I got nothing.'

'My secretary sent it a week ago.'

'I suppose my mad son-in-law found it,' Handley said, 'and burned it.'

'Anyway, I sold "Abraham in Flanders", "The Prodigal Poacher" and "Jacob and Esau". I've had offers for four others. Then there are royalties on reproductions. Comes to nearly £3,000.'

'Was there a chit in the envelope?'

'I believe so.' He took a cheque book from his drawer and showed the stub for £2,952.

'Write me another,' Handley said. 'And give me a drink. My hand's trembling.'

'If you don't mind,' Teddy said, 'I'll see first whether or not this one's been cashed.'

Handley flushed. 'Don't you trust me?'

He poured a large brandy. 'Absolutely. With my life—and that's saying something. But I've got to do it this way to satisfy my financial people. It's only a matter of days. If you're short of a thousand I can give it you on account.'

Handley sat down. 'I'm not that short—yet.'

'Tell me how your work is.'

The lost cheque worried him. 'The crack-up's coming. But work's all right. The community's bursting at the seams. Four people dropping out. I was thinking of asking Daphne to join. You as well.'

'Very kind,' Teddy said sarcastically. 'But I don't like the country. Fresh air brings back my asthma. Why don't you have lunch with me? We'll split a bottle of good wine at "The Flayed Ox".'

'I'm off to Rowney's for a stock of paints and paper. Anyway, I've got to look for the cheque. I'll go back home and tear the place apart.'

'Just do some more marvellous work,' Teddy said.

'I sometimes think I'll never even paint a door again.'

'A good sign. Something's bubbling in you. You're a fine artist, Albert.'

Handley stood, sick of being where he was, though he didn't know where else he wanted to be. 'I'd often prefer it if there wasn't so much money coming in,' he said, anger breaking through his pleasant humour. 'I've worked half my life on begging letters and the dole, and suddenly I get swamped with ten thousand a year. I'd much rather get fifteen hundred so that I can scrape along just one notch above the bread line.'

Greensleaves didn't like this sort of talk. 'Your work's the same, whatever you earn.'

'Yes, but if I got enough to eat and nothing else I wouldn't stick to what made me rich, but would do something different. It'd be more interesting.'

'For God's sake don't change your style,' Teddy exclaimed, and Handley noted with satisfaction that he'd never seen him so agitated.

'It's exactly what people want. You're in a bad way. What's eating you?'

Handley pushed his face to within half a foot: 'You're eating me—with chutney and pickle. You've got my liver in your fangs. And, naturally, I don't like it.'

Teddy felt a strong impulse to kiss him, but resisted because he didn't relish the savage punch-up that was sure to follow when his gesture of goodwill was misconstrued. 'I don't understand you,' he said, as Handley drew away.

'I don't savvy myself. But I've always painted exactly as I liked, and the fact that I've made money in the last few years hasn't changed my ideas a bit. I'm not that sort of bloke. If Enid and I had to live in a tent so that I could experiment with other styles, we'd do it. I'm not saying I'm going to, but it might come one of these years.'

Teddy smiled with relief. 'Every artist has to develop and widen his talent. As long as he keeps on the broad road of it, and doesn't wander into dead-ends and byways.'

'You can leave that to me. I certainly shan't do the sort of black melancholy crap that's hanging in your gallery this morning. I never was one to frighten myself to death. Anyway, thanks for the invitation to lunch. I must do my shopping and get back to Enid.'

They parted on the usual good terms. Handley drove towards Percy Street, but got glued in traffic for half an hour around Oxford Circus, so that by the time he'd found a meter-bay, and bought his painting materials, it was well into lunch-time. He sat alone with a quick pizza on Charlotte Street, mulling over the fate of the fat cheque that never got to him.

Chapter Forty-six

Saying good-bye to Maricarmen, in the cool and early morning, was like making his farewell to a woman at the end of a fiery sexual affair. She had, after all, taken a hard line on killing him, and two people couldn't get closer to actually enlacing than that. He thought she must feel it too, when they shook hands and looked at each other. She smiled, as if to mark this closeness, but it quickly died on reaching the point when there seemed to be almost no barrier between their intimacy.

Through the frigid cant of departure Dawley knew that what they meant to each other could never die, no matter where she went—even though they might not meet again. The Rambler slid through the front gate. He watched it go up the village street and out of sight.

It was a green day, when the mind swung neither one way nor the other but simply followed any event that turned up. He sensed that the community would not now get back into its routine because Cuthbert and Maricarmen had taken whatever impetus it had. There was a heap of mail on the kitchen sideboard, but nothing for him. He poured a mug of coffee, then cut a thick slice of bread and put a lump of butter on his plate. 'So they've gone.'

'I'm fond of them both,' Myra said, 'but Maricarmen was like ice, as if she hardly knew what she was doing.'

He wolfed his breakfast. 'She'll wake up. Everyone does.'

She thought of herself: 'I wonder if they do?'

'That's the way it usually goes. It's a fair system.'

Ralph came in, hands rough as if he'd been shifting earth. He stood by the mail, and slipped a long envelope into his pocket. 'I'll see to him,' he offered, taking the dish of porridge to feed Mark. She was glad to let him, and sat opposite Frank.

'Been digging somebody's grave?'

'Filling one in,' Ralph smiled. 'Somebody else dug it. I'm keeping fit, really. Cuthbert advised me to do more physical work. He said it was good for me. It would teach me how to think.'

Dean came into the kitchen. 'I can smell coffee.' He looked refreshed, but worried, as if he'd already been awake for an hour. 'Cuthbert's gone?'

'You didn't say good-bye,' Frank said, reaching for the honey.

Lines creased the skin of his low forehead. 'I'm sorry. Do you think Cuth's off for good?'

'It's hard to imagine,' Dawley said.

He took the coffee pot from the Aga, and poured two mugs: 'One's for Enid,' and went back upstairs with them.

'He's asking for trouble,' Frank said.

Myra refilled their cups. 'He *is* fond of Enid.'

'I'll say.'

The letter in Ralph's pocket called out to be read as he went upstairs, so he opened it at the first landing. There was no sun to see by and light was dim, but as he looked at the clear typed lines, his left hand began to tremble, then the right. He leaned against the window to re-read the first paragraph, for he had gone no further. The words assaulted his senses, and his legs shook so that he was forced to sit down. He grew dizzy, and held the letter away. Then he became positively tired, as if he hadn't been to bed all night.

With forceful tightening of the sinews and eyes, he read it from start to finish, till every word was plain, and the meaning had shot right through to his marrow. He wanted brandy, but laughed at the idea. There would be no justification any more in stealing Handley's. The end of the world sat in his lap, coolly written on two sheets of stiff lawyer's paper.

His lips were as dry as leaves that had been in the sun for a month, about to disintegrate at the next breath of wind. Mandy wouldn't like

to be brought out of her warm dreams and back into tl
world. She would want to know, of course, that they w
could now grow up to any age they would like to be.
letter a third time he saw that his proper upbringing ha
for this event, but he still wondered how Mandy would

He went into their room, and sat calmly on the end of the bed, folding the letter into an inside pocket. The pressure of his body disturbed the mattress under her. Or perhaps she heard the click of the door, for she drew the bedclothes over her face.

'What time is it?' Her voice, though normal, shocked him so that his whole body jumped.

Beginning to shake slightly, he controlled himself. 'Time to get out of bed.'

'It's never time for that.'

He nudged the rise of her haunches. 'It is now.'

No one else could have caught the alarm in his voice. She swept the clothes free, and sat up, a violent move which unsettled him, though his heart stayed quiet. 'What's the bloody matter now?'

'Nothing,' he said.

'There is. Tell me.'

'You look adorable. I love to see you wake in the morning.'

'Don't keep me in suspense.'

'I have a letter.'

She pulled the fine blonde hair from her face. 'I'm dying for some coffee.'

He stood. 'I'll get you some.'

'What letter?'

'I'll tell you over coffee,' he smiled.

'Tell me now. Don't torment me.' The familiar look of disturbance was in his eyes, the sheen of blight preceding a fit that could last for weeks. Her dream had been nondescript and pleasant, part of a wide contentment that had come after making love last night. But she had noticed before how such deep sexual delight between them contributed to his imbalance next day. The same bleak feeling of waking up to its first signs were on her. 'What is it?' she whispered.

'An aunt died, and she's left me her house, a lot of land, and two hundred and ninety thousand pounds.'

An awful despair tore at her heart. Tears poured down. After his last g melancholy stretch she told herself that if he had another she'd be it only for the loony-bin. Her control was snapping at this latest flight of his mad fancy. She leapt out of bed and put on her dressing gown. 'Don't say any more, please. Let's just go down and have a big breakfast, then you'll feel better.'

'It's true, my love.'

'Leave me alone,' she screamed. 'You're trying to kill me. You want to send *me* crackers! I know you do.'

It was difficult to stay calm, but the knowledge of the money made him more sure of himself than he'd ever been. Yet at the same time the sight of her weeping was the strongest assault on his self-assurance. Seeing at last what he'd done, he held her, and kissed her cheeks, taking away the salt of bitterness.

She sobbed against him, and when he was about to speak broke in: 'Don't say anything else about this story, please.'

His voice was quiet when he retold what was in the letter, but the cooler his voice, and the more convincing his tone, the more she knew he was lying. His worst madnesses had begun with such a sane and realistic display. He took the letter out, wondering why he hadn't done so at first. 'Do me the favour of looking at this, before you go off again.'

If only she hadn't come to. It was bad enough waking up, without having such problems. He noticed how she was afraid to take the letter for fear it was just another trick, but maybe most of all in case it turned out to be true. It was difficult to hold himself into the new life of firm control, but he had to get used to it, for it was certainly here to stay.

She read the first sheet, then the second, her face turning white as she went from one to the other. She looked at Ralph, her eyes rolling with panic. They closed and she fainted clean away, bumping on to the floor like a newborn child, the letter fluttering.

Ralph felt like a hero. When your wife fainted it was something definite. Life was real. You could do something about it. The power of money was marvellous. He took a bottle of eau-de-Cologne from the dressing-table and rubbed it on her forehead, then over her nose.

Her head moved. She opened her eyes when he got her on to the bed. He went quickly downstairs, pressing through the crush of the kitchen to fill a tray with bread, butter and coffee.

Chapter Forty-seven

It wasn't a good day for a walk, and called for macs in case it rained. Mist lay along the main street, but thin and ready to disperse when Frank and Myra went uphill, a mobile mist spewed about by a new-born breeze.

The route they took out of the village ascended from Cuckolds' Cross to Thieving Grove, a narrow and winding road running a short distance over a plateau of open fields, till the land descended abruptly towards the next village. They passed the housing estate, where Myra remembered canvassing at the last election with her husband George, glad to find at least a few Labour voters in the neighbourhood.

In recalling him she also thought of the book Frank had written on Algeria, and some time ago spoke of it to the publisher who had brought out George's book on the poetry of landscape. The publisher, it seemed, was waiting eagerly for Dawley's manuscript, hinting that anything mentioned by Myra would be a fair gamble for his up and coming firm.

He also knew she was acquainted with Albert Handley, from whom he wanted a book of engravings. Unlucky in his approaches to Teddy Greensleaves, he was willing to try a roundabout way. Myra was aware of this and, knowing Dawley's narrative to be worth any printing risk, was quite happy to hold out some promise of a book from Albert, who had in fact agreed to a combined deal of his material with

Frank Dawley's memoirs. She explained the scheme as they walked slowly uphill.

'You mean I'll be a writer?' he said, inwardly pleased.

'Why not?'

'Maybe I'm too old. Most writers are dead by thirty,' he joked. 'Still, it'll be good to earn some money. You've supported me long enough.'

'Are you worried about that?'

'Not in the way you mean. But I believe in the equality of the sexes, so I'd like to contribute my slice.'

'Don't be impatient.'

'I'm not, as long as you marry me.'

She smiled: 'Well, I'm having our second child.'

'You mean you don't have much option?'

'I don't, do I? But I'll still marry you. As long as I don't lose *my* equality!'

'I love you. That'll help.'

'So what else matters?'

'If I thought love was the only thing that counted,' he said, 'I'd hang myself, or take to the road. But it's important enough for us to stay together, which of course means getting married.'

They stood by a gate at the top of the hill, the church of the next village coming out of the mist below. Opposite was the triangle of wood known as Thieving Grove, a few acres of heavy-smelling green thickets. 'You don't give me much to go on,' she said, knowing that the less ponderous they were about the future the more secure it would be for them both. But she was unable to live like that. She wanted some statement, no matter how vague, a formula of commitment no matter how uncertain—to come from his own lips. For she also knew that what he said, he stuck to. And he knew it, too, which was why he'd say very little.

'I'm here,' he pointed out—unnecessarily, she thought. 'I won't run away.'

'I don't care whether you do or not.'

'So that's it,' he started. 'A minute ago it was equality. I'm all in favour of that, but what sort do you mean?'

This touched her rawly. 'Together we can seem strong, and even be strong. But apart, things aren't so firm.'

He looked at her, a woman with a light in her eyes that would take a lifetime to penetrate, but what riches would pass from one to another in the process! Last night he had relished her small breasts and firm hips, and now when she turned a gaze on him he found it hard to meet.

'Human beings are like that,' he said. 'I don't expect anything else. I'm not too proud to lean on you if you'll do me the honour of leaning on me! I not only love you, but I like you as well, and I can't say more than that. I never was much good at lovers' speeches, but our love's gone beyond that by now. It's going into the fire of life and God knows what it'll find there. The best love goes into it, and if it's worth anything it never comes out because the flame won't relax its grip. In many ways it's a savage flame, jealous on both sides, but it holds us together in bed at night so that we feel part of the earth and each other. Can I say it'll go on longer than that? Whether the flame lasts till we die depends on what we've got in us. But who can say? Who can promise or prophesy? I feel it in you, but only you can tell me whether I've got it in me. I don't even know whether it's love or not, and that's how I feel, and all I can say about it. After that it's normal everyday humdrum life and work and care—while knowing for sure that the fire burns in us both for as long as we want it to. I've grown to dislike strength. I distrust it now, so I know it's not strength. It's something beyond. I'm not strong, and I'm not weak either, and maybe it's the same with you, though I'll let you say so if you like, and if you don't I won't mind! It's just a rooted feeling I've got, because we've been through a lot together, and for each other, so it's had time to get there, though I saw it first thing, when you left your husband that day and came to my room in Camden Town. If you remember it as long as I do we're in that flame for good. The trouble with me is—and I know you've always felt this—that I don't explain things. I don't talk, I don't say much. It's not that I'm inarticulate, because my mind is continually talking and explaining and saying things to itself. I just don't think many things are important, or worth bringing to my lips. It's not even that I'm too lazy to talk, either, because I'll often go out of my way to do things or work. Anyway, it always takes less energy to talk than it does to listen, or say nothing. While you talk you make energy to go on talking. I'm sure of that. You start to tell lies because you get carried away. You get too much energy, so you say things that don't matter.

I suppose that's why I don't or won't say that I love you in so many words, because I believe that things should speak for themselves, though they hardly ever do, so I have to end up saying something. And anyway, if the comforting and tormenting flame is bright enough, there's no need to point it out. It's almost sacrilegious to show it for what it is, not because I'm afraid of it going away but because I feel embarrassed at stating the obvious. Maybe I'm wrong. In the beginning was the Word, and I should speak, but at the same time I know that one should not use the Word in vain, and who's to say whether it's vain or not till it's finally over and we're dead?'

She stood a few feet from him, her face turned away, listening to his measured words while a thin rain fell. He could have gone on talking. When he once began, it sounded even more natural than not talking. But he stopped, and stepped over to her, took her by the shoulders and kissed the back of her neck. 'You weren't listening?'

She turned, which he was glad of so that he could kiss her lips. 'What have you left for me to say?'

She looked at him, a faint apprehension on realising from the set of his face that she was likely to be with him for a long time. Luckily, she was in love, and so was he, but how long could they make it last? She would never think it wrong to ask such a question of herself.

'Tell me your side of it whenever you like,' he said.

'I will.'

He took her hand. 'If ever it's necessary.'

'It will be,' she said, 'time and time again. I think I'm a normal sort of person, and I live my life trying not to be alarmed by it.'

They walked down the hill and, half-way to the village, had to stand in towards the hedge to let a car go by. It was the Morris Traveller from the house, and Myra waved when she saw Enid at the wheel. Dean was sitting beside her, and in the back were several suitcases, and Dean's bulging rucksack.

Frank stared, but they did not look at him, or give any sign of having seen Myra—though the car passed within a foot of them. The windscreen wipers were going against the rain, but Enid's beautiful and slender face was stony and set at the road, an expression of misery and determination from which her blonde hair was swept back neatly into a tail.

Dean beside her looked happy, though bemused, and rubbed a hand over his bunched features as if rain were falling directly on to them. The windows were partly open, and the radio was playing a song by that new group called The Beatles.

Chapter Forty-eight

Maria was in the kitchen, and he asked her where Enid was.

'Don't know,' she said sulkily.

He put the perfume on the dresser, and saw some letters resting against a mug. The first had no stamp on, only his name in Enid's handwriting. He took this and several others into the living-room, and saw at a glance that none conveyed the overdue cheque from Teddy Greensleaves, so he ripped Enid's letter quickly open.

'Dear Albert,' he read, 'I have gone away with Dean and I'm not coming back, not to live with you, anyway. I've left you and the children so that I can live another life, because I'm in love with Dean and he's in love with me. By the time you get this we'll be on the sea for Ostend, because we are going to Turkey, to live there a while. After then, I don't know where. I drove the Morris to the station at Bedford, and left it in the car park to collect whenever you like with the spare keys.

'I suppose you've found out by now about the cheque from your gallery. I signed your name on it, and put it into my account, so that we'll have a bit of money to start us off with. We also took the money from the tobacco tin in your studio. I hope you don't mind, but I had to do it this way because I didn't want any fuss. I know you'd have given me the money if I asked for it, but I couldn't face the bother when I told you what it was for. In any case, I have worked for it all these years.

'I'm sure you won't mind me going away, because it was finished a long time ago. There's no more we can find out about each other. It's plain a mile off, and we both know it. It's a big wrench for me to leave the kids, but I'm sure you'll take care of them. I know I can rely on you for that at least. Well, Dean is waiting in the car, and getting impatient, so I have to go.'

He threw the letter aside. It was fairly short for such good riddance. He could hardly believe his luck. Free at last. Locked into the domestic prison at eighteen and now, at forty-four, liberated by the armies of adolescent passion! Released by a curt letter from his skedaddling all-in-all wife! But did she think you only lived as man and wife so as to get to know each other? She must have got such a shallow idea from that flat-faced little bastard Dean.

What a noble creature she had proved herself at last, going away with the first mug she falls for. He really couldn't think too badly of her, though they had been a long time together, and she had taken a lot of his life with her, just as she had left a good bit of hers behind.

He sat for a while, till he heard Rachel and Paul coming in from school. Myra was calling them to order, and he thought that at least there was one good woman in the world. A spiky bomb was lodged in his entrails, pressing on every pipe and vein as if, should it explode, his eyes would be the first to go. Maybe she had taken none of his life with her at all, and that as soon as the boat left England the full weight of what she was doing would cut every minute she had spent with him out of her system forever.

Obviously they had been planning it for weeks, and he had been so blindly engrossed in his painting that he'd not noticed a thing. Yet even if he hadn't been working they'd have been brewing it up. He couldn't blame his art for everything, and that was a fact. They'd hated each other at times, but he loved her, just the same, and loved her still when the pain wore off for a moment, and before it came back.

But he had to pay some price for getting rid of her, and if that price was to have his love destroyed then long live love! It was good that life could be lived again and again no matter what happened, providing the love of life remained. He was glad it had stayed long enough with Enid to let her go off for a new start with a youth of eighteen. She deserved happiness after the bleak decades with him. And if he wanted revenge for her going away, he was already assured of it in the sort of person she'd decided to live with. It was an unworthy thought, and he was sorry it came, but it was some comfort at this desolate moment.

She'll be back, he thought. Maybe she changed her mind at Dover, when the sea breeze hit her, and will come haring home again. Not if I know it. I hope not. I don't want her. Enid's not one to suffer making up her mind for nothing, and neither am I. The older you get the more you learn not to waste anything. Waste not, want not, as the terrible old adage goes. She's on her way. I'm not on mine, though. She'd had a few weeks to get ready for this, so I expect she's further on the road to recovery and change than I am, but my road will lengthen, as soon as I come out of this black spin, and then there will be no more turning back for me, either.

Life felt strange. He didn't know what to do. He wanted to get up from the armchair and go to the garden, to savour his newly awarded freedom, but he couldn't, because Enid wouldn't be there for him to tell his impressions to when he came back afterwards. It was like thinking what an interesting experience dying would be, but then realising that you'd have no one to share it with.

He stood, and put the letter in his pocket. He swayed, as if about to sit down again, then he straightened his back and walked into the kitchen—the hub of the house.

Dawley saw him, upright and pale, but with a smile on his lips, and Handley could tell that Dawley knew when he looked at him. 'She walked out,' he said. 'Didn't you see 'em?'—as if Frank might have stopped them.

He poured Handley some tea. 'They drove by me and Myra when we went for a walk up the hill. We realised what was happening, but there was nothing we could do.'

'Who walked out, Dad?' Rachel asked.

'Your mother.'

'Shall you tell her off?'

'She won't be coming back.'

'Dean as well?' Paul asked.

'Him too,' Handley spat. 'Lace that tea with whisky.'

Frank opened the bottle. 'I'm sorry.'

'Don't be,' Handley said. 'It's all God's work. That is to say, mine. We ask for whatever happens to us. But I'm still sound in wind, limb and brainbox.'

'That's fine, then.' Handley had been dealt a near mortal blow, but Dawley knew he would survive—as one had to.

'I'll sit for an hour or two in John's room,' he said. 'There'll be a bit of comfort there. If you see Mandy or Adam, tell 'em their mother's gone on a trip with Dean—to Turkey. They'll understand. I'll explain it to 'em though, if they don't come in till later.'

He walked upstairs, slowly, one step at a time, not so much out of shock and grief, but so that he wouldn't upset his teacup brimming with whisky. He stood for a moment by John's door, then opened it and went in.

The first subliminal flash showed him the old room, the altar and shrine and relics of his saintly brother's life, among which he'd wanted to efface himself and take comfort in recalling that more cosmically devastated love. He needed to sooth his own galling hurt that to his shame and chagrin was taking him over more and more. But he stepped back almost to the landing.

The room was spare and neutral, and had nothing to do with John or any memories at all. Books, maps, radio gear had gone. Only a small photograph of John had been left on the shelf. It was as if the room had been scooped out by lightning. The neatness and order had created a prison—or a hospital.

He wondered who was trying to drive him mad, but laughed at the idea and drank half his whisky-tea. He took out a long thin cigar and lit it, then sat in the wooden armchair. He was proof against madness. One shock destroys another. This desecration of John's life could only be the combined work of Cuthbert and Ralph. It was a cauterisation of memory.

He sat with hands over his head, as if shells were exploding all around him. They were bursting thick and fast. He'd have to get away from this house and go to Lincolnshire, back to the ancient battlefield now grown over and green where he had spent most of his life with Enid and their children. He didn't really want to be close to her any more, but he needed some connection with reality—which was always the past.

He regretted John's revolver being dropped into Gould's Lake. If it had still been in the cigar box he might have used it, and followed his brother's footsteps along the only road that honour and a cure for pain demanded. But he pissed on honour: he didn't need honour to show how brave he was. Such pain as this could be over-lived, though he didn't think so at the moment.

Yet it was a pity the revolver had gone, he thought, lifting his head, because no matter what his arguments he might still have killed himself. There was something to thank Maricarmen for, after all.

He finished the whisky in a few more minutes, and the stripped room began to feel spiritually healing. In the old version he might have given himself up to the agony of his loss, but in this strange chamber he was not so sure that there would have been any good in that, because there were certain people on earth who had lost far more.

Chapter Forty-nine

With such an inheritance Ralph was at last able to show what kind of man he could be. As the owner of five hundred acres of the richest agricultural loam in Lincolnshire he soon became reconciled with his parents. He took their advice on how to buy and what to plant, and where to invest the lump sum he had acquired—though he had this checked by a Boston lawyer before finally acting.

He was rich enough, albeit within the dreams of avarice, to satisfy himself in all he modestly wanted. His house, Skeat Court, was bigger than he'd imagined in his fantasies while locked in the Handley Community, but it was comfortable enough not to give him any more ambitions, which meant that his madness was cured.

At thirty he was the father of three sons, and it was having children, as much as his good fortune, which helped to draw him closer to the elder Spilsbys. Mandy loathed them as much as ever, and did not hide it—at first. But Mabel Spilsby, her mother-in-law, grew gentler as the children came, and Mandy put up with her because whenever the mood took her she could dump the kids there and take off in Ralph's large Royce to the motorway, in an effort to chase out the smouldering discontent till such time as she would know what to do with it.

Handley's sons went to Oxford, but their revolutionary knowledge did them little good. They discovered that those students, who were supposed to hate the medieval authority and deformed human ritual of the university, were appalled when they produced a foolproof blueprint for burning much of it down. So Adam and Richard studied all they could, got honours degrees, and departed for the United States to do more research.

Adam stayed there, but Richard came back for a while, then went to Israel where he spent many years in labour and study on a kibbutz. It was the closest in life he could get to a perfect form of democracy as far as he was concerned, as well as being an everyday existence which also had its dangers because it was close to the Syrian border. It was this peril in which the people lived that eventually enticed him into it for good. He married a girl there, learned Hebrew, and stayed.

Albert Handley's sole purpose in life was to get letters and paint pictures. But he left Myra's compound to have a house built on the site where he had once lived in Lincolnshire—which still belonged to him. Paul, Rachel and Toby stayed with Myra, a neat arrangement that did not disturb their schooling, and left Handley free to plan and build.

Scorched bricks under the tangled mound of bushes and thistles were finally cleared away. Rotting and burnt timbers were pulled clear, and the foundations of a bungalow laid. An adjacent studio with enormous glass windows was added later.

His wooden studio was dismantled and transported to his old garden, and he lived in it, with Eric Bloodaxe for company, the Rambler Estate car standing outside. He painted pictures and sent them to Greensleaves' gallery, but many hours of each week were taken up with builders constructing his new house, moving among heaps of bricks and timber, dodging dumper trucks and concrete mixers, peering over drawings, and arguing about the finish of the work.

Ralph and Mandy came to the housewarming party, as well as Dawley and Myra and his three young children. Greensleaves travelled from town with Daphne Ritmeester.

The house was placed near the brow of a hill, its lights glowing for miles around. Local people who'd known him for over twenty years saw that the Handleys were back—after an absence which now seemed like no time at all. The local tradesmen sent vans up the muddy green-arched track laden with food and drink. Except for absent faces it was like old times, and Handley, upright as ever, smoking his long Schimmelpenninck, led his guests from room to room showing off his house as if it were a new car. Finished canvasses, awaiting transport to London, decorated every wall.

'It amazes me where you get your energy,' Teddy said, sipping his champagne—and then putting it down on a box. It was so dry it scorched his tonsils.

Handley tapped himself on the groin. 'I store it here!'

'Oh you don't,' said Daphne Ritmeester. 'I can't believe it!'

'A dynamo,' Handley said. 'I haven't had a woman for three months. The last was a girl of eighteen from some art college. Got the shock of her life to find me living on a construction site. She thought I was the foreman and asked where Albert Handley was. I didn't let on straight away. Said I thought he'd gone to Boston and would come back tomorrow—from his hotel to see how the house was progressing. I got on with her all right, even though she did think I was the foreman. After she'd slept two nights with me in my hut I sprang it on her gently. Then she stayed another two nights and left. A lovely young girl. We managed fine with my old dynamo.'

'You don't change,' Daphne said. 'That's why I never lose faith in you.'

'I'll be sleeping in the hut tonight,' he said, 'because friends and family have taken over the bedrooms.'

'I shall love to see it,' Daphne said, holding his hand. 'Does it smell of creosote?'

'I gave it a new coat,' he told her softly, 'specially for you.'

He led a hermit-like existence—except for the dog, and occasional visitors—though Daphne came now and again to see him. He thought of Enid, and remembered the coffee she made in the early Lincolnshire mornings. He hadn't had such a cup since she'd gone. He hadn't noticed it was so spectacularly good at the time. Yet it was, and he knew it now that she was no longer here to make it and share it with him.

It wasn't much to remember her by, yet everything else came with it. He had only to breathe the pure Lincolnshire air in the early morning to be reminded of her—and smell his own rotten coffee-brew coming through the window. We never value what we've got, he thought. If only man didn't always want something better—which turned out to be no good when he got it.

He heard from Cuthbert and Maricarmen, that they had set themselves up as sculptors in a village in the Pyrenees, but used their house as a sort of transit camp for Spaniards who had to cross the border illegally out of Spain. Those who came through in the perilous snows of winter were glad to find some haven that would help them on their way. Handley sent money, to finance the work of which his brother John would have approved. He knew also that Cuthbert would help people to get into England if ever it were necessary.

Cuthbert told how he had gone with Maricarmen to Algeria and, after a ten-day search, found Shelley's grave in a desert village between Aflou and Laghouat, guided there by directions which Dawley had written down for them. The people remembered when the group of guerrillas came, and how one of them who was sick had died that same afternoon. They led Maricarmen to his grave by the wall of their own small cemetery, still marked by the pyramid of stones that Dawley had built. Cuthbert observed her. She smiled, as if it were one desolation over and done with. Whatever was left in her would be for him, and it was more than enough. It had to be, though he felt it was more than he deserved. Life grew out of death. He saw it happening already. They paid a mason to build a permanent stone for Shelley. After photographing it, they got into their car and drove back to Oran.

Eric Bloodaxe, in the ripe fullness of age, its dream-world forever intact, guarded him day and night. The torment of losing Enid, which he put down more and more to callous neglect of her, stayed a while, and then the hardest bit of it eased after the new house was built on the ruins of the old. He worked hard at his painting, and though his reputation in the art world waned for a while, it then revived. He enjoyed his freedom for the first year in Lincolnshire, but was glad to send for his three children who, back in their old territory, made him feel more like himself again. It turned his agony on to remembering Enid, yet even that did not last. Unnecessary pain soon wears away.

Five years later a letter came from a town on the south coast, relayed from Myra's address, and he recognised her writing crossed out on the envelope. After a long time wandering between the Mediterranean and India she and Dean had made enough money on smuggling (she didn't say what, but he could guess) to buy a small hotel, where they had settled with their two children. He was welcome to have a free holiday any time he was down that way, she said.

He dropped the letter on to the fire, and went into the frost to cool off. He wouldn't spend any more effort on her than that. He was happy that she was happy with Dean, but what was happiness? He didn't know, and never would, though they were all entitled to it. Only the oblivion of work gave an illusion of it. He heard from her again, that her happiness palled and she couldn't get rid of Dean. He wouldn't leave her, she said—maybe wanting Handley to go down and sort things out, and perhaps ask her back to Lincolnshire.

But he didn't want to return to all that piggery, though it did occur to him from time to time that one day he might get married again. After all, he didn't want to live on Vinegar Hill for the rest of his life.

Chapter Fifty

Dawley and Myra got married at St Pancras Town Hall, accompanied by the two children already born to them, and Handley who acted as best man. Nancy had divorced Frank for desertion, and she had used her freedom in the same way—as an end to independence.

Myra's house seemed empty. Maria and Catalina had gone back to Spain. The caravans were vacant, and so was the flat over the garage. When Handley took his children Myra and Dawley were left with Mark, and Saul the new baby. The community had died.

Frank's book was published, and went through three hardcover reprints in a year, and then into a paperback edition. It was not popular with the reviewers, but became well-known nevertheless, especially among young people and students, for it not only covered the adventurous times in Algeria, but contained his observations on street-fighting and guerrilla warfare, so that it became a technical handbook on the subject. Though it was weak on the political side, many organisations invited him to give talks and lectures, and out of these he got ideas for future essays.

But as time went on he did not know how to reconcile his revolutionary principles and writings to his life as a normal family man. It bothered him most when he was happiest, because he was happiest when he was in the garden with his children, feeling he had no right to be happy with so much misery and devastation in the world. But he could not avoid loving Myra and the children and being happy. They talked about the problem, but he could find no answer. The main thing was that the question continued to gnaw at him.

He woke up at four one summer's morning, a slit of light at the blind. Lately he'd not been able to sleep much, and instead of tormenting himself with it he dressed in silence, and walked downstairs.

The sky was low and milky across the paddock, as if it would turn into a hot fine day. A snail lay on one of the steps, a slimy track behind, so he stepped aside to avoid crushing it. The gate squeaked on its hinges: he'd oil them later. The far hedge was tall and dark, blackberry creepers reaching out and putting new tentacles tenaciously among the grass, digging their roots in.

It seemed the end of life, this beginning of the day in which the birds were so loud from neighbouring fields and trees that it sounded as if they were getting ready to take over the earth—hoping that all men had gone from it during their brief sleep.

This end of life was the fire of life, in which the flame was often invisible, nonexistent. How could one live without this flame? You didn't have to see it to believe it was there. If it was in your heart you could see it spring up in all different places. As long as it stayed in your heart your revolutionary principles were not at variance with the way you lived.

He could wait, and warm himself at his own flame, and let others share it when they needed it. Waiting and guarding your own flame with the faith of your life was justification enough. Because when the call came, when he had waited until he knew what to do, when it was necessary to go out to a cause and do something, then he would do so—but always finally remembering, and being troubled by, the words of Handley's brother John. In the meantime the flame stayed plain, and as long as you loved those nearby you would know what to do when the time came.

And if it never did? he asked himself with the healthy bite of scepticism. While the flame of his heart stayed with him he did not need to answer that question. Life in any case was brief enough. If it never came he still had to live. Yet he knew beyond all doubt that it would come. The world that he knew was made that way.

Feeling good to be alive and up so early, he went back to the house to make breakfast for his family.